Oblivion

Kris Lynn

Broken Typewriter Press
5001 1st Ave SE
Ste 105 #243
Cedar Rapids, IA 52402

Broken Typewriter Press
http://broken.typewriter.press

Version 1.0.0

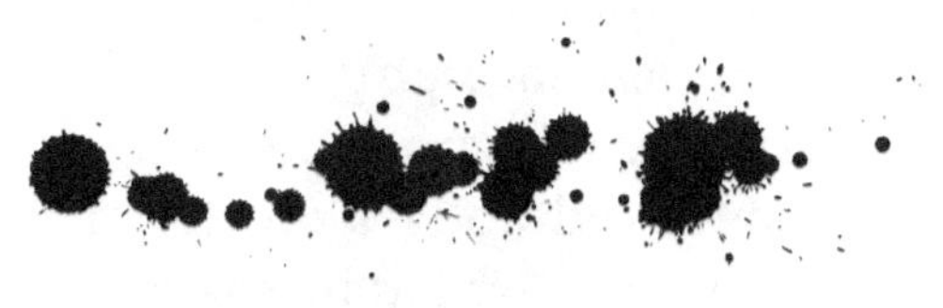

Chapter 1

The End of Anonymity

BLOOD: by Trinity Morgan.

Such an anticlimactic title for something that was very nearly my entire existence. I spent two years preparing for this night. I even quit my job. And now my defining moment was here. Tonight was my first art show.

This was my chance to make a name for myself, and more importantly, a chance to escape my own personal hell; my dismal, one bedroom apartment in Sunnyside, New York. Everyday the walls inched closer, creeping in to suffocate me. I did what I could to make this dump feel like home by hanging artwork everywhere and decorating in calming colors. But *nothing* would ever make this place shine.

The plaster on the buttercream colored walls was deteriorating, exposing rusty pipes underneath. My patchy carpet and faded linoleum were the same ugly shade of shit brown. The air conditioner never worked in the summer, and the temperature rarely reached sixty-five in the winter. Since my only bedroom had been turned into a makeshift studio, my bed also served as my couch, and my dresser became my TV stand. The only furniture to even hint that this was a living room was a dingy, faded blue recliner circa nineteen-eighty.

A white garment bag lay across the ancient comforter on my bed. I spent six hundred dollars on the black designer dress waiting inside. That dress would be the nicest thing I had ever worn, but it also represented half of next month's rent. If I didn't sell some paintings tonight, it would become a serious liability.

I removed the dress and slid it on with a smile. The satiny fabric felt more like lingerie than outerwear. The open back plunged down to my tailbone, with two strips of fabric draped across my shoulder blades. The hem was short, and the front dipped low enough to show some cleavage. I would have paid twice as much for it.

The dress also left my entire tattoo exposed. The obscenely nude woman being swallowed in the flesh of my left arm was a half-sleeve version of one of my own works. I could only afford such a large piece because I gave the artist a painting in trade.

I did a slow twist in the mirror and readjusted the clip that tamed my long tresses. My naturally blonde curls had always been one of my favorite assets, but at this moment, I wanted to chop my hair off and dye it black. That seemed much more appropriate for the subject matter of my show.

A quick glance at the clock told me it was six twenty. Don, my overweight, over-the-hill agent, promised to send a car for me at six forty-five. Can't have his artist take the subway to the show. That would look unprofessional to potential buyers.

I needed to hurry and finish getting ready. I gulped the last of my vodka and Kool-Aid and sat at my rickety old computer desk, the only spot I could comfortably apply makeup. I already had some on, but obsessing about my face seemed like a good idea. I grabbed the mascara first, and carefully applied another coat while I stared into the muted green of my own eyes, wishing they were several shades brighter.

Immediately to my left was the photo of my foster parents

that I felt compelled to display in a weak attempt to make up for our lack of communication. Their judging eyes bore a hole into my forehead right now. They never loved me enough to bother making our little family official, for there was no real adoption, but they didn't hate me enough to send me away either. I hadn't returned to Missouri to visit Sara and Hank Anderson since I moved to New York four years ago. I considered not telling them about the show, but I felt I owed them. The news did not go over well.

Sara and Hank didn't approve of my choice of careers. Painting was frivolous and I needed to grow up and get a real job. Even more horrifying in their eyes was *what* I painted. My artwork scared them. They viewed it as a crime against God, outright blasphemy. What kind of person drew pictures of monsters and people being torn limb from limb? The obvious conclusion, to them, was that I was insane. My drawings as a child led to a steady stream of psychologists who only confirmed their suspicions, at which point they turned to another venue. The Church.

I spent almost every day of my childhood there, while priests tried to drive the demons from me. I don't think it worked. And I despised Sara and Hank for it. I reached over and slammed the frame down on its face.

My paintings were too much for some people. But I was compelled to paint them. If I can't get my visions out, I find myself in mental anguish. And no matter what my foster parents, or anyone else, thought about my artwork, I found it beautiful. Maybe I was a little dark and twisted. That doesn't have to be a bad thing.

A majority of my most recent paintings depicted women being tortured in some way or another, but that wasn't where the controversy originated. This show was about something else.

I cut myself one night as I worked on a painting of a young woman in bondage. Without realizing it, I smeared a decent amount of blood right on top of the paint, and then a great revelation came to me. How could I ever portray a more graphic scene than by using *real blood* where she was supposed to be bleeding? Granted, this was not the first time anyone thought of this, but it was the perfect fit for my brand of artwork.

My agent said it was genius. That was not the standard reaction from everybody else. Maybe that's why I was so nervous about tonight. What if everyone ran out screaming? Or worse, maybe they'd finally commit me this time.

There was one painting in particular I was apprehensive about showing. I had never done a self-portrait before. So I finally decided to devote myself to one. The painting itself was rather large, five feet by three feet, and showed me as I normally depicted others; naked, tortured and tied down, bleeding and writhing in pain.

For all my other paintings, I used pigs' blood mixed with acrylic paint (to hold the color). This one I felt had to be more personal. I drew my own blood by making a shallow incision into my wrist with a razorblade. I did what I could to collect an adequate amount of that precious liquid while still keeping my wound manageable. It was a somewhat failed attempt. I almost blacked out, but the rush experienced from such an endeavor was phenomenal.

The sound of my phone ringing interrupted my thoughts. I grabbed the cheap cell phone and flipped it open. The screen inside just showed one word, Slave. I grinned and pulled it to my ear.

"Hello, Luke."

Lucas Steele was, or thought he was, my boyfriend. He was a heavily tattooed mechanic, which is what I told myself I was looking for, so he was the closest thing I had to a real relationship.

"Hey, sexy." I could hear the smile in his voice. He always seemed happy to talk to me. I rarely reciprocated his enthusiasm, but I was almost always glad to hear it.

"You have impeccable timing you know. I'm about to leave."

"Yeah, yeah. Just calling to wish you luck. Not like you need it."

"I do need it. I'm about to have a panic attack." That sentence was more honest than I intended it be.

"Are you sure you don't want me to come with you tonight? I could change real quick and meet you there..." He trailed off. I knew he didn't really want to go, but I was flattered he at least pretended. Besides, I definitely did not want to appear tied down to anyone tonight. A date was out of the question.

"No, don't worry about it. Maybe we can meet up afterwards. I look way too good to make this an early night."

He laughed. It was a warm and inviting laugh, his usual. For someone who looked as intimidating as him, it almost didn't fit. He wasn't overly tall or muscular, but the shaved head, metal jewelry and extensive tattooing overshadowed the kind chocolate eyes and sweet smile. He really was an easygoing and compassionate guy, much too nice to date a chick like me.

I cut him off mid laugh, "Hey, I really need to get going, the car's gonna be here any minute."

"That's alright. Just call me afterwards, okay?"

"Yeah, I will." Probably.

"Good luck."

When I shut the phone the screen read six forty-four. A wave of anxiety washed over me. I ran to the kitchen cupboard and grabbed a pill bottle from the middle shelf. My Xanax. These little babies worked miracles. Twenty minutes from now I'd have no worries. They were not prescribed, but that didn't keep me from having a steady supply. I popped a couple in my mouth and swallowed without the aid of water. The remaining pills went into my handbag, and out the door I went.

I sprinted down the hallway to the elevator as fast as I could manage in heels, shoes much too ridiculous to take the stairs. Another wave of anxiety sank in as I waited for the exhausted old thing to come to a whining stop. The doors cried out in protest as they strained open. It was empty, thank God. Not that I was very heavy, but any extra weight in here terrified me. I'd be surprised if these elevators had been inspected in the last ten years. One of these days someone was going to get stuck, and I just hoped it wouldn't be me.

Seven tense floors down, past the filthy entryway and mailroom I saw a green Camry waiting for me outside. Don's drab car. Not exactly what I had in mind. Showing up in your agent's passenger seat was hardly more dignified than riding the subway.

I slipped inside and gave him a big smile. I didn't even have a chance to say 'hi' before he was all business.

"There will be some pretty big names in attendance tonight," he beamed. Don had a lot of faith in my abilities, or at least my abilities to make him money. "I'm sure they'll be more interested in your stuff than that crap Ivan passes off for sculpture."

"Still bitter he didn't pick you for his agent?"

He didn't seem amused. "This is serious. You're lucky I'm so good at my job. Gallery New York doesn't normally show unproven artists. You'll have to seriously work it if you want to make any money."

I folded my arms across my chest. "I thought that was your job."

"I got you the booking, that's more than most agents could do." He paused and looked me over. "Good call with the dress. I was worried you'd show up in a tank top."

"I look better than you do," I teased, but I wasn't lying. Don was past his prime for sure. He probably had been attractive in his youth, but that was long behind him now. Twenty years ago the art world chewed him up and spit him out. So he gave it up, put on some weight, and started pushing other people's work instead of his own.

Located in the middle of West Village, Gallery New York attracted the art world's A-list for their clientele. That's probably why my show was a double booking. To ensure the gallery's success this evening, my possibly controversial paintings were paired with a man named Ivan Stately. He was a sculptor with a decent following, whose pieces were mostly semi-erotic abstracts of the female form. I thought they were boring and predictable, but what did I know? His stuff sold, and that's all that really matters.

The place was already packed when we arrived. Several large banners outside depicted various samples of my paintings and Ivan's sculptures. The bold print across the top read *Presence of*

Life by Ivan Stately and introducing BLOOD by Trinity Morgan. There were also smaller, individual signs for Ivan, with sultry imagery for *Presence of Life.* The ones dedicated to me were a lot bolder, with *BLOOD* in red dripping capitols, and the tortured eyes of my pretend victims. I definitely liked mine better.

The kicker was the marquee. I will never forget the joy of seeing my name four feet across in lights. I stopped in my tracks to stare up at it. Don had to drag me by the arm to pull me away.

Inside, the gallery was one large rectangle with a bar in the back. My paintings were spaced evenly on the white walls, and Ivan's sculptures were scattered around the middle, smaller ones on pillars and larger pieces directly on the beige tile floor. The classical music played quietly under the bright lighting. It was wall-to-wall people, all of which were dressed to kill. At least in this dress, I wouldn't look as outclassed as I felt.

Two minutes after arriving, Evelyn Counter, the curator spotted us and waved us over.

"Trinity Morgan, so very nice to see you again." She flashed me a plastic smile.

"Nice to see you too, Evelyn." I gave her a fake grin as I gagged on her overuse of perfume.

"It looks like we may have an excellent evening. Your work complements Ivan's quite nicely."

Complement Ivan!? I opened my mouth to snap at her, but Don took one look at my face and intervened. "Your decision to book them together looks to be panning out nicely. Ivan never brings in this size of a crowd on his own." He had the smile of a proud parent, not the type of thing I was used to seeing in my life. "After tonight, everyone's going to know who Trinity is."

"Yes, I'm sure everyone here will have strong opinions of her work," Evelyn addressed Don, but she eyed me suspiciously. "One way or another."

I clenched my teeth and cussed her out silently in my head. "I guess we'll have to just see, won't we... I'm going to get a drink."

I stormed off before she could say anything else. In hindsight, that was probably not the best way to handle things. But I never claimed to be mature.

As I approached the bar, the young blonde behind it smiled at me. "Would you like some complimentary champagne?"

"I would love some." I separated each word to emphasize the urgency. While she poured me a glass, I leaned against the bar to try and get a read on the reaction to my paintings. I could see quite a few people looking at them, and no one was screaming. I took that as a good sign.

The bartender set the glass of champagne next to me. I lifted it to my lips immediately. "Thank you."

"You're welcome," she said. Her smile looked innocent. I wondered if she would still smile at me after I've had ten glasses. "Are... are you Trinity?" She asked shyly.

"I guess I am...just haven't decided if that's a good thing yet." I took another drink then watched the bubbles rise from the bottom as I lowered the glass. It was almost empty already. "I think I'm going to need another of these, if you don't mind."

"Oh, of course!" She grabbed the bottle again with a flush in her cheeks. "I just want you to know I really like your paintings. They're...they're kinda scary."

I laughed. "Thanks, I'll take that as a compliment."

She nodded in agreement and set another glass next to me. I slammed the last of my drink and traded it for the full one. Then I thanked her again and walked away.

I weaved slowly through the crowds of people, wondering what I was supposed to do this whole time. I passed a group that was hovering over one of Ivan's larger sculptures, the torso of a woman dancing out of a wave. They seemed to think it was a masterpiece. *Idiots,* I snickered to myself. I made my way towards a couple that were staring up at one of my creations. I tried not to be obvious about eavesdropping by pretending to look at a sculpture as I snuck in on their conversation.

The woman looked appalled. "That's disgusting. What kind of person would like this stuff?"

"You're being too sensitive." Her date replied.

That wasn't the reaction I hoped for, so I kept moving. The people gathered in front of the next few sets of paintings seemed to be enjoying themselves more. I heard a couple words of praise as I walked by and smiled to myself.

During my journey through the crowd, I spotted the resting place for the one painting I should have left at home. My self-portrait hung isolated and emphasized like none of the others. I stopped twenty feet away and stared up at my own sick version of my face. I felt just as vulnerable and naked as I looked in that painting.

Just as I was about to walk away, an elderly woman, dressed in an exorbitant sequin dress and gaudy gold jewelry, paused to look at my doppelganger; she covered her mouth with her hands and starting ranting something I couldn't make out from this far away. She resembled someone who had just found the rotting corpse of a rat in her bed.

"You can't please everyone, can you?"

That smooth, deep voice sounded like it was spoken right into my ear. I spun around to see who could have gotten so close without me noticing.

The man standing next to me turned my brain to mush. His eyes caught me first. They were so intense and beautiful, an odd shade of brown that came across almost red, with golden centers and dark lashes. His jet-black hair was parted over his right eye and hung in layers down to his chin. He wore a dark blue dress shirt, untucked with the top few buttons undone, revealing a glimpse of what I imagined to be a chiseled chest. He had broad shoulders and thick arms, the type of look that required countless hours in the gym.

"Some people have no taste." He nodded in the direction of the old lady, and held his hand out to me. "Vino Amante."

I released a breath I didn't realize I was holding, and feebly reached out to take his hand. The second we touched a current pulsed up my arm and spread through my chest. My heart lost its rhythm for several beats. I couldn't believe I was reacting like this.

"I'm Trinity Mor..."

"I know," he interrupted. "You looked lost. I felt compelled to come introduce myself... My family and I attend a lot of these things. It's been awhile since I've come across anything that's piqued my interest." His eyes lingered over me. "I'm very glad I came tonight."

Why was this man affecting me so much? I was twelve all over again and he was the first boy to ever talk to me. I swallowed hard and reached a hand up to my necklace. "Um, thank you. I'm glad at least someone appreciates my work."

"I'm sure I'm not the only one. You've captured the perfect expression of rapturous pain. Gives me a chill just looking at it."

I made the mistake of looking back into his eyes and was stunned again. It took a second to regain my wits. "Wow, thank you. That's not the reaction I've been getting from most people."

"Maybe you're surrounding yourself with the wrong people."

He aimed a sly smile at me, and all my baser instincts took over. My whole body overheated. Was he hitting on me? I sure hoped so.

Vino leaned in and lowered his voice. "Do you mind if I pick your brain a bit? I have a few questions that I'm dying to ask you."

"Yeah, sure." Having him that close affected every muscle in my body. I lifted my forgotten drink and took a sip to calm my nerves. "What exactly do you want to know?"

Vino turned to the painting we were standing closest to, and motioned to the woman crucified in the center. "Is this what you dream about at night, torturing young women to the brink of death?"

"I—I guess I do." My answer was dumb enough to make me giggle. After a moment, a better explanation came to me. "As far back as I remember I've always drawn this sort of thing. When I was a kid everyone just thought there was something wrong with me."

"I don't see anything wrong with you." He looked me up and down again for emphasis before he continued. "You used animal's blood for these paintings, didn't you?"

While I was busy swooning, I managed to nod. "Pigs' actually. I got it from the deli down the street from my apartment. They thought I was crazy. Don't think I ever did tell them what it was for."

I thought he would laugh, but he must not have got the joke, because he continued as if I never answered him. "And that one..." He pointed to my self-portrait. "That's your blood on that painting, isn't it?"

I sucked in a quick gasp of breath. *How could he know that?* I didn't remember telling anyone. "Yeah—How?"

That response he found hilarious. "You just told me. Had a hunch, that's all."

Real funny. I'm glad he was enjoying himself. I was going to have a heart attack by the time this conversation was over.

Then his laughter came to an abrupt stop. His head turned to the side as if he was listening to something coming from behind him. I watched his eyebrows drop down and a grimace spread across his face. But I only caught a glimpse. When he noticed me watching, he smiled again. It wasn't the sly smile he'd been showing me just moments before. This one was fake.

"It appears my father has arrived. He wants to speak with you," he said.

I looked around us to see who he was talking about and saw no one, so I searched Vino's face for an answer. He was still smiling, but his jaw muscles were flexed like he was clenching his teeth, and his hands were balled into fists.

That's when I saw them.

The crowd parted by some invisible force as two men and a woman glided towards us. The man in front was just *unreal*, easily the best looking person I'd ever seen. He reminded me of a seasoned rock star, regal even. He was tall and lean, but the way he carried himself implied strength. The grey vest he wore hugged his chest over a long-sleeved white shirt with the buttons at the neck undone, and the cuffs at his wrists rolled back. His scarlet tie had been loosened and pulled down a few inches, a casual look that must have been painstakingly planned down to the last detail.

His slightly graying blond hair was just long enough to be combed back with a few strands strategically falling down his forehead and into his eyes. Those eyes, those radiant, god-like eyes, seemed to emanate with their own light. A blue glow so deep and bright it would never be duplicated. Flanking either side of him, the other man and the woman were a matched set. Only a few inches separated them in height, and they had the same thin build. They were dressed in all black in feminine and masculine versions of the same suit. Their chestnut hair was thick and straight, hers to her mid back, and his in a short, messy spike. The features of their faces were almost identical, large deep-set eyes and small pouty lips. I couldn't tell if their eyes were hazel or green, but they were frightening.

I was dreaming, wasn't I? I *had* to be hallucinating. People did not look like this. They did not have this *presence* about them. I knew my sanity was riding a fine line, but this was unbelievable.

The blond man walked directly up to me with the most hypnotizing smile and grabbed my hand. It shocked me, and I'm sure I jumped. A sickening warmth radiated through my body as he slowly lifted my hand to his lips. Without looking away from my eyes, he leaned forward and kissed the top of my hand. My heart seized, and I felt like someone punched me in the gut.

"Good evening, Trinity. My name is Sebastian Amante. These are my children, Amelie and Andras." He released my hand and motioned to the two at his sides. The fluidity of his movements were so graceful they looked rehearsed, like a ballet.

Sebastian turned his attention to Vino then, who was standing with his arms folded over his chest. "Vinicio, you always find such lovely friends."

Vino shrugged and looked around the room without answering. He didn't seem to be looking at any thing in particular, just avoiding Sebastian the way a rebellious teenager would never look directly into the eyes of their scolding parents.

Sebastian didn't notice, or care. His startling blue eyes bore into mine as if he was searching for something. "Your work is quite impressive. I'd love to have one for my collection."

"I'm glad you like them," I said, struggling to compose myself enough to have an adult conversation. Something about this man felt wrong, I couldn't put my finger on it but my subconscious was screaming for me to run away. "Which one did you have you eyes on?"

"Several, actually." Sebastian paused to look at Vino, who was trying to walk away. His back was already facing us, but he stopped immediately and mumbled something under his breath. Sebastian turned his attention back to me as if nothing happened. "You have a very unique gift, my dear. I'm amazed you went unnoticed for so long." He studied me for a moment. "Those women in your paintings, the expression on their faces is sheer perfection. So real it makes me feel as if I'm right there, torturing them myself, causing them all that pain. For you to have visualized this so accurately..."

"You speak like you have experience in that area." I took a nervous drink from my glass, emptying it.

The evil intent behind his smile said more than any verbal answer he could have given me. But it was so sexy, I melted anyways. "Let's just say I find beauty in the same elements you do."

He reached out to take the empty glass from my hand, letting his fingers linger over mine for longer than necessary. That small touch flooded my body with unnatural warmth again. This time it was accompanied by a surge of hormones. I could feel the blood rush to my cheeks.

From the look on his face, Sebastian noticed my reaction. He handed my glass to Amelie without looking away from me. "Would you mind getting us a few drinks? It appears Trinity needs a refill."

I was utterly lost in Sebastian's features. Somehow, the laugh lines around his eyes managed to make him even more attractive. How old was he? I wouldn't have put him a day over forty, but if these three were really his children, that wasn't possible. Vino looked at least thirty, and the other two couldn't be much younger. That meant that he was probably in his fifties. He was just so flawless it didn't make sense.

"There was one painting in particular that I refuse to leave here without." Sebastian turned and pointed across the room, aiming directly at my self-portrait. "That one there. The subject matter is to die for."

What!? Why on earth would he want the one of *me*? I couldn't imagine anyone actually owning that piece, let alone hanging it up in their home and looking at it everyday. I frantically tried to pull myself together. "Why that one?"

His expression transformed into something more devious, as if there was some private joke that I was missing. "It is by far your most exceptional piece. It's much more personal than the others, I can see the emotional investment you put into it.

"I was wondering," Sebastian continued. "Could I also commission you to do a piece for me? You would be well compensated."

"Yes, of course," I blurted out before my brain had a chance to tell me I should find out more about what I was getting myself into.

"Fabulous!" He reached out to take my hand, and that nauseating warmth radiated through me again.

I felt the urge to pull away but couldn't. I blinked a couple of times to clear my head and regain some composure. "What exactly did you have in mind?"

"We can discuss specifics later, dinner perhaps, Wednesday?" He said. "I'll send a car for you at seven. If that's alright with you, that is."

"Wednesday works."

"It's a date then." He glanced in Vino's direction. "We'll make an occasion of it. I'll bring the whole family."

The twins, as I assumed they were, returned with two drinks piece, providing a much-needed distraction. Amelie handed one to Sebastian, he took it without acknowledging her. Andras gave me his extra. I mumbled a quick, "Thanks." He didn't answer.

Very slowly, Sebastian lifted my free hand to his lips again. The second they made contact it sent a jolt through my heart. The room and all the people around me faded away. I was paralyzed, stuck there in that moment, where there was nothing but *him*. I wanted to run away in horror, and yet, I never wanted him to break that touch.

When he peered up at me again, a triumphant expression on his face proved he could sense the power he held over me. He looked positively sinister right then, and all I could do was stare into his eyes as they burned with some invisible fire that melted the blue into swirling, liquid pools. There was no way what I was seeing as real. But I didn't care. I never would have dreamed there could be something that gorgeous.

He sighed and lowered my hand without releasing it. "I suppose we really must be going. I look forward to seeing you again, Trinity."

"It was really nice to meet you, Mr. Amante." My voice came out weak and quiet. My mind was still spinning around somewhere, trying to find its way back to reality.

"To you, my dear, it's Sebastian." He winked at me, a gesture so seductive my heart doubled its speed. I was putty in this man's remarkable hands, and we both knew it.

Then he released my hand and we were back in the crowded gallery. "Wednesday," he reminded me, and walked away.

The other three didn't bother to say goodbye, they just disappeared into the crowd. I stared after them in wonder. Did all that really happen? Had anyone else been affected the same way I had? A quick look around the gallery provided no answers. I couldn't see one person in the room who was so much as looking in my direction, let alone the direction of the strange group I was just with.

When the feeling came back to my legs, and I felt confident about moving again, I made a beeline to the restroom. I needed to be alone. I threw my handbag on the counter and leaned into it, staring at my face in the mirror. My eyes were a little wild, but otherwise there was no physical proof I lost my mind. I reached up and pulled the skin down on my right eye to take a closer look. No, nothing out of the ordinary. I would have splashed water on my face too, but that would have destroyed my makeup.

I shook my head a few times, then reached into to my bag and popped a few more Xanax, chasing them down with my champagne. At least it wouldn't be long until I was too intoxicated to remember what was bothering me. I lowered my head and closed my eyes, taking a few calming breaths. The door opened and another woman walked in. I didn't pay any attention to her as she occupied the nearest stall. I took one more deep breath, smoothed out my hair and dress, and left the bathroom.

Out in the gallery, everything was back to normal. There was no sign that I just had a mental breakdown in the midst of all this. The strange, beautiful characters that captivated me were gone, leaving behind no trace. I had control of my own mind again, all the people were real, and the room and everything in it was just as it should be. As far as the rest of the world was concerned, the encounter never happened.

Chapter 2

Sanity

When I emerged from unconsciousness the next morning, my head spun like a roulette wheel and throbbed like I'd been hit with a mallet. The light coming in from the window was excruciating. I was naked, and this was definitely not my bed.

A familiar laugh filled the room. "Morning, sunshine."

Lucas. What a relief.

"I bet you feel awesome. I'm even hung-over, and you had quite a head start on me."

Did I? The previous night was a blur. Great, this old guessing game again. "What did we do last night?"

I rubbed the sleep out of my eyes to help adjust to the brightness of the room. Lucas leaned against the door of his bedroom with a towel wrapped around his waist. The skin of his well-toned body was damp and glistened in the morning sun, making all his tattoos look brighter. He was always a sight without his clothes, more ink than skin. A colorful collage of cars, pin-ups, skulls, and flames with a giant cross covering the expanse of his chest. I'm sure this would turn a lot of people off. But I loved it. To think of how many hours he spent under the needle, and all of the pain involved... that was a special brand of sexy.

He strolled over and took a seat next to me on the bed. "You asked me to pick you up from the gallery, remember?"

The light bulb in my head sputtered and switched on, *the art show*. "Oh yeah, that rings a bell."

"I'd hope so. It's all you've talked about for months," he said. "It's a shame you don't remember. You were in top form last night."

"That bad, huh?"

"Not bad. I enjoyed it anyways."

I leaned into him and hid my face in his chest. "Shit, you might as well give me the play-by-play."

Lucas wrapped his arms around me and kissed the top of my head. "Okay, I think it was nine when you called me to come get you. Something about losing your mind, or hallucinating or something. You weren't making much sense. And you never did tell me what it was about. But you said you wanted to drink. So we bar-hopped till close and then came back here..." He trailed off again. I got the hint. "Oh, and your agent called. Apparently you weren't supposed to leave the show. You had me check the message. The guy's pissed."

I shrugged that last part off. Don should be used to my behavior by now. "Nothing embarrassing?"

"You danced on a bar, and I almost had to punch a guy."

Typical, that wasn't too far out of the norm for me. "I don't see you punching anyone."

He laughed. "That's why I said almost."

The fresh scent wafting off of Lucas' skin accented how disgusting I felt. "I need a shower."

"Well, you know where it is. And I stocked the bathroom for you, since you refuse to leave anything here. I'll have coffee ready by the time you get out."

"That sounds great, I'll be quick." I kissed him and hopped out of bed.

An unopened toothbrush waited for me on the bathroom counter. And new bottles of shampoo, conditioner, and body wash were in the shower. This was a bad sign. I needed to be more careful about how often I was staying over. Don't want Lucas getting all serious on me.

I turned the water up to its hottest setting and eased my way into the shower as I tried to piece together my forgotten night. Broken images floated by of my artwork, my dress, the crowd at the gallery, and then… *him*.

Sebastian. Glorious, terrifying Sebastian.

That was why I wanted to drink. Why I wanted to forget. Those liquid-blue pools he called eyes were they only part of the evening that came back to me with perfect clarity. Although I was sure my memories were not accurate. There was no way that they burned the way I remembered. And it was simply not possible that looking into them had caused my entire world to vanish.

His whole family had that strange presence to them. Vino was insanely sexy, but the second Sebastian showed up he wanted nothing to do with me. And those twins acted more like bodyguards than children.

At least I wouldn't have to see them again… until Wednesday. I was officially done enjoying my shower.

When I left the bathroom, I found Lucas waiting on the couch in his boxers, flipping through the stations on his flat screen. His two-bedroom apartment was well decorated for a bachelor pad. He used lots of bold, primary colors with masculine furniture. The walls were covered with tastefully framed prints of classic cars and pop art. All the finishes were new and the rooms were spacious. He may not have been rich, but he was doing a lot better than I was.

When he heard me enter the room he turned around and smiled. "Feeling better? There's aspirin on the counter if you need it."

Damn saint. I chuckled to myself and pictured him with a halo around his head. "Hangover's almost gone, actually. I'm ready to start drinking again."

He laughed at me. "Drinking is the last thing I want to do right now."

"Wuss."

After I popped a few pills and poured myself a mug of coffee, I snuggled in next to him on the couch. Lucas didn't allow me much time to get comfortable before he moved my cup to a safe distance and threw me on my back. He grabbed a handful of wet tresses at the base of my skull and kissed me. When he reached for my towel, I laughed at him.

He hoisted himself off me. "What?"

"I really have to get going," I said in between giggles.

"It's Sunday. What on earth could you possibly have going on?"

"Stuff."

Lucas pulled out his classic pouty face. "Fine, I'll go put some clothes on."

"Sorry." I said. I didn't mean it. And even though a morning romp would have been fun, I just wanted to keep him on his toes.

I threw on last night's dress and he put on a wife-beater and shorts. Then we jumped in Lucas' daily driver; a Jeep Wrangler that he threw some large tires on and made several of off-road adjustments to. I didn't understand why he would waste money on something so unnecessary for city living. His truck would have been more at home on a gravel road in the country. He did have a second car to redeem himself, although I've never ridden in it. This one was a classic Camaro that he kept at the garage he worked at. He took me to see it a few times, and it was impressive. But it was far from being completed.

Before we parted ways at my place, I leaned over and gave him a long kiss. "I'll call you later."

"I'm taking you out Tuesday. No excuses."

I rolled my eyes. "Sure."

He made me promise twice before he let me leave the jeep.

I barely had my apartment door shut before I ripped my dress off and threw on a fresh pair of panties and a tank top. My head was still spinning, so I popped a few Xanax, then gathered every blanket and pillow I owned, tossed them in a pile on my bed, and buried myself in the pile of fluff. I would have eaten too, but I hadn't bought groceries in weeks.

A nap sounded like the best idea in the world right now, but despite the pills, I couldn't sleep. I flipped on my ancient twenty-seven inch TV instead. I was too broke to afford cable, so I don't know how many infomercials I watched before I was bored into slumber. When I woke up it was dark outside. The screen of the TV cast a dim light around my tiny living room, creating a dream-like ambiance that made me question whether or not I was really awake.

Something didn't feel right. I stretched and took a quick look around me. In the corner by my desk there was a mass on the floor that I didn't remember. I squinted to try to make out what it was. A pile of dirty clothes, maybe? But I normally threw my clothes in a different corner. I rubbed my eyes again and sat upright in my bed.

Then it *moved*.

It quivered first, like the shadows were pulling together and darkening. The shape elongated from a round lump to what almost looked like a stubby body. It turned the deepest color of black, then an arm reached out and touched the wall. Slowly, another arm emerged and it crawled several feet up the wall before disappearing into the shadows.

A scream stuck in my throat and I couldn't breathe. My heart pounded so strenuously that my chest ached. I stared at the corner, but it was empty now. The desk sat by itself just as it always had.

Of course nothing was there. I was seeing things again. I jumped out of bed and turned on the light, then inspected every inch of the room for anything suspicious. I lifted up every article of dirty clothing, secured all my windows and crawled on my hands and knees to look under the furniture. I even checked the bathroom and studio, just in case.

Once I was sure there was nothing out of the ordinary, I went to my kitchen to grab myself a drink. My phone was on the counter not too far from the fridge, and the red light in the upper corner was flashing. I picked it up and flipped it open. There were two missed called from Don. I hesitated over the buttons. This was not going to be a pleasant conversation.

It only rang twice before he picked up. "Look who finally decided to call me back."

"Yeah, sorry."

"You left before the show was over—who knows how much money you cost us." He mumbled something unintelligible under his breath. "I should raise my percentages for this."

"I am really, really sorry. I had to leave."

"And what could possibly have been more important than last night!?"

I took a deep breath, trying to buy some time to come up with a good lie. "I got sick. I didn't want to puke all over the gallery."

"So you drank too much then? That's just great. You couldn't manage to stay sober for one night?"

"No, I think it was nerves, they've been bad all week. I'm still shaky today." That was not technically a lie. I just stretched the truth a bit.

"Nothing I can do about it now," he grumbled. "You better not be lying to me."

"I swear on my life." Okay, *that* was a lie.

He sighed on the other end of the line. "I'd be angrier if almost half the paintings weren't spoken for by the time the gallery closed yesterday. And Evelyn is leaving the auction open until Tuesday."

That brought a smile to my face. "Did you say almost half?"

"Yes, I did. Despite bailing early… You had a barely mentionable review in the Times today, and the major one will come out in *The New York Artist* on Friday. I'll be out of town so it's up to you to keep an eye out for it."

"I will."

"There is one more thing," Don said. "One of the collectors at the show insisted he take two paintings home immediately.

One of them was your self-portrait. I don't know why the curator allowed it."

Suddenly, I felt nauseated. That was the one *he* wanted. Did that mean Sebastian had it pulled from the auction? What kind of person would have that much influence?

I snapped back to reality. "That's odd, I wonder why she did that." My voice was cool enough it would have even fooled me.

"I'll call you then, alright? And answer your phone next time."

I laughed. "Okay, I promise."

I flipped my phone shut and flopped down on my bed. I tried to clear my head by making pictures out of the flaws in my ceiling. As usual, the stains became faces and creatures. Chips in the plaster became evil eyes and cracks became sharp teeth. Not exactly calming. So I rolled over and stared at the TV, paying very close attention this time so I wouldn't think about Sebastian.

I didn't do much the next day. I have a tendency to be lazy. My dinner tonight was a thirty-three cent package of ramen that was so bland I could barely finish it, and a glass of Kool-Aid spiked with the cheapest vodka money could buy. This was a typical meal for me. I hadn't been eating well lately. My financial situation was partially to blame, but that wasn't the whole truth of it. The majority of my diet consisted of booze and pills. I constantly spent money on those two items instead of purchasing silly things like food.

Once I had eaten all I could stand, I took my cup and went to sit at the narrow window by my TV. The view directly outside was over a corroded fire escape, and peered directly into the apartments of the building next door. I threw open the window looked to the alley below. No one was out there, just dumpsters and metal stairs. I sighed, what I wouldn't have given for one tree.

The air smelled faintly of garbage, but was still fresher than my stale apartment. I closed my eyes and listened to the sound of a couple arguing several floors down from me. A few obscenities were loud enough to make out over the sound of nearby traffic.

I chuckled to myself. That's what happens when you move in with someone. And people wonder why I live alone. I opened my eyes to try and tell which apartment it was coming from.

Directly in front of me was a face. It was corpselike and floated in mid air, with empty chasms for eyes and rotted lips framing a distorted mouth. I couldn't see any teeth, or a discernable body. It appeared as a shadow, like a blurry photograph.

I screamed and fell to the floor with a loud thud. The apartment echoed with the impact. I crawled backwards until my head hit the corner of my coffee table. The creature was gone, but my fear was building. I started hyperventilating, and I was sitting in what used to be my drink. The terror wiped my mind blank. I couldn't move. I couldn't even blink.

I had to get out of here now, but it was still an agonizing minute before I could jump up and sprint out of my apartment. I didn't slow down until I reached the door to my favorite drinking establishment, a full four blocks away. I paused to wipe the sweat from my forehead, and check how soggy my shorts were, then walked inside and made a beeline to the bar.

Kearney's was a dingy Irish tavern with seating for less than fifty. It looked just like the other hundred Irish bars in the city; green walls, Celtic art and Guinness signs. Tacky gilded emblems covered the wooden bar that stretched along the far wall. The lights were dimmed too low and the music was randomly picked by whichever drunken idiot had shoved cash into the jukebox. It felt like home to me. Much more so than the apartment I was avoiding.

I waved down my usual bartender, Jackson. "I need whiskey, lots of it."

He laughed. "Straight to business tonight, huh? What's the matter with you?"

"You don't want to know."

I folded my arms on the sticky bar and rested my head on them while I waited for Jackson to make my drink. That face was at the front of my mind. What was that thing? And why did it seem so familiar? I swear I had seen something like it before, but where? A movie? No, I doubted it. In person? That was even more unlikely. Someone's artwork maybe?

That was it. I'd seen similar faces in someone's artwork. And not just anyone's, it was *mine*.

I had drawn this creature before, or something very similar to it. If I remembered correctly, any artwork of mine that depicted that sort of thing would have been pencil drawings from elementary school.

No wonder Sara and Hank tried to get me help. They really were trying to get the demons out. I laughed to myself. It was all in my head. Visions from my imagination couldn't hurt me, physically anyways.

Jackson sat my drink in front of me. I slammed half of it and smiled at him.

"Tragedy averted?"

"You could say that." I rattled the ice in my glass. "Whiskey heals all wounds."

"So I'm told..."

When I woke up at noon the next day, I put myself on a mission. I was determined to find my drawings of that creature. I had to prove to myself that I'd had hallucinations like this before. And I knew exactly where to look.

The congested closet hidden in the back of my makeshift studio housed most of my older works. I pulled everything out and organized it in piles by year on the floor. I came across a green sketchbook with holes cut out of the cover. It was the one that got me in the most trouble. I was in my dismembering phase, and starting to play around with the idea of sex as a form of death. Somewhere around sixth grade, I think. I made the mistake of taking it to school one day and all Hell broke loose. The principal called Sara and Hank to the office, along with a child psychologist. They grounded me for months, and sent me for daily meetings with our priest.

I flipped through the pages, drinking in the nostalgia of it all. I didn't have many happy memories from back then. Maybe that's why I was so bitter about life now. It was such a typical tortured artist story I had to laugh. At least the artwork was worth it. I hoped.

After an hour of digging, I finally found what I was looking for. A box buried at the bottom of the closet, hidden beneath everything else I had ever drawn. It was wrapped in duct tape and covered in black marker scribbles.

I blew off the dust and opened the box, choking on the musty puff of air that drifted in my direction. Nearly all the notebooks inside were the ruled spiral kind typically used for classrooms. They were all worn and yellowed with age. The corners were crumpled from being shoved under my mattress to hide them from my foster parents.

I grabbed the one on top and started rummaging through it. Almost all the drawings inside had the same theme; hazy creatures with rotted faces.

Half way in I found myself staring at one and unable to turn the page. It was a large shadow in front of the tree outside my childhood bedroom. A distorted face with hollow eyes and decayed lips sat in the middle of the densest part of black.

Bingo.

This was an almost exact replica of what I saw last night. I was having flashbacks from my own wild imagination. It brought a new sense of tranquility to the carnival ride of my deteriorating sanity.

I threw on a skimpy jean skirt and a colorful tank top. My usual look for the summer months. The jewelry I picked was a set Lucas gave me a month earlier; a metal beaded necklace with stylized flame pendants and matching earrings. I let my hair fall where it wanted and checked my reflection in the mirror. I gave myself an eight. Casual, but still cute enough to make it look like I put some effort into my appearance.

The wait for Lucas was painful. Even after I polished off my bottle of vodka and popped several pills, I found myself pacing my living room and checking the clock every three minutes. When the text indicating that he arrived finally came, I skipped out of my apartment so fast that I forgot my purse and had to let myself back in to retrieve it. Was I really this excited about seeing Lucas? Or did I just need to get out of my apartment?

Outside, his jeep was parked parallel to my front door. He was leaning against it with his arms folded, looking very James Dean. I ran up to him and threw my arms around his neck.

He planted a kiss on me. "Someone's in a good mood today."

"Just happy to be going out."

Lucas opened my door to let me inside. "Do you care if Teddy and Conchetta go to dinner with us?"

"A double date could be fun." Or at least it would be a distraction from the wickedness going on inside my head. "Where're we going?"

"Bien Comer. They'll meet us there at seven."

"Should've guessed, that's the only place they ever want to go."

Teddy and Conchetta were snuggled together in a booth towards the back of the restaurant. Teddy was a tall, pudgy black guy with an eyebrow ring and extensive tattooing. He was a fellow mechanic at the high-dollar garage Lucas worked at and had a personality almost as cuddly as his name. He also held the title of Lucas' best friend.

Conchetta, on the other hand, was a Puerto Rican girl several years younger than Teddy, and was not a big fan of mine. She was always dressed up and tonight was no exception. She had on a revealing dress with large flowers on a black background. Her makeup was done to perfection and her shoulder length black hair was pulled back in a silver barrette. I always thought she was out of Teddy's league, but maybe that's why they got along so well. Teddy worshiped the ground she walked on.

We ate dinner, drank margaritas, and I had to listen to Teddy and Conchetta tell me how happy they were to be together a disgusting number of times. They kept up the whole charade for the entire meal. I didn't understand that type of devotion and it made me want to vomit.

"Would you like to join me for a cigarette, Trinity?" Conchetta's faint accent made the question sound more like a proposition.

I didn't usually smoke, and I had suspicions about her motivations for inviting me, but I reluctantly agreed and I got up to follow her outside. Knowing her love of all things Trinity, I prepared myself for an argument.

Conchetta offered me a cigarette and motioned for me to join her on the rusty metal bench. "I was hoping we could take a couple minutes for some girl talk."

"Okay…" And we're already off to a bad start.

"You've been dating Lucas since before I met Teddy, right?"

I took a deep breath and gave myself a moment to think of an answer that would shut her up. "We've been friends for awhile but it's only recently been… official."

She looked like I just clued her in to some huge piece of gossip. "How serious are you two?"

"We're not. But if we get there I'm sure you'll be one of the first to know. My career has center stage right now. I don't have time to deal with much else."

"If you're not serious, then why are you with him?"

I threw my cigarette to the ground and stomped on it. "Why are you asking so many questions about us?"

"I'm just looking out for Lucas. You never hang out with us and you constantly blow him off. You didn't even come to the company picnic last month. It's about time someone said something to you about it." Conchetta glared at me. "I have a friend who really likes him and would treat him a lot better..."

"You can tell your friend to back off." I snapped. Who cares if I didn't want to be serious? He was still mine, and I was not about to give him up. "Do me a favor and mind your own damn business."

"Sorry, forget I said anything." That was the last thing she said to me all night.

Lucas drove back to his place, as he always did after our nights out. I never argued with him not to. We made it back in piece anyways, and I plopped myself down on his couch.

He joined me a few seconds later with two glasses of water. I opened my mouth to protest but he stopped me. "Not everyone gets to quit their job and sleep till noon."

"Preemptive strike. Had to prepare myself for fame, you know. Jobs are for losers."

He laughed. "I may be a loser, but you're the one sleeping with me. So what's that make you?"

"Stupid, I guess." I climbed onto his lap. "So you should probably take your clothes off before I wise up."

"Yours first." Lucas pulled me into a kiss before he lifted my shirt over my head. He sat back and looked me over with a big grin on his face. "Have I told you how sexy you are lately?"

"You can always tell me again," I said.

Lucas flipped me onto my back and stripped me of my skirt and panties. He slipped his shirt over his head and positioned himself over me, then started covering my neck with slow kisses. "Something about you is so different," he said. "I've never had so much trouble keeping my hands off someone."

I giggled, ignoring the mushy part of his statement. "Then it's a good thing I like them on me so much."

He started kissing a path down my chest. His trail of kisses continued down my stomach and stopped just shy of the intended area. I squirmed in anticipation. He laughed and lifted my leg in the air so he could start kissing down from my knee.

The build-up was tormenting, and wonderful all at the same time. "Quit teasing me!"

He smiled at me and switched to the other leg, starting the whole process over again. This time he didn't stop.

Chapter 3

The Big Day

The shrill scream of Lucas' alarm assaulted my ears. This was my least favorite part of having a boyfriend with a day job. Sleepovers were always interrupted.

Lucas hit the snooze button twice before I rolled over and snuggled against his chest. "Good morning," he whispered in a scratchy, sleep-ridden voice.

"Too early," I mumbled.

He laid there with me until the alarm made itself known again. This time he gently slid out from underneath me and sat up to turn it off. The sudden emptiness in my arms left me feeling hollow.

I traced the curves of the pin-up girl on his ribcage with my fingers. "Just lay here with me a little while, will you?"

He turned around and leaned over me with his trademark sweet smile. "Work, remember? I can't be late. Not all of us have fame and fortune waiting in the wings."

"Very funny." I pulled him down and forced him to kiss me.

Mornings weren't normally my thing, but today I craved the closeness.

Lucas laughed at me, but maneuvered himself so he was supporting his body above mine. "Isn't this normally where you try to get rid of me?"

"I could use a distraction, I have a big day ahead of me." I kissed him again and he seemed to take the hint. Things escalated swiftly thanks to the fact that we were already sans clothes from the previous evening. But when I wrapped my legs around his hips, he pushed away from me.

And he laughed at me again. "Alright, you better stop that. I need to get in the shower or I'm not gonna have enough time to get you home."

"Then don't give me a ride. I think I'll survive if I have to take the subway."

He turned to look at the clock. "We won't have enough time to get ready. You really wanna ride the subway with no shower?"

Damn him and all his thinking. "I don't care about that right now."

Lucas started nibbling on my earlobe. "Always getting your way—I'll just leave you a key, then you can officially have free run of the place."

I was so wrapped up in my moment of triumph, I barely paid attention to what he said. It all sounded like yes to me. Not that he'd ever said no before.

I stayed in bed while Lucas got ready. I must have fallen back asleep, because when he kissed me to say goodbye, I practically jumped out of my skin.

"Gotta go. Make yourself at home. Key's on the counter."

Shit! That's right, Lucas was giving me a key. "Have fun at work."

"Yeah, I'm sure it'll be a blast. Call me as soon as you get the details from the show, okay?"

I shooed him away with one hand and buried myself under the sheets. "In case you haven't noticed, I'm trying not to think about that right now. Thanks for bringing it up."

He chuckled and kissed the top of my head. I cringed. Lucas said goodbye and I didn't answer. I was mad at him for mentioning the key. The anger was completely irrational, I didn't care. He disappeared and I went back to sleep.

Sometime around noon I woke up again. I threw a pillow over my face to block out the light and have myself a little freak out session. After two full years of working full time and painting on the side, I left my monotonous data-entry position to finish preparations for my art show. It had been a head-first leap of faith into dark waters. Today I was going to find out what was waiting for me below the surface. I hadn't allowed myself to get excited about Don's previous comments over the show. Now my nerves were about to kill me.

My dinner plans for this evening were equally nerve wracking. The Amantes were terrifying. Or maybe just my reaction to them was terrifying. Either way, trying to impress a group of the rich and powerful was not how I wanted to spend my night.

At least I had no hangover today. That would make things easier. I got ready quickly and headed to the kitchen to raid Lucas' fridge. After settling on a microwavable breakfast sandwich, I spotted the key on the counter. It taunted me. How had I allowed this to happen? Lucas knew me too well to ask me outright if I wanted it. He was such a dirty trickster. A key to his place meant a lot of loyalty on his part, yuck. I should dump him. That would teach him to try and get serious on me.

I sighed and picked up the key. Of course I wouldn't do that. There were certain aspects of our relationship I wasn't ready to give up. And I had no time to audition a new toy. I shoved it in my pocket, not quite ready to commit to putting it on my key ring. Maybe I could still give it back, or accidentally leave it here next time I came over. I could trick him the way he tricked me. Worth a try at least.

Thanks to my uncompromising libido, I had quite the trek ahead of me. The trip from West Village to Sunnyside was multiplied exponentially when you had to navigate the subway system. Unfortunately, the station closest to Lucas' place was packed and filthy, and today it smelled of body odor and garbage.

I went to the end of the platform where the fewest people were waiting. The next car was scheduled to arrive in less than fifteen minutes, so I passed the time by watching the crowd around me. They all moved together as one current coming from the street and through the station. I imagined them flowing down a stream. The constant chatter of voices became the babble of water running over rocks. Then the current turned red and transformed into blood pouring onto the platform and spreading in all directions like it spilled from a mortal wound. That put a smile on my face. I should paint it.

When I got bored of that, I stared down the tunnel to my right. Two sets of tracks ran parallel to each other and disappeared into the distance. Vertical steel beams ran down the middle at three-foot intervals, serving as a wall between the two tracks that allowed you to view the platform on the other side of the street. Fluorescent lights ran in one long line directly above me. The last two lights in the row were out, so the tunnel was darker than normal. The artificial glow accented all the rust on the steel and made everything look ancient and cold.

And just wrong.

About fifteen feet away from me, at the bottom of one of the beams, was a small black lump. It didn't appear threatening, though it was probably a safety issue for anything to be there. I took a step forward to get a better view.

The shadows surrounding it started to swirl around themselves and darkened into an object that almost appeared solid. Then slowly a pair of black eyes began to standout in the middle. The rest of its nearly skeletal face grew and stretched away from the mass on a long neck that bent in the middle. Short arms split that at the elbows into two separate pairs of forearms and hands emerged next. Then long legs hinged to the side came out of the back.

It was gangly and disgusting, with short scraggly hairs sticking out in tufts from several places on its body. Its face was long and hollow, and covered in winkles. The eyes were exactly like the face outside my window. Exactly like my drawings.

I stopped breathing. My chest seized, and a deep chill ran through me. Fear rendered my body immobile. The creature looked me straight in the eye, slowly swaying its head back and forth as if it was making sure I noticed it.

Then it started to crawl along the median towards me. It reminded me of an undead kangaroo. Each arm reached out with two hands and pulled it forward while its disproportionate legs hopped in small lunges.

I gasped and took a step back. My heel landed on top of someone else's toe.

"Watch it," an irritated voice barked behind me.

I spun around before I realized what I was doing. The man was already walking away, but he was the least of my worries. I turned my back on that creature. I snapped my head around just in time to see the next train come barreling down the track. The creature was gone. And by the looks of things, I was the only one who saw it.

The rush of air and shake of the platform that came with the arrival of the train brought me closer to reality. I could finally breathe again, but I was hyperventilating. My heart beat so hard I felt it pounding in the back of my ears.

As the crowd around me pushed forward, I mechanically followed to the door of the nearest car. It was standing room only by the time I made it inside, so I grabbed the first pole and stared down at my feet. I really was losing my mind. That had to have been a hallucination, right? It was so familiar, there was no other explanation. But it looked *real*. And it looked like it was coming right for me.

Too much more of this and I was going to have to check myself into the mental hospital. Kudos to me if I could really think something like that up, but I never wanted to see anything like it again.

Hanging around to late with Lucas just so I could get laid was not worth all this. I should have let him drive me home when he offered.

Don didn't call me until five. Thanks to several little blue friends liberated from my pill bottle, I was feeling much better. Light as a feather, my eyes droopy, I giggled at the fact that Don sounded more excited about this conversation than I did.

"Despite your behavior, Saturday night was a success. You actually did better than most the pros I deal with. Two-thirds sold. People are just eating this shit up—Well, there were a few exceptions. But I'm willing to bet there will be a line for your next show."

I could barely contain myself, stuck somewhere between bouncing up and down and squealing with joy. "That's the best news I've ever heard in my entire life, you realize that right?"

He laughed. "It gets better," There was a moment's pause. I'm assuming for dramatic effect. "Your bank account's been well padded. Would you like to know the numbers?"

"No, of course not. That's not the whole reason for doing all this, now is it?"

"Exactly. No one ever hires an agent to make them money," Don said, proving his immunity to my sarcasm. "Anyways, fifty-seven was the final number. Minus taxes and my fifteen percent, you're just over forty-four grand. Not too shabby, if I do say so myself. Check's already in the bank."

I had to set the phone down so I was adequately free to dance around enough to relieve my excitement. That was an awful lot of money for someone like me. Even if it was nothing compared to two years salary. While I shook ass, I ran over the numbers in my head. If two-thirds sold that should have added up to about forty-five thousand. Not fifty-seven. I snatched my phone and threw it against my ear. "Wait a minute, I don't get it. Why is it so much—? Not that I'm complaining."

"I should hope not," Don said. "Two of your paintings sold for more than twice what we were asking. Your self-portrait alone brought in thirteen grand. This big time collector scooped it up along with the one of the two women bleeding out on the bed. His name's Sebastian Amante. Apparently the guy has disgusting amounts of money, and he buys tons of art. But that's all anyone really knows about him."

There went the end of my dancing. "Sebastian bought two?"

"Yes, did you get to meet him? What's he like? I've never actually seen him."

How could I answer that question? My perspective was completely warped. I didn't know how Sebastian would appear to someone who wasn't having a mental breakdown. "Uh, he seemed nice. He's really hot."

Don laughed. "Of course that's the only thing you would notice about him. Well, maybe I'll get to meet him someday. If he seemed interested in your work we might get lucky and he'll come back for more."

From his answer, it was obvious that Don had no idea about my dinner plans for the evening. It must be beneath someone of Sebastian's stature to clear the event with my agent.

Don and I went over every last detail of the show. As important as that should have been, I was done paying attention. I made up an excuse to let him go and decided to start preparing for my night.

The short black skirt and nearly backless silver top I set aside for this evening was my favorite outfit. It only covered the necessities but was classy enough that you barely noticed. I kept on the jewelry Lucas gave me. They were no crown jewels, but aside from what I wore to the show, they were the nicest things I had.

Sebastian said he'd send a car at seven. I never told him where I lived, and if he hadn't talked to Don, I'm not sure how he would get that information. I checked the clock every three minutes until six forty-five before my nerves forced me out the door. It wouldn't take fifteen minutes to get downstairs, but I just couldn't take it anymore.

I forced myself to walk at a calm pace downstairs, and took one last calming breath before stepping outside. Directly in front of me was a man in a black suit, standing next to a shiny new Lincoln of the same color. He was approachably handsome, brown hair, brown eyes, and average height and build. When he saw me exit the building, he gave me friendly smile.

"Miss Morgan?"

"That's me."

He held open the back passenger door and motioned for me to step inside. "I'm Steven. I'll be your driver this evening."

I nervously slipped onto the cool leather seat. "So where are we going?"

He gave me the same steady smile. "It's to be a surprise, ma'am."

Steven didn't say anything else as we drove into the heart of Manhattan. When he stopped the car, we were parked at the front door of Blue, one of the fanciest restaurants in the area.

Inside, Blue was overwhelmingly modern, clean straight lines, minimalistic design, and zero clutter. Well-dressed people filled every table, and blue lights illuminated everything. Steven nodded to the maitre d and escorted me toward a set of elevators. As far as I knew, the restaurant was on only one level, but Steven hit the button for the top floor. I would have waited a month to get a table, and here I was being nodded up to a private room.

By the time the doors opened up to the entryway, my nerves were shot. I felt like I was getting ready to step out on stage for the first time. Only I was naked, and I forgot my lines.

Steven led me through another door. This room had the same style as the restaurant on the first floor, only this one was almost completely framed in windows. A long mahogany table was in the center and a glass waterfall backlit with a bright ultramarine light was on the wall opposite me. Every line in the room pointed to the chair that sat in front of that waterfall, and the glorious man who sat in it.

My heart came to a halt when I saw Sebastian. My memories had done the man no justice. He was leaning back in his chair with his hand under his chin. The light from behind surrounded him in an angelic blue aura. It bounced off the stylish black suit he wore, accenting his strong features and gleaming off the gaudy diamond in his ear.

Amelie sat directly to the right of him. She looked like a supermodel tonight. Her hair had been curled and pinned partially back. Her eggshell gown was loose and low cut, showing off the definition of her shoulders and arms, and revealing more than was necessary of her perky rack.

Andras sat on Sebastian's left. He had on a dark brown suit with a dress shirt the same hue as Amelie's dress. He was her mirror image, sitting in the exact position and looking almost as beautiful as she did. I found it creepy that they were dressed alike again.

Vino was all the way in the back of the room. He was lounging on one of the couches with his feet up, and staring off into space out the window. He was dressed similarly to the way he was at the show, an untucked burgundy dress shirt with the top two buttons open and black dress pants. His hair was pulled back in a ponytail, but quite a bit of it hung loose in the back and spilled into his face. Every aspect of his posture and expression said he did not want to be here.

I followed his gaze through the window to the lights of Time Square. In my four years of being a New Yorker, I had only seen this area from above a few times. Under normal circumstances, it was one of my favorite things about the city. Tonight I had something even more spectacular to look at.

Sebastian abruptly stopped his conversation with his daughter as I approached the table. Then he smiled at me, and my world became a happier place. "Trinity, how wonderful to see you again. Please, come have a seat with us."

His velvety greeting hit me with a force that nearly knocked the wind out of me. *Not this again.* "Hello, Sebastian," I said awkwardly.

A man dressed the same as my driver came out of nowhere to pull out a chair for me. There were three other men just like him waiting off in the corner. Apparently, Sebastian brought a whole staff with him.

Sebastian made a show of sweeping his eyes over me. He raised his wine glass and gave me a wink of approval. "Don't you look positively delicious this evening. Perhaps I should have asked my family to stay home."

I turned bright red. I might have even giggled.

"But we are here for business, aren't we?" He sighed and motioned to his left and right where the twins flanked him. "You remember my children, Amelie, Andras," he nodded to the corner behind him. "Vinicio."

"Yeah, nice to see you guys again." I wasn't normally at a loss of words, but right now, I could barely remember how to speak.

"Pleasure's ours, I'm sure." Amelie answered, without hardly looking at me.

"Beautiful view from here, don't you think?" Sebastian crooned. "My favorite place to eat in the whole city." He paused to watch one of the servants pour me a glass of wine and hand me a menu.

I smiled in answer as I opened the leather bound booklet. There were no prices inside, just a list of eight entrees that they were serving that particular evening. I was the only person who received one, and the servant who gave it to me was still waiting at my side to take my order. I pointed to the duck and handed it back to him. I didn't know much about dining in fancy restaurants, but I was sure this is not how things were normally done.

When I made eye contact with Sebastian again, he grinned at me like he was up to something. "That's exciting news about your art show. Eighteen paintings in one night is quite an accomplishment."

How in the world would he know that? I took a deep breath and tried to appear calm. "Things went better than I expected. I guess I have you to thank for some of that."

Sebastian dismissed my gratitude with a wave of the hand. "I knew you were something special the second I walked in the door. I like to think I have an eye for that sort of thing."

Coming from him, that compliment seemed like high praise, even if he complimented himself in the process. "Well, no reviews have come out yet, so I'm trying not to get too far ahead of myself."

He shook his head. "You have nothing to fear. Like I said, I have an eye for these things, I could probably narrate everything they're going to say before it gets put down on paper." He paused to take a drink from his wine. "I suppose we should get down to things, don't you think?"

Those were happy words against my ears. I couldn't handle much more small talk. "Sure."

"I'm not asking for much. Just a painting."

"Sounds easy enough, what exactly did you have in mind?"

He took another sip of wine before he answered me. "I would like you to do a portrait for me. One of a slightly larger scale than the two I've already purchased."

I cringed internally about that. He had my self-portrait in his possession already. That meant there was a picture of me, nude and in bondage, somewhere in his home. The fact that he was the one who owned it gave things a whole new perspective.

Two women entering the room with carts of food interrupted us. They were barely allowed inside before Sebastian's servants took the carts from them and sent them away. It shocked me how fast they were. I ordered less than five minutes ago. It didn't even seem possible to get all the way downstairs and back up in that amount of time.

The servants placed all the plates on the table at the same time. As before, Sebastian paid no attention to the people serving him. I was the only one who thanked them, or even looked at them. And both of the twins glared at me in unison like I wasn't supposed to talk to the help.

Sebastian took a bite then cut another chunk off the slab of meat and held his fork up to study it. "Did anyone else order the veal? It's fantastic."

His eyes darted towards the back of the room. Apparently his question had been directed towards Vino, who had yet to claim his meal. When he didn't leave his spot on the couch, Sebastian's happy demeanor faltered and his upper lip twitched an almost infinitesimal amount. "Don't you think you're being rude to our guest?"

Vino slowly stood and made his way to the table to take the seat on my right between his sister and me. He glanced at me with a face devoid of any emotion. "My apologies, Trinity. My mind was elsewhere. It's nice to see you again."

"Nice to see you too."

Without the smiles and charm Vino showed me this weekend, he was much more intimidating. I shied away from him and turned my attention to the plate in front of me for a distraction. The duck breast was nestled in a pile of rice, drizzled lightly with sauce, and surrounded by a bouquet of vegetables. It was almost too pretty to eat. I cut off a tiny piece and took a sample. It tasted even better than it looked.

"They really know what they're doing down there, don't they?" Vino leaned towards me while he spoke, watching me like I was some sort of science experiment.

My heart sputtered when we made eye contact. "Yeah, you guys have great taste."

"Only the best—back to business shall we?" Sebastian chimed in, bringing everyone's attention back to him. He took a sip from his wine and held it away from his face, propped up on one elbow dramatically. "I suppose you'd be wondering what I might like to pay for such an endeavor?"

My curiosity was piqued. Nerves and anxiety aside, this was the part I was most excited about. "I'm sure whatever it is will be way more than I'm worth."

"You have no idea what you're worth." Sebastian paused to laugh. "I was thinking, twenty thousand up front, and at least much that amount upon completion."

My eyes bulged out of my head. Forty thousand was ridiculous for one painting. I opened my mouth to answer, but wasn't allowed.

"And I'd appreciate it if we kept your agent out of this. I'd hate to see the man get a cut for doing nothing, wouldn't you?"

"I'm under contract, I don't know how I'd..."

He cut me off again and shook his head. "You needn't worry about that. We have ways around such things."

I ran over the morality of omitting the man who got me my big break so I could make more money in my head. Money won. "In that case, sounds like a good deal."

"Wonderful," Sebastian leaned forward in his chair and put his elbows on the table with his hands together in the steeple position. One side of his mouth curled up in a devious smirk. He looked exactly like a comic book villain about to unravel his sinister plan. "There are a few minor details we need to discuss first."

I knew there was a catch, and by the look on his face, it must be a doozey. "Alright, shoot."

He chuckled quietly at my reply, and his eyes bore into mine with that same ferocity they had at the show. They started to radiate with their own light again and flicker like they were made of flames. "My first stipulation is relatively easy. You will do this painting at my estate and you will use the supplies we provide. All you will need to do is show up."

That sounded more like a bribe than a stipulation to me. "That doesn't sound so bad, when did you want to start?"

"Stipulation number two." He raised his eyebrow at me. I got the impression I wasn't supposed to interrupt. "We start tomorrow, seven p.m. sharp, and every night that fits into my schedule thereafter until completion. I will have a car waiting outside your place at six thirty."

He waited for me to answer this time. No days off would be rough, but I was not about to say no. I nodded my agreement. "I can handle that."

"Good, good." He glanced around at the other three at the table. They were all watching me now. The twins leaned forward with their heads cocked to one side in sync. Vino sat back with his arms crossed, staring at me.

The table in front of me started to stretch out. All of the others around it slowly grew further and further away. I could feel my heart beating faster and my breath picking up speed. Things started to spin and grow blurry...

Then Sebastian cleared his throat and everyone but him looked away from me. The room and I went back to normal. "My last stipulation is the important one. You see, our business venture will leave you privy to certain… sensitive information. I need to be sure you will keep quiet in regard to such things."

I swallowed at the lump in my throat. It was several long moments before I could compose myself enough to speak. "Of course, non-disclosure agreement, I know how those work."

He finally smiled again, but it was not a nice smile. "Paperwork holds no value. Let's just say, straying from our agreement would be of great consequence to you. You cannot tell a soul where you are or who you are with. As far as anyone needs to be concerned, you know nothing of my family or I."

The fact that he was smiling as he calmly issued such a vague threat, gave his words a viciousness that shook me to the core. I wanted to look away from him and found myself unable. It felt like he was commanding me to, taking my will away and sucking me in. I forgot who I was, where I was and every other thought that had ever entered my mind.

I'm not sure how long I was trapped like that. He just looked away, and I was free, back in the room with everyone else like I had awoken from a dream. I should be on medication. Maybe this guy was a little scary, but this was ridiculous. I needed to get it together if I was going to have to see him every day. Hallucinations and panic attacks were a horrible way to make a good impression.

"So what will it be, Trinity? All I need is your word of approval." Sebastian was back to his dazzling smile, appearing as benign as he was able.

I nodded. My hands were clammy and I felt sweaty. I hoped no one noticed. "Yes."

"Well, now that we have all the unpleasantries aside, I have a gift for you."

A servant came to my side immediately. He held out a large black jewelry box. I hesitated before taking it from him. "I can't…"

Sebastian interrupted me before I could get anymore out. "A small token of our newfound friendship. It's nothing, really."

I took him at his word and opened the box. What lay inside was definitely not nothing. It was a thick, silver colored chain, flat and more than half an inch wide in a modern, seamless braid. There were also matching earrings, hoops that twisted slightly at the end. I was pretty sure they were platinum.

"They're beautiful."

"Please don't be afraid to wear it. I would hate for it to spend its life in a box."

I reached up to unclasp the necklace I was wearing and he snapped his fingers to alert a servant to assist me in the matter. Once the switch had been made and I changed out the earrings, he leaned back in his chair and nodded his approval.

"It suits you."

I blushed, the threats from a moment before long forgotten. Complements and shiny presents were the easiest way to gain my forgiveness. "Thank you, it's a wonderful gift."

"I'm so glad you like it." He picked up his wine and took a larger then average drink, finishing the glass. In one fluid movement, he sat it on the table and stood up. "I'm saddened to admit that as much as I enjoy your company, we must be going." He let out an exaggerated sigh. "Duty awaits."

Sebastian made his way around the table and the twins silently left their seats. They nodded to me at precisely the same time. "Till tomorrow," Amelie said as they both stepped back to wait for their father.

Every step closer that Sebastian took made my heart beat faster. I rose to meet him and he stopped with mere inches between us to casually take one of my hands in his. His touch sent a jolt through me exactly as it had on Saturday, and the same nauseating warmth started to spread through my body.

He looked me in the eye and smiled, slowly lifting my hand to his lips. The second they made contact my surroundings disappeared again, leaving behind a reality that consisted only of him. He closed his eyes took a deep breath, savoring whatever it was about this moment that he found so satisfying. It felt like forever before he lowered my hand away from his face.

He winked at me again and my brain shut off. I was so smitten with him that the logic that he was twice my age and utterly out of my league wasn't setting in.

"You did not disappoint, my dear. I will see you tomorrow." His deep voice seemed more than a sweet promise, it was also an order. One that I would blindly obey.

I couldn't regain my composure until he released my hand. "Yeah, see you tomorrow."

Sebastian smiled at me one last time and turned to take his leave. It wasn't until he walked away that Vino finally rose from his chair. He paused to turn to me. His eyes had changed to a deep shade of crimson and he stared into mine with an intenseness that made me blush.

I gave him a weak smile. "Good night."

"Good night." He repeated indifferently, then strolled over to where Sebastian and the twins were waiting.

They all disappeared through a back door that I hadn't remembered seeing earlier. I was alone in the room, except for Steven, the driver who had been assigned to me. When I picked up my handbag and the jewelry box off the table I noticed all the plates had already been cleared. I only remembered taking a few bites, and never saw anyone come to retrieve a single item.

Steven came to my side to get my attention. "Shall we get going ma'am?"

I trembled as I turned to look at him. "Yeah, I suppose so."

Chapter 4

Sebastian's Flawless Face

Steven dropped me off at my filthy apartment after dinner. My mind was spinning past exertion, my heart was racing, and I felt sick. By reflex, I reached for my bottle of Xanax and found it empty. Not a good sign. They usually lasted twice this long.

Sobriety was not my friend. I longed for the sweet escape and calming numbness of intoxication. Whatever wine I consumed this evening hadn't done the trick, and my place was dry. Until today, I didn't have the money necessary to keep a liquor cabinet. I would change that as soon as possible.

The springs in my bed squeaked in protest as I plopped down and threw a pillow over my face. Processing the plethora of information I received today was overwhelming. My art show did well, I had forty-four grand in the bank, and my loser boyfriend tricked me into taking a key to his apartment. Then there was dinner, and the selling of my soul, as I saw it.

I couldn't believe I agreed to work *every single day*. That's not even the worst of it. It wasn't my ludicrous reactions to Sebastian either. It was the consequences he mentioned. What could possibly be so important that he felt the need to threaten me? Was he doing something illegal? Maybe he was a mob boss, or a drug lord. That might be cool, but I doubted it. Whatever he was into, it had to be bad. And yet, I didn't think bad of him. I felt quite the opposite actually.

Strange how I could be so frightened of someone, and then crush on them to such a degree.

In my frustration, I threw my pillow across the room and sat up. It was only ten. I didn't feel like going out, and there was no way I could go to sleep, so I settled on dragging myself to my desk. My virus-ridden, fossil of a computer was something else I hated about my life. It was so slow I normally got mad and unplugged it before accomplishing anything. I flipped it on and waited, giving it the evil eye the whole time so it wouldn't think about trying anything funny.

The logic behind my actions was simple. I was curious as to how much money I had. Hearing Don rattle off numbers over the phone was one thing. But seeing it in my bank account, that would be something special.

When I arrived at my bank's homepage, I logged in and held my breath. I even crossed my fingers. Much to my amazement the computer didn't freeze, but that's not why my jaw dropped.

The balance wasn't forty-four thousand, it was sixty-four. A separate deposit was made today for twenty grand.

Sebastian already paid me.

That meant Sebastian knew what bank I used, probably even my account number. Don was the only other person who knew that information, and Sebastian made it clear he would not deal with him.

In a mindless attempt to hold in my overactive heart, my fingers found the exorbitant chain wrapped around my neck. The magnificent gift only added to my anxiety. I was already in deep, and I hadn't even done one hour's worth of work.

The sound of my ringing cell phone interrupted my thoughts. I picked it up while it was still ringing but didn't answer. I didn't feel like talking. Lucas could wait.

The next morning the only thing on my mind was shopping. I made it through three clothing stores before Lucas called me again.

My eyes rolled skyward as I answered. "Hey, Luke."

"Why didn't you call me back last night?"

"I was busy... hold on..." I pulled the next shirt from my pile over my head.

"What are you doing?"

"Trying on clothes. What's with the twenty questions?"

"You didn't call me. I'm allowed to have questions." There was a loud exhale into the receiver. "If you're shopping that means you have good news, right?"

I adjusted my cleavage in the mirror before answering him. "I banked, actually, made a total killing."

"That's great! We should go out tonight to celebrate."

"Can't, I have to work."

Lucas was silent for a moment. I'm sure he was trying to get the concept of me and work to fit together. "Alright, you lost me—will you just pay attention for one damn minute and tell me what's going on?"

"Fine." I suppressed the urge to mess with him and sat on the tiny bench. "So, I found out I made a boatload at the show, then I had a meeting to pick up a new project, and now I am out spending money. That pretty much sums it up."

"What kind of project is it?"

I sighed. "A portrait for some super-rich guy. He doesn't seem to understand that people need days off. I have to paint every night from now until it's finished."

"Wow, that's going to be rough. I know how well you and work get along."

"Ha, ha. You're so fucking funny." *And you're interrupting my shopping,* I added internally.

Lucas' warm laugh filled the receiver. "I thought so…" he paused. "Did you say you're trying on clothes?"

It didn't take a genius to see what he was getting at. "Sorry, I'm fully dressed right now."

"A guy can hope."

That one brought a smile to my lips. He was so hopeless. We said our goodbyes, and I went back to changing clothes. Things would be different not seeing Lucas every day. But I refused to tell myself I'd miss him. I'd call him this weekend. That would be good enough.

My last outfit was purchased at four o'clock. By this time, my bank account was several grand lighter and I was worried about my deadline. I hailed a cab and made one last stop. The liquor store.

I strutted through the door in my new designer sunglasses and smiled at the cashier. "Do you have a cart?"

The forty-something Asian woman gave me a suspicious look. "Over in the corner."

With a quick nod, I put my shades on top of my head then grabbed the first cart and headed down the aisles. I picked out several bottles of wine, a new wine opener, gin, rum, tequila, whiskey, two bottles of top shelf vodka, and the most expensive scotch they had. I topped it off with some mixes on my way to the counter and grinned. This was a joyous occasion.

The woman stared at me. "Big party tonight?"

I laughed. "Sure, why not."

Seven hundred dollars later, I made my way back to the cab I paid to wait outside. My chivalrous cabbie even helped carry up my bags. I made sure to keep him from going in my apartment and tipped him an extra twenty. I was feeling generous today. Which was probably the reason behind his kindness. That, and the fact that my ass was hanging out of my shorts.

I made myself a drink, threw all the bags on my bed, and stood back to admire them. I'd never been able to buy so much stuff before. It was exhilarating. I didn't even have room for all this. It was a good thing my lease was up in three months. I needed more closet space.

Pants went in one stack, dresses and skirts in another, shirts on the bed, shoes and accessories on the floor. It probably wasn't a good idea to spend so much, but shopping was great therapy. I could have thrown everything into a pile and swam in it like Scrooge McDuck.

When six rolled around, I was still lost in my piles of booty. I struggled to pick out an outfit, and settled on a skirt with an off the shoulder green top. I applied some of my new make-up, spritzed myself with new perfume, and slipped on a new pair of brown strappy sandals. The jewelry set Sebastian gave me finished off the look. The necklace hadn't left its spot around my throat for longer than required to take a shower. I even slept in it.

Promptly at six-thirty, I stepped outside to find Steven waiting for me with the same black Lincoln. Tonight he drove into Tribeca, the city's richest precinct. We parked in front of an all-black skyscraper and he escorted me inside. As before, he paid little attention to the valets, the door attendant, or the man at the front desk. We were buzzed through a set of steel doors, then Steven punched a code into a keypad and led me into an elevator.

There were no buttons inside, only an emergency stop knob and a phone. After a long silent ride, we walked through a short hallway with only one door. Steven entered another code and granted me access into Sebastian's apartment.

As I stepped inside a deep shiver ran through me. The bright room was enormous, a lot bigger than my whole apartment. The outside walls were windows with intricate wrought iron decoration. The inside walls were white, with paintings and other artwork hung everywhere. It was hard not to too run up and inspect them all. Rugs and exotic plants covered the polished wood floors. Large sculptures drew attention to a spiral staircase that led through the exposed rafters of the high ceiling. The contemporary furniture was accented by a few classical pieces. One of which was a chesterfield couch that sat parallel to a ceiling mounted theater screen.

The twins were sitting on the couch. Amelie was leaning

against Andras' chest, and he had his arm around her. They looked more like lovers than siblings. He turned his head and put his mouth next to her ear. I couldn't tell if he whispered something, but she smiled and spoke.

"Hello, Trinity."

I nervously adjusted my shades to the top of my head. "Hey, guys."

Amelie appeared to be listening to what Andras said again. I didn't hear a word. "Our father's waiting for you upstairs. Your escort will see you find your way."

Steven led me past them through an arched doorway where a second set of elevators waited. This lift was nicer than the one from the lobby. The interior walls were plush, like the inside of a luxury car. He pushed one of the unmarked buttons and we went up two, maybe three floors.

The doors opened to the top floor of the building. If you paid no attention to the fact that it was twenty degrees cooler, you would have thought we were back outside. The room was all windows; even the ceiling was a glass dome. Only one wall ran the length of the room in back. To my left was an enormous infinity pool surrounded by upscale patio furniture. It spilled onto a hidden ledge with more tropical plants so it appeared the water poured into a jungle and then down the side of the building. On my right was a large canvas and easel set up in front of a black partition. The canvas had to be seven feet tall, and the table next to it was covered in supplies.

In the back corner of the room was a sitting area with a white, semi-circle sectional covered in red throw pillows. Sebastian sat in the middle of that couch, accompanied by four women. There were two redheads and two bleached-blondes. All of which were voluptuous beauties with large breasts and tiny waists that looked remarkably alike. They barely looked old enough to drink, and all wore different versions of the same black lingerie. Another matched set.

The woman to his right was kissing her way up to his earlobe. The one to his left was nuzzling his shoulder and reaching into his open shirt. There was one sitting between his feet, resting her head on his thigh. The last girl was behind the couch, leaning into him and playing with his hair. The worship in their eyes was hard to ignore as they seemed to take the greatest joy in just being able to touch him.

Sebastian wore a serene grin on his face. His arms were draped over the back of the couch and his tie was loosened half way and pulled off to one side. Both his shirt and his vest were completely open, exposing his enticingly firm chest and stomach.

I felt like I walked in on an orgy. It upset me on a level I never expected. Everything in me wanted to be disgusted by this, but I was more disgusted with myself. I was *jealous*.

He watched me calmly, holding my gaze as a sickly satisfied expression spread across his face. The women continued to paw at him, and he just sat there, staring at me as I walked towards him.

Then he gently pushed them away as if they were unwanted dogs. When they were clear of him, he stood and leisurely headed in my direction, rebuttoning his shirt in slow motion. I couldn't take my eyes off him. He positively oozed sex. It seeped from his pores and wafted off him like the finest cologne. The mere scent of him was intoxicating.

"Trinity," he purred. "Just the person I was thinking about."

I blushed. I hoped he meant that to be as inappropriate as it sounded. "It's nice to see you again, Sebastian."

He left his vest open and reached out to take my hand. That same warmth spread through me with his touch again. It radiated up my arm and into my chest, sending a flurry through my senses. He kissed the top of my hand again and held me in his gaze for much longer than necessary.

There was something utterly dirty about the way he was looking at me, and I was totally okay with that.

Sebastian released my hand and made a sweeping motion to the room around us. "Do you find this an appropriate place to work?"

I blinked a few times and forced myself to glance away from his face. "It's perfect, must be the best view in the city. I hope I don't get distracted."

"I promise there are better views than this. As for distractions..." He gave me a seductive wink. "We seem to have a lot of those around here."

All I could do was stare at him with a dumb grin. He gave a slight tilt of his head to indicate the area to my right. "Shall we?"

Was he motioning to the canvas, or the women? In a momentary flash of panic, my eyes darted towards them. They were silent, motionless, and watching Sebastian with an eerie longing. Their separation from him looked painful.

He chuckled under his breath and began gliding towards the canvas. He buttoned his vest, straightened his tie, and smoothed his hair into place with his fingers. His movements captivated me enough I almost didn't notice how perceptive he had just been about my reaction. I was going to have to watch out for that.

Sebastian snapped his fingers and a servant rushed ahead of us to stand next to the partition. It was only then I realized Steven was gone. I had no idea when he left my side.

The canvas was massive up close. In terms of a portrait, its size was ridiculous. I'd be lucky to finish in a month. There were two chairs in front of it, a small round stool and a comfortable looking office chair. A full-length table on the right side held a wide selection of paints and brushes, several palettes, and nearly every other supply I could think of. There was even a small telescopic cart to use as a portable workstation.

I ran my fingers over a group of brushes and picked one up to get a closer look. The handle was a polished red wood and the bristles were soft animal hair. It had expensive written all over it.

"This is nice," I sat it back down and turned to him with a smile.

"If there is anything I can get for you, please let me know."

There was only one thing that I could think of. "I could use a drink, if you don't mind."

Sebastian laughed. "Of course, of course. I should have known." He looked to a servant and issued an unseen command that sent him running. "Can you think of anything else?"

I shook my head and pointed to the partition. "What's with all the secrecy?"

He leaned down, uncomfortably close, and reached out to take my hand. "You and I have no secrets."

A voice from somewhere deep in my subconscious whispered that I was supposed to perceive that comment as menacing. It was silenced quickly. Even as that weird sensation flowed through me again, I was more compelled to go into his arms than shy away from him.

He winked at me and released my hand. "You'll have to forgive me. I'm afraid I'm growing a touch dramatic in my old age."

I giggled. I actually let out a stupid, girlie giggle. "I can probably manage some forgiveness, in your case."

Sebastian laughed. "That's good to know. I hope I don't exceed your tolerance for it."

He issued another silent command and the servant slid the partition out of the way. There was a stage set up behind it; four stairs leading up to a small platform, covered in burgundy velvet and sprinkled with white flower petals. In the back were more tall tropical plants and a set of mirrored abstract sculptures in white.

In the center of the platform was a throne that appeared torn out of a medieval castle. The black wood was carved with swirling patterns and decorated with gold inlays. Its high back and seat were upholstered in red silk with a stencil sewn around the border. I didn't have to ask who would be sitting in that throne.

There was a proud look in Sebastian's eyes. "What do you think?"

"Dramatic was the right word, I've got my work cut out for me."

He laughed again. "I have faith in you, my dear. Do you need a minute to situate yourself? Or would you prefer if we got straight to work?"

I mulled it over for a second. "Might as well get to work. This thing's not gonna paint itself."

Sebastian smiled at me with a naughty joy. "Wonderful."

He waved to the women and they all rose in unison. They were almost close enough to touch him before he turned away from me to walk up the stairs and take his seat. He sat tall and erect, slightly leaning on his left elbow. His right arm draped gracefully over the opposite rest. He sat his right calf casually on his left knee, balancing himself. He crossed one leg over the other to balance himself out visually. He looked regal and at ease. It was as if the throne was made especially for him and he had ruled in it for years. Sebastian was breathtaking.

One by one, the women positioned themselves around him. The two ginger-haired beauties each took a side of the throne. The one to his left stood, leaning against the throne like a stripper pole. The other knelt on the opposite side and handed him an antique golden chalice with rubies embedded in it. It seemed cliché, but it fit the scene so well I couldn't object. He held it off to his left, propped up at eye level away from his face.

The first blonde sat at the foot of the throne, leaning backward with one leg extended down the stairs. The last woman sat on the first stair and turned sideways, holding herself up with one hand on the platform and one leg out to mirror the other blonde's.

The servant returned with a glass of red wine. I eagerly accepted it, sat on the stool, and let the view sink in. All the women just stared forward with the same sensual look in their eyes, holding their provocative positions like statues. No one showed much emotion except for Sebastian, who wore his sinful grin as he studied my reaction. Amazingly, I was calm. Work mode switched on, and my emotions switched off. It was easier to look over the scene when I saw everything objectively, and ignored their faces. In my mind I broke it down into composition of color and shapes. Everything was perfectly balanced, top to bottom, left to right. Even the colors were in perfect harmony. It had the right ratio of darks to lights though the entire spectrum. This would make for an exquisite piece. I couldn't have planned it better myself.

I grabbed a piece of charcoal and walked up to the oversized canvas. Mindlessly, I started blocking in the shapes of where everything went, paying no attention to detail. I don't know how long I did this, but before I knew it, the entire canvas was covered in ovals, triangles, and lines, a rough plot as to where things would go.

Cleaning up the bodies was the next task. I concentrated on the curves of the women, and the sexy way they carried themselves. I roughly sketched their lingerie, their long hair, the placement of their facial features. They all looked so much alike I felt I was drawing the same picture repeatedly. The last one took half as long as the first.

My kneaded eraser was balled up against the stem of the wine glass in my left hand. I wondered how many times it had been refilled and came up with no reply. That made me briefly aware of my surroundings again. It was dark outside now, and the overhead lights had taken over. There were even spotlights moved in around my subjects. I couldn't recall seeing anyone wheel those in.

I had purposely avoided drawing Sebastian. He hadn't moved an inch. It was as if someone had pushed the pause button on life. I took a deep breath and started sketching out his clothes, his hands, and the chalice, saving his face for last.

When I finally looked at his eyes, it instantly broke my concentration. I took a sip from my drink and hit the reset button in my head. I studied the distinguishing silver highlights in his hair, his arching eyebrows, the lines too attractive to be called crow's feet, his angular nose, soft lips and strong jaw line. I hesitated when I had to look in his eyes again. There was no way I'd be able to capture those piercing baby blues in a way that would give them the respect they deserved.

The nub of charcoal in my hand was hovering over the canvas, but I hadn't drawn anything. I wasn't studying Sebastian for artistic purposes anymore. I was ogling him.

He noticed.

His smile grew wicked as his eyes bore into my soul. Even from ten feet away I could see every detail as his irises caught fire again. Violent flames whipped the blue and melted it to liquid. Then the black centers of his pupils grew to engulf the blue flames and extinguish them. The black kept spreading, slowly crawling out to conquer the white. What was left was emptiness, a black hole that went plunging into forever. Sucking me and what was left of my sanity into it.

The canvas may as well have been gone. I was still holding the charcoal to it, but the reason for doing such a thing eluded me. I was falling into the abyss of his eyes like a dream, sinking with no end in sight. The room around me faded away, until all that remained was darkness. Darkness, and *his face*. That flawless face, marred only by the fact that the eyes were gone, and the skin around them was shadowed with black veins.

I was trapped underwater, unable to breathe and staring up at him through the murkiness. Reaching upwards, waiting for him to pull me out and save me from drowning. A weight was on my chest, pushing me further down, taking away my reality. There was nothing left of me, my mind and body were gone. They were swirling around in those waters somewhere out of reach. The only thing I could feel was the pit that had formed in my stomach from falling so long.

Plummeting deeper and deeper...

Descending into oblivion.

But no matter how far I fell, he was right there. Just out of reach, and wearing that vexing grin as he watched me tumble helplessly. That smile with all its cruel intentions was mocking me, enjoying my pain.

And then it changed. His smile *grew*. It twisted up at the corners into an inhuman sneer. The lips distorted and decayed as they stretched outward and up like an evil joker cartoon. His once perfect teeth were now a set of jagged, uneven fangs.

His handsome face was gone, and all that remained was a monster. More ghastly than anything I could have ever dreamed. So far from human, and so, so horrible.

There was the sound of broken glass, and something splashed against my bare ankles. I gasped loudly, and clutched at my chest. The frantic rhythm of my heart burned me from the inside.

That split second snapped me back to reality. I don't know what I was doing, or where I was until then, but the shattered glass of my drink now lay at my feet. The red wine had splattered the marble and left dark droplets covering my skin and sandals. It looked remarkably like blood.

My eyes closed on instinct, fighting off the waves of panic. I was light-headed enough I feared I would faint. I wanted to run away, run right out that door and never come back. My previous hallucinations were nothing. I had never been so frightened in my entire life.

"Is something the matter?" Sebastian's voice had an ominous ring to it. I felt like I had been left out of some sick joke again. Almost as if he knew *exactly* what was wrong.

Gathering the strength to look up at him was a struggle. His face was back to normal but the expression on it had me stunned. His chin was tilted down so he was peering through his eyelashes, with one eyebrow raised. He wore a vicious smile turned up in one corner. He looked so malicious, and *satisfied*. It was gorgeous.

Something else overpowered my fear as I looked at him. "Wait," I blurted out. "Hold that pose."

He got a kick out of that. "As you wish."

I frantically started drawing again, trying to capture the look on his face accurately. I ignored the servants who came to clean up my spill. It felt so strange. I was compelled to keep working and unable to process anything else.

When I finished his face, I stepped back to admire my work. All of my subjects were loosely sketched out. The only area of the painting with any detail was Sebastian. He had been drawn with perfect clarity.

Sebastian seemed to notice the hesitation in my head. "I think that's enough for tonight, don't you? I'm beginning to tire of sitting here."

I did not want to stop, but I didn't want to tell him no. "Sure, we can stop here."

He took a sip from the chalice and handed it to the woman next to him. Had he been drinking from it this whole time? I couldn't remember. He stood slowly and started down the stairs. The women parted to make room for him but otherwise stayed in their spots.

My heart picked up speed as he neared. Without my work to distract me, I remembered only too vividly what I had seen earlier. Visions of his distorted face flashed through my mind and I froze in fear. I prayed he would keep his distance.

Of course he did not. He strolled right over and threw an arm around my shoulders as if we were the best of friends. He studied my progress for a moment and gave me a light squeeze. "Magnificent. It's going to be a masterpiece."

I fought against the warmth as it spread through me and closed my eyes. It had a voltage to it, an electricity that charged my entire body. If he knew he was doing this to me, would he still touch me so much? Hell, I bet that's the reason why he touched me at all.

"I'm glad you like it." I finally muttered, forcing my eyes open.

He kept his grip on me; it was probably the only thing holding me up. "Like is too weak of a word. And don't worry about your supplies. The servants will see they are put away properly." He looked down at my feet and laughed. "I think your shoes may be ruined."

They hadn't even lasted one day. The wine had thoroughly saturated the leather, and my skin. There was no way it was going to come out. "I guess I'm a little clumsy."

"That's just adorable." He finally let me go, steadying me as I caught my balance. "If you'll excuse me, I'm going to retire for the evening."

All I managed was a bashful nod. He picked my hand up to kiss the top of it again. I stopped breathing when he did it and he smiled. I was in turmoil. Something inside was screaming, *run away*. But I didn't want to.

He took a couple steps and made a motion towards his harem. "Ladies…"

They all stood together and made their way over to him. He threw his arms around two of them and cast a glance over his shoulder to issue one last wink. "Good night, Trinity."

"Good night."

I watched them walk away with conflicting emotions. He whispered something and the women giggled before they disappeared through a large door at the back of the room.

Steven was at my side immediately, and he had a big smile for me. At least he was just a normal person. "Are you ready to go now, ma'am? It's late, you must be exhausted."

I looked out the glass ceiling at the sky. It had been dark for hours. "What time is it?"

"Getting close to one."

My mind wandered as I followed him silently towards the elevator. Fantasies about what was going on behind that door tried to creep up on me and I repressed them. That was a road I was not ready to go down. Not even in my head. The last thing I needed was to picture Sebastian having sex with those women every time I looked at them.

The ride home was surreal. Steven didn't talk much, just smiled and acted polite, like everything was normal. If every night was going to be like this, I don't think I'd survive it. I had absolutely no control over myself around Sebastian. Whenever I suppressed candid visions of him, I would catch a glimpse of what his face turned into. I didn't know which was worse, wanting him or fearing him.

Maybe I should go see a shrink. I could afford to now, and I definitely needed it. What I saw was terrifying, but that feeling, the falling, and drowning… That was plain psychotic. I'm sure they have pills for that sort of thing.

But why did Sebastian look like he knew? Like he did it on purpose, and he enjoyed it.

I shuddered. No, there was no way that was true. That would mean that what I saw was… *real.*

The contents of my stomach were about to make an appearance again. Damn, I needed a drink.

And where the hell was Vino tonight? Everyone else was there. Did he live somewhere else? Would I ever see him again?

Steven couldn't get me to my place fast enough. I sprinted upstairs and headed straight for the kitchen. My tiny freezer bestowed upon me the gift of a new bottle of Ketel One Vodka. It had been resting in the icy box alongside a few of its comrades, and almost no food. I freed it from its aluminum top hat and took three long swallows, savoring the burn. They were followed by a smile, then two more gulps. I didn't bother with getting a glass. The cupboard was too far away, and washing dishes was not my specialty.

I sat down at my decrepit kitchen table with my old friend. He was the only one I had right now, the only one I could confide in. No matter how desperate things got, he was right there by my side. There was always comfort waiting at the bottom of a bottle.

After a pull, I banged the bottle down on the table as a toast to our partnership. A piece of the dented metal trim fell off. As I bent over to pick it up, I lingered mentally on my mismatched chairs and the rips in the linoleum beneath them. Man, my place sucked. I took another long drink and laughed at myself.

Chapter 5

The Switch

The life of an alcoholic is a never-ending series of bad mornings and long, forgotten nights. This particular morning, I woke up fully clothed and sprawled diagonally across the bottom of my bed. Both my right leg and arm hung over the edge, the TV blared, and my bottle of Ketle One lay open on the floor. Lucky for me, there was not enough left inside to spill in this position, so I had no mess to clean up. But this also meant that I drank an entire bottle sitting by myself in my shit-hole apartment.

To a normal person that might have been depressing. Personally, I was fine with it. After all, that was why I bought the damn bottle. I didn't entertain guests often.

I had a vile taste in my mouth, and was experiencing a painful level of dehydration. So I gave myself a satisfying stretch, dragged myself to the kitchen, and drank right out of the sink faucet. After depleting half the city's water supply, I ripped my clothes off right where I was standing and threw them in a pile on the linoleum floor.

The familiar pains of my hangover were nothing to me today. I had too much on my mind to worry about trivial things like a headache or upset stomach. Sebastian filled my every thought. Three images kept flashing in procession through my head; the serene smile he wore as the women pawed at him, the monster that replaced his face, and the satisfied grin he wore after I came back to reality.

My friends in the cupboard called to me again. Maybe whiskey would make a good breakfast companion. Too bad calling in sick wouldn't be an option for me. Though I doubt Mr. Terrifying would be angry if I showed up drunk. From what I could tell, he found my alcoholism entertaining.

I opted for milk instead of whiskey. Unfortunately, the milk had started to turn sour and it churned in my stomach. I needed to eat, but I bought clothes and booze instead of food, so I had limited options. After a considerable amount of rummaging around I found the remnants of a loaf of bread. I put the two heels in the toaster and wiped off a knife from the sink so I could cover them with a hefty serving of margarine.

The churning stopped after I ate. If I had been smarter, I would have taken this opportunity to clean, to buy groceries, or even to shower. Instead I texted my "pharmacist" and asked him to swing by later. I kicked myself for not doing so yesterday. That was a serious lack of judgment on my part. The refill of my non-prescriptions was usually at the top of my list.

He answered back almost immediately saying he couldn't make it until five. It was only ten-thirty, so I crawled back into bed. I had plenty of time for a nap.

The second time waking up went much better than the first. My hangover was gone and my head was clear. I energetically hopped out of bed and took a long shower. I stayed in until the water temperature froze me out; which wasn't saying much for my place. Getting ready was effortless for the first time in days. I picked out another jean skirt, I had quite a collection now, and a low cut sequined top. I grabbed another new pair of sandals, since my shoes from yesterday had gone into the trash. And of course, I wore the necklace Sebastian gave me. Then I ordered Chinese and picked at it in front of the TV while I waited for my visitor.

My "pharmacist" was in and out in less than five minutes. I purchased samples of just about everything he had; Xanax, Vicodine, Oxycodone, and a few random others I thought might be fun. Why the Hell not? I could afford to be experimental.

It took every ounce of control I had not to pop a handful of pills and pour myself a stiff drink. I settled on two Xanax and a weak one. I could get a little buzz going; no one would blame me for that.

I stepped out my front door promptly at six-thirty. I'm not gonna lie, I felt pretty good. I was actually looking forward to my ride with Steven today. He was the last normal person I would see tonight.

But when I got outside, Steven was nowhere to be seen. There was no black Lincoln, no friendly smile to greet me. Instead, the spot directly in front of my building was occupied by a silver convertible Bentley with the top up. I didn't know my cars well enough to know what model it was, but with something that beautiful, who cared about its name.

I had to slide my sunglasses down the bridge of my nose to admire it fully. I stood there, stupefied with my mouth hanging open, and hoped no one was inside to see me drooling over it that way.

Of course, I was not that fortunate. The passenger window rolled down and an enraged voice called out. "Are you going to get in, or what?"

Was he talking to me? I leaned over slightly to get a peak, without appearing too obvious, and spied Vino glaring at me from the driver's seat. Apparently someone woke up on the wrong side of the bed today.

I couldn't have cared less about his mood. That Bentley was too distracting. I skipped over to it and gave myself a moment to cop a feel from the seductive curves leading to the handle. The door felt weightless as I opened it and slipped inside. The quilted leather seat was probably the most comfortable thing ever put in a vehicle. I touched everything around me, trying to get the full experience and shivered. I couldn't tell if I was cold, or if I was just that turned on by this car.

"Wow."

Vino watched at me with a sour look on his face. "I take it you like my car."

Again, I didn't care about his attitude. I was still in awe of this machine. "I would have sex with this car."

The fury on his face finally broke, and something completely lecherous took over. "I'd like to see that."

I don't know what reaction I expected, but it was not that one. The sinful gleam in his eyes proved he meant what he said. I nervously looked away from him. "Maybe later..."

He shrugged and whipped the car into traffic. The inertia pinned me against my seat before I could buckle myself in. *Show off.* I almost said it aloud, but he looked angry again so I figured I'd better not press my luck.

Whatever pissed Vino off, he took out on his car. He was speeding, cutting people off, running every intersection, and generally driving like a dick. He ignored me the whole time, and turned up the radio to an ear-splitting volume. That was fine with me. I was much too worried about being splattered across the windshield than trying to make small talk. His choice of music did throw me off a little. Crunk style rap, and the stereo sounded set up specifically for this preference. I thought the bass would rattle the teeth out of my head. It didn't seem appropriate for who I assumed he was.

We made excellent time to Sebastian's, but I guess when you ignore every single traffic law ever written, there's not much to slow you down. Once the car was in park, the music was muted, and my heart was out of my throat and back in my chest where it belonged, I finally got the guts to pose a question to him.

"Why didn't Steven pick me up today?"

Vino sighed as if he were in disgust of having to explain himself. "That's my job now."

"Why? What happened?"

His lip twitched in an irritated sneer. "It's part of my punishment."

"Punishment for what?"

He whirled towards me and leaned closer to my face. His eyes burned like I remembered Sebastian's. But there were no blue flames; Vino's seemed to pulse with electricity like red livewires. It was enchanting.

His tone was not. "Insubordination." That was as close to a growl as I had ever heard a human's voice. "Why is it any of your business?"

I shrank away from him and tried to match his tone, unsuccessfully. "It directly affects me, so that makes it my business."

I immediately regretted saying that. His eyebrows drew together in the center and his eyes squinted into small slits.

"Get out of the car."

This couldn't be the same man I was so taken with last weekend. He was so likable and charismatic that first night. I even thought he might have been into me. Guess I was wrong.

I reached for the door handle as fast as I could and sprang out of the car. Vino took his time getting out to come and lead me inside. He tossed the keys to the valet without giving him a glance and ignored the greeting from the man at the front desk. Once we were inside the elevators, he leaned against the corner and folded his arms across his chest. He could have been wearing a billboard that screamed *keep away*.

Either out of cowardice, or that silent command, I pushed myself into the opposite corner and made myself as small as possible. I shivered and looked down to the floor to avoid him. His feet were as jolting as the bitter expression on his face. The ridiculous shoes he was wearing must have cost a fortune. They were pointy-toed, black leather dress shoes with big buckles and silver dyed snakeskin on the top. I had to bite my lip to keep from laughing out loud. It definitely took some of the fear out of the situation.

He took me as far as the second elevator and blocked the doors with his hand. His eyes were still angry and pulsing, but his words had lost their bite. "Sebastian's not here. I'll come back for you later."

It was nice to know the rules Sebastian set for me obviously did not apply to him. But I was not going to pry for an explanation from Vino. The second I stepped out of the elevator he shut the doors and disappeared.

A servant stood by the canvas waiting for me. As I approached, he was all smiles. "Good evening, Miss. Morgan. My name is Charles."

I smiled back at him. "Hi, Charles."

He presented a bottle of red wine. "Chateau Le Pin?"

I nodded and he went about pouring me a glass. "Mr. Amante sends his sincere apologies. Unfortunately, he has been detained by business, but he assures me he will arrive as soon as possible. I am to make sure you have everything you require."

"Thanks, but I don't think I'll need anything." I took the glass from him and sampled it. It was delicious. "On second thought, you could leave that bottle here."

"I would never dream of forcing you to pour your own drinks. I'll stay close, but out of your way." He motioned to a box sitting among the art supplies. "Mr. Amante has left a gift for you. If you need anything at all, please don't hesitate to ask."

He left me with a bow. I waited until he was nearly out of sight before I nervously picked up the box. I lifted the lid slowly and peaked inside. It was a pair of brown strappy sandals. The exact same pair I destroyed last night, correct size and everything. Normally, I loved getting presents, and this would have been a sweet gesture. In this situation it seemed ominous, like it came with invisible strings attached.

I set the offensive box to the side and sat down in the office chair. How did he know *everything* about me? At least he wasn't here to see my reaction, since everything I did seemed to amuse him. I suppose my fear of receiving another gift would be hilarious.

I leaned back and eyed my surroundings for a few minutes. My intentions were to sit for a lot longer, but the painting called to me. I sighed and stood up. It would be a lot easier to concentrate on the background with everyone gone. Time to work.

I'd been drawing for several hours by the time I finally noticed someone else enter the room. I'm not sure how, and I heard no footsteps approaching, but I knew Sebastian had arrived. I felt an internal tug, commanding me to look at him as if a magnet connected us. I fought against it for a moment, setting down my worn charcoal nub and cleaning off my stained fingers. In the end, the need to see him won out.

And oh my, was he a vision tonight. He strolled casually towards me with a big grin on his face. His outfit was different from his usual look. There was no vest or tie paired with his black Italian-cut suit. The electric blue dress shirt underneath was untucked and unbuttoned one button too low, showing a chest that was begging to be touched. He wore a silver colored pendant on a long black chain, two rings on his right hand and the diamond in his ear was even bigger than normal. This look was topped off with a black fedora donned with a band matching the loud blue of his shirt.

Out on business my ass. That wasn't an outfit for a business meeting. A man only dresses that way when he's trying to pick up some tail. But I couldn't argue the effectiveness of this look. It sure worked on me.

I pictured him onstage with backup dancers. Two scantily clad women dancing around him as he crooned into a microphone and sashayed to a sexy beat. What made it more real was the fact that I knew, without asking, that he would be a good dancer himself.

I pulled myself out of my fantasy and smiled at him. "I was beginning to think you wouldn't show."

He closed the distance between us and reached out to take my hand for his customary, heart-stopping kiss. "It would have broken my heart to stand you up."

Always with the sweet talk. If Lucas would have said that to me it would have been so cloying I might have puked. Coming from Sebastian, it made my heart sing. I tried to remind myself how petrified I was of him, but looking up at him right now, all logic vanished from my brain.

He released my hand and studied my progress on the canvas. "You work fast."

I glanced at my work and nodded. The entire background was sketched in detail. The plants, the sculptures, the stairs, the throne, and even all the flower petals were ready for paint.

"You're a good motivator."

That answer pleased him. His smile was exuberant. "Maybe you should take a break… I've had a long day. I could use a strong drink and the company of a fine woman."

I blushed. "And yet here you are with me, that's got to be a disappointment."

Sebastian laughed. "You don't have to feign modesty for my sake. I happen to appreciate a good ego when it's deserved." He winked at me and motioned for me to follow him. "Come, there's something I wish to show you."

Another shudder ran through my body as we stepped into the elevator. I really wished he kept his apartment warmer. I didn't want to have to start wearing more clothes.

Sebastian looked me over. "I apologize it's not warm enough for you. I'll see to it the heat is turned up." He slid his suit coat off as effortlessly as if he had no bones and held it out for me. "Please, take my jacket. I would hate for you to be uncomfortable."

He helped me slip into it, and I hugged it around myself. I closed my eyes and inhaled, basking on his heavenly scent that emanated from the silky lining. "Thanks."

He dismissed my thanks as the elevator doors opened to an immense gallery. It made the one my show was in look like a closet. The long room stretched out across the entire floor and opened into to another vast room. Classical music played quietly from unseen speakers. Everything but the artwork was white, even the short benches that were centered down the middle isle. There were large entryways directly to our right and left, leading to more big, open rooms. Sliding display panels hung along the length of the right side with paintings both on them and on the walls behind them. The left side was split into sections by rotating partitions that displayed more artwork. Some of these were straight, and a few had been turned in one direction or the other. It looked like everything in here could be moved or adjusted in some way to make a hundred different galleries out of just this one.

My jaw dropped, my eyes felt like they bulged out of my head like a cartoon, and I had to reach out and grab his arm to steady myself. I was in so much shock, I barely noticed the weird sensation that went along with touching him.

"You've got to be fucking kidding me."

He laughed. "I thought you might enjoy seeing this. Feel free to look around."

Charles interrupted us by hurrying over with a tray carrying two martinis. He looked uneasy. "I apologize for the delay Mast— Mr. Amante." His eyes shot wide open and fear spread across his face. He bowed his head and did his best to hide it. "It won't happen again, sir."

"I'm sure it won't." Sebastian reached out and grabbed the two glasses, handing one to me. "Now leave us."

He nodded several times, backed up, and scooted away. I ignored the odd exchange and took a sip from my new drink. It was a vodka martini with the right hint of olive. Sebastian knew my favorite.

The artwork closest in vicinity to us was in stark contrast to the modern surroundings of the gallery. It was old, sixteen or seventeen century. Even the statues looked ancient. I almost pushed Sebastian out of the way to walk up to one of the larger ones.

The painting in front of me depicted soldiers taking babies from women and killing them. They were writhing and grabbing at each other while climbing over the bodies of the fallen children. It was both disturbing and awe-inspiring.

"This is amazing."

"Rubens, 'Massacre of the Innocents.'" Sebastian called out from behind me.

I turned to look at him and he was standing so close I jumped. I could have sworn he was quite a ways behind me. "I'm trying to remember the story behind it..."

"King Herod ordered the murder of the children in Bethlehem around the time the Christ child was born. It's from Matthew, chapter two."

Ok, now I was confused. Did he just quote a bible verse? "I didn't peg you for the churchy type."

"I'm not." He shook his head. "But my position requires me to be well versed in the scripture. Perhaps someday soon I'll explain it to you."

Sebastian kept his distance and allowed me to wander about for a while. I was beginning to notice a pattern in the artwork; everything had a similar theme to it. Most of the paintings showed some form of death, torture, or evil being. Anything that wasn't macabre was generally nude women. The area we were standing in had a lot of influence from the darker side of the romanticism era with some baroque art thrown in among them.

I was staring up at a painting of a creature eating a small man that might have been done by Francisco Goya, when Sebastian gently put his arm around my waist to lead me away. The warmth came in waves again, but much milder than before.

"You'll have all the time you please in here. There's something you need to see."

"You promise I get to come back?" I pleaded.

He chuckled and pulled me tighter against him. "Any time you wish, my dear."

I slid my arm around him before I made the decision to do so, and walked with him. I was compelled to do it. It felt right, and at least he said I would get to come back. That would be a nice little perk to our arrangement.

As we traveled further into the gallery, the nature of the art-work changed. The large room at the other end of the floor was entirely medieval themed. Two suits of armor framed out a red couch, and a long glass case in front of the window carried all sorts of golden artifacts. The only permanent wall was covered in hanging weapons; swords, battle-axes, even several shields, a few flails and a mace.

Sebastian laughed at me as I strained my neck to look at them, but we walked by without slowing. "All in due time."

I resisted the urge to force him to stop and followed obedi-ently. We ignored a whole room on the left and headed for an entryway on the right. The artwork in this room was much more recent. There was a painting I knew had to be Dali. It fea-tured lumps that appeared to be distorted bodies in an embrace while they carved into each other with forks and knives. There was so much I wanted to look at, and so many famous artists I recognized. This gallery could have been made especially for me. It was a struggle not to pout like a little child as we passed them.

Directly in the center of the room we were in was an extra ell jutting out from the side of the building. This was last floor to have the extra room, so the ceiling was one big piece of glass open to the night sky.

This room was much smaller than the others, but still at least twenty feet deep. One wall held more sliding panels, the second one in held something I was very familiar with. My self-portrait, staring down at me with tortured, crying eyes. I cringed at the sight of it. It didn't belong among artwork of this caliber. It was a lot like throwing a pebble into a pile of diamonds. No matter how shiny the pebble was separately, it would be dull next to their gleam.

Sebastian studied me with an amused look on his face. "That's not the reaction I was anticipating."

I couldn't help but laugh at myself. I should have been hon-ored. It was probably rude not to be. "I'm sorry, it was just un-expected."

He gestured to my painting with a graceful wave of his hand. "I don't believe I made it clear how much I like this one."

"I think I got the gist of it." Why else would he have paid more than twice what I was asking?

Sebastian spun me around to face him. His eyes erupted into brightly burning flames again, and his expression shifted into something more sinister. I held my breath, having him that close was so intense I don't think I could have breathed if I wanted to.

"That look on your face... It tells me much about you, Trinity." He used one finger to tilt my chin upwards and leaned down so we were only inches apart. "You enjoy pain. And you yearn for someone to show you the most pleasurable ways of experiencing it."

His expression looked so ravenous, and unbelievably sexy. Was what he said a proposition, or a threat? I mentally checked the proposition box.

He laughed and took his hat off to toss it on a nearby bench. When he turned back to me he looked almost sweet. "I have a good feeling about us. Don't you?"

Us, that was a beautiful word. My dumb grin stayed planted on my face as I lost myself in his eyes again. I kept telling myself it wasn't real, that it was just another hallucination. But I didn't want it to be. There was nothing in this world more fascinating than those flames and the swirling pools they hailed from. And whatever shade of blue they created, was now my favorite color.

We stood there, trapped in each other's eyes for a wondrous minute. I thought he might kiss me. It's what I hoped for anyways. But he didn't even come close.

Instead, he stepped away and turned towards the blank wall at the end of the room. It was the most easily viewed wall, and spotlighted like no other area of the gallery. "This is where I intend to place our current project."

"It's fitting, I like it." Of course he would put a portrait of himself in the most prestigious place of the floor.

"I'm glad you approve... The other painting I purchased from you is hanging in my bedchambers. I debated putting your portrait there also, but I came to the conclusion that when all is said and done, you and I should be together."

I knew he was referring to the paintings, I really did. But that's not what registered. I'm sure that was his intent.

He reached out and swept a piece of hair out of my face. "I suppose it is getting rather late, isn't it?"

I shrugged, having no idea what hour it was. Time seemed to stand still when I was in his presence. "Guess I hadn't really noticed."

Sebastian laughed at me again and led me back through the gallery to where the elevators were. Even with his jacket, and alcohol-warmed blood, it was still cold inside. I hugged the jacket around myself again and became aware that I no longer had a drink. I had no idea where it went.

When the doors opened he put his arm around me again. We were back on the top floor. "I was thinking I'd give you Saturdays off. There are other matters I need to attend to tomorrow."

I almost hugged him. "Oh, that's great, I suppose you know how well artists do with schedules."

"I was more concerned about you growing tired of me."

Tired of him? I didn't see how that could be possible. "I wouldn't worry about that."

That was clearly the answer he was looking for. "I thought you might wish to see my bar before you left. I believe Vinicio is waiting there to escort you home."

Our destination sounded splendid. I just wasn't happy about who waited for us. And I enjoyed my time with Sebastian too much to want to go home.

He led me past the pool, my workstation, the huge couch, and through the large doors at the back. The same doors he escorted those women through last night. Inside, the lights were dimmed, and club music played at a reasonable volume. There was another half dome glass ceiling and the exterior walls were the same patterned windows as the other side. An all black bar with a white marble top lit by hidden blue lights ran the length of the wall to our left. There was a man in a white shirt and a tie behind it, the only servant I'd seen without a full suit on.

At the far end of the room resided a hot tub that looked big enough for twenty people. Black couches and love seats were scattered about around sturdy circular coffee tables. There were two long platforms down the middle with a pole reaching upright from the center of each. This room wasn't a bar. It was a private strip club.

Off to the side, lounging on one of the love seats, was Vino, with his flashy shoes on the coffee table in front of him. He was reading a paper, which I found odd considering the hour. He bent down the top half to look at us expressionlessly when we walked closer to him. He then slowly folded the paper and set it down, took his feet off the table and sat upright. He moved so fluidly it was as if he were underwater.

He picked up a rocks glass with some kind of brown alcohol in it and took a drink. "Done for tonight?"

"I believe so." Sebastian looked down at me with the same sinful grin. "Unless, of course, you would care to stay and have a few drinks with me."

Every cell in my body wanted to say yes. It was as if something snapped and all of a sudden the only command my brain could register was *submit*. I longed for Sebastian. He was suddenly the most glorious person in the world and my muscles ached to touch him. I was helpless to do anything but stare into his searing eyes. I could feel myself moving closer to him, reaching out to him…

And then he looked away. I had control of myself again. As suddenly as the feeling came, it went. I blinked a couple times to clear my head. When I looked up they were both watching me.

"Perhaps we should get you home." Sebastian grinned at Vino, who looked four shades of pissed off.

Vino stood up slowly and made his way over to us. "Ready to go?" The question was directed at me, but his eyes were on Sebastian.

"I'm ready." I almost whispered it. You know the old adage 'you could cut the tension with a knife?' I would have needed a chainsaw. I could feel their hostility like it was an electric current in the air. But all they were doing was staring at each other silently, Sebastian with a pompous grin and Vino with poorly hidden outrage.

Sebastian turned his attention back to me like nothing was wrong. "Sunday then?" He took my hand and lifted it for a kiss.

My heart sputtered. "Yeah, I'll see you Sunday."

I slipped out of Sebastian's jacket and handed it to him. The second the air hit my skin, I shivered. He reached out and touched my cheek with the back of his hand. "Are you sure you don't wish to wear it home? I rarely wear the same suit twice. It won't be missed nearly as much as you will."

I blushed again. That was painfully charming. "Thanks, but I'll be fine."

Vino was already several steps ahead of me. He stopped in front of the door and held it open without looking in our direction. I took that as my cue, said goodbye to Sebastian, and followed him out. I swear I could see the anger rolling off him, like a red aura or waves of energy. I didn't dare try to talk to him.

Two valets waited out front to let us into Vino's magnificent car. I savored every second as I took my seat, forgetting my last few awkward minutes and touching every surface I could. I was in love. If they could only make a man as perfect as this car...

Vino stared at me from the driver's seat. I jumped from the intensity of his gaze. "Sorry."

His anger disappeared momentarily and he raised an eyebrow at me. "The offer still stands."

"What offer?"

He tilted towards me with an immoral smile. "I'll let you ravage my car if that's what you really want."

I'm sure I turned bright red. "I didn't mean literally."

He leaned back in his seat and started the car. "Suit yourself."

Vino didn't have anything to say to me for most of the ride home. It was an uneasy silence, and I was freezing. But I refused to ask him to turn off the air, or turn down the music. I sat there staring out the window thinking of what I was going to do tonight. It was only one in the morning, three hours was plenty of time to get in a few drinks.

I pulled my cell out of my pocket and turned it back on. I saw Vino watch me from the corner of his eye so I casually turned the phone so he couldn't read it. Lucas had sent me a text asking me to call him whenever I was done. I certainly wasn't going to call him right now. I wouldn't be able to speak over the obnoxious music and Vino would hear every word. I would rather none of them found out that I was seeing someone. As much as I liked Lucas, trading up was always an option.

I scrolled through the short list of numbers instead. I had always been somewhat of a recluse, which I liked. The only time it caused problems was when I wanted someone to drink with. Of the few friends I had, I decided I didn't really want to see any of them, and slapped the phone shut.

Maybe I would call Lucas after all. This car did have my blood pumping...

The vehicle jerked to a stop. My seatbelt pulled against my chest, nearly knocking the wind out of me. I braced my hands on the dash and gave Vino a dirty look. We were at my building.

"Thanks a lot." I hissed.

He winked at me. "You're very welcome."

I didn't answer. I just reached for the door handle and stepped out. I was about to slam the door when his annoyed voice snapped back at me. "You forgot your shoes."

I didn't remember to grab the box when we left Sebastian's. I hadn't even seen Vino touch it, but there it was in his hand. I reached in and took the box from him.

"Thanks." I meant it that time.

He didn't answer me. He didn't even look at me. The second my door was shut he peeled out and sped away. I stood there, staring after him until he was out of sight. Once I was sure he was gone, I pulled my phone out and dialed Lucas' number.

Chapter 6

Sex, Drugs, and Hallucinations

"You need to come get me." I ordered in my most seductive voice.

As always, the sucker fell for it. "Sure, where are you?"

"Outside my place."

"Give me fifteen minutes." Lucas was too easy.

I hung up the phone without saying goodbye and leaned against the outside of my apartment building. There was almost no one out at this hour in Sunnyside. This neighborhood is boring at night, with not much for bars and no late night stores or restaurants. I felt comfortable against the cold brick, half hidden in the shadows. I passed the time studying the buildings around me, trying to make patterns out of which windows had their lights on. But I tired of that game quickly and started scanning my surroundings for something else to hold my interest.

Across the street from me, a narrow alley divided two apartment buildings. With only one streetlight on our block, no light penetrated it once the sun went down. At the line where the light shifted to darkness there was a slight quiver in the shadows, like leaves blowing around in the darkness. But there was no tree close enough to supply any. I focused on the movement as it sped up then started to swirl and pull together. What appeared to be leaves before was collecting in the middle and slowly darkened, creating a face.

I could feel terror trying to rise out of my chest. Panic started bubbling up from the base of my spine. I closed my eyes and took a deep breath. I was not going to allow myself to get freaked out by something that was in my imagination.

When I opened my eyes, the face was still there, and clearer, appearing much closer to a solid object. The distorted features came across in full detail now. Its face was flat, smashed in like a bulldog or a hairless Persian cat, except the skin hung off the bones like a decaying corpse. There were tiny rotted holes where the nose should have been, and its mouth was wide and twisted. Its eyes were nothing but big black holes. Exactly like my previous hallucinations. And just like I had seen at Sebastian's.

My fear was gone. An irrational anger replaced it. I hated that creature, and hated every other ludicrous hallucination that dared to threaten my sanity. I was done. It was time to get a grip on things.

I would confront it. That would prove that it was fake, and my mind would be forced to revert back to normal.

I pushed myself away from the wall and took a step forward.

The face moved towards the light so I could make out the emaciated frame of its body. Bony arms, with knobby elbows and enlarged hands possessing only three digits, sprouted out of shoulder blades that protruded from its back at an odd angle. Every one of the creature's ribs poked through the skin above a sunken stomach.

This creature revolted me. And that only pissed me off more. I tucked the box I was carrying under my arm and stepped forward.

My hallucination crouched to the ground and cocked its head to the side.

I took another step.

It did too.

All the muscles in my body tensed. I could feel the panic trying to sneak its way back and grab me by the throat. I gritted my teeth and clenched my fists for another step.

That did it.

The creature started crawling towards me, out into the dim glow of the far away streetlight. Staying down on all fours, its head bowed down towards the dirty cement of the sidewalk. The hind legs were hinged out to the side in a way that probably inhibited it from standing upright. They moved up and down the way a spider's legs would, with the knees almost touching each other above its back with each step.

I pushed myself forward. No turning back now. I'd stomp right on that thing's head. That would teach it.

The creature opened its mouth for a silent scream and picked up its pace. As it howled without making any noise, its mouth distorted and stretched, showing rows of uneven teeth. It scampered towards me with a purpose now, weaving from side to side with irregular steps. The creature made it all the way into the street before it froze. The scream on its face dropped, giving way to sudden fear and its head snapped to the right.

Then the creature ran away. It didn't run so to speak, it just *went*. It abandoned the shape of its body, leaving an elongated shadow that shot into the alley.

How frustrating. Apparently my mind was not going to cooperate with proving itself wrong tonight. I had to hand it to myself though, I was pretty imaginative. That thing was even creepier than the last one, definitely worth putting down on paper.

I stood on the curb, gaping into the shadows where my little friend disappeared, trying to will it into existence again with my mind. I was so deep in concentration, that when a vehicle pulled up next to me I shrieked.

I whipped around and almost fell into Lucas' Jeep. I gave him a big smile to cover it up and leaned on the open window of his passenger door. "Need a date, big boy?"

"Don't you know it. What's the going rate?"

"One soul." I flashed him the most sinful look I could manage.

He shook his head and pretended to think it over. "That's a pretty hefty price. What if I told you I already bartered mine away?"

I opened the door and hopped in, throwing my box on the seat next to me. "I'm sure we can work something out."

That was a funny concept, Prince Charming over here without a soul. He had the brightest white aura of anyone I knew. I bet you mine had to be black. I chuckled at my internal thoughts. "So where are we going?"

"I was about to ask you that." He leaned over and gave me a quick peck.

I grabbed him and forced him into a deeper kiss. It felt healthy, and *normal*. I didn't want it to stop. "Maybe we should stay here."

He laughed. "Can you at least make it to my place?"

"My place isn't good enough for you?" I snapped, shoving him back to his side of the truck.

Trying to be mad at him was difficult with his warmhearted laughter in my ears. And he was right, my place sucked. I crossed my arms anyways and sighed dramatically.

"If you want to stay here, I'm game." He finally said.

Even though he gave in, the mood was officially ruined. "Let's go get a drink."

Lucas frowned. "You're no fun."

I laughed to myself. That's not what I'd been hearing lately.

He made no move to start driving. Instead he turned to me with his version of a mischievous smile. It wasn't very effective. "What if I offered a bribe to get you to come to my place?"

"I like bribes..."

He reached in his pocket and pulled out a folded cellophane from a cigarette pack. Inside were two circular blue pills with a stamp on the front. "We still haven't celebrated your new found fame."

My eyes popped open. "You naughty little boy, I thought you were against that sorta thing."

"Normally… But you're not. So I figured I would make an exception." He waved the cellophane around in front of my face.

I snatched the small package out of his hand and took a closer look. There were little smiley faces stamped on the front of those pills, how appropriate. It was obviously ecstasy. I couldn't believe Lucas had these. He was usually so straight-laced. Aside from all the drunk driving, he rarely did anything illegal.

"You sure know the way to a girl's heart." I opened the package and pulled out one pill, then popped it in my mouth and swallowed without the aid of a drink.

"So my place then?"

"Yeah…" I took the other pill out and positioned it in my teeth, then grabbed a handful of his shirt and yanked his face down to mine so he had to kiss me. While we were in this semi-forced embrace, I slid the pill into his mouth with my tongue.

We didn't kiss very long before he pulled back and grabbed a bottled water for a drink. What a wimp. He put the bottle down and shifted the truck into drive. Then he took a double take in my direction, staring at my neck with a peculiar expression on his face.

"That's some necklace…" The words sounded concerned but he grinned and shook his head. "I'm not even going to ask you what you paid for that."

I lifted my hand to the wide band of the necklace. It had barely left its home around my throat since Sebastian gave it to me. "It wasn't as expensive as you'd think."

"Hey, it's not my business what you do with the money… What's with the box?"

Yet another subject I didn't want to discuss with Lucas. "Shoes, it's a long story."

He laughed at me again. "That's such a nice way of saying 'I don't feel like telling you' "

"I will later," I lied.

We drove straight to Lucas' apartment. With most of the traffic nonexistent at this hour, it was a quick ride. A couple blocks from his place the first wave hit me. I hadn't rolled in a long time; it was too expensive for a poor chick like me. And it did horrible things to your body on a chemical level, not that I worried much about that. But the feeling was unbelievable. My heart sped up and my body felt like it wanted to float away. I took a deep breath, the cool air tasted lovely and felt extraordinary in my lungs. Even the seat of the truck was holding me in a splendid embrace.

As I watched longingly out the window, the dark shades of night were more radiant then ever and the streetlights twinkled like they were reflected in water. The fascinating scenery had me in a daze until the Jeep came to a stop. When I turned to my left, I found Lucas grinning at me with a wild look in his eye. Before I could say anything, he grabbed me for a prolonged kiss. My whole body trembled from my overwhelmed senses.

I pulled myself over so that I straddled him in his seat. Every touch was magnified a hundred times over, that one sense overpowering all others. I considered ripping his clothes off right there inside his truck, but he had other ideas. He grasped my arms with both hands and lifted me off him, laughing hysterically the whole time.

"I should have tried bribes a long time ago." He paused for a moment to calm himself. "We've got all night, I think we should at least make it inside."

With the help of the cool breeze feathering my skin, I felt lighter then air on the walk to his building. I was positively giddy and had a skip in my step. It was the kind of happiness only found when chemically induced.

Lucas gave me a quick slap to the rear when we entered his apartment. I giggled and pounced on him, knocking him into the wall of his entryway. We were all smiles, and laughs, and recklessly bumping into everything as we tripped over each other into the nearest room, which happened to be the kitchen. He lifted me onto the countertop and kissed me urgently, reaching his hand to its familiar place at the base of my skull. The cold countertop felt spectacular under the hot skin of my thighs. I threw both arms around his neck, wishing momentarily that he had some hair for me to grab onto while we pawed at each other.

It was the silly, fun-loving type of fooling around that accompanied severe intoxication when two people are comfortable with one another. The kind Lucas was famous for, and one of my biggest attractions to him.

Lucas leaned back to pull his shirt over his head and I ran my hand down his chest, tracing the colorful tattoos with my fingertips. He pulled me against him and I closed my eyes as he slid his hands up my sides, pushing my blouse over my head. I shook my curls loose of the fabric and they tumbled onto my skin, tickling my back and shoulders. I giggled again and opened my eyes.

The person looking back at me was not Lucas.

It was Sebastian, with his radiant blue eyes blazing, and his sly smile tempting me.

He stood silently between my thighs and brought his hand to my cheek, then caressed it gently, and tilted his head to one side.

I stared at him in disbelief. Lucas may have been a walking piece of art, but in my current condition, the shirtless Sebastian resembled a marble god.

This was simply not possible. I was here with Lucas, right? I was still in his kitchen, sitting on his countertop. This could not be Sebastian in front of me, but...

I wanted it to be him.

Then Sebastian leaned in to kiss me, and I was done rationalizing. I wrapped my arms around him and threaded my fingers through his golden locks. He slid my hips forward on the smooth counter, pulling every inch of our torsos together and hiking up my skirt in the process. Our bare skin glided across each other's like silk on silk.

The combination of the drugs raging in my system and the excitement of finally getting my hands on Sebastian, put me through wondrous sensory overload. I reveled in his touch. I ached for Sebastian. It felt so real, kissing his lips, holding his body, pulling his hair. I was utterly convinced he was really there, and thrilled about it.

With Sebastian's strong hands pinning me against him, my bones and brain turned to goo. One hand traveled upwards to grab a fistful of my hair and pulled—hard, forcing my head to snap back and give him access to my throat. I locked my legs around his waist and gave into him completely. I would have let him do anything to me at that moment.

Lost in euphoria, I whispered Sebastian's name. He removed his lips from my skin and straightened to look me in the eye. I smiled at him lovingly; the grin he reciprocated was anything but. One side of his mouth curled upward and the flames in his eyes had such ferocity they should have singed his eyelashes.

Then those veins crawled out of his irises again. They engulfed his eyes completely and stained his skin. His smirk started twisting and warping in that inhuman way...

I screamed and shoved against him as hard as I could. My head smacked into the cabinet behind me with a loud thump. The pain caused my eyes to shut and I reached back to cover the throbbing part of my skull.

A hand covered mine and I jumped. My eyes flew open, and a concerned Lucas stared back at me.

"You okay?"

I blinked a few times and forced a laugh. "Thought I saw a spider."

He leaned forward to inspect the lump on the back of my head. "Must've been a big spider."

"Enormous..." I threw my arms around his neck and clung to him in a desperate attempt to calm myself. Thank God, it was Lucas. I kissed him, just to make sure, and he laughed at me.

"Maybe the kitchen wasn't such a good idea." He lifted me by the waist and slid me down the front of him, letting my body catch on all the necessary places. Once my feet were planted on the floor, he grabbed my ass.

Yep, this was definitely Lucas. I shook my head and laughed, then pulled him by his belt into the bedroom.

The smell of fresh coffee stirred me into consciousness the next morning. I was alone and naked in Lucas' bed, but he left a large white t-shirt lying just off to my right side. I stayed there for a while and gave myself a good stretch. My whole body was sore and my head hurt. It was hard to tell what was hangover and what had been caused by possibly hours of coitus. I swept clumps of damp curls out of my face and smiled, remembering the shower we took last night. Blissful memories of the hot water pelting my over-sensitive skin, the heat of Lucas' hands, and lips, and… that was the best shower I ever had.

I was surprisingly unaffected by my hallucinations the previous evening. After all, vigorous physical activity is a great way to clear your head. And visions created by drugs are soon forgotten. I threw on the shirt and headed down the hallway.

Lucas was sitting on the couch in his boxers. He greeted me with his usual inviting smile. "Good morning."

I walked over and sat on his lap, wrapped my arms around him, and buried my face into his neck. The effects of the Ecstasy had all but completely worn off, but the sensation of his skin against mine still felt better than normal.

"How come you're always up so early?"

He chuckled and kissed the top of my head. "It's eleven-thirty."

"Still too early." I yawned and stretched up to kiss his cheek. "I had fun last night. We should do that again…soon."

"Sex and drugs was right up your alley, huh? Who would've guessed?"

I punched him playfully. "Whatever. You ready to take me home?"

Lucas sighed. "Seriously? You just woke up."

"So… I've got stuff to do, it's my only day off."

He hugged me tight against his chest. "And it never occurred to you to spend the day with me?"

I'm sure he meant that as a joke, but he hit the nail on the head. The idea never crossed my mind. "I told you I have stuff to do, I can't really make that happen."

"You should at least stay and let me cook you breakfast. There's no reason for you to make your escape just yet... And besides, you've already showered. You're practically ready for the day."

That one made me laugh. I doubted I got very clean during my last shower. "Fine, I'll stay, but you're taking me home after we eat."

"Yes, ma'am." He rested his cheek on my hair. I took that to mean he was pouting. "Are we at least doing something later tonight?"

"Probably, that's a long ways away."

Lucas didn't answer; he knew better then to push the subject. If he wanted a chance to see me it was always best to play it cool. Amazing how he picked up on that stuff, treating me like I was some wild horse he was trying to rein in.

True to his word, Lucas cooked me bacon and eggs, the only breakfast I'm sure he knew how to make. I took a few bites to make him happy and filled up on coffee. He took me home not more then fifteen minutes later.

The rest of Saturday went all too quickly, and I accomplished almost nothing. I spent most of the day lying around, only leaving to finally buy some groceries and get a new computer. Lucas got stood up, and I passed out early. However, I did spend the whole day drinking, so I guess that counts for something.

Sunday was much of the same, except I didn't leave at all. I started drinking early and I sampled a few pills that were itching at me. I knew I had to go to Sebastian's, but I couldn't help myself. Addiction is a bitch. That cruel temptress seduced me a long time ago, and she was still sprawled naked across my bed.

I was more intoxicated than I intended to be by the time I went downstairs. But I felt great. Who cared if I got in trouble. That enticing Bentley was out front again, it still took my breath away. I practically skipped up to the door, and almost stumbled into it when I got to the curb.

Too bad my own personal buzz kill was waiting inside for me. I may have been glowing from my intoxication-induced joy, but Vino was as sour as ever. He barely even looked at me. I had enough liquid, and pill, courage to try to break the ice as he whipped the car through traffic.

"Have a good weekend?" I asked.

He looked me up and down accusingly from the corner of his eye. "Not as good as yours must have been."

Why did he have to be such an ass? I crossed my arms and stared out the window for a moment before my anger got the best of me. "Steven was a much better chauffer then you." I snapped.

"Steven is no longer with us." He stated flatly, without looking in my direction.

I snapped into an erect position in my seat. "What happened? Did he get fired?"

Vino finally cracked a smile. "You could say that."

Of course he wouldn't give me a straight answer, anything to aggravate me. I didn't say another word to him the whole drive there. Not even on our way into the building or upstairs. It was a good thing I was so far from sober; I don't think I could have handled all that anxiety otherwise

Everything upstairs was as I left it Friday, only the company had changed. The twins were on the red couch today. Amelie was lying across it, propped up on her elbow with her feet on Andras' lap. He stroked her calf with one hand. It was creepy.

"Hello, Trinity," she said. "We came to watch today, if you don't mind."

"Yeah, sure." I threw her one of my fake smiles. "The more the merrier."

Andras stared at me in silence. I wondered if I would ever hear him speak. It was as if Amelie spoke for the two of them.

On cue, Sebastian waltzed through the large doors from the bar, followed by his procession of women. They weren't hanging on him as they had the other day, which was a relief. Instead, they followed silently about five steps behind him.

He floated over to me and ran the back of his hand against my cheek, then leaned down to wink at me. "Good evening."

I blushed; his face was excessively close to mine. "Hello, Sebastian."

The wicked smile he flashed proved he had me figured out. "Someone's had a good day today..."

At least he didn't look mad. I would have been. If I was paying someone this much money, and they showed up three sheets to the wind, I would fire them.

"Caught me." I lifted my hands up to the surrender position.

Amelie laughed quietly from across the room. I don't know if she was happy I might get in trouble, or if she just found everything I do amusing also.

Sebastian's eyes flashed over to her and she shut up immediately. "You weren't being very evasive..." He looked back into my eyes and raised his left eyebrow. "There's not much you could do to offend me. We're all about enjoying ourselves around here."

That was an understatement; this guy was all about carnal desires.

"That's good to know." My intoxication had me feeling rather cocky. Even being next to Sebastian was almost easy right now. I'd have to show up like this everyday.

"How do you feel about working outside today?" He asked.

He didn't really want to move all this stuff did he? Everything was already set up. I opened my mouth to question him but Sebastian shook his head as if he could hear my thoughts. "We don't need to go anywhere. Just watch."

He pointed to the ceiling. I looked in the direction he aimed, and the glass dome started opening from the center and sliding silently down the sides so more then half the ceiling disappeared. Even the windows in front of the pool were on tracks that slid out to the right and left. The entire sky and city was open to us now. And at this elevation, there was no trace of the city smells below as a soft breeze circled around us.

This day was getting better and better. "That's a nice trick," I said.

"I've been known to have a few up my sleeves." He laughed the kind of laugh that made me sure he had plenty of tricks I would rather not find out about.

"I was wondering one thing…" Sebastian looked as if he was getting ready to reveal something spectacular. He reached in his suit coat and pulled out a folded section of newsprint. "Why have you not read your review yet?"

Then it hit me, I never grabbed this week's copy of *The New York Artist*. It came out on Friday and I was so distracted by Sebastian I forgot about it completely. "Oh my God, you're right."

When I reached up to take the paper from him, he maneuvered it out of my reach with a swift, graceful flick of the wrist. His devilish grin lit up his whole face. "I am the first to show you this…? Am I the only one looking out for you, Trinity?"

I folded my arms across my chest. "Are you going to let me read it, or not?"

"I guess I have my answer, don't I?" He handed it to me and sighed dramatically. "It's exactly as I thought it would be. These people are so predictable."

I unfolded the paper and read it quickly. It was only two paragraphs long since the review covered Ivan's sculptures also. And Sebastian was right, again. They loved it, stating that my work was bold and sexy, and that I had an eye for the macabre. I wanted to jump up and down. The smile on my face felt like it would split my cheeks open.

Sebastian positively gloating. "You could thank me, you know…"

"Yes! Thank you!" I blurted out. "You definitely made my day!"

He reached out to put a hand under my chin. "Glad I could be of service."

I melted at his touch; such a small gesture seemed to impart so much meaning. And the way he was staring at me reminded me of my strange, drug-induced fantasy from the other night. The sexy parts, anyways. I stared back into those glorious eyes, not wanting him to look away. When he finally did, it nearly broke my heart.

"Let's get to work, shall we?" Sebastian sighed again and slipped out of his jacket. He swung it over one shoulder and waved to the women I had all but forgotten about. They kept their distance as he made his way to his seat on the throne. Then one by one, they mechanically moved into their spots around him and froze like statues.

I watched them for a moment, studying their faces. Something was off. This did not have the same feel as it did a few days ago. Did the women switch places? They all looked so much alike I couldn't tell. No, it was the expression on their faces that was different. Before they all seemed sultry and provocative, with impish little grins and longing eyes. Today those eyes were dead, blank of emotion. Their faces were expressionless voids, like someone had sucked the life right out of them.

They reminded me of zombies, beautiful, half-naked zombies.

I shook it off and grabbed my charcoal. That little oddity was rather trivial compared to all the other weird crap I had to explain to myself. I began sketching the finishing details on one of the women and stopped mid stroke. This girl had a tattoo of a butterfly on her ankle. That had definitely not been there before. And it was not a new tattoo either, the colors were faded and the lines had thickened and softened, it had to be several years old.

This girl had not been here last time. I was sure of it. I searched the others for differences, but came up dry. I couldn't have picked if any of them had been here before or not. Would there be different women everyday? I guess it didn't really matter; there was only one face counted in this painting.

I worked diligently for a couple hours, paying attention only to the canvas in front of me. I finished all the sketching and even started to apply color. I managed to avoid ogling Sebastian the whole night, so when I snuck a glance and our eyes met

I blushed. He looked bored out of his mind.

"I'm growing tired of sitting here… Do you think you can manage without me?" He rose before I had a chance to answer, and effortlessly weaved his way through the women on the stairs.

"Feel free to take the night off," I said.

He chuckled. "Yes, I think I will."

The twins appeared out of nowhere next to me. "This is going to take a while, isn't it," Amelie stated rudely.

"Probably." I snapped back. She obviously did not know anything about the artistic process.

She ignored me and walked to Sebastian's side with Andras in tow. Sebastian said his usual flamboyant good night and they took their leave. It was just the zombie women and me then, alone in this massive room.

Vino came for me sometime before midnight. He looked as angry as ever. He didn't have anything to say to me on the ride home. I hoped that would wear off soon. It was getting old, and I was really beginning to hate the guy.

I fell into the routine of the next few days amazingly easily. The strange play set out before me had an eerie rhythm to it that I flowed into naturally. Up by the crack of noon, drinks with lunch, then spending money until five. Lucas would normally call about this time, I didn't always answer. My hostile chauffer was always on time to take me to the ecstatic Sebastian, who would greet me like I was the person he wanted to see most in this world. I would be allowed a few hours to work before he would get bored and take off. Then I would hop back into that alluring Bentley and head home to start the whole thing over again.

I never stayed sober enough to let anything bother me. All the outlandish things going on inside my head didn't mean much. I was even seeing a lot less of my hallucinations; very rarely would I catch a glimpse of something completely dismissible. The only thing that still reminded me I was losing it, was Sebastian's searing eyes and scorching touch. But it wouldn't be a stretch to say I was enjoying that part.

Friday arrived before I knew it, and another night was wearing down. Many of the basic colors were blocked in on my painting, no detail yet, but it was coming along. Sebastian didn't say anything as he left his spot to come stand by my side. He watched me paint for several minutes then rested a hand on my shoulder.

It was impossible to work with him touching me, so I turned around to face him and he dropped his hand. "You're turning in?" I asked.

"You may call it an evening also if you would like." His eyes were distant, and that forever smile he always wore was nowhere to be seen.

He took one of my hands and kissed the top of it, closing his eyes and hovering there with his lips barely skimming the surface. My heart sputtered frantically to regain its rhythm. That still made me dizzy. He sighed and lowered my hand without releasing it.

"I'm leaving town for a few days," he finally murmured. "Just a short business trip. We'll reconvene on Wednesday."

"Sure, don't rush back on my account." Days off were always a good thing, but days without seeing Sebastian might be rough.

"I was hoping you'd tell me how much you were going to miss me." He paused and his smile reemerged. "But I suppose that's too much to ask for from someone like you."

I blushed, he was right, he was *always* right. I would never admit to something like that. Even if it *was* true. "You think you have me pretty figured out, don't you?"

"That is precisely the reason I am going to miss you."

More riddles. Why was it always so hard to tell what he was talking about? "Because you figured me out?"

His wicked laughter filled the room. "Perhaps I'll fill you in one day...for now I just want you to know that if you require anything in my absence, there will be plenty of people here at the estate to assist you."

"Thanks, but I'm sure I'll be fine."

He leaned closer, forcing me to stare into his blazing eyes. They turned my mind to mush. "I do have a favor to ask..."

Anything, my heart cried out. I'm glad I didn't verbalize that part. "What kind of favor?"

"Try to behave yourself. I couldn't bear it if something unfortunate happened to you while I was away."

That sounded suspiciously like a threat. Normally a comment like that would make me want to prove exactly how much trouble I could get in and still make it back in one piece. But everything he said always had some sort of hidden command sent down to the deepest pits of my subconscious. There would be no way for me to disobey him.

"I'll do my best. No promises." I stammered. I had to at least try to make him think I still had a will of my own.

"I suppose that will have to do..." Sebastian winked at me. I'm pretty sure he saw through my act. Then he glanced towards the elevators and his smile faded. "It appears your ride has arrived."

I followed his gaze to see Vino leaning against the wall with his arms crossed and his usual sour expression. I frowned.

Sebastian laughed at me. "I promise he won't bite." He reached a hand up to caress the side of my cheek one last time. "Not that I would keep him waiting."

Chapter 7

Vinicio

Vino barely acknowledged my existence as we left Sebastian's apartment. I waited for the normal hatred to roll off him as we walked silently to his magnificent car, but nothing came. I snuck a glance out of the corner of my eye when we climbed inside. He still wasn't paying attention to me, but at least he didn't look like he wanted to hurt me.

He appeared calm enough that I attempted small talk. "Happy to leave town?"

The hint of a smile formed on his lips. "I'm not going anywhere."

Now it started to make sense. With Sebastian gone for five days, Vino would be free of his burden, free of me, and free of whatever was going on between them. I shot him a taunting smirk. "I get it, you're just happy dear old daddy is leaving you alone."

"I've never referred to him so fondly... but yes, that might have something to do with it."

Wow, no smart remark. He must be in a good mood. "You don't like your dad much do you?"

His smile vanished. "What's with all the damn questions?"

"Sorry, just curious." I folded my hands in my lap and stared out the window.

My thoughts wandered back to my art show, it felt like such a distant dream. Vino was the one asking the questions then. I would have jumped his bones that night, but I could barely see the attraction now. This was a completely different person sitting next to me. The charm and charisma were gone; all that remained was an irritating jerk. So what if he was hot. Next to his father's distinguishing handsomeness, he was downright pretty, like a girl. Well, maybe a female bodybuilder.

Vino drove as erratic as ever, but he wasn't paying attention to the road. His eyes were boring a hole in the side of my face. I tried to ignore him but the whole no-look-driving thing scared the crap out of me.

I turned to yell at him, and the calm expression on his face stunned me into silence.

"What's your opinion of Sebastian?" he asked.

That caught me off guard. What did I think of Sebastian that wouldn't sound crazy when explained to Vino? Glorious, perfect, *terrifying*. I ran through the words in my head and decided to go with something else entirely. "He's definitely got quite a presence. It's hard to get used to."

"A presence, you say..." Vino laughed. "You have no idea."

"Humor me."

He shook his head. "You'll figure it out eventually."

"That tells me absolutely nothing."

"Aggravating isn't it?"

"Infuriating is more like it...Will you pay attention to the damn road?! Why can't I get a straight answer from you people?! I'm starting to get tired of being fucked with all the time!"

Vino winked at me and I just about lost it. I wanted to hit him, but I clenched my jaw and settled on punching his door. This brought on another fit of laughter so fierce I thought he would wreck the car.

I crossed my arms again and ignored him the rest of the ride home. When he pulled the car to a stop outside my building, I jumped out without saying a word, making sure to slam the door behind me.

"Good night Trinity." He called after me, laughing as he sped off.

Thank God I wouldn't have to see him for five more days. That would definitely be the best part of my week.

Around three the next day, I received a call from Lucas asking to change our plans for that evening. He offered to take me to this fancy jazz club I'd never been to. It seemed out of the norm for Lucas, but I didn't question him. It was a great excuse to get dolled up and wear another new outfit.

He told me he would meet me there at eight thirty, another odd suggestion coming from Lucas. Maybe this was some new strategy to keep me interested. It did work after all, I felt excited about tonight.

I had several pre-date drinks, then threw on my sexiest black dress and the highest heels I had, accessorized with a thick silver belt and Sebastian's necklace. My make-up and hair took almost an hour, but the end product was worth it. I felt great. I looked hot. This would be an exceptional night.

The cab to get to the club cost me thirty-five bucks, but I didn't care. This place was worth the cash. It reminded me of a club from the fifties or sixties, plush red leather and a bold color scheme with old paintings and cigar motifs. A woman in a sequined cocktail dress was singing a bluesy ballad on the stage up front. The sunken area around the stage housed several layers of tables with white covers. Booths framed the outside edge with lattice and plants. Circular ones in the back were twice the size, and visible only from directly in front.

I walked up to the bar and took a seat on the ultra-plush stool with a shiver. They sure kept the air cranked in here. A statuesque woman in a white shirt and black tie greeted me. She had long, dark brown hair, lovely hazel eyes, and an exceptional smile. If I were a few more drinks into the night, I'd have a problem not hitting on her.

"What can I get you, hunny?"

"Vodka martini, dirty, with lots of olives," I replied.

"Better use Diva for that, and bring me three fingers of Macallan 55." Interrupted a deep voice from behind me.

The bartender's eyes flew wide open. "Yes, sir."

I cringed as I watched Vino slide into the seat next to me with a devilish grin.

"Don't mind if I buy you a drink, do you?" he asked.

"Only if you promise to go away." I dragged out every word to emphasize my annoyance, and put my hand to my forehead.

He laughed and casually put his arm around the back of my chair. "Aren't you happy to see me?"

"No." I spat. Not seeing him was supposed to be one of the perks of this evening, and besides, how would I explain his presence when Lucas showed up?

"You're hurting my feelings, you know. I did just buy you one of the most expensive drinks on the planet."

"I think you can afford it."

"I suppose you're right."

When the woman behind the bar came back with our drinks, the look on her face was classic, sheer surprise and confusion at our little exchange. I'm sure she didn't often see someone so furious over being bought a top shelf drink. Not to mention the fact that the best looking guy in the bar was paying. When Vino held up a credit card without looking at her, she didn't say a word, so I did.

"You might as well throw two shots of your best tequila on there too."

She nodded and fetched them immediately. It took maybe forty-five seconds for her two pour two shots and bring them back to us. I snatched the one she set in front of Vino before it even left her hand, and slammed it.

He laughed at me again. "What? No toast?"

"Fuck you." I slammed the other shot.

He was unfazed. The bastard even winked at me. "You do look rather tempting tonight…"

I sneered at him; it was too late for compliments. "I have my drink, you can go now."

Vino showed no signs of leaving. He just smiled at me as if he was up to something. He lifted his beverage and took a long drink, taunting me with his silence. He took his time studying the liquid in his glass, then swirled it under his nose and took a deep breath. Then he gently set it down on the wooden bar and smiled to himself, peaking at me from the corner of his eye.

"You can wait for Lucas all you want, but he isn't going to show up."

That was a big slap to the face. *How did he know about Lucas?* I reached for my martini and took a gulp to rid myself of the lump in my throat. I ended up having to take two.

"They distill the vodka through crushed diamonds, you know. I've seen bottles go for over a million. Granted, the bottle your drink came from probably only cost a few hundred." Vino's calm voice held no trace of the ominous comment he made a moment ago.

I ignored him. "Where's Lucas?"

"I'm sure he doesn't even remember asking you out."

What the hell does that mean? I wanted to scream it. Vino's only purpose in life must be to make me angry. I took a calming breath before speaking. "Tell me where Lucas is."

"Don't worry. Your boyfriend is fine." He emphasized the word boyfriend to make it sound like an insult. "Why don't we grab a table? There's quite a bit we need to discuss."

"Why would I go to a table with you?! I can't stand you!"

Vino raised his eyebrow. "You'll like me a lot better sitting in the best seat in the house, drinking the most expensive drinks money can buy, and feeling the envy of every woman in here… And I've even chosen to let you in on our family's big secret. I know you're just dying to know the truth."

I wanted to say no, but that was a sweet deal. He bribed me with everything I could ask for in this situation. I took another pull off my drink. "Fine, I'll hear you out, as long as you keep these martinis coming."

"That's what I thought."

He stood up and locked his arm in mine to lead me away. It felt like a soft electric current flowed out of him and into me. I ripped my arm away before it could distract me, and shot him a dirty look.

Vino picked a private booth in the back with a reserved tent on the table. He coolly picked it up and tossed it aside. Whoever intended to sit here tonight was out of luck.

He slid in just close enough so that we weren't touching and put his arm behind me. "What do you think of this place?"

More small talk, I wasn't in the mood. "I like it, too bad the company leaves something to be desired."

"Feisty, aren't we?" He laughed and paused to take a drink, drawing it out longer than necessary. "I picked this place because I thought you would enjoy it."

That was the last straw. *He* picked this place? What was he talking about? Lucas was supposed to be here with me, not him. I gripped the stem of my glass so violently it should have cracked. "You better start giving me some answers or I'm leaving."

"Have some patience... that's why we're here after all." He sighed. "You can at least try to enjoy yourself."

"Fine," I gave him one of my fakest smiles. "Please, just explain what happened to Lucas."

"I assumed you wouldn't willingly go anywhere with me, so I had him help me out a little... He won't have the slightest clue about it tomorrow. He is completely unharmed and unaware that we are together."

So Lucas was okay, but Vino obviously did something to him. I suppressed my urge to freak out. If Vino was in the mood to give answers, I needed to take full advantage.

"Alright, I can deal with that... So what's with the change in attitude? I thought you hated me."

"I never said that."

I groaned. "Answers, remember?"

He shrugged. "My problem was never with you. I don't like being ordered around, that's all."

"You still could've been less of an ass."

Vino ignored the comment and made a gesture towards my neck. "You should take that off before we continue."

My fingers wrapped protectively around the smooth band at my throat. "Why?"

"We'll get to that part, for now, just trust me. You definitely want to take off that necklace."

"I don't trust you one bit."

"Yet I'm the only one who will be honest with you," he said, giving me a stern look. "Just take the damn necklace off, or I'll remove it for you."

I didn't want to find out how he would remove it, so I quickly unhooked the clasp and set the necklace on the table.

Vino grabbed the necklace and shoved it in his pocket. "I'm tired of tailing you in secret. If I'm going to have to follow you everywhere, I might as well have some fun with it."

"You've been following me?" I choked on the words as they came out.

"Don't flatter yourself, it wasn't my idea. It's part of my punishment."

I should have expected Sebastian to send someone to watch me. It was just harder to swallow with that person being Vino. "Do I get to know what you're being punished for?"

That put the grin back on his face. "Maybe later... There's something important I need to ask you first." He paused for a serious moment. "What have you noticed that's different about Sebastian?"

I took a drink. That was a tough question. "I don't know how to answer that."

He thought it over for a second. "Let me rephrase... I know you see things that aren't normal about us."

Before I could answer, he gently cupped his hand under my jaw line, and tilted my face so I was inches from his. His eyes changed again, and pulsed to a silent rhythm. The contrast of the gold against the red and brown was fascinating. That current flowed through my body again, relaxing every muscle. Any anger I felt towards him instantly vanished.

He laughed quietly and eased away from me. "My case in point."

It took a moment to catch my breath. I could feel the blood raging under my skin. "I don't know what you're talking about."

"You naïve girl. Do you need another demonstration or will you just come clean?"

I tried not to look at him and smiled to myself, another demonstration would have been nice. "Okay, so I react a little strongly to you two. I don't see what that has to do with anything."

"Tell me what you saw."

I did not want to respond to that. I stalled by grabbing my martini.

"Tell me what you saw." He repeated, at twice the volume.

"Your eyes… they move," I admitted in defeat.

"What did you feel?"

That one took longer to answer. "A current… or electricity, maybe."

"Very few people have ever been sensitive enough to notice those things."

"It's not all in my head then?"

"No. It's real," he said. "Does that frighten you?"

That was a valid question. In truth, I actually *liked* it. Knowing his alluring eyes and sedating touch were real was an appealing concept. And it meant that I wasn't crazy. "It's kind of a relief, actually. Much better then thinking I'm going insane."

"Guess I expected that." I could hear the disappointment in his voice. "What about Sebastian, what do you see when you look at him?"

Sebastian's perfect features came to the front of my mind. Thoughts of his radiant eyes gave me the warm fuzzies. If those blue flames and swirling pools were real, my life just got a whole lot better. Then those gorgeous eyes turned black and his smile distorted. Happy thoughts gone.

I started shaking with fear. "No, no... that can't—"

Vino laughed at me again. "Thought so. You caught a glimpse of him didn't you?"

I shook my head, then slammed the last of my drink. That was *really* Sebastian's face I saw. He showed himself to me and scared me *on purpose*. My beautiful Sebastian was the most terrifying thing I'd ever seen in my life.

Vino turned his attention away from me to waive his glass at a waitress. The busty brunette pranced over to our table. She was more than happy to greet Vino. "What can I get for you, sir?"

"Another round would be nice." He winked at her and she blushed, then skipped away.

I waited until she was out of hearing distance and summoned all my strength to ask the one question that rolled around in my head. It just didn't come out very coherently.

"Are you—you're not..."

"Human?" He shrugged. "That's up for interpretation... my mother was. Sebastian on the other hand, he's never been anything close."

"Then what is he?" I whispered, not to keep others from hearing, but because I didn't want to hear the answer myself.

Vino thought about that for a second. "The easiest explanation is that he's a demon, though I'm sure if you asked him he'd try to tell you he had god status." He started laughing at some internal joke. "Second in line to Hell's unobtainable throne... In fact, that's where he is right now. He's been summoned. If he wants to keep that precious status of his, he has to obey."

"He's in..." I stammered.

Vino nodded.

"Why are you telling me all this?"

"Because it's really going to piss him off." He gave me a self-satisfied grin. "You know, you've caused quite a little stir in our family."

I didn't know what to think about that. A family of monsters and I was the one causing problems? "How is that possible?"

"Do you remember the night we met?"

I nodded. "My show, how could I forget?"

The look on Vino's face scared the shit out of me. I'd best describe it as ravenous, sadistic maybe. It was the kind of look where I knew he was about to do something I wouldn't like.

Just as I started to protest, he grabbed me by the back of my neck. I yelped, expecting violence, but the physical assault I received was of a completely different variety. He pulled me into his arms and held me against him.

I was furious… for about two seconds. I wanted to slap him, or yell at him, or do anything but give in. Which is exactly what I did. I didn't have the resolve to fight against that current. It felt phenomenal, like taking a handful of sedatives.

Vino smiled, and leaned down like he was going to kiss me. I tried not to notice things like how thick his arms were, how hard his chest was, or how silky his hair felt as it fell into my face. But I did.

Right before his lips made contact he turned his head to the side and put them outside my ear instead. Then he whispered in a slow, sweet voice. "I had other plans for you that night… until that vile father of mine stepped in"

He hovered there, leaving me hanging on his words. My muscles went limp. I felt him take a long breath, inhaling the scent of my perfume. He chuckled as he exhaled and purred into my ear again.

"He said killing you would be a waste."

I panicked and shoved against him as hard as I could, trying to break free of his embrace. I could have been pushing against a boulder. He didn't release his hold on me, he didn't even move one muscle.

"Shh, Trinity. I'm not the one you need to fear. Besides, I've been given strict orders not to touch you," he said. "Really is quite a shame, though. It was going to be beautiful. Your last moments would have been filled with pleasure like you could never imagine… You would have loved it, I promise."

His voice contained not one hint of malice. He believed what he said, and he sounded truly disappointed I would miss the experience. Those last words rang in my head over and over. *You would have loved it.* He was talking about killing me! But here, still trapped in his arms, I could almost picture it his way. Death by his soothing touch would probably be rapturous.

Vino released me and leaned back against the booth, throwing his hands behind his head. He was the picture of perfect serenity, as if a giant burden had been lifted. I felt the complete opposite. Now that we weren't touching, a black wave of anxiety swept over me and I trembled uncontrollably.

I was glad to see the waitress coming back with fresh drinks. She smiled adoringly at Vino as she set them on the table and cleared away the empties. He ignored her completely this time. She looked heartbroken.

I couldn't care less; I just wanted the drink she delivered. More than half was gone by the time I was through with it, but I didn't feel any better.

Vino watched me with a smile on his face. "It's a nice thought, isn't it?"

"I don't see how dying could be enjoyable." I wanted to kick myself for even thinking along those lines earlier.

He laughed. "I thought you fantasized about that sort of thing… The women in your paintings don't seem to mind dying."

Vino and I had this conversation before, the night of my show. I just hadn't realized he was being so literal at the time. "Those are just paintings."

He leaned closer to my face and squinted his eyes. "Then how do you know what expression a person wears as the life is sucked out of them? No one could capture it that accurately unless they'd seen it."

"Is… is that why you wanted to kill me?"

"You haven't figured that out by now? That's only what brought me to the gallery. I was curious, thought maybe you were connected to our kind somehow. Your portrait is what made the decision for me. Even dried and mixed with paint, the smell of your blood was tantalizing. But the look on your face, it was so different from the others. It was like you were longing for death… I wanted to be the one to bring it to you," he said.

"Then I shook your hand and found out about your *sensitivities*. And well, let's just say I wasn't very happy to see my father that evening."

Vino was honest, I'll give him that much. But I didn't know how to process what he was confessing. It was a good thing I'd been drinking so heavily, because I was a wreck. I grabbed my martini with unsteady hands and slammed the rest of it. Then I pulled the most insane move possible at that point. I sought out the one thing that I knew would give me instant comfort. I leaned back into his arm.

Exactly as I expected, that calming current swept over me in a flurry. My muscles relaxed and my head cleared. If only I could find something like that in pill form...

Vino's head snapped in my direction and I felt him tense up. I closed my eyes and shrugged. "That feeling, it's... pleasant, soothing even. Do you feel it too?"

He pulled his arm out from behind me, breaking our connection. "You haven't paid attention to a damn thing I've said to you."

I ignored his rudeness and turned to look him in the eye. "What is it? Why do I feel a current?"

I reached out to touch his arm and he swiftly maneuvered it out of the way. He scowled at me but answered anyways. "Our bodies draw in the energy from everything around us. You're channeling it somehow."

Why was Vino suddenly offended by me touching him? He was practically groping me a moment ago. I watched him take a few more drinks and avoid looking in my direction. His scowl slowly gave way to bewilderment. Then he started laughing.

"I tell you I was planning on killing you, and you want to cuddle? Now I've seen everything."

When put that way, it *was* pretty funny. I was one messed up chick.

He swept one side of his hair behind his ear and chuckled to himself some more. "I think that's our cue to call it a night."

"I still have a lot of questions." I pleaded.

He finished his scotch. "You know enough for my purposes."

I sighed. Two drinks, what a lousy date. "Do I have to go back to my place?"

"I don't care where you go." He sounded insulted that I would assume it mattered to him.

"You're not giving me a ride? I thought you had orders to follow me."

Vino got up out of his seat and glared at me. "That doesn't mean I plan to chauffer you around everywhere."

"What about our tab?"

"I'm paying at the bar. Don't follow me." He stormed off.

I got out of our booth and leaned against the table. It didn't take long to figure out his reasons for paying at the bar. He wanted to hit on the bartender. The one I thought was so pretty, but her annoying giggle was loud enough to be heard above the music, even this far away. I'm sure he was just trying to get under my skin.

I reached for my phone to check the time. It was only about ten, and I was too dressed up to go home. I wondered if I should call Lucas. What really happened to him tonight? Where did he think I was? The line between reality and fiction had been seriously blurred. I decided to go ahead and text him, try to feel the situation out before actually speaking to him.

I sent something uncomplicated, just a 'what are you doing' message, and hit send. I looked back up to see if Vino had finished flirting and about jumped out of my skin. He was standing right in front of me, way too close for me not to notice.

"What, you strike out?" I shoved the phone back in my purse, hoping he didn't notice what I was doing.

He laughed wholeheartedly. "You're not very perceptive are you? I never strike out. Her laugh was atrocious. I have better taste than that."

I grinned at him. He may not have meant it that way, but I took that as a huge compliment.

We walked to his car silently. The gravity of my situation slowly crept up on me. By agreeing to do this painting for Sebastian I was putting myself in serious danger. And *demons?* That

was some biblical shit, literally. I should have paid more attention in church.

I had just fastened my seatbelt when my phone beeped. I
reached for it and hesitated, worried about what it might say.

The Bentley roared to life. "Aren't you going to get that?"

"I was thinking about it." I snapped, flipping my phone open
with the screen positioned so Vino wouldn't be able to read it.
The message from Lucas was simple. 'Out with Teddy join us'

"What's Lucas want you to do this evening?"

"None of your business."

"Whether I like it or not, everything you do is my business
now."

I hadn't really thought about that. How close had he been
following me? "What do you mean by everything?"

"Exactly that, everything." He drew the last word out into
three long syllables.

"Since when?"

"Last Friday..."

My heart jumped into my throat. Last Friday I was with Lucas, and the ecstasy. "And how close were you following me?"

An evil smile spread across his face. "Was there something I
wasn't supposed to watch?"

All the blood rushed to my cheeks. "You could say that..."

He winked at me again. "I'll admit, I did enjoy that part."

This was bad, very, very bad. I wanted to throw up, and then
punch him in the face. He just admitted to watching Lucas and
me that night, that long, wonderful, now tainted night. How
could I ever look him in the eye again? He saw everything; every
kiss, every thrust. That was unbearable.

Vino was in hysterics. "Didn't think you were the shy type."

"I'm no exhibitionist." I spit as much venom into those words
as I could. "You could have given me some privacy."

"Where would be the fun in that?"

I folded my arms across my chest for an old-fashioned, childish pout. "I'm pretty sure I hate you right now."

Vino took a while to calm himself down. "You're not the only
one this is affecting, you know. Do you really think I *want* to

follow your ass around? Watching you is ruining my nightlife. If I have to be miserable, so do you."

I didn't even look at him. "I don't feel sorry for you."

"I don't expect you to be... But since the old man's out of town, this presents a golden opportunity to catch up on some me-time." He waited to make sure I was paying attention. "In other words, I'm taking the night off."

We came to a stop in front of my building then. I reached for the door handle and Vino's voice stopped me. "Don't do anything stupid. You do not want to be on my bad side."

Vino's taillights were still in view when I pulled my phone out to call a cab. My head throbbed, my stomach was upset, and my nerves were shot. I was suffering from a serious case of information overload. I fished out several pills from my purse and popped them, not checking to see what they were. All I wanted right now was to see Lucas, and to drink away my last couple hours.

The shadows quivered in the alley off to my left. I closed my eyes, not wanting to find out if I really saw something or not. If everything Vino said tonight was true, then there was a good chance these were not hallucinations. I wasn't ready to test that theory at the moment. Luckily, my cab appeared in a matter of minutes, and I was on my way to the bar.

Lucas said he was at Chain, a trendy club located in Soho. Oddly enough, it was the same bar I met Lucas at over a year ago. He took me back to his place for the first time that night, and has pursued me with vigor ever since. I was only now beginning to appreciate that. I needed someone that was genuinely interested in me for normal reasons. At least I would get one more night with him where I could pretend I hadn't been dropped in the middle of a nightmare.

When I walked into the bar, I found Lucas sitting at a high-top table with Teddy and Conchetta. I practically ran to them and threw my arms around him. "You have no idea how happy I am to see you right now."

He held me for a long moment. "Did you have a bad night or something?"

"If you only knew..." For a moment I thought I would cry. Luckily I caught myself in time to hide it.

I said hello to Teddy and Conchetta, but didn't pay attention to their replies. I was too busy studying Lucas. I reached out and threaded my fingers through his. I felt nothing but the warmth of his skin. I was actually disappointed. As irritating as I found Vino, he was so stunning. And that current, I wished everyone could do that.

"Is something wrong?" Lucas whispered. "You seem a little off."

I shook my head. "I'm fine. It's just been a long night."

"Well, if it helps, you look great." He pulled me closer for a quick kiss. "It's going to be hard to keep my hands off you."

That did make me feel better. I loved compliments. "You don't need to keep them completely off me..."

"There's the Trinity I know."

I convinced Lucas to leave about an hour later. I just wanted to be alone with him. My intoxication had almost reached the blackout point by this time, and I could think of nothing more satisfying than a good old-fashioned release of stress with my non-threatening, *human* boyfriend.

We were in the parking lot outside his building when I saw something move again. I fought the panic that tried to sneak up on me and clung to Lucas. Twice in one night? That was not fair. My little visions had done a good job of leaving me alone most of this week. Why did they have to bother me now?

Ignoring my sighting didn't make it go away. The creature stepped out of the shadows. It looked similar to all the others. Black eyes, rotted face, but this one had four scraggly arms and a tail that looked chopped off at the end.

It followed us all the way up to the building, hopping from shadow to shadow and appearing solid for only moments at a time. I should have been afraid, anyone else probably would be. But no one else had just been told that a *demon* fantasized about killing them. And I doubted there were many others who were pining after a man, who wasn't a man at all, that just happened to be visiting Hell at that moment. I almost laughed. It all sounded like a cheap horror movie.

By the time we were inside, I couldn't see the creature anymore, not that I cared much about it. As we stepped into the elevator, I grabbed Lucas and pulled him to me with near excessive force. He kissed me with almost as much fervor. It was like we hadn't seen each other in years.

When we pulled out of the kiss, he kept me held against his body. "I really missed you this week. I'm starting to hate your work schedule."

I didn't want to think about the painting. "I don't have to go back until Wednesday, so I at least get a little break."

His smile was filled with genuine excitement. "That's great news. Maybe you can finally spend some time with me."

That's exactly what I planned on doing. I really did not want to be alone. "We'll see, depends on how nice you are to me"

He pinned me against the wall of the elevator, then leaned down and kissed my neck right below my ear. It sent a tremor through my whole body. That was the same spot Vino lingered when he confessed his plans for me.

Lucas laughed quietly, oblivious to that real reason for my reaction. He whispered into that same ear. "I guess I'll have to show you exactly how nice I can be."

Chapter 8

Desperation

The following morning, Lucas took me out for breakfast at his usual spot. Neddie's was an old boxcar restaurant down the street from his place. Booths with red vinyl seats lined one wall, a vintage bar with a worn countertop lined the other. The palpable smell of grease, maple syrup, and stale coffee clung to every surface and chased you for hours after leaving. This place probably couldn't pass health code, but they sure made a mean breakfast platter.

The sexy outfit I wore last night had a much sloppier effect this morning, made worse by the lack of makeup and the addition of sunglasses to cover the bags under my eyes. I looked ridiculous sitting across from the ever casual Lucas in a wifebeater, shorts and sandals, like there were blinking neon lights above my head stating 'I slept at his place last night.'

Normally, I would have been more concerned about my appearance. Today, I was just happy to be with Lucas. I could have tethered myself to him. Who knew my life could change so drastically in one evening.

Now that Vino's words had a chance to sink in, I realized how grim my situation really was. I didn't particularly trust Vino, I just felt like he told me the truth. So I believed everything he said. Which meant that Sebastian was a monster, and I was seriously fucked.

First thing I did upon waking, besides Lucas, was raid my pill stash. Needless to say, I was already wasted. I don't think he knew, or if he did, he didn't comment on my current condition.

I mostly picked at my plate, chopping up the sausage into tiny pieces, and stirring my hash browns until they were mush. Lucas affectionately studied my mindless actions. "Eventually you'll waste away to nothing you know."

"My liver will give out way before that happens." *If I don't get slaughtered first.*

"If you ate more, it might last longer."

I put my fork down on my plate. "Are you lecturing me?"

"No, no… just think it's cute that's all." He smiled the same delightful smile he normally reserved for me. It almost made me feel better.

"That's me, Miss Adorable." I raised my mug of black coffee in a sarcastic toast.

"So where's that fancy necklace of yours? I figured you'd never take something that valuable off."

The mention of that necklace made me queasy. I hadn't seen the exquisite gift since Vino shoved it in his pocket. He never told me what the big deal was. I did my best to hide my inner turmoil from Lucas. "Didn't want to lose it, just being cautious I guess."

"Wow, you being cautious, that's a new one."

I kicked him lightly under the table. "You're hilarious."

Lucas made a face like I hurt him; it was not at all convincing. "You know, I've been thinking… Maybe we should take off for a couple days."

"Like a vacation?"

"Sort of, my parents have a time share in Montauk. I should be able to get time off work pretty easily."

That dashed my hopes. I immediately went into defensive mode. He just said the one word that would be the deal breaker in our relationship. "I'm not meeting your parents."

"That's not what I meant." He laughed and shook his head. "They're not even there right now. They left early this year so the place is gonna be vacant the rest of the week. I got a call saying it's all mine if I want it. I just thought you might like to escape with me for a few days."

If only Lucas knew what a sales pitch he just tossed my way. No shit, I wanted to escape. I suddenly felt so happy I could cry. This was perfect. I could simply run away. Granted, this was only a temporary fix, a band-aid over a bullet hole, but it was the best option I had. And if we left fast enough, maybe Vino wouldn't know. Or maybe he wouldn't want to travel to keep tabs on me. As long as he wasn't watching right now, I might be in the clear.

"So what do you think?"

"I'm in. You've got me all to yourself." *I hope.*

We were on the road in under two hours. I rushed Lucas the whole time, hoping we would disappear unnoticed. I had no way of telling if we accomplished this. Vino stalked me for a whole week, he had watched my most private moments, showers, changing, sex with Lucas, all without me ever knowing. That was a daunting thought.

As I made patterns in my head from the passing blurs of scenery out my window, Vino's voice whispered in my ear. *Don't do anything stupid.* I turned around and checked out the back window, just to make sure he wasn't following. There was no silver Bentley in view, but I didn't feel any better.

I popped a few more pills with Lucas watching me from the driver's seat. He made a face but didn't say anything. I usually put forth an effort to keep the drug abuse to a minimum around him, but today was not a day for discretion.

Our voyage to Montauk took two and a half hours. The resort town sat near the point of the peninsula, past the Hamptons. We pulled into a gated community of townhomes at about three in the afternoon. They were all cheesier versions of beach homes that you might see in warmer climates. Behind them, a wide sand path led between two tall mounds of grass towards a barely visible beach.

Lucas parked his truck in front of one of the smallest townhomes in the row. I didn't complain. It was a beach house; therefore, I would be spending all my time on the beach... and away from demons.

"It's not much to look at inside," Lucas admitted. "But there's a private beach just past those dunes, it's beautiful, much nicer then the ones near the city."

"As long as there's a bed and a shower I think I can manage."

"Two beds actually," He laughed. "The shower's kinda small though, it'll be tight with both of us in there."

Classic Lucas, mind in the gutter. "Can we go swimming first?"

"We can do whatever you want, all weekend, I promise."

I threw my arms around him and hugged him as tight as I could. I almost started crying. Man, I was a mess.

Inside, the townhome looked like any other cheap hotel, two full sized beds with tacky flower-covered comforters and a thin dresser that boasted a pint-sized flat screen. In the modest kitchenette cramped in the corner to our immediate left, was a mini-fridge, a microwave, and little else. The wall at the back of the room had a set of cheap double doors that opened up to a decent sized deck. Not bad by any means, perfect when you're only staying a couple of nights.

I threw my suitcase on the bed and unzipped it, pulling out a flimsy purple bikini with a cartoon skull on the back left cheek. It was a full size smaller then the suit I bought the year before. Lucas had been right this morning, if I lost any more weight I'd look malnourished.

"That's hot." Lucas commented when he saw the tiny swatches of fabric.

"Thought you'd say that." I forced a smile and winked at him. It felt creepy the second I did it, reminding me of two others who liked to wink at their prey.

I stumbled internally over that word. Prey: helpless and vulnerable to attack, unable to defend oneself. Yeah, that pretty much sounded like me.

To my own shame, it applied to Lucas also, which completely reversed my role. The hunted now a hunter; though this hunter would only bring him heartbreak. Mine promised death, and most likely eternal damnation.

After donning our swimwear, we went to the beach. Bright sun, a refreshing breeze, and an ocean horizon. The sand was remarkably pale for New York, and it was almost empty. Rocks framed either side of us, splitting the beach into two sections as it wrapped around the timeshares. The abandoned lifeguard tower had seen better days, but the peeling paint and broken boards only added to its charm. I could even see a lighthouse in the distance. This place was definitely worth the trip.

Lucas spread a blanket on the sand about twenty feet from the water, and motioned for me to sit. I grabbed him and kissed him first. "You weren't lying about it being beautiful. I could live on this beach."

"For the next two days, we can do exactly that."

I flopped down on the blanket, threw my arms behind my head, and inhaled the salty smell of ocean air. He laid down next to me, propped himself up on one elbow, and leaned close enough to kiss me. I waited for it, but the contact never came. He carelessly traced his fingers around the curves of my stomach, circling my naval and playing with my bellybutton ring.

I closed my eyes and tried to relax, tried to concentrate on only Lucas, and the peaceful moment we were sharing. But Sebastian waited behind my eyelids. He snarled at me through jagged fangs and glared at me through empty eyes. Now that I knew what he was, I couldn't even picture the version of his face that captivated me these past two weeks.

"Do I wanna know what you're thinking about?" Lucas asked quietly.

"It's nothing important." I snuggled in close to him and buried my face in his chest, grateful for the warmth of his skin, the heat of the sun, and the small amount of comfort I received from the two.

He wrapped his arms around me and held me close. I could tell he knew something was wrong, but he had a knack for figuring out when I didn't want to talk, so he never questioned me. I felt so helpless, so hopeless. I had to pull myself out of this. My life had been a steady stream of unhappiness since the day I was born. I hadn't let it get me down yet. True, this situation may be slightly more catastrophic than anything else I've dealt with, but moping around wouldn't make it any better. The best thing I could do right now was try to enjoy myself.

After a few minutes, I leaned back and smiled up at Lucas. "How about a swim?"

He kissed me. "That sounds fun."

We spent the rest of the evening acting like any other normal couple. The more time I spent alone with Lucas, the more I could feel my troubles sinking below the surface. We went to a restaurant a few miles away, ate seafood and enjoyed Long Islands. My nerves were still shot, but at least I was able to have fun with him. Though I'm unsure how many pills or drinks I consumed in the process.

By the time we made it back to our room, it was completely dark, and had been for hours. We stopped inside only to grab our blanket and a bottle of wine. Then we made the journey down to the water, camping out in almost the exact same spot we had earlier. The moon was a thin sliver in the sky, barely illuminating the petite white caps of the waves as they crashed against the shore. The whooshing sound from the ebb and flow of water gave the evening a tranquil ambience. Everything else around us was silent, and no other person on the entire beach. I'm sure the beach closed after dark, but the risk of being scolded for trespassing was the least of my worries.

Lucas opened the bottle and passed it to me. With no artificial light around, it was dark enough I only knew what he was doing because I heard it. I was disappointed I couldn't watch Lucas as we sat there chatting. The thought of him sipping wine was comical, too highbrow for a guy like him. My little grease monkey was more of the beer and tequila type.

I leaned into his chest and tilted my head back to kiss the hollow spot where the side of the chin meets the neck. He chuckled. "You know, one of these days you're gonna have to admit how much you like me."

"You're delirious." I lied.

"I hardly think so." He took the wine from me so we could lie down together. "Now, don't freak out, but I have a suggestion."

Uh-oh. "You better quit while you're ahead... I still like you for the time being."

"But you *do* like me." He leaned down and kissed my neck, slowly making his way up my throat and briefly kissing me on the lips. "I've missed you a lot lately. It's got me thinking about us, about where we're going... Don't worry, I'm not going to push any four letter words on you, and I don't want you to answer me tonight, but I think you should consider moving in with me."

"Luke..."

"I just want you to think about it for a while. You've got a couple months until your lease is up, right? I won't pressure you. If it comes down to it, and you don't want to live with me, then I'll help you find a new apartment myself."

That whole spiel sounded rehearsed. I'm sure he planned this whole moment. Damn, he was so persistant.

Lucas may not have said the "L word," but I could hear it in his voice. And it hurt me on so many levels. I cared enough about him that I didn't want him to feel that way, because I didn't feel the same. I liked him, I needed him, but I didn't love him. I wish I did, but I doubted I was capable. I wasn't comfortable with that emotion, and no one had ever felt it toward me before. Not even my foster parents loved me. Sure, I'd heard them say they loved each other, but those words were never uttered in my direction.

But the worst part of all this, I wanted to tell him yes. I wanted to live in a world where we could be happy together. A week ago, no, two days ago, I would have turned him down immediately and told him he was a moron. I needed to believe that these new feelings towards him weren't created out of desperation. Because if there was anyone out there who was right for me, it was Lucas.

If I did tell him yes, it would only make things worse. After what Vino told me last night, there was no way I was going to just walk away once the painting was finished. Even I was smart enough to figure that out. I wasn't in control of my own life anymore, and Lucas was going to suffer for it.

I turned my head away from him to hide the fact that I started to cry, and came up with what I imagined to be a typical answer for me. "I'll think about it, but don't get your hopes up."

"That's all I'm asking…"

He tilted my face back towards his. I swiftly wrapped my arms around him and locked our lips together, praying he couldn't see my tears in the darkness.

Physical intimacy was as close as I could get to emotional fulfillment, so that kiss escalated quickly. And this was the perfect setting for it, a soft blanket on the cool sand, all the whispering sounds and smells of the ocean, and relying on our sense of touch under a curtain of darkness. Again came the thought, *so what if we got caught?* Someone could be ten feet away and they would barely be able to see us.

Then it hit me. That veil of black worked both ways. My heart sank to my stomach, and I was suddenly very afraid. Someone probably was watching, and I bet he was furious.

I pushed away from Lucas and caught my breath. "What if someone sees us?"

"I doubt that's possible. I can barely see you and I'm three inches away. What's with the sudden nerves? This is way more private than my parking lot…"

I cringed, I'm sure Vino saw that little episode too. Lucas leaned down to kiss me again and I stopped him. "Maybe we should go inside."

"No fun." He murmured as he pushed himself up and started grabbing our stuff.

I adjusted my swimsuit and stared into the darkness searching for clues of demons, then clung to him as we walked up the trail to our tiny townhome. Once inside, I bolted and covered the doors completely, then drew the blinds and locked the windows. Lucas sat patiently on the bed and watched me as if I were a crazy person.

I realize the best way not to get caught having sex is to avoid it completely, but my libido had a mind of its own. Besides, there was no way that someone was inside this room with us. I couldn't imagine how a person could see through walls and curtains, but then again, a *person* wasn't exactly what I was dealing with.

The next morning, we hit a bunch of novelty shops, followed by lunch at a restaurant on the shore. I was heavily sedated again, and feeling much better. Lucas laid it on thick, and I didn't object. Having someone dote on me so completely felt delightful. I appreciated his affections more than ever today, and I was mad at myself for not noticing how wonderful he was sooner.

It was a beautiful day outside, the brilliant sun scorched in the cloudless sky, and crisp ocean air had me almost forgetting my problems. I hadn't seen one hallucination, or creature, or whatever they were, and Vino was nowhere to be found. I was beginning to think we were really going to get away with this. I didn't want to ever go home.

We spent the afternoon swimming, and just enjoying each other's company. When the sun started to set, we made our way toward the end of our gated community to a small bar that overlooked the other side of the beach. The timeshare we were staying in was one of the furthest from it, so we had to walk down the parking lot past the larger units to get there.

As we rounded the corner past the biggest townhome, I saw something that stopped me in my tracks. Pulled in sideways across two parking spaces, and sticking out into our path, was that exquisite silver Bentley. A shiningly ominous reminder of what I was trying so hard to forget.

Lucas saw it about the same time I did and let out a long whistle. "Nice... it's got the Le Mansory package." He grabbed my hand and started pulling me eagerly towards the car.

I dug in my heels and yanked back at his hand. For a moment, I was too scared to speak.

Lucas' eyes were wide and excited. "One quick look? I promise to be fast about it."

"No!" I finally yelled.

He froze, and looked completely confused by my reaction. "What's the big deal?"

I scrambled for a believable excuse. "What if the owner comes out and gets mad? I'm sure they don't want anyone to come near it."

Lucas laughed at me. "Is that what you're worried about? I work at one of the best-known garages in New York. Anyone who spent that much money on a car would have heard about us. I'm sure whoever owns this would be happy to talk to me."

That was a horrible visual. Vino striking up a conversation with Lucas... I shivered just thinking about it. "Please, let's just go get drinks."

He frowned and gave a longing look at the car. "I did say we'd do whatever you wanted, didn't I?"

We gave the car the widest berth possible. Lucas stared at the magnificent piece of machinery the whole time, straining his neck to inspect it from all angles. I couldn't blame him. I had a similar reaction at first. Right now, all I wanted to do was kick it, or maybe take a sledgehammer to it. Anything to cause the thing damage would have sufficed.

Vino left his car sitting there for just this occasion. He knew we would see it. Why else would he park it in such a ridiculous way? And it was common knowledge that mechanics like Lucas can't resist shiny things on wheels. My vacation was officially ruined.

The entrance to the bar was not more then a couple hundred feet past that townhouse. We headed to the patio and took a seat at a table under an umbrella. I couldn't relax in my chair. I might have been hovering over it. Adrenaline burned through my veins and my breath came in short, shallow gasps. When the waitress showed up, I let Lucas order for the both of us, since I was having a hard time paying attention to anything he had to say. I don't even remember what she looked like. I was too busy scanning my surroundings for stalkers.

Three drinks down and still nothing. I hadn't even taken one bite of food. My coaster was torn to pieces, sweat poured out of my pores, and every time the door opened I almost flew out of my seat. I knew my raven-haired assassin was around here somewhere, watching me, laughing at my agitation. Very possibly dreaming up ways to harm me.

"Trinity," The tone of Lucas' voice implied this was not the first time he'd said my name. "What in the world are you so worried about? I've never seen you this jumpy."

"Jumpy? I hadn't noticed." I tried my best to play it off and gave him a fake grin.

"I'm sure. You haven't heard a word I've said since we've been here."

"Yeah, I have."

Lucas shook his head. "Tell me one thing I've talked to you about in the last half hour."

He had me there. I was coming up dry. Not one word he said sank in that whole time. "I'm fine, just daydreaming, I guess."

"Look, I know something's up. In as long as I've known you, you have never acted like this. Who are you looking for?"

I reached for my drink to buy myself a few seconds. I couldn't think of any logical excuse. "I'm not looking for anyone, I just— I don't know."

Lucas sighed. "You don't have to tell me what's bothering you, but it might help. That's what I'm here for, right? It's my job to make you feel better." He hopped up and gave me a quick peck on the cheek. "I'm going to get shots, when I get back you'd better be smiling, or you can't have one."

That added another rip to my heart. Did he really have to be so considerate? I couldn't confide in Lucas. It was as simple as that. If he at least got mad at me, it might make that fact a little easier.

As I watched Lucas walk away, my fear and grief started to give way to rage. How dare Vino ruin my night. If that asshole was really going to do something, then why the fuck wouldn't he just get it over with? Then my logic kicked in and I remembered something very important. Vino wasn't *allowed* to hurt me. Putting his car there was a bluff. He was just trying to scare me, and doing a standup job of it.

By the time we left, it was late, and I had still not seen anything out of the ordinary, so I started to calm down. That was, until we had to walk past his car again. Lucas tried to be nonchalant about getting closer as he stared. I kicked some sand at it when he wasn't paying attention and smiled. I hoped Vino saw that. I would have rather been kicking the sand in his arrogant face.

I must have mumbled something under my breath, because Lucas stopped and turned towards me with the most peculiar expression. "What did you just say?"

"I dunno, why?"

"What do you have against this car? It sounded like you were cussing it out."

We were too close to the Bentley for comfort. I grabbed his hand and pulled him along. "Nothing, don't worry, I wasn't cussing. I'm just a little worn out that's all. Can we head back to our room, watch a movie or something?"

He gave me a look like he wasn't buying a word I said. "Of course, anything you want."

When we returned to the townhouse, we picked some suspense movie on pay-per-view and snuggled in together on one of the beds. The movie could have been anything; I had no real plans to watch it. There were only two things on my agenda, sleep, and avoiding being watched having sex with Lucas. Luckily, as long as one came fast enough, the other wouldn't become a problem.

That night, I had several nightmares. I was burning alive in one, falling in another, but the one that got to me was the one with Sebastian. I won't go into details, but let's just say it started out like a porno and ended like a splatter film. Thank God, Lucas was in bed with me. I attached myself to him like life-support. Who knows how he slept through it.

The schedule the next day went pretty much the same as the prior one; beach, shopping and lunch at some tacky tourist trap. But I was acting completely neurotic the whole time. And Lucas was a little more standoffish. I kept thinking I saw Vino around every corner. I knew he was there, watching me. I constantly felt eyes on the back of my head, but never located their source. Whether he was able to hurt me or not, this was a terrifying exercise in paranoia.

I was almost relieved when we packed up our things and started our long journey home. I slept the whole way, too exhausted by my anxieties for anything else.

Lucas, being the gentleman he was, carried all my things upstairs for me. Once his arms were empty, I jumped into them.

"You're not sick of me yet?"

"No, I kinda don't want you to leave." That slipped out before I could stop it.

"I think that's a good sign."

And there I go getting his hopes up again. That rip in my heart tore a little further. I kissed him, rather forcefully, perhaps saying more than I wanted to with the action. Lucas had to put forth some effort to pry me off him. He seemed to think that was hilarious.

"I'll call you when I get off work tomorrow, ok?"

I nodded and he slipped out the door. When the latch clicked shut, I leaned against it and pressed my cheek against the peeling paint. It took all my willpower not to collapse.

I'd been with Lucas for over a year, and treated him like dirt the whole time. And he stayed with me anyways. He was loyal to me when I wasn't loyal to him, and never once gave up when I was too stupid to commit. I saw him for what he really was these last few days… too good for me.

I sniffed back a few tears and stepped in the shower to bathe in my own self-pity. When the water went cold, I still felt alone, and miserable. I wrapped a towel around my torso, and grabbed another for the mess on top of my head. I opened my bathroom door and the air from the other side swirled in around me, stinging my wet skin, and causing my whole body to tremble. I must have left a window open. I let my hair fall into my face as I scrunched and shook my curls to blot them dry. Then I turned and walked blindly into my living room to solve the problem.

Not three steps out the door, I crashed headfirst into a wall. It sent a jolt through me, which caused my wet heel to slip on the cold linoleum. I shrieked as I tumbled backward, fell flat on my ass, and almost dropped both towels in the process. Stunned, sore, and confused by the sudden change in layout, I swept the wet mass of hair out of my face to look around.

There were no real changes to my apartment. I hadn't walked into a wall. I walked into Vino. And he did not look happy.

I stared at him in shock with my jaw hanging open. I had a moment where all time stood still and the reality of what just happened didn't want to sink in.

Vino stood perfectly rigid with his arms crossed, and he glared at me like he wanted to rip me into pieces. His hair hung in his face and his eyes glowed a deep red, illuminating the contours of his features. For the first time since the night I met him, he looked like a being from Hell.

"We need to talk about that stunt you pulled," he said.

I quickly adjusted my towel to make sure nothing was hanging out, and swallowed back the fear that was trying to strangle me. "What the hell are you doing in here?"

"I already told you."

I stood on shaky legs to yell at him. "Get out of my apartment!"

"No."

I tried to stand my ground, but he was twice my size, and had that whole scary-demon-thing going for him. Plus, I was practically naked, and much more frightened than I was trying to let on. In the end, I lost the staring match quickly. "Can I at least get some clothes on?"

That one made him smirk. "Nothing I haven't seen before."

I turned bright red, marched into the bathroom, and slammed the door. I reminded myself he couldn't hurt me about ten times, then muttered obscenities while I threw on my robe and combed my hair. When I came back out Vino was still petrified in the same place. I was afraid to approach him. He looked as scary as the Devil himself.

I stepped around him and sat down at my dingy kitchen table. "There was no rule saying I couldn't leave town for a couple days."

His paralysis finally broke and he came to stand across from me, his lip twitched slightly. "It was implied."

I folded my arms across my chest and looked away from him. "So I'm supposed to know rules that no one told me about, that's just great."

"You knew I'd have to follow. Were you purposely trying to piss me off?"

"All I wanted to do was go to the beach. I did nothing wrong."

"What do you think Sebastian's going to say about this?"

I *was* worried about that one. "Well, what do you think he's gonna say when I tell him about our little date the other night?"

Vino leaned down, putting one hand on the back of my chair and one hand on the table. His face was not more then six inches from mine, his cold breath blew lightly across my skin. "The whole point of that was for him to find out about it."

I held my breath; there was no argument for that one. He was being careful not to touch me, but I could feel the energy rolling off him like static in the air. The ferocious disposition in his eyes took all the beauty out of that rhythmic pulse of red and gold. He glared at me for a moment without backing off. It was intense; my heart was beats away from breaking through my ribcage.

"I won't do it again… what else do you want me to say?" I whispered, too frozen in fear to manage much else.

He smiled. It was not at all pleasant. "You can say you're sorry, and that you are going to do everything I tell you to from now on."

I barely executed a nod. "I'm sorry…"

"And?" The air around him cracked with the strength of his energy, it made me instantly sick to my stomach. I only had one option left, submission.

"And I'll do whatever you ask." I looked down at my lap, my will utterly broken.

"That's more like it." Vino lingered over me for a second and slowly backed away. He grabbed the other chair and spun it around so he could straddle it in front of me. Then he rested one arm up on the back and stared at me through his thick lashes.

I shivered in the uneasy silence, afraid to look him in the eye. This was a hard task with him directly across from me like that. It felt like hours before he finally spoke again.

"I was only ordered to refrain from killing you. Don't think, for even one second, that I would hesitate to end anyone you come in contact with." He paused to let it sink in. "And that in-cludes your ridiculous boyfriend. One step out of line, and he dies."

I gave him another weak nod, acknowledging the severity of the threat. There was no question that he meant every word.

"It won't nearly be as satisfying as killing you, but watching your face as I reach in and rip the heart from his chest might be a fitting consolation prize… It would make for the perfect metaphor don't you think? A much more literal translation of what you were conspiring for him anyways."

Tears welled up in my eyes as the vision of Lucas' unbeating heart came to the front of my mind. How could I have put him in this much danger? Was I really that selfish that I didn't even once think about what Vino could do to him? Lucas was a good person; I couldn't let him get hurt because of someone like me.

My visible anguish only added fuel to the fire. "I considered confronting you earlier, making you plead for his life there on the beach… but the look on your face as you searched for me was so rewarding, I've decided to give you another chance."

The levee broke then, and I cried quietly to myself for a while. Vino stayed put, and watched me. I tried to console myself by focusing on how stupid the shoes I was staring down at were. Another pair of fancy dress shoes, with big shiny buckles. The snakeskin on top was dyed to match the crimson of his shirt. His ludicrous fashion sense didn't make the situation any less threatening this time. I was still miserable, and freezing. My skin was covered in goose bumps, and I was starting to tremble again.

My tears eventually slowed on their own, and I summoned the courage to glance upward. All the anger had washed out of Vino's face, even his eyes had stopped glowing. But his expression was blank, unreadable.

For a moment, I almost thought he felt bad for making me cry. Logic told me I knew better. I looked away. "Can I close the window? It's really cold in here."

"It's sixty-five degrees outside. That's not why you're cold."

"That doesn't make any sense, my air doesn't work." I muttered towards the floor.

"You don't pay attention too well do you? I explained this the other night."

I very clearly remembered everything he said that night, and there was no mention about changes in temperature. "You'll have to spell it out for me, I guess."

He put a hand up to his forehead and squeezed his temples. "Try to stay with me on this. Think about it on an elemental level; any warmth you feel in the air is caused by some form of energy. Be it from the sun, the presence of other beings, or whatever heating device has been placed nearby…"

I nodded. As preposterous as that sounded, it made sense. "And you're a magnet for energy."

"Exactly. So get used to it."

My thoughts drifted to documentaries I had seen on ghosts, with cold spots of swirling energies and collecting mists. A funny realization hit, it was the same way my hallucinations seemed to be put together. Maybe those people in the footage were looking for the wrong thing. "Do those little creatures collect energy too?"

"I wondered if you could see those."

Finally, verification they were real. "Only recently, I think. There were some drawings from when I was a kid, but I don't remember."

I looked back up at him. Now Vino appeared more curious then anything. "Were you trying to confront that one the other night?"

I could picture that creature with the silent scream and spider legs crawling towards me from across the street. The memory was a lot more frightening now that I had a different perspective on it. "I was trying to prove to myself it wasn't real."

He choked back a laugh. "How'd that work out for you?"

"Something scared it away before I got close enough. I suppose that's a good thing now."

"You're welcome... Seems my chivalry knows no bounds these days."

I silenced the back talk about exactly how un-chivalrous he was. I didn't want him getting all nasty again. "Do you mind explaining that one to me?"

He sighed but answered my question anyways. "Those lesser demons, or whatever you want to call them, keep their distance from us. They're nothing more than animals. We're even more of a threat to them then we are to you humans, so if one of us is around, none of them will be... I caught the little guy off guard, he ran for miles."

That explained a lot. No wonder I hadn't seen anything since Vino started stalking me, until the one night he left me alone. "Can they tell I can see them? Every time one pops up it's coming right for me."

Vino stood up and slowly pushed his chair back under the table. "They're just as drawn to you as we are, I suppose. But I doubt they could do any harm, they're barely strong enough to hold their form. Unless they're completely solid, I don't think they can even touch you. Then again, as sensitive as you are, who knows?"

Very reassuring. It really was coming at me from all sides now. If one group of monsters wasn't coming for me, then the other would. Awesome.

Vino wasn't paying much attention to me right then, he was studying my dingy apartment with a disappointed look on his face. "If I'm going to have to be here all the time, you need to make some changes… I expect you to clean up tomorrow and buy some new furniture. This place is intolerable."

Yeah, I noticed he said 'here all the time,' but I was not about to tell him no. "First thing in the morning."

He smiled, it was almost friendly. "That's what I like to hear. Keep up that attitude and we just might get along."

I couldn't ever see that happening, but nodded anyways. He pulled something long and silver out of his pocket, and dangled it in front of my face. "You may want to be wearing this when we go back to the apartment. Wouldn't want Sebastian getting too upset with us, now would we?"

I forced myself to take the elegant necklace from his hand. "You never told me what was so important about this."

"Didn't I?" He wasn't fooling anyone; he was messing with me. "Perhaps I'll explain that later. I have to get going."

He fluidly made his way towards the door, and left me holding the heavy necklace, staring after him. When he reached the doorknob, he stopped and laughed under his breath. "And by the way, drawing the curtains is not an effective way to keep me from seeing what you're doing."

I gasped. The heat of embarrassment flushed my face. Apparently, I gave him another free show. I should have slept with Lucas on the beach. "How—?"

Vino gave me a sly wink. "I have my ways. I'm not about to tell you all my secrets, you know."

With that, he was gone.

Chapter 9

The other side of the story

I awoke the next morning with a heavy heart, not something I'm accustomed to feeling. Hangover? Easy. Embarrassment over some drunken action? Sure. But *guilt*? I hadn't felt something like that in years. Allowing harmful emotions in is a bad idea. I just plow forward and let the calming effects of intoxication chase those thoughts away. That was rule number one for living the way I did.

But now that I let the guilt slip past my defenses, it was destroying the wall of protection I used to close myself off. Every horrible thing I ever did to Lucas was a fresh memory now, opening up wounds I never knew I had.

If I had been a moral, self-sacrificing person, I would have made a vow to never speak to Lucas again. I should sever contact completely to keep him out of harm's way, and give him a chance to be happy with someone who deserved him. But I was weak. If he wasn't already at work, I would have called him right then.

When I finally pulled myself together enough to get up and make coffee, a new thought entered my mind. All this wasn't my fault. It was Vino's. He may have been too scary for me to do anything about it, but at least my blame was in the right place.

I didn't want to clean my apartment, especially since Vino told me to. But I also didn't want anything to happen to Lucas, so I complied. To calm myself for the task at hand, I dumped several shots of whiskey into my coffee, popped a few pills, and blasted some heavy metal. I cursed Vino in my head, hoping my choice of tunes bothered him. I knew he'd be able to hear this, wherever he was watching me from. In my experience people who listened to rap just didn't appreciate distorted guitars and screaming lyrics the way I did.

Cleaning my living room, or bedroom as it functioned, was the easiest part. It was the only room I ever cleaned on a semi-regular basis. I hit my make-shift studio next, I figured I wouldn't need it for a while, so I shoved all the art stuff to one side and made room for whatever dresser I planned to purchase today. Twenty-five years worth of supplies took up a lot of space. Even organized in neat piles it filled a whole wall and nearly reached the ceiling.

My kitchen and bathroom were last. I wasn't good with all the gross stuff. I did manage to scrub my shower for the first time ever. You'd think a couple of frat boys lived in this place.

When I finally finished, I collapsed on my bed and looked at my clock. It was three already. It had taken me five full hours to clean three and a half tiny rooms. How was I supposed to shower, shop, and make it back here by six-thirty? I was already bombed, and all I really wanted to do was take a nap. This evening would be rough if I didn't get any time to sober up and rest.

I missed my monotonous data entry position; I could always call in sick there. And there was no impending doom if I didn't do exactly as told. If I had known painting would get me into all this trouble, I would have broken both hands so I would never be tempted to do it again.

My foster parents had the right idea. I think I forgave them now, how could I be mad anymore? If I had listened to them in the first place, I wouldn't be in this whole mess. I may have ended up miserable and unfulfilled, but I at least I wouldn't be worried about whatever untimely demise was headed my way. And I definitely would not be stuck in this godawful world of make believe.

About ten minutes later, I rolled out of bed and forced myself into my tiny bathroom to take the fastest shower I've ever managed. I was in such a hurry that I cut myself twice shaving my legs. Getting ready became reduced to throwing on the first matching outfit I could find and covering my face with as little makeup as I thought I could get away with.

There was a furniture store a few miles away, but I needed to find something a little trendier. So I took a chance and headed into Manhattan, praying that I would have enough time to purchase a few items. It was four-fifteen when I walked through the door of my target store. A handsome, middle-aged man in a black blazer greeted me immediately. He had a slight accent that I couldn't quite place, Russian maybe?

I didn't allow him to make any small talk, simply stating that time was of the essence and I only had an hour to purchase as much as humanly possible. The dollar signs lit up in his eyes as he rushed me through two floors of showrooms. Everything in this place looked ultra-modern, so it was easy to just point to the first thing that caught my attention and move on. I picked out a small all-white sofa with no arms, a bright red chaise lounge, new dresser, and a sleek, black bar table with matching sixties-style stools. Everything else I needed would have to wait, my time was up. I had to admit, as brief as my experience was, I thoroughly enjoyed myself in the process. I'd never had enough money to buy new furniture before. The next chance I got, I would have to come back.

The only downfall to the occasion, besides the time restraints, was the substantial amount I had to fork out for delivery and removal of my old stuff, but I had no other choice. Years of unhealthy living had left me frail and helpless. Moving furniture was out of the question. I can't even rearrange things unassisted.

My phone rang as I stepped into another cab. I was delighted to see it was Lucas, although the nickname 'Slave' I had programmed in my phone felt awful. I'd have to change that.

"Hey, Luke."

"What's up, sexy?"

The sound of his voice brought a big smile to my face. "Just bought some furniture, wishing I could take the night off right about now."

"Is that your way of saying you miss me?"

Yes. "It's my way of saying I should have never taken this job. It's not worth what they're paying me, even if the amount is ridiculous."

He laughed. "That's not something I ever thought I'd hear from you."

"No, shit."

"What, is the guy you're working for being a dick? I know firsthand how hard it is to deal with rich people."

"No, that's not the problem. He's been really nice to me. It's just..." What could I tell him? The man I'm working for is a demon? His son threatened to kill you last night? That sounded crazy. The less Lucas knew the better. "It's just, well... they're kinda intimidating."

"Is there anything I can do to help?"

I needed to change the subject, and fast. I probably already said enough to put him in more danger. "I'll be fine. Don't worry about it... Are we gonna spend this weekend together?"

"Of course. I have to catch up on some hours Saturday during the day, but I'll find something fun for us to do that night."

I stayed on the line with him for the rest of the twenty-five minute ride home. I don't remember the last time I talked on the phone that long.

It was almost six when I walked in my front door. My head was pounding, and my bed looked so comfy. It beckoned to me from across the room. I couldn't help but lie down, just close my eyes for a couple minutes...

"Trinity..."

My eyes burst open as I jumped out of my skin and into consciousness. I bolted upright and was further startled to find Vino standing at the foot of my bed with his arms crossed.

"We need to leave." He gave a nod towards the kitchen, where a Starbucks bag sat on the counter. "Be downstairs in ten minutes. I'll be in the car."

He disappeared out the door before I could say a word. I probably wasted two minutes staring after him, wondering what just happened. I must have been dreaming. Vino didn't really show up with coffee for me, did he? I jetted to the kitchen and tore open the bag. There was a giant cup and some sort of a Panini inside. I hadn't eaten anything yet today, so I quickly devoured the sandwich. The clock on my microwave read six twenty-four. I'd been out for a half hour and didn't even remember falling asleep. I shook it off, ran to the bathroom to freshen up, and popped a few more pills before bounding out the door.

My coffee and I were downstairs in record time. I climbed in the passenger seat and gave Vino a weak smile. "Thanks, by the way."

He remained expressionless. "It wasn't for your benefit. I'm the one who'll get in trouble if you're late. I'm sure I don't need to tell you what will happen if you spill that coffee in here."

"I'll be careful." I made a show of putting both hands around the tall cup.

As soon as he was sure I had a firm grip, he let the car roar to life and whipped us out into traffic. It was a good thing that I chugged half my beverage before getting down here, the g-force during the drive would have spilled it all over me otherwise.

We rode in an uneasy silence for half the drive, then Vino turned and gave me a look like he expected me to say something.

I recoiled on instinct. "What'd I do?"

He pulled the necklace out and dangled it in front of me. I'd been in such a hurry that I forgot to grab it from my apartment. "I bet if you sobered up your memory might improve."

I snatched the necklace out of his hand. "You've had a drink in your hand almost every time I've seen you, what's the difference?"

Vino shook his head. "Unfortunately, alcohol doesn't have quite the same effect on me. I only wish I could be as lit as you are all the time. You humans have it so easy..."

Serves him right. I hope his life was as miserable as he was making mine. "Sucks to be you."

I reached up to put the heavy silver band around my neck and halted, worried about what would happen. I lowered the necklace back down to my lap and pleaded to Vino. "Don't suppose you'd tell me what the big deal about this is?"

He studied me for a minute before he said anything. "With as pitiful as you look right now, I might as well. But you still have to put it on after I tell you." He waited until I gave verification I would do as he asked, and went on. "It serves as a connection between the two of you. While you are wearing it, no matter how far away you are, he'll be able to sense your presence and whatever your emotional state is. It also amplifies whatever control he has over you. To what extent I'm unsure."

I held my breath. I'd been doing that a lot lately. I had barely taken the necklace off the first week and a half after Sebastian gave it to me. There was one moment in particular that stood out in my mind; I was wearing that necklace when I had my twisted fantasy about him taking Lucas' place.

"That's awful."

"If I'm near you it will probably make things worse. So until the day comes that you are unable to remove it, keep it off when I'm around... I don't need him wondering what we're doing all the time."

My hands started shaking. "I won't be able to take it off?"

"Eventually. I wouldn't worry about that right now." Or rather, it sounded like he didn't care to explain right now. "You might as well put it on, we're almost there. And it wouldn't hurt if you composed yourself."

Calming down was next to impossible at the moment. "Can I ask you one more question?"

He raised an eyebrow. "Shoot."

"What does he want with me?"

"It's best for you not to dwell on that part."

I struggled to fight back the tears. I could see no possible way for me to ever find a way out of this. "I promise I can handle it."

Judging from the look on Vino's face, my comment was hilarious. "Doesn't look like it to me... I may have a few theories, but I honestly don't have an answer for you. I'm the last person Sebastian would confide in."

One more deep breath, and I wrapped the necklace around my throat. "If he asks, you were just really mean to me on the way over."

"As believable as that is, he's more perceptive than that."

I expected an ominous atmosphere in Sebastian's apartment, but it was quite the opposite. Today was another beautiful summer day and the roof was open again. The twins were lying by the pool, looking like an ad for a beach resort, Amelie's toned body barely covered by a blue thong bikini. Andras had on tiny, European-looking trunks that matched the color of her suit to a T. He reminded me of a fly-weight boxer, thin, but ripped. Having a perfect body must be one of the prerequisites to being a demon. But as good as they looked, it was gross they were barely wearing any clothes with only their family. They both turned around to ogle us with anticipation, but issued no greetings.

The servants were in their normal positions and there was no sign of the women today. Sebastian sat alone on the couch, lounging with his feet up on the coffee table and a sly grin on his face. He looked so devastatingly handsome that I momentarily forgot I was terrified of him. I couldn't take my eyes off him. Our brief absence from each other must have caused me to lose whatever tolerance I had built up to his allure.

When we approached, he rose and opened his arms to us. "It's been too long."

Vino said nothing, and I barely uttered a hello. Sebastian came out from behind the coffee table to give me his normal greeting, grabbing my hand and lifting it to his lips. Knowing what I knew about him now, my imagination ran away from me, and I watched him bite my hand off in my mind. My heart sputtered uncontrollably, but I still felt drawn to him. He chuckled. I'm assuming at my nerves, since I knew he could sense them now.

When his lips made contact with the top knuckle, it felt like my whole body wanted to shut down. My chest burned and my temperature went through the roof. I was suddenly very light-headed, barely clinging on to consciousness. My knees started to buckle…

Then Sebastian caught me with one arm to keep me from losing my balance. He laughed quietly as I felt the voltage of our embrace drop suddenly. "You're quite a fragile little thing aren't you? You'll have to forgive me, I forgot how careful I need to be in your presence."

He gave me a moment to straighten myself out and backed off, releasing me completely. It felt like a fresh breeze had entered the room, I was free and able to breathe normally again.

He studied me with the most enchanting smile. "It really is such a joy having someone with your sensitivities around. It's been centuries since I've found anyone with such an exquisite gift."

I nervously pushed my hair back behind my ear. "Feels more like a weakness to me."

Sebastian shook his head slowly and reached out to take my hand again, this time controling himself so only a slow current flowed through me. "It is in every way a blessing. You should cherish what you've been given."

His gaze shifted over to Vino, who was standing arms folded, trying to ignore him. I caught Sebastian's happy expression falter for barely a second before he spoke again. "Well then, much has happened in my absence… We should have a chat."

He led us through the doors into the bar, keeping his hold on my hand the whole way. Though he was taking care to be gentle, it was still difficult to walk with the distraction of the electricity between us. As we slid into a couch in the middle of the room, he wrapped his arm around my shoulder so I was snuggled against him. Vino sat in the chair directly to my left, and propped his foot up on the table in front of us. A servant had shown up with a tray of drinks before we were even settled in our spots.

Sitting that intimately with Sebastian was very unsettling. He had to have noticed. Not to mention the sickening current that was starting to get stronger again. It made me queasy. I wanted to reach forward and grab the martini glass in front of me to calm my nerves. But I found myself unable; bound to Sebastian by some invisible rope.

"You look positively exhausted, my dear." His hypnotizing voice oozed directly into my ear.

My thoughts flashed to Vino and all the excuses I had for my appearance, but I decided to play it cool. "I've had a long day, that's all. I'm alright."

Sebastian ignored my comment, and turned his attention to Vino as if he read my thoughts. His tone changed completely as he stared at him. "How do you suppose we deal with our current dilemma?"

Vino rolled his eyes, looking much like a resentful teenager. "You already know what you plan on doing, so just get on with it."

"Impatient, aren't we?" Sebastian snapped.

As the words came out that current rolled off him in waves, pelting against me like I was trapped in a storm out at sea. It halted my breath and made me nauseous. But within seconds it stopped abruptly, and he had perfect control again, so much so that I could barely feel anything at all. His expression went back to the usual naughty imp, completely composed like nothing had happened.

Vino wasn't even looking in our direction anymore. Sebastian paid him no attention. "I see no need for punishments. I would never have burdened you with such information so early on, but what's done is done. It's best to not dwell on past events."

Vino didn't move, even his voice was monotone. "Am I free to go then?"

Sebastian sighed. "No, I think you should stay at the estate. Your brother and sister were so looking forward to seeing you. It would be rude to disappoint them."

I saw Vino grimace; there was some hidden meaning to that sentence I couldn't pick out.

Sebastian turned his attention back to me. "You don't have to paint tonight. I was thinking we could keep each other company... I promise to behave myself."

I knew I didn't really have a choice, no matter how nice he made the offer sound. His invisible hold on me vanished at that point, and I was finally able to lean forward and grab my drink. I took my time sipping the smooth vodka, enjoying the burn as it drifted down my throat, trying to buy a few more seconds away from his embrace.

When I was done I set the glass down and turned to face him. "That painting isn't going to finish itself. Aren't you worried about having some sort of a timeline?"

He flashed his usual breathtaking smile. "Not in the slightest. Time is always on my side, I'd rather spend my night enjoying myself than worrying about imaginary deadlines."

I tried to force myself not to fall for his charm. It didn't work. "I can't argue with logic like that, now can I?"

Sebastian winked at me, but spoke to Vino. "Why don't you keep your siblings company for awhile. We could use some privacy."

Vino didn't make any acknowledgment other than swiftly rising from his seat and leaving the room. I was alone with Sebastian then, worried about what torture he might inflict upon me, and equally hopeful it might be something I liked.

"I want to apologize for my son's behavior. You see, Vinicio enjoys playing the villain, always trying to scare everyone out of their wits all the time." He let out another dramatic sigh. "I may not agree with his methods, but I can't argue their effectiveness. I doubt I'll ever have to hear about you leaving town again."

I cringed. "I'm sorry, I—"

He raised a hand to stop me. "I'm not in the least bit upset. It's nothing more than what I expected. Your boyfriend poses no threat to me."

There was a strong emphasis on that last part. Of course it would be beneath him to worry about something so trivial. When it came down to it, we both knew I would do whatever he wanted. Lucas wouldn't even register as a speed bump.

"I don't want you to be frightened of me, Trinity. I was rather hoping you liked me, but I understand where that might be difficult for you."

I smiled shyly and took another sip of my drink. "I'm trying not to be intimidated, I swear."

Sebastian nodded. "That's good enough for now... Do you mind if I ask what details my son told you? I wouldn't want you having your facts wrong."

It was of no use for me to lie to him, not after what I learned about the necklace today. There was no way to tell exactly how much he could sense. "He went pretty light on the details, just told me enough to try and scare me. He was pretty clear on the fact that you didn't let him kill me though. I should probably thank you for that."

Sebastian waved it off. "No need. I admit it was for purely selfish reasons. Under normal circumstances I wouldn't have interfered, but I was beginning to grow bored again and you presented a perfect remedy."

"How is that possible? You have everything a person could ever want."

He laughed. "I suppose you're right, but it all grows tiresome quickly. Humans have such short lifespans they need to cling to every moment. I have lost all sense of time now, just wandering around for eons, trying to find ways to fill the hours."

Just how long was he talking about? He seemed so nostalgic, remembering things that I would never be able to comprehend.

"I think I should tell you my side of the story. Set things straight; maybe ease your mind a bit."

"I'd like that." That was an amazingly true statement. I was fascinated by him, no matter how frightening he was.

"I thought you might." He made a motion for me to lean back with him on the couch, with no silent command this time. "Please?"

Even without him forcing me, I still wanted to do what he asked. I settled back in, leaned against his shoulder, and closed my eyes as the rush of endorphins gave me goosebumps.

He let me have a minute to collect myself and kicked up his feet. "I promise I'm not the horrible monster my son makes me out to be... Well," he paused to chuckle to himself. "perhaps a little. But I have a feeling that you're going to enjoy our friendship.

"I'm sure by now you've gathered that your artistic abilities aren't your only reason for being here." He bent his elbow so that his hand was behind my head, gently twisting a strand of my hair between his fingers. "I have much bigger plans for our future, but you needn't worry that pretty head of yours. We have a painting to finish, and I would hate to destroy our professional relationship... You'll come to me on your own accord soon enough. I would never take you against your will. Go ahead and live your life, date whomever you want. Time means nothing to me. I can wait."

I couldn't think of a response to that. He sounded so acidicly sweet, his charisma was overpowered by the sinister undertones. All I could do was nod, wondering what silent response I really gave him.

He brought the strand of my hair closer to his face so he could take a long whiff. "You see, what my son failed to tell you, is the true nature of what I am. I have the freedom to live my life completely governed by carnal desires. Whether it's money, power, or sex, anything I want, I just reach out and take. It's a life with no consequences... only pleasure."

It sounded wonderful when he put it like that. "That doesn't sound so bad."

"You wouldn't worry about the moral aspect of that would you? Most humans would be disgusted at the thought of taking whatever they wanted. Isn't it Christian teaching to feel guilty for your sins?"

I shrugged. Christianity had played a very small part in my life as of late. "I don't see what you're getting at."

"I'm getting ahead of myself." He reached out and stroked my cheek with the hand that wasn't wrapped around me. It made my blood rage under my skin. "You're quite suited for this lifestyle, my dear."

"Why would you say that?"

"The disturbing visions in your head are full of torture and despair when they are not preoccupied with sex and desire. There's scarcely a kind thought in there. It shows in the things you do to those women in your paintings. I bet you'd actually enjoy watching someone die."

He stopped to see if I would disagree, I couldn't, so he continued. "You're completely immoral and give no regard for anyone but yourself. The only person close to you seems to be that boyfriend of yours, and you even treat him with utter disrespect. The way you toy with him and take advantage of his kindness, using him for physical pleasure then tossing him aside when you're done, that takes an uncommon cruelty. And then there's all the boozing and drugs… You just do whatever you want, sin with a smile on your face. It's like you've been preparing to join us."

No one's ever called me out like that before. But he was right, especially about Lucas. It hurt me to my core. I looked down at my lap and fought back the onslaught of tears.

Sebastian tilted my chin up so I had to look at him. His radiant eyes ignited as he gave me a reassuring grin. "That's not an insult, Trinity. In fact, it makes you nearly perfect in my eyes. I don't think you understand how truly special you are."

In an unexpected move, he leaned in to kiss my forehead. A calming flurry swept over me and every unhappy thought fled from my mind. The loving gesture felt so natural I didn't question it, until he pulled away and whispered one last sentence. "And those pictures you see in there hold some of the most magnificent imagery I have ever seen."

It took a moment to register what he was talking about. When the pieces clicked into place, they didn't create anything pretty. "You're not saying—oh, please don't say you can read my mind."

"No, no," he said. "I'm much more in tune to emotions. But yours come across as pictures, you practically project them at me. Truthfully, it's a mystery even I haven't been able to decipher. I've never encountered anything like it before."

That made me sick. Who knew how much he had seen, or how many of my sick visions he'd been privy to. "Do I want to know what kinds of things I'm showing you?"

"It's nothing to worry about," he assured. "Glimpses, really, mostly still pictures, sometimes a brief flash from some whimsical scene. Only enough to keep me guessing," he raised an eyebrow in my direction. "I was surprised to see how often my face appeared. It's quite flattering, you know."

I nervously leaned forward to slam the rest of my drink. "I knew I shouldn't have asked."

By the time I settled back into my place, a servant had already come with a refill. I kicked up my feet and crossed my ankles this time. I felt pretty confident Sebastian wasn't planning to hurt me, so I might as well go with the flow.

We sat there, cuddled up on the couch like that, for quite a while. We talked about everything, and nothing at all. It was romantic, in an eerie sort of way. I could feel myself easing up more and more with each passing minute. The fear I felt previously dissipated like scattering ashes. As promised, he was on his best behavior. The power rolling off him was calm, and he was careful to not say anything that would alarm or embarrass me. Even his eyes barely moved, I would catch a flicker off and on again, but no real pyrotechnics.

That sophisticated charm was thick, and laced with unconventional compliments. I was positively swooning. There wasn't a woman alive who wouldn't be smitten with him right now. But there was also something vaguely unnatural about it. A blinking warning light in the distance, slowly growing more sporadic and dimming with time.

We eventually made our way to the gallery, at my request, wandering the opposite side than we visited on my previous journey here. A large area directly in the center had the windows removed and an extra set of burly metal supports installed. Those I-beams held a thick slab of fresco more than twenty feet long that appeared to be torn out of a cathedral from the fifteenth century.

The painting on that slab depicted a hoard of people being thrown into Hell by angels in suits of armor. Creatures I would have called demons a week ago, tortured these people as they writhed over each other in a dense mass. It was a graphic version of what awaited the earth's sinners. I was immediately drawn to it.

Sebastian was pleased. "Luca Signorelli, 'Damned cast into Hell,' fifteen-o-four."

He knew every detail about every piece he owned. I tried not to seem overly impressed, to no avail. I gawked at the massive painting, wondering how many millions he would have paid to acquire such a piece, when his silky voice broke my train of thought.

"What is your vision of Hell, Trinity?"

I turned to face him and put a hand to the back of my head, scrunching up my hair a little. "I don't really know anymore. When I was little I used to associate it with flames and people burning, but most of my adult life I've avoided the thought all together. Enough people tell you that's where you're going and it all turns into one big joke."

Sebastian laughed. "They were speaking the truth. I could tell the second I laid eyes on you."

"Hilarious." I gave him a childish eye roll.

As he gently reached out to take my hand, his eyes started to burn again. "I'm serious. You are truly a damned individual. Any one of us can see it."

That startled me, all of the times I had heard that in my life had been nothing compared to hearing it from Sebastian. This was absolute. He really *knew*.

His voice was soothing and melodic as he continued. "I don't tell you this to frighten you. There is nothing wrong with your fate. This…" he motioned to the painting in front of us. "This is not Hell. I could argue that Hell is the putrid life people lead denying themselves the most important pleasures to buy their way into Heaven… But the actual, tangible place that everyone is referring to, is nothing like this.

"Hell is not a bad place, I happen to quite like it myself. I've spent hundreds of years there, and it is still my home. I need you to know that damnation is nothing to fear."

Sebastian pulled me against him and wrapped his arms around me in a classic lovers embrace. The intensity of being held by him in such a way sent my hormones into chaos.

"I want you to envision something for me, think for a moment about what it would be like to always have everything you've ever wanted; the very moment you want it. You could satisfy every craving, fulfill every desire, give in to every temptation, without ever feeling guilt… Imagine experiencing unadulterated bliss, all the time."

He slowly lowered his face down to mine, edging our lips closer and closer. "That, my love, could be my gift to you."

If seduction was a superpower, Sebastian had it. My entire body burned with anticipation.

But he didn't kiss me.

He hovered there, millimeters away from contact, torturing me with my own desires. His lips were so close I could *taste* him. I tried to lift on my toes to close the distance myself, but he locked me in place with that invisible hold of his. I felt an ache from deep within, a need unlike anything I'd ever experienced. I was about to break. If I didn't start crying, I would scream.

And then he backed off, as if he could tell I'd reached my limits.

"Soon, Trinity," he whispered.

While I struggled to retrain my lungs to breathe, my mind flashed with a thousand lucid pictures… all of him.

Sebastian winked at me, a clear sign he caught my drift.

I turned bright red. "That's not fair."

He laughed. "I believe I mentioned something earlier about keeping things professional…"

We wandered around the gallery for a long time. I prodded him to explain everything he knew about most of the artwork there. He was so well educated that I felt like a child asking about the color of the sky, completely ignorant and outclassed. But he seemed so happy to tell me whatever I wanted to know, that it didn't bother me. I loved every minute of it.

Sometime after midnight, Vino stormed in. "If you plan on making this an all night event, can I at least be allowed to leave?"

"I didn't summon you." Sebastian answered calmly.

Vino glared at him. He was definitely mad again. "You've usually left the estate by this hour."

Sebastian sighed. "If being in your own home causes such agitation, I suppose I'll let you take my lovely Trinity home. It is getting rather late."

He took my hand and lifted it to his lips, sending a sexy smile my way while he lingered there. "I'll see you tomorrow, my love."

I blushed. That one little sentence seemed to say so much. When he released my hand and motioned for me to follow Vino, it took a tremendous amount of effort to leave his side. I craved Sebastian's company like I had wanted no one else's, ever.

Vino didn't say a word the whole way to the car. It didn't bother me one bit. I was still riding the high of the evening. Maybe Sebastian was a monster. I didn't care.

We were barely a mile down the road when Vino broke his silence. He barely shifted his gaze away from the road and stated flatly, "Necklace."

I reached up and unhooked the clasp, throwing the necklace into my purse and onto the floor. Vino smiled and turned towards me. "It all sounds like a fairytale when he tells it, don't you agree?"

"He did paint a more colorful picture than you did."

He laughed at me. "It's amazing how every time you open your mouth you manage to prove what an idiot you are."

"And every time you open yours you prove what an ass you are," I grumbled.

It took him a little longer than was appropriate to collect himself and choke out the laughter. "He left out a few things, you know."

"I figured as much." *Had Vino been eavesdropping?*

"You really are going to Hell."

"Heard that one."

He was not impressed by my attempt at a comeback. "Oh, Hell is a utopia for those who sit on its thrones. But for a damned, human soul...it's everything you've ever dreamed and more. That is, assuming you still have a soul when he's done with you."

I had some difficulty masking the chill that swept over me.

"Did you ask him how many times a day he has to kill to keep that body of his up here?"

My jaw went slack.

Vino caught me that time. "That's right. You heard me correctly...how many people, a day, does it take to stay here in *that body*."

"He didn't mention that one," I whispered.

"Clever editing."

I swallowed at the lump in my throat. "How—what does he do to them?"

By some miraculous feat, Vino managed to smile even bigger. "Out of all the questions you could have asked right now, that's the one you choose? That says quite a lot about you." He leaned closer to me and lowered his voice. "Let me tell you something about killing, Trinity... it is the single most rapturous thing in life. Nothing else compares. Nothing even comes close. Not even sex."

He stretched the last sentence out so I would understand. "And in case you're wondering, that is the one thing that my entire family agrees on."

In other words; no matter what sweet promises Sebastian whispered in my ear, he would eventually kill me. And I'd let him do it.

Chapter 10

Poor, Poor Lucas

I slammed the door when I entered my apartment. It rattled a little, but was otherwise fine. I, on the other hand, was not. I could see my brain exploding in my head. The pressure would probably rupture my eardrums and pop my eyeballs out of the sockets. I wouldn't make an attractive corpse.

So I guess I'd say I felt frustrated...and my head hurt.

Leave it to Vino to ruin my perfectly good mood. A few moments ago, the most handsome man I'd ever seen escorted me around a fairytale, with promises of a life I could only dream of. Then pretty-boy out there had to go and rip apart the illusion.

I didn't want to believe Vino. I tried rationalizing reasons why he would lie to me, and believe me, there were a lot. But in the end, he sounded more honest than Sebastian. His enticing words were always laced with a darker intent.

But Sebastian's face swam around in my head, even if that wasn't really his face at all. Thoughts of his almost kiss, and the life he promised, flooded my desires. I wanted him in all his gloriousness, no matter what the price.

This was not love I was seeking; this was lust, and power. Two things that had a lot more meaning in my life. And I was surprisingly unbothered by the number of people that he allegedly had to kill to make this possible.

Why couldn't Vino have just kept his mouth shut? I peeled off my sandals and threw them across the room, then stomped to the freezer and pulled out the Patron. Once I had it in hand, my anger washed away, and was replaced by sadness. That was Lucas' favorite tequila.

Here I was gushing over Sebastian, without even giving Lucas a second thought.

I didn't know what to do at that point, so I plopped down on my bed, and started chugging from the bottle.

A knock at my door woke me up. I rolled out of bed and fell to the floor, still in a drunken stupor. I stumbled to the door in yesterday's clothes, and opened it without thinking.

Three deliverymen were on the other side. I forgot they were coming. Two were actually young and muscular, looking very blue collar in black harnesses. The third one was a good ten years older and had a gut. Can't win 'em all.

I let them inside and showed them the furniture I wanted gone. Then I started coffee and freshened up in the bathroom, since I looked horrible, but at least my place was clean. I couldn't help flirting as I watched them do all the heavy lifting. It put me a good mood. Strong men had always been a turn-on for me. Plus, I always liked attention.

It took about an hour for them to haul everything in and get rid of the old crap. There wasn't much room to fit furniture in here, so the couch was placed against my bed, almost like a step to help you crawl in. The fact that it had no arms made it look good there, like it was planned out. The chaise was kiddy corner from the couch, giving it a good view of my bed, the TV, and the door. The immediate difference new furniture made in my place was astonishing. I made the decision to go shopping again right away. I might as well spend as much money as possible, since I probably wouldn't live long enough to justify saving it.

After a quick shower, a few pills, and the hair of the dog, I threw on a green dress and the sandals Sebastian replaced for me. I clipped part of my hair back, grabbed my purse, and paused at my kitchen counter to chug the rest of my coffee. I spun around to take one last look at my new digs and jumped, dropping my keys on the floor in the process. Vino was lounging across my new red chaise, with his hands behind his head like he'd been there all day.

"Not bad," he commented flatly, "I would have got the couch in black."

"How'd you get in here?"

As always, he ignored my question. "Where are you off to this morning?"

I slammed my purse down on the counter. "What does it matter?"

He turned in the chair so he could give me a dirty look. "I asked you a question."

"I asked you one first."

Vino sighed and gracefully got up from his seat, took the whole three steps necessary reach me, and bent down to pick up my keys. His shirt was one button lower than normal, so I caught a glimpse of his muscled chest. I could make out a thick black line in the area normally covered by fabric as he stood up. I squinted and leaned over to try to see what it was.

He raised an eyebrow and dangled the keys in front of my face. "Don't be difficult. Just tell me where you're off to."

I grabbed the keys and snapped back to my erect position. "Shopping, I'm going shopping." A smile slowly grew across my face. "Do you have a tattoo?"

"Is that such a hard concept to grasp?" Always answering a question with a question, how aggravating.

"Can I see it?"

"No."

"Didn't think you were the shy type." I quoted him, in the hopes my taunting would trick him into giving in.

"You have horrible logic."

I reached out to move his shirt aside, and he snatched my hand before I made much progress. The sedating current rolling off him hit me again, relaxing my muscles and sending a rush of adrenaline. I could feel my checks flush. I'd forgotten how much I liked that feeling. He had been so careful not to touch me since our night at the jazz club.

Vino dropped my hand with a frown. He looked genuinely repulsed by my response to the exchange of energy. That was so odd; it was the exact opposite way Sebastian acted towards me.

I tried to ignore him. "Why won't you just show me? I promise not to tell."

"I don't think you're worthy to see it." He flashed a criminal smile and leaned towards me. "And besides, we wouldn't want you falling in love, now would we?"

My jaw dropped. As if seeing him with his shirt off would instantly make me fall for him! "You're such an ass!"

"You keep saying that..."

Vino reached into the cupboard behind us, pulled out a rocks glass, and held it up to the light to inspect for cleanliness. After making a disgusted face at his discoveries, he grabbed the ratty towel hanging from my semi-functional, olive green stove, and wiped it out. Then he reached for the Johnnie Walker Blue and filled the glass to the brim.

I crossed my arms and murdered him with my eyes. That was a two-hundred and fifty dollar bottle of scotch he was helping himself to.

My mood left him undaunted. "So where are we going shopping?" He asked politely.

"What do you mean, 'we?'" I growled.

"I like shopping," he said, "and I don't feel like putting the effort into following you from a distance today. So I guess I'm driving." Vino took a long drink of the brown liquid, finishing more then half of it, and set the glass on the counter next to him. "Well...?"

"You barge into my apartment, piss me off, and then expect me to hang out with you all day? I think you're the one with horrible logic."

He laughed. "I thought you liked me."

"You threatened to kill my boyfriend, I can't stand you."

"You didn't seem too hung up on him last night."

That hurt. My scowl dropped and my lip started to quiver.

Vino took one look at me and sighed. "Look, we're stuck together whether we like it or not. I'm just trying to make the best of a mutually shitty situation. So just let me drive."

Riding in that luxurious piece of machinery did sound a lot better then taking a cab, too bad he'd be trying to ruin my day the whole time. "I need more furniture. I want to replace everything in here."

He nodded and finished the rest of his drink. "That's a good idea. But we're picking you out a new TV first. I don't know how you can stand to live in this cesspool." He turned and started walking out, then stopped and eyed me from the door to make it clear I was intended to follow.

I have to admit, it felt pretty satisfying to let people see me being escorted by this hunky man in his expensive car. Every woman we passed gave him serious "fuck me" eyes; an astonishing number of men did too. They all gave me jealous glares. That was definitely good for the ego. Too bad Vino had to ruin it by making sure to acknowledge the better-looking ones, of both sexes. It sucked he had to be so damn intolerable all the time.

He picked the stores, of course, commenting that he had better taste then I did. I just went along with it. Every place we walked into the employees waited on us hand and foot. Vino was never nice to them, not outright mean, but unpleasant enough to show that he felt they were beneath him.

As we climbed back into the car after our third store, he un-hooked the latches on either corner of the windshield. Then he pushed a button and the top of the car folded back and hid itself in a compartment near the trunk.

"Would you like to hear a story?"

I squinted at him through my sunglasses. "Is that a trick question? You only tell me things that are going to bother me."

He shrugged. "I thought you wanted to know why I was being punished."

"Oh! In that case, spill it!" I knew he was baiting me, but I didn't care. This was going to be good.

Vino pulled out into traffic, relatively slower then normal. "Finding new ways to piss Sebastian off has been a hobby of mine for many, many years. As far as I can tell, I'm the only one who's been able to get away with such things. Most of the others were destroyed at the first sign of disobedience."

"Others? How many others are we talking about?" I grabbed the majority of my hair with one hand, and held it to the side of my neck to keep it from blowing in my face.

"Let's just say my father's made repopulating the world with our kind a top priority. The actual numbers would be unfath-omable to someone like you. Two thirds, at least, have been de-voured or destroyed for being disappointments. And yet I'm still here, completely unharmed and continuously throwing a wrench into his plans. Perhaps he likes the challenge, couldn't tell you exactly why. But for any reason, I've been forced to stay with him the longest, and I'm not happy about it. So sometimes I have to give him a little reminder."

"Did you just say devoured?"

"Doesn't matter, you don't need to know the details." He waved it off like it was a completely insignificant comment. Didn't sound like it to me. "Anyways, after that last little tiff, the one about killing you, I was angrier than usual..."

He waited to see if I'd react. I didn't, so he continued. "Do you remember the day I came to pick you up for the first time?"

"Yeah, you were being a complete bastard, and making lewd comments, as always."

He laughed. "You're the one who wanted to have sex with my car. Where did you expect that was gonna go?"

I rolled my eyes at him. Vino continued with his narrative. "That has nothing to do with the story. What I wanted you to remember was what had been different, besides the fact that I was there. A reason that you would be unable to work on that wretched painting."

I spent a moment trying to remember that night. Sebastian said he had a long day, that's even when he decided to give me Saturdays off. Neither fact gave me any clues. "There were two days I didn't paint, but the apartment looked the same to me."

"Your ignorance causes me great pain sometimes." He shook his head. "Must I always spell everything out for you? I'm not talking about the apartment. I'm referring to your subjects."

My subjects? That was just Sebastian, and the women. The attractive matching set that I couldn't tell if I had ever seen before, except for the one with the butterfly tattoo. The ones crawling all over him that first day, and then not again after. They were different, all of them.

"Those women…what did you do?"

His eyes started pulsing again, and smirk spread across his face. "What do you think I did to them?"

"I'm guessing you killed them?" I whispered, though it wasn't necessary with the sounds of the passing traffic.

He winked at me, with wild strands of black whipping past his eyes. "I'd be happy to tell you the details."

I stared at him without breathing. Did I really want to know what he did to the four of them? Could I really handle hearing a first person account of murder?

The short answer was yes. I was a sick, morbid person.

I took a deep breath and nodded. "Tell me."

"You're one twisted chick, aren't you?" He laughed and pushed his hair behind his ear, the wind blew it back out instantly. "Anyways, after you left that first night, Sebastian took off, as he normally does, and left me alone to watch after those annoying juveniles. Their constant chatter was driving me crazy, so I decided to shut them up."

Vino rolled up the windows to cut down on the airflow and leaned towards me. "They thought I was there to party with them, I even had a drink first… one particularly irritating girl was telling me she thought Sebastian had the nicest apartment in the city. I couldn't stand the sound of her voice, so I ripped out her sternum, along with half her ribcage." He chuckled and rearranged his hair again. "The bitch never saw it coming. It was so quick, she just stood there, gaping at me with an enormous hole in her chest. When those idiots finally figured out what I'd done, she'd already been dead on the ground for a full minute. They went into hysterics, so I made sure to rip her into extra small pieces for them.

"They begged for their lives as I moved from one to the next, dismembering them, and showering the room in their blood. By the time I got to the last one, she was clinging to me and crying, swearing she would do anything if I just let her live…And I did, for a few moments, just long enough to let her get her hopes up. I tore her head clean off."

I was speechless, but not from fear. Vino seemed to approve of my reaction. "It took days to get the room clean. All the furniture, the rugs, even the drapery had to be replaced. I had to wash my hair twice to get all the gore out. So maybe it was a bit messy and wasteful, but the look on Sebastian's face was worth it. He was positively livid. I haven't seen him that mad in centuries."

I stared wide-eyed at him for a while, imagining the ferocity of him ripping those four beautiful women apart. I could picture the tears streaming down their cheeks as they pleaded with him to be let go, only to see his fierce eyes and sadistic grin as he took the greatest pleasure in ending their lives.

That vision wasn't as disturbing as it should have been. I knew what I was supposed to feel after hearing something like that, but I was more disappointed I didn't get to see it firsthand.

However, that gruesome portrayal contradicted all the other references he'd made to killing. And that was not how I'd imagined it when he talked about ending my life.

"Is that what you were going to do…to me?"

Vino's smile dropped instantly, and he slammed on the brakes. Several horns blared and tires squealed as I was thrown forward into the dash. My seatbelt yanked against my chest and scraped my bare collarbone. Then he whipped the car to the left, further throwing me around in my seat, and inspiring more honks and shouts from other drivers. When the car came to a complete, jerky stop in a narrow alley, Vino whirled towards me, looking completely offended.

"That is not what I had in mind for you." He snapped.

I released my grip on the dashboard and took a few frantic breaths, still jostled from his erratic driving. "Then tell me what you would have done!"

His eyes were bright, and more violent then I had ever seen them. The red overshadowed every last trace of brown. "You really want to know?"

"Yes."

He seemed to debate answering me. I heard the car crack somewhere; I'm unsure whether it was the steering wheel or the shifter giving way under his grip. "What I did to those women was an act of rage. I purposely allowed them to suffer. For you...there would have been no pain."

He reached out and touched my cheek with the back of his hand. I gasped as the soothing flurry swept over me.

"*You*," he said, "would have begged me *not* to stop."

Then he dropped his hand, turned forward, slammed the car into drive, and peeled out down the alley. "That is all I will tell you."

We didn't go to any more stores after that. Vino's earlier good mood had vanished, he was quiet and moody again. I couldn't get a word out of him unless I asked a direct question, and even then, he barely answered me. He dropped me off in front of my apartment with out issuing a goodbye. It didn't bother me. At least he wasn't being rude, I can handle indifferent.

My long forgotten cell phone rang soon after I got home. I knew who it was before I even picked it up. Lucas would be getting off work right now. I held the phone in my hand and watched it ring, making no motion to answer. It had only been two days since we got back from our mini-vacation, but it felt more like ten years.

I sprawled across my new couch, still holding the now un-ringing phone in my hand. What was I going to do? I shouldn't call him back, but I still cared about him, and I really wanted to see him. But after the evening I spent with Sebastian, there was no question who would win in the end. I would have kissed him, if he allowed it. Hell, I would have done a lot more than that.

I debated for ten minutes, and called Lucas. The excuse I gave myself was that ignoring his calls would be childish, and it would only hurt him more. He didn't hide the fact that he was happy to hear from me. We chatted for a while about trivial things, and confirmed plans to get together this weekend. Then he brought up a subject I didn't want to talk about.

"How'd work go last night?"

I didn't have a repeatable answer for that. "As good as can be expected, I guess."

"So what's this guy like? What makes him so scary?"

"I don't know."

Lucas took a moment to answer. "You're being awful evasive about this. Why won't you tell me what you're doing?"

"I was told not to."

Another pause. "But I'm your boyfriend. Doesn't that allow me a little more information?"

"Normally..."

I heard a sigh over the receiver. "Should I be mad you're hiding things from me, or worried you're in some sort of trouble?"

"Neither. Everything is gonna be fine. I'll probably be done in a few weeks and everything can go back to normal." That was a bad lie. Apparently, I was incapable of doing the right thing.

Lucas didn't buy it. "You don't sound very confident about that."

"I said I'm fine... I need to get ready. I'll call you tomorrow."

I shut the phone before he had a chance to reply, and threw it across the room.

Vino didn't talk to me the whole way to the apartment, and he disappeared as soon as we walked in the door. Sebastian was as chipper as ever. I felt overjoyed to see his face. Even after everything I knew, when I saw him, all I could think of was the offer he made the night before.

Sebastian was wearing hushed pink today, with black suspenders. On him, the ensemble looked insanely masculine. He threw his arm around me and pulled me close. "You look beautiful this evening. That dress is perfect on you."

I blushed. "You keep filling my head with stuff like that, and I might start to believe you."

"There you go, pretending to be modest again." He slid a finger under the strap of my dress and tugged on it playfully. "You wouldn't dress in such a way if you weren't trying to be tempting."

Coming from anyone else, I probably would have taken that as an insult. But the way he was smiling at me insinuated that he was the one being tempted, so I let it slide. I stared at him with a stupid grin. He'd reduced me to a bumbling idiot in just a few sentences.

The door to the bar opened then, pulling me back to reality. A servant led Sebastian's harem into the room. He didn't acknowledge their entrance, but I still felt an irrational twinge of jealousy at the sight of them.

That is, until I studied them closer. They moved in an unnatural synchronization as they found their spots on the stairs. They seemed so lifeless, with dead eyes and expressionless faces. My mind unwillingly jumped to visions of the previous set, begging for their lives as a magnificent and bloody Vino ripped them to shreds with a smile on his face.

Sebastian's entire demeanor changed, he lost it for a moment and shocked me. I went weak in the knees, if he hadn't had an arm around me, I might have fallen over. When I looked back up he was peering down at me with a scowl on his face, his brilliant blue eyes were burning. "I see someone's been telling you stories."

Touching must give him a direct link to my brain; I'd have to remember that. "He didn't scare me as much as he wanted to."

"It's the fact that you are unafraid that troubles me."

That was not how I expected him to answer. "I thought you didn't want me to be frightened."

"Yes, you are completely correct." He grinned, playing it off perfectly. "Why don't we get right to work today?"

I agreed and we proceeded to my area. Everything was untouched, perfectly clean, and in the exact place I had left it before our break. It had been almost a week since I'd touched any of it, but I needed no adjustment time.

Sebastian didn't take his normal spot on the throne. Instead, he pulled over the office chair and sat down behind me, saying he wanted to watch the process for a while. It made me nervous at first, but two brush strokes in, everything else disappeared.

Maybe half an hour later, I was jerked out of my zone by Sebastian's hand on my shoulder. I lowered my brush and turned around.

He smiled innocently, or as close to it as he could manage. "Don't let me interrupt...please, continue."

So he was trying to peek into my head. I shrugged. "Alright."

My zone was harder to find with him touching me. I had to really concentrate for the first few minutes, but his constant contact eventually became encouraging.

I couldn't tell if it was ten minutes, or sixty, when he returned to his spot on the chair. I have no idea when he left either, but it couldn't have been long after. He didn't even say goodbye. In fact, I didn't see him the rest of the night. I expected him to come and see me off before Vino came to get me, but no show. I was really disappointed.

Friday came and went quickly. I didn't see Vino until the usual pick up time, and it was uneventful at Sebastian's. He greeted me as if we hadn't spoken in weeks, and even posed with the women for a couple hours before formally dismissing himself. It broke my heart to see him go.

On Saturday, I did absolutely nothing, except watch as more muscley men hauled large pieces of furniture into my tiny apartment. I was drunk by the time Lucas came to get me. Always the gentleman, he came all the way up to my door. When I answered it, he scooped me up in his arms and spun me around, planting an enthusiastic kiss on my lips.

"Well it's nice to see you too." I giggled.

A big, warm smile lit up his face. "What can I say—I missed you."

That brought on a huge wave of guilt. He hadn't exactly been the only one on my mind. "That's enough mush, thank you."

He shrugged and set me down. Lucas looked rather debonair this evening, wearing black dress pants and a sport coat over a grey shirt with the top two buttons unhooked. Completely covered like that, only three tattoos showed. Two were traditional sparrows on the top of each hand. The other was the top portion of a cross. It commanded my attention tonight, because I knew that under his shirt it dominated his whole torso, stretching from bellybutton to Adam's apple, and out on both shoulders. With the cross being surrounded by so many other tattoos, I never paid much attention to it. Now, after everything I'd been through recently, those top six inches creeping out from his collar spoke to me. It seemed to be an omen, painting Lucas in a white light, representing the last thing of virtue in my life. I pictured him with a halo and wings, since he was probably the closest thing to an angel I'd ever see.

That really put my feelings for Sebastian in perspective. I wondered if he owned a pitchfork.

I ran my fingers down the middle of the tattoo, and pulled his shirt down another inch. "You look hot, what's the occasion?"

He reached a hand behind his head in a boyish fashion. "We're trying out a new club tonight. They have a dress code."

"Will I pass?" I did a quick spin for him. I wore another revealing dress today, this one deep purple with a loose, plunging neckline. If I'd had anything more than my modest B-cup, I would have had to tape it.

Lucas gave an approving nod. "No one would refuse you anything in that… besides, I think the code is mostly for the men that show up. From what I've heard, any hot chick that wants in is usually allowed."

"Sounds like my kind of place."

Lucas threw his arm around me and walked into my apartment, scanning the room to take in the new scenery. "Someone's been busy. If you don't look at the walls or the floor, this place looks great."

"Gee, thanks." I gave him a light elbow to the ribs. "I wanted to buy more, but I ran out of space."

"At least you only have a couple months left here," he said, obviously hinting at the fact that there was plenty of room at his place.

My mind went into another direction. I knew I had even less time than that, because I'd probably be dead before my lease was up. "Yeah, yeah. Let's get outta here. I'm anxious to see where you're taking me." I grabbed his hand and tugged him towards the door. This night was going to be really bad on my newly formed conscience.

Lucas drove to the lower east side and parked in front of a row of tall buildings. We hopped out of the car and instead of going into one of the crowed bars on the street, we turned down a dark alley. On the side of an old building was a set of stairs going to a basement, guarded by a large man in a black suit and sunglasses. There were no signs indicating that this was a bar, with no visible windows and no line outside. The man looked us up and down for a minute, without removing the unnecessary shades, and nodded. Then he reached one hand out and unhooked the velvet rope barrier to let us in.

The doors opened to a set of wide stairs that went down into a basement. Another equally large man in a black suit was waiting at the foot of the stairs to check IDs, and collect cover charge. Once both checkpoints were cleared, it opened up to a maze of iron partitions, and a room that looked more like a bordello then a nightclub. The walls were covered in pleated red fabric, and lined with muted sconces. Black bar tables were strewn about the middle of the room, with a variety of booths on the outside and more partitions leading to private areas.

The bar itself was lined with red lights and mirrors. There were several women bartenders behind it, all of which wore some form of lingerie and high heels. The wait staff was dressed similarly, but with aprons cocked to one hip. Loud rap music played overhead, and several patrons, mostly women, danced on a small dance floor.

We grabbed one of the only available booths, and ordered a round from one of the nearly nude waitresses. I turned to give Lucas an appreciatory hug, but the look on his face stopped me.

"You wouldn't believe what I saw right outside your place today," he said.

My heart sank, there's no way this was going to be good. "Was someone trying to rob the corner store again?"

"No, it was that car we saw in Montauk, the Bentley. Had to be the same one, there were a lot of extra options on it. What're the odds?"

I wondered how Vino would react if I punched him in the face, because that's what I was going to do the next time I saw him. I covered my reaction the best I could. "Yeah, that's weird. You must be a magnet for nice cars."

"Maybe you are." Lucas leaned back in the booth and studied me. His tone grew serious. "I can tell something's up. Your behavior's been off these last few weeks, even for you. What are you hiding from me?"

I nervously grabbed my drink, the only thing that could save me right now. "Things are just a little...complicated."

"Does this have to do with the job?"

I didn't answer.

"Are you seeing someone else?"

I shook my head.

"Then tell me what's going on."

That was not an option. I should have broken up with him, right then and there. But I was far too selfish for that. I needed Lucas, even if I wanted something else more.

"I'm sorry, Luke. There are just some things you have to keep to yourself."

Lucas didn't say anything for a painful moment. "What am I supposed to do?"

I could feel the tears trying to break free. "Yell at me, demand answers, call me a liar… leave me."

"I don't want to do any of those things," he said. "I'm not even mad. I'm more worried than anything. I wish you would just tell me, but if you really can't, well…I guess I'll just have to trust you. I don't want to waste our one night a week arguing."

I leaned against him and laid my head on his shoulder. This would be so much easier if he would fight with me. "I don't deserve to be treated like this."

He wrapped his arm around me and kissed the top of my head. "I think you do, you just haven't figured it out yet."

Our natural chemistry did a wonderful job repairing the damage caused by our previous conversation. So within minutes, we fell back into our usual routine. I found myself daydreaming about what it would be like if I did move in with him. I knew it could never happen, but I bet it would have worked out. Sure, we'd start arguing about bills, my laziness, things like that. I'd never lived in a home with someone glad to see me every day, someone who cared about me, and didn't just take care of me because they were obligated. I probably would have been happy.

Over the next few hours, we ordered a lot of drinks, shots mostly. The number was based more on how fun it was to be waited on by half naked women than an actual want. We joked about how bad the waitresses feet must hurt, made out a little, and generally enjoyed each other's company. I was so relaxed around him that I actually forgot about everything else going on in my life, for a while.

As we arrived back at our table after leaving the dance floor, Lucas scooped me in his arms and planted one on me. The kiss lasted longer than was appropriate for public, and I was glowing when he set me down. While Lucas slid into the booth, I turned around to check for a waitress. Just as I started to flag one down, I spotted something that ruined my night.

Vino, the king of all buzzkills, was lounging in a booth almost directly across from us, with his arms around two women. That egotistical asshole was staring right at me with a big smirk on his face. The two women were exquisite, as if I expected anything else. One was a tan brunette, wearing the skimpiest dress I had ever seen, and the other was a chesty Latina with gorgeous long hair.

He winked at me and leaned over to whisper in the Latina's ear, without his eyes ever leaving my face. She gave a seductive smile in my direction and blew me a kiss.

I just about died. That was a bold move, even for Vino. How was I going to pull this off? I quickly plopped down next to Lucas, and waived to the nearest waitress.

She made her way to us and leaned over our table, giving us a nice view of her cleavage. "What can I get for you?"

"We're going to need some shots.   At least two apiece…tequila sounds good."

Lucas laughed. "Do I want to ask, or am I supposed to shut up and drink?"

"Let's go with option number two."

I risked a glance at Vino, who was still watching me with that self-satisfied sneer as his two dates hung all over him. He looked so much like Sebastian had that first day, like an orgy was about to break loose in front of me. I wanted to puke. I gave him the most pissed off glare I could manage, and turned my entire body around so I was facing Lucas, and there was no way I could accidently look in Vino's direction

I slammed the rest of my drink, and tried to come up with a strategy. Now was probably not the best time to punch him,

I'd have to explain my actions to Lucas. And leaving was pointless, he'd just show up wherever we went. So I decided to try to ignore him, which wasn't a very good plan, but it was the only one I had.

I made as much small talk with Lucas as I could manage, I barely heard a word he said. I could feel Vino's eyes boring a hole in the back of my skull. I was on the verge of a complete freak-out.

"Maybe we should take off."

Lucas looked completely caught off guard. "I thought you liked it here?"

"I do, but I'm ready to go."

Lucas called over another scantily clad lady and went to hand her his credit card, but I stopped him. "I've got it tonight. I think I owe you by now."

He reluctantly allowed this, and kissed me in thanks.

When we got up to leave, I put extra effort into looking in any direction besides Vino's table. Unfortunately, I tried so hard I walked right into someone's chair, and Lucas had to catch me to keep me off the floor. While I was rebalancing on my heels, I accidently made eye contact with Vino.

He was laughing his ass off. At least the women didn't see it, but that was because they were too busy groping each other on his lap.

"That mother—"

Lucas stopped in his tracks. "What?"

Shit, I didn't realize I said that aloud. I shot him a big, fake smile. "It's nothing, people were just laughing at me for tripping. Let's get out of here before I sober up enough to realize I should be embarrassed."

Lucas gave the room a chivalrous sweep with his eyes, as if locating the cause of my embarrassment would save me from it. The expression on his face changed as something over my shoulder caught his attention. Judging from the direction, I could only assume what he saw. I didn't have the guts to turn around and see for myself.

I didn't have much to say to Lucas on the walk to his truck. I came to the conclusion that I would never have a moment alone with him again. So I gave up, it was pointless to continue. This had to be the last time I ever saw Lucas.

"So where are we going?" He asked.

"I'd better go home."

The rejection set into his features as he opened my door for me. "I'm not coming with you?"

I shook my head.

"Can I at least ask you why?"

I opened my mouth to answer, but nothing came out. I was such a coward, I couldn't even look at him anymore.

We rode in agonizing silence the entire way to my place. When we pulled out front, I turned to him to try to give him some sort of an excuse. But I took one look at the pain on his face and started crying.

I grabbed his shirt and pulled myself across the seat to kiss him. "I'm so sorry," I said, in between sobs. "I do really like you. I—I should have told you earlier."

"It's ok, I knew." He smiled, though I could tell he was close to tears too. "I love you."

I kissed him again, because I couldn't bear to hear anymore. "I wish you didn't." I threw my arms around him and hugged him as tightly as I could. My tears threatened to choke out my words. "Goodbye, Luke."

I jumped out of the Jeep as fast as I could. Lucas called out to me as I stepped away, but I didn't stop. I took off running towards my apartment instead.

I was a big, festering ball of unhappiness the next morning. I couldn't bring myself to get out of bed, so I just buried my head under the covers. If breaking up with Lucas was the right thing, then why did it hurt so much? I knew I didn't have a choice, but if I did, would I have picked Lucas over Sebastian? I cared about

Lucas, as a person, I couldn't say that about him. But Sebastian was everything a girl could ever want, right?

My brooding was interrupted by the sound of rustling papers. I flipped back the covers and spotted Vino lounging across my chaise. I would have been furious, if I wasn't so depressed. He was reading a newspaper with his hair back in a messy ponytail, his shoes off, and still wearing yesterday's clothes. He probably wanted to rub it in my face that at least one of us had a good night…yuck.

"What the Hell are you doing here?" I threw one of my pillows at him, but my aim was off, it hit the side of his leg. He didn't even flinch.

Vino lowered the paper to grin at me, and I caught an eyeful of something I wasn't expecting. His shirt was completely open and flopped out to both sides, which, since he was a man, shouldn't have been a big deal. But not very many men looked like *that*.

I expected him to be muscular, but he barely looked real. Vino had the kind of airbrushed perfection only achieved in pictures. He could have made the cover of *Muscle and Fitness Magazine*, though he could have been on the front of *Skin and Ink* too. There was a massive, mirrored tribal across his chest… and coming up from below his belt onto his abs. It looked painted on, and unnaturally black. Very distracting. My mind went blank for a couple seconds.

He noticed. "Good morning, sweetheart."

I flopped down on the bed and covered myself with the blanket, grumbling into my remaining pillow. "You didn't have to do that last night, I wasn't breaking any rules."

"You're the only one that gets to go out and enjoy themselves? I was only doing the same thing you were."

"My date's still breathing."

Vino laughed. "They didn't suffer, if that makes you feel any better."

I groaned. "Why are you here harassing me? Isn't there something else you could be doing?"

"No."

I pretended to go back to sleep, hoping that maybe if I ignored him long enough he would get bored and go away.

"Aren't you gonna get that?" he asked.

About that moment, there was a knock at the door.

I bolted upright in my bed. "You got an explanation for this?" I hissed quietly.

Vino shrugged and resumed his reading.

There was another knock.

"Trinity?" That voice sent me straight into panic mode; Lucas.

"You need to get out of here...now." I ordered at the lowest volume I could manage.

Vino turned the page of his paper. "No."

"Trinity, I know you're home. Just open the door," Lucas pleaded.

"I'm coming—hold on, you woke me up..." I jumped out of bed ran over to Vino. "Please, I'm begging, just leave."

He smiled at me. "How can I? There's already someone at the door, that's the only way out."

I grabbed my hair with both hands and yelled at a whisper level. "Just use whatever magical fucking way you always do to get in here! Don't do this!"

Vino ignored me and went back to reading his paper. I grabbed my robe in an attempt to cover up the fact that I was only wearing underwear and a tiny tank top. The sheer robe didn't cover much more than the underwear did. This didn't look good.

I stopped at the door and took a deep breath, then slowly turned the knob and slid out into the hallway. I closed the door behind me before Lucas could see inside.

His kind, chocolate eyes looked so troubled. "I'm sorry to drop in on you like this, but I—I just have to know why. Just please, tell me why you're leaving me."

"Lucas..." I threw my arms around him and buried my face in his chest. "I'm sorry, I can't tell you what's going on, but you can't be here right now, you have to leave."

He held me for a moment, then gently pushed me back to look at me. "What's going on, why can't I come inside?"

I looked at the floor, unable to stand another second of those painful eyes. "You have to go, Luke."

His fist clenched. "Tell me what's going on, now."

"I can't…"

He reached out for the doorknob, and my heart stopped. I knew what his assumption would be if he went inside, and that was only a best-case scenario. What if Vino killed him for being here? I grabbed his hand and pleaded with him, tears starting to fill my eyes. "Please, don't…"

Lucas hesitated for barely a second, and stared down at me in outrage. Then he turned the handle and swung it open, stepping inside enough to block me from closing the door. Vino was impossible to miss, still lounging on the chaise as if he didn't have a care in the world. He lowered his paper enough to smile and give smug little wave.

Blind fury spread across Lucas' face and his entire body tensed up. "Now I get it."

I grabbed his shirt and tried to pull myself to him, but he pushed me away. "It's not what you think! I'm not sleeping with him!"

Vino chuckled to himself in the background. I reached out for Lucas.

He grabbed my hand before I could touch him. "You really are as bad as everyone told me, aren't you? How long has this been going on behind my back?"

Tears streamed down my cheeks. "Lucas, please… You have to believe me."

He dropped my hand. "You really think I'm stupid, don't you. I'm tired of your games, Trinity."

Vino had set down his paper by this point, and turned to get a better view of the action. Lucas glared at him. "I hope you know what you're getting yourself into."

He laughed. "She is an immoral little monster, isn't she?"

That did it, I snapped. "Shut your damn mouth! I have had about enough of you!"

Lucas let out a tortured laugh. "It's good to see you're enjoying yourself. I'm outta here." He stepped around me and stormed down the hallway.

I started after him, not caring how many of my neighbors witnessed this spectacle. "Lucas, stop! Just let me explain!"

He spun around, his eyes didn't look kind anymore, they were filled with hatred. "It's a little late for talk. I gave you every chance to make this work and you toyed with me the entire time. No, there's not a single thing you can say…Go back to your new play-thing."

Lucas turned and resumed down the hallway, disappearing into the stairwell. I stood there and stared after him for a long time, not bothering to wipe the tears dripping from my eyes. I eventually sat down against the cold wall and hugged my knees into my chest. I couldn't get the look on Lucas' face out of my head. I was the cause of all that pain, and there was nothing I could do about it.

My apartment was the last place I wanted to go, but unless I wanted to hit the town in my underwear, that's where I was headed. I drug my heels on the way back, not wanting to see Vino's arrogant face. Why was he here anyways? Rubbing his night in my face didn't seem like much motivation. Then it hit me, like a baseball bat to the dome. He did this on purpose. Why else would he be show up this early, half dressed in yesterday's clothes with his hair all over the place… He knew Lucas was coming and set me up, purposely making it look like we slept together.

I was done crying then. My vision turned red. I wanted to kill Vino. But how do you kill a demon? I was weak by human standards, what could I do against him?

I stomped through the door and slammed it shut with as much force as I could muster. The door hinges rattled in protest and specks of plaster shook down from the ceiling.

Vino peered over his paper and grinned. "Isn't it customary for you to cook me breakfast after this sort of thing?"

"I fucking *hate you!*" I screamed at the top of my lungs.

He winked at me. "Well, I'm quite fond of you, lover."

I grabbed the first thing I could find, a small ceramic vase from my counter, and hurled it at him. My aim was much better this time; it would have hit him in the face if he hadn't caught it.

The only thing Vino moved was his hand. "You're going to have to do better than that."

I spun around and reached into my crowded silverware drawer, and wrapped my fingers around the first knife they found. When I turned around to throw it at him, he was right in my face, so close it was a miracle we weren't touching.

"So you want to kill me, do you? Please, feel free to try."

My hands were trembling. As much as I wanted him dead, he was so intense this close up that I couldn't even move. He reached out to take the knife from my hand, and placed the blade against the skin of his chest. "Go ahead, I'll give you a free shot. You want to get revenge? Plunge the knife into my flesh. I dare you."

I wished I had the guts to stab him, but I just looked down in defeat. "Wouldn't do me any good, would it?"

He took the knife away from his chest and started rolling up the sleeve of his shirt. "If you hit my heart you might kill me. But miss by even a fraction, and well… let me show you what will happen."

Vino touched the knife to his forearm and waited to make sure I was watching.

Then with a downward thrust, the blade disappeared behind a gush of red. The thick, crimson liquid erupted in all angles, spilling to the counter and splashing onto the cheap linoleum below.

I knew none of my knives were sharp, but the blade slid through his flesh like he was slicing through soft-serve. Vino showed no hesitation, nor the slightest implication of pain. I heard the sound of metal scrapping against bone before he withdrew the blade.

Suddenly, the blood slowed to a trickle. The flesh inside his arm swiftly pulled back together, and the skin shut by itself, as if by some invisible zipper.

Vino casually tossed the blade in the sink, and twisted his arm around to show that there were no wounds.

I waited for him to back off, but he just stood there, imposing on my personal space. I wouldn't give him the satisfaction of looking at his face, but when I looked down, all I could see were his abs, and the solid black forms scrawled across them. I decided to close my eyes.

He sighed and leaned against the counter next to me. "I did you a favor. You should be thanking me."

"I'm interested to hear the logic behind that one."

He leaned his face down so that I was forced to look into his eyes again. "He's alive isn't he? This way we don't have to worry about him coming back."

I folded my arms across my chest. "You did it for your own sick enjoyment."

"That was a very small part of it."

He gave himself a moment to rebutton his shirt, wipe the blood off his arm, and roll down his sleeve. I stayed frozen in my spot, staring towards my window and cussing him out in my head. When he sat on the chaise to slip on his shoes, I fantasized about him dropping dead right there. Maybe his head should explode, I bet he couldn't regenerate that.

Vino started laughing and made a gesture towards my feet as he walked to the door. "Sorry about the mess."

I looked around to find a thick splatter of blood all over the floor, the cabinets, the counter, and my bare feet. A morbid reminder that there was nothing I could possibly do to get even.

I hated Vino more than I had ever hated anything in my entire life.

Chapter 11

Questions

Few people ever get to experience the joy of cleaning large quantities of blood. So I would call my task at hand a testament as to how far out of the normal spectrum my life had become.

Blood becomes a thick, syrupy mess rather quickly, and dries from the top down like Elmer's glue. So every time I would wipe what appeared to be a gelatinous sludge, the surface tension would break, and the crimson liquid inside would squirt out, making the puddle twice the size of the original. Once I mopped up all the pools, I was still left with a crusty, burgundy stencil that required a butter knife to scrape away.

I am perfectly fine with blood on a normal basis, so this should have been a cakewalk. I painted with the stuff for Christ's sake. I've cleaned up bloody messes a hundred times before. But the sheer volume was revolting, and with the emotional state I was in, I was having difficulty holding it together.

After all of Vino's blood was gone, I showered, and collapsed on my bed. My psychological turmoil exhausted me, and aside from getting completely wasted, there wasn't anything I wanted to do. I ended up sleeping all day and didn't drag myself out of bed until I felt I was out of time to get ready.

I had to force myself out to the car. I should have stabbed Vino when I had the chance. Who cares if it wouldn't have hurt him. The extraordinary feeling of thrusting a knife into his flesh would have been satisfying enough. I gritted my teeth as I slid inside, careful not to look in his direction.

Vino chuckled as he watched me hook my seatbelt. "Hello, Trinity."

"I'm officially not talking to you."

"And why would that be?"

I crossed my arms and took a deep breath, trying not to completely freak out. "Because I *hate* you."

"And I thought we shared something special. Does this mean you won't be asking me to stay over again?"

I closed my eyes to hold back the rage. When that didn't work, I bit my cheek and dug my nails into my palms so hard I broke the skin. "You should die a slow, horrific death."

"At least you're right about something." He said, as he erupted into laughter.

I ignored him the best I could for the rest of the drive. He did eventually give up and quit pestering me, but by that time we were almost to the apartment, so it didn't really matter. I had been wearing the necklace the whole time, hoping that if Sebastian caught any of this he would be mad at him. But then again, that may have been the motivation behind Vino's actions.

Vino escorted me as far as the living room and disappeared down a hallway, leaving me to ride the elevator by myself. When the doors opened, Sebastian was waiting right outside. I took it as proof he knew how upset I was and had come to console me. Just the sight of him brought so much comfort. I know it was completely irrational, but I wanted to run to him, and jump into his arms to tell him all the things the bad man had done to me.

I managed to compose myself better than that, though not much. He picked up on my needs and opened his arms to me. I went into them without hesitation. Sebastian hugged me the way a man should, strong and supportive, with one hand holding my head to his chest and his cheek resting on my hair. He became my protector, someone to be adored and worshiped. I wanted to melt into him.

"It seems I've found myself having to apologize for my son's behavior yet again. I gave you my permission to do as you pleased, he should have respected my wishes and not interfered." Sebastian loosened his grip enough to lift my chin with one finger. "I wouldn't have Vinicio as your escort if I didn't believe it necessary. He is my own personal bodyguard, and there is not one creature on earth more qualified to keep you safe. His orders are to protect you, not cause you distress. You have my word I will devise a very nasty way to punish him for you."

That brought a big smile to my face; I hoped it would be painful.

Sebastian laughed. "You are one delightful human. Let's get to work, shall we? It'll do you good to get your mind off things for a while."

I would have rather stayed in his arms all night. Much to my disappointment, that offer wasn't on the table, so I agreed and got to it.

Sebastian was right, again, painting was therapeutic. I managed to accomplish a lot that night. He stayed for hours, without ever taking his eyes off me. I finally felt comfortable enough that I spent the entire time working on him. If I had another full week of nights like this, I could be close to finishing the painting.

I was worried about that. What would happen when I was done? Would Sebastian come through with his promise of a divine life of sin, or would I be disposed of?

The next few days went off without a hitch. The painting was going great, Sebastian was as charming as ever, and even Vino was growing tired of his game. I missed Lucas, a lot, but I forbade myself from calling him. I even packed away my phone so I wouldn't be able to. I'd done enough to the poor guy. A genuine saint like that deserved to be with someone who wasn't destined to burn in Hell for all eternity.

By Friday, I felt relaxed in my strange new life of horrors. I was vegging out in my apartment, drinking by myself again, when Vino showed up out of nowhere. I still hated him, but I was much less passionate about it. So when he materialized behind me, I just rolled my eyes.

"What do you want now?"

"I missed you. We never hang out anymore."

I groaned and flopped down on my couch. "Yeah, I'm sure that's it. How do you plan to ruin my day this time?"

Vino eased his way onto the couch and threw his arm behind me, being careful to avoid contact. "I thought we could go out for lunch, that's all. No strings attached, just a meal and some drinks."

I glared at him, being nice always meant he was up to something. "I'm not buying it."

"Don't you trust me? I've come prepared with bribes…"

"There's not a bribe on this planet that would get me to go anywhere with you."

He dipped his head so he was speaking into my ear. "They're good. You should hear me out."

"What then? What could possibly convince me to spend time with someone I wish was dead?"

"Oh, you're breaking my heart." He gave me a fake pout. "I have no ulterior motives, I swear… and I'll admit, I was getting off on you hating me, but I'm tired of that now. Besides, I want to go out, and the only way I can do that is if you come with me."

I shook my head. I was not about to do anything that would make his life easier.

"My first offer is information. I know you have questions, and I'll answer every last one for you. All you have to do is come with me."

"Not good enough. That just means I'll have to talk to you... and will you back the fuck off? It makes my skin crawl having you breathing in my ear."

Vino laughed and eased away, about six inches. "I stole Sebastian's car for the occasion. You're going to melt when you see it."

That got my attention. What car would be worthy to have Sebastian drive it?

"It's a Bugatti, most expensive car on the market."

I couldn't keep the smile off my lips. I should have been ashamed.

"Alright, I cave." I gave him my best 'try anything and die' stare. "Let's do lunch, if you pull anything I won't hesitate to make a scene."

"Best behavior." He put both hands up in a sign of surrender, then rose from the couch and motioned for me to follow.

When we got outside I did melt, smolder was more like it. The car parked in his usual spot made the Bentley look like scrap metal. The black paint had a metallic sheen that made it appear soft to the touch, and the rims and trim were gold. It looked like it was moving a hundred miles an hour standing still. This wasn't a car, it was sex in vehicle form.

I bounded to the passenger side and proceeded to run my hands all over it. The body panels looked like fabric, with a copper weave built in, but they felt like glass. I giggled, and had to ask, "What kind of car did you say this was?"

Vino walked over and opened my door for me. It felt strange having him make such a small gesture. "Vincero d'Oro. Basically a Bugatti Veyron with a Mansory package on it like my car has... Sebastian was trying to show me up."

"Well, he definitely succeeded."

I slipped inside and allowed him to shut the door for me. The interior was as exotic as the exterior, and molded perfectly to its passengers. It even had mood lighting built into the seats. I made sure to touch everything within reach.

Vino laughed and got into his seat, faster then I would have thought possible for being on the other side of the car. He watched my reaction without turning the key. "No comments about ravaging this one?"

"Not even you could piss me off in here. Make as many lewd comments as you want."

We ended up at some fancy restaurant about forty minutes away. I hadn't paid attention to what neighborhood we drove into, the ride itself was enough for me. I didn't want to leave the car, but when the valet opened my door, I felt obligated.

A young brunette led us to a private booth towards the back, where we ordered food and drinks. If I didn't hate the guy so much, it would have felt like a legitimate date. But once the happy thoughts generated from the car subsided, I was annoyed by his presence again. And this new nicey-nicey stuff just irked me more.

I finally gave into my anger and hissed at him. "So what, you're trying to be my friend now? That's not exactly how this works."

"You're not still mad about that are you?"

"I have never been so mad at anybody in my entire life."

Vino smiled and took a long drink from his rocks glass. "Of all the human emotions, hatred seems to be the most powerful, especially in people like you. And the look on your face when you wanted to kill me… it was beautiful, you should have seen yourself." He winked at me. "Any of that passion you want to send my way is always appreciated. But having you mad at me was getting old, and having Sebastian enjoy it so much took all the fun out of it."

"He was enjoying it?"

"He thought it was hilarious, but he'd never tell you that. You know it was all working out in his favor, don't you? The madder you are at me, the more you'll want him. What's the first thing you did after I upset you?"

As twisted as that was, it made perfect sense. Vino got my boyfriend out of the way, and I ran straight into Sebastian's arms. "Does this mean you're apologizing to me?"

"Not at all. Whether you want to admit or not, I did you a favor."

"No, you did not." I snapped at him.

"Do you really believe Sebastian was going to let Lucas live? The only reason he wasn't ordered dead already was because Sebastian found it amusing how you were using him. If I had relayed what was really going on between you two, he would have had me off him immediately." He leaned closer to eye me. "*I spared his life for you*... feel free to thank me at any time."

I wasn't expecting that, but it didn't excuse his actions. "He loved me, and now he thinks I was cheating. What you did was wrong."

"You're saying you've always been faithful to him?"

I grabbed my drink, looking for an escape. "Mostly."

"Then what's the difference of him thinking you slept with me? You couldn't do much better."

"Asshole."

"Oh please, I'm not telling you anything you don't already know." He leaned one elbow on the table. "I am the person you hate most in this life, and yet if I wanted to, I could take you right here on this table, in front of all these people. You wouldn't refuse me and you know it."

I didn't justify his comments with an answer. What a narcissistic jerk. As if I would ever sleep with him! Who cares if he had a body fit for Mt. Olympus, or how intoxicating his touch felt. He was a horrible man, and I couldn't stand him.

Then my mind flashed to the night at the jazz club, and his thick arms, his hard chest, his silky hair...and the way I immediately gave in to the bliss of his embrace. I'd never had hate sex before. It'd probably be an epic struggle for dominance. Somehow, I doubted I'd come out on top.

"You're thinking about it, aren't you?"

I slammed my drink on the table and moved to get out of the booth. I'm not sure which disgusted me more, his ego, or my own shallow thoughts. Either way, I was leaving.

Just before I was out of reach, Vino grabbed the fabric of my shirt to keep me in place. I stopped, only because I was afraid of ripping the garment.

"Sorry, alright. I didn't mean it. Stay, I promise I'll be good."

If I wasn't so opposed to touching him, I would have slapped his hand away. "You made that same promise earlier. Look how well that turned out."

"But I apologized. Have I done that before?"

"No."

"So give me another chance."

"You don't deserve one."

He let go of my shirt. "I won't disagree with you. Just stay."

I sighed and resumed my position next to him. "You're lucky you brought that car, otherwise I'd be outta here."

He laughed, it almost sounded nice. "I knew that was my only chance."

We sat in an uneasy silence until the waitress showed up with our food. I took a couple bites, but mostly picked at mine. I wasn't really hungry, and with Vino staring at me the whole time, I was even less inclined to eat.

"Why do you deny yourself nourishment?" He asked suddenly.

"Huh?"

"You rarely eat. I don't even have to, yet I ate more yesterday than I've seen you eat the entire time I've been watching you. Why don't you consume what you need to sustain yourself?"

I shrugged. What a weird thing to ask. "Not hungry, I guess...drink most of my calories anyways. What do you mean you don't need to eat?"

"It's more of an indulgence, gluttony maybe. We get all the energy we need through other venues. Just because I don't need it, doesn't mean I don't enjoy it." He took another bite off his plate, chewing it slowly. After he swallowed, he sat his fork down and lounged back in his seat. "I fully intend to answer all your questions, you might as well start asking."

I had a million questions swarming around inside my head, so I started simple. "How do you keep getting in my apartment?"

"It's hard to explain, I'll show you sometime."

Vague, but I guess that was an acceptable answer. "Can you like, manipulate flame, move stuff with your mind, things like that?"

"I'm not very good at it. Everyone's abilities are different. I wasn't blessed with those particular gifts." He raised an eyebrow at me. "Muscle's much more impressive than parlor tricks."

I pretended I didn't hear him compliment himself and moved on. "Can you possess people?"

"I wouldn't be much of a demon if I couldn't."

"Is this what you did to Lucas, when he made the date you showed up for?"

Vino didn't answer right away. "Not exactly, I just momentarily influenced his behavior."

I took that as a yes. "You swear you didn't hurt him?"

"I swear."

I'm not sure what he would swear on, since the bible was out of the question, but I believed him. I gave myself a moment to pull Lucas out of my head by sipping my drink. I even took a few bites of food. "What does Sebastian really look like, if that's not his body and all?"

He finished his drink and waived it at the nearest waitress. "I can't tell you that. If you start trying to picture him other than he is now he might go into a rage."

I almost thanked him for the warning, but decided against it. "Then what do you really look like?"

That put a huge smile on Vino's face. "This," he gestured to himself with both hands, "is all me. I was born naturally into this body and I will forever be just as gorgeous as you see me now."

"You're not as hot as you think you are."

He laughed. He knew I was lying. I changed the subject before he could call me out. "Is Steven dead?"

"Who?"

"The guy originally assigned as my escort, or whatever."

It took a few seconds for the light of recognition to go off behind Vino's eyes. "Yeah, he's dead. Sebastian gave the order, so I took him out."

"That's awful."

"Orders are orders. When I'm told to off someone, I do it."

"But I thought you were Sebastian's bodyguard? Why would he have you kill someone who couldn't pose a threat?"

"Is that what he told you? Bodyguard—that's rich, my father needs no bodyguard." Vino started laughing again, it didn't sound very nice this time. "I've been given about the same status as a pit-bull. My purpose in life is to intimidate, and attack when Sebastian yells 'sic 'em.' As long as I'm obedient he won't put me down."

No wonder Vino was such a dick. That must be a lousy existence. "If you're his attack dog, then watching me really is just a punishment, isn't it?"

He sighed. "Of course he needs to keep his newest treasure safe. But that doesn't necessitate someone following you around every second."

I waited for him to continue, he didn't. "You wanna elaborate?"

"No."

"You said you'd answer all my questions. Maybe I should leave."

He scowled at me, but gave in. "If your dog bites you for taking his bone away, what's the cruelest way you can think of to prove your dominance?"

I shrugged.

"You tie him down and dangle the bone in front of his face."

Vino made a point of not looking in my direction when he told me this. And I wasn't exactly comfortable with being compared to a dog bone, but it was nice to hear I was so desirable. I almost felt bad for him. Then I remembered that all Vino really wanted to do was kill me. Since that was the case, Sebastian could rub me in his face all he wanted.

"Okay, so tell me this, why the Hell am I such a demon magnet? This whole energy thing, the stuff I see, the stuff I show

Sebastian… Where does it all come from? Did something happen to me, or was I born like this?"

Vino looked relieved to have the attention away from himself. "Were your parents gifted?"

I shook my head. "I don't know anything about them, and my foster parents refused to tell me."

He thought it over. "I'm going to go ahead and guess that it's natural, but you must have had some kind of contact or interference from one of our kind. I don't see any reason for us to be drawn to you in such a dramatic way otherwise."

I couldn't remember much from my childhood, if something had happened, I doubted Sara and Hank would tell me. "So it's a dead-end then? I thought you guys were supposed to know everything."

"Sorry, can't help you there. If something is locked in your memory banks, you're going to have to figure it out on your own."

"That sucks." I grumbled, picking at my food.

He watched me for a minute more and went on. "Well, there might be a way to shake something loose, but you'll need to ask Sebastian for help."

I couldn't concentrate on painting that night. My mind wandered whenever my brush left the canvas. The question I asked Vino at lunch was rattling around in my head.

Sebastian watched me with obvious concern. "Is something on your mind, dear? You seem preoccupied."

He rose from his spot on the throne, and made his way past the women. He rested his hand on my shoulder, a gesture normally meant to give comfort, but I'm sure he was just trying to see in my head.

I struggled for a moment against the feeling that swept over me. "Yeah, there's something I've been meaning to ask you actually."

"Ask me anything. I'm all yours."

He snapped his fingers and the women left in unison. I summoned the strength to pose my question as I watched them. "I'm trying to figure out what happened to make me so different from everyone else, why I see and feel things other people can't"

"I've been wondering that myself, but I don't think I can be of assistance."

"Are you sure? I thought you could sense things, you've been able to pull everything else out of me."

He laughed and put his arm around me. "I would love to see every thought that's been in that pretty little head of yours, but it's more complicated than that. You'd have to know it before I would be able to, and even then I wouldn't get all the details."

"So there's nothing you can do to help me remember? Vino said you might be able to…"

"He did, did he?" Sebastian's eyebrows lowered. "I don't think it's a good idea to try something like that."

"Please?"

"I'm not sure you understand what you're asking. Humans block painful memories to protect their psyches. It's best not to tamper with such things."

"Whatever it is I can deal with it." I put as much confidence in that sentence as I could.

"You are handling the rest of this quite well, but…" he reached out and stroked my cheek. "I don't wish to see any harm come to you. Especially by my hand. There is no way for me to know what you're going to see, or how disturbing it might be."

"If something happened to me, I want to know. I think I have a right to know." I was begging by this point, I probably looked pathetic.

Whatever Sebastian saw in my eyes must have won him over, because he pulled me into a tight hug. "It's going to hurt. And there's no guarantee that I won't cause you damage."

I nodded into his shirt. "A little pain can be a good thing."

He laughed. "I'm glad you see it that way."

Sebastian tilted my face towards his and leaned in closer. "Don't be afraid," he whispered, as his eyes burned their last flames. Black engulfed the blue of his irises and conquered the white, creating black holes.

I plummeted into that abyss again. But he held me up this time, and slowly lowered his lips down to mine. The surge of endorphins, paired with the force of the electrical current, over-whelmed my senses. My heart stopped, and my lungs seized, my body froze, weightless and burning with unnatural warmth. The one thing I had ached for was now so intense I was barely coherent enough to enjoy the fact that he finally kissed me. I could feel myself slipping, slowly losing consciousness...

Chapter 12

Lost in a Dream

My eyes opened to a familiar room, my childhood bedroom. Misty purple walls and puffy pink curtains, the way my replacement mother, Sara, figured a young lady's room should be. There was an old, wooden crucifix hanging on the wall where it had always been, taunting me from across the room. I was in pain, so much so that I couldn't tell where it came from. Throbbing and burning sensations hit me from all angles, and radiated from somewhere deep inside. My body wanted to writhe and twist in protest but could not. I was being restrained by something.

I looked down to see the straps holding me to my bed peeking out from under my blanket. My arms were on top of the stained and torn quilt, shackled at the wrist and elbow. They were mine, but they were the bruised, emaciated limbs of a little girl, covered in scratches and welts, and splattered with small amounts of dried blood.

My foster parents were huddled over me, praying silently

with tears in their eyes. A third adult stood at the foot of my bed, a priest wearing ceremonial robes, with a rosary in one hand and a bible in the other.

His eyes closed as he chanted a prayer. "God, by your name save this child, and by all your might defend my cause..."

A bloodcurdling scream broke loose and I convulsed against my restraints. "Go to Hell!" I spat at him.

"Hold her down!" He yelled.

Hank pushed down on my chest, pinning me harder to the bed, and Sara held my knees in place. I fought them as hard as I could, spewing obscenities and violently thrashing around. My head was the only thing I could lift, so my neck was strained to its full extent as I searched for something to bite at.

"Holy Lord, almighty father, everlasting God and father of our Lord Jesus Christ, who once and for all consigned that fallen and apostate tyrant to the flames of hell..." The priest paused and made the sign of the cross above me with his rosary. "Hasten to our call for help, and snatch from ruination and from the clutches of the noonday devil, this human being made in your image and likeness. Strike terror, Lord, into the beast laying waste in your vineyard."

I screeched and whipped my head from side to side. Thick, warm tears streamed down my cheeks. He reached into his robe and pulled out a large vile, poured a clear liquid into his palm and sprinkled it onto my face. It scorched my skin like a thousand tiny torches. I screamed until I choked on it, coughing up a small amount of blood onto my ratty nightgown.

"What's happening to her!?" Sara shrieked in the background.

The priest ignored her, placing his hand on my head and securing it to the mattress. "I command you, unclean spirit, whoever you are; along with your minions now attacking this servant of God...I cast you out, along with every satanic power of the enemy, every spectre from Hell, in the name of our lord Jesus Christ. Begone and stay far from this creature of God..."

A voice that was not mine escaped my lips at that moment. It cursed and yelled things that I did not understand, tearing my throat from the inside. My whole body was on fire now. It wasn't pain anymore; it was far beyond that. My soul itself felt as if it was being ripped in two.

The hand on my forehead was removed as I continued to yell. The priest spoke above the noise. "Begone then, in the name of the Father, and of the Son, and of the Holy Spirit…Lord heed my prayer, and let my cry be heard by you."

The crucifix fell from my wall and crashed to the floor with a loud thud. The priest held his bible in both hands and braced himself. "May God show you mercy…" he chanted, as he brought the bible down hard across my face.

I bolted upright with a shriek, panting in wide-eyed terror. What did I just see? And where was I now? I must have left one dream and ended up in another.

The bed I laid in was easily twice the size of my bed at home. It was merely a mattress on a contemporary platform, dressed with the softest sheets I had ever felt. I brought some of it up to my cheek for a quick feel, inhaling the lavender scent. My clothes had been changed too; I was now wearing a long, silk nightgown that I had never seen before.

Everything in the room was modern and minimalistic, decorated with a blinding white and accented with hushed blue. An oriental style sitting area was ten feet out from the foot of the bed. And a singular black sculpture, that stretched more than halfway up to the fifteen foot ceiling, stood in contrast to the crisp brightness of a wall of windows.

On the wall directly across from me was a large painting of two nude women embracing on a bed. They were kissing, and carving at each other with small, ornate daggers. The white sheets entangling them were stained crimson with blood.

I knew this painting well, and I knew the blood on those sheets was real.

Because I'm the one who painted it.

This was the other painting Sebastian purchased from me. Which meant that I was in Sebastian's bedroom, in *his bed*. And I was most definitely not dreaming.

I remembered last night vaguely, and only one moment stuck out: the kiss. Just the thought of it made my hormones surge, though I couldn't remember if I had even enjoyed it. All that came to mind was Sebastian saying not to be afraid, and his eyes going black… then I was being assaulted by a priest.

The door opened and I jumped. A young woman in a button-down shirt and dress slacks entered the room. She was carrying a black garment bag and pushing a cart. "Good afternoon, Miss Morgan. My name is Julia."

"Good afternoon…? What time is it?"

"Four-thirty, ma'am. I've brought you a change of clothes." She hung the garment bag on a hook and pointed to the other end of the room towards a bathroom. "Everything you need should be through those doors, please take your time."

"Did you just say four-thirty, in the evening?"

"Yes, ma'am. If there is anything else you require just page the intercom and I will be right up. Mr. Amante is in his study, it's down the hallway, he'd like for you to join him once you're ready."

"Yeah, um, thank you." I stammered. Years of drinking and drugs had conditioned me for a lot of disorienting awakenings, but this one took the cake.

As Julia nodded and left the room, I crawled out of bed and I almost fell over with a serious case of vertigo. My legs didn't want to support my weight at first either. I gave myself a moment and stumbled toward the stainless steel cart where the wonderful smell of fresh coffee emanated from. On my way, I unzipped the garment bag to take a peek. There was a short, off the shoulder black dress inside.

I got ready as fast as I could; only pausing briefly to marvel at the chamber too big to be called a bathroom. Every product I could ever need awaited me on the counter and the shower was straight out of a resort. It had a built in stereo, steam enclosure, and nine showerheads, including a ceiling mounted rain head.

It felt strange showering alone in such a massive room. I wondered how many servants Sebastian had bathe him every day.

Once finished, I slipped on the dress and checked myself in the mirror. It fit me perfectly, accenting the curve of my breasts and hugging my tiny waist. As if I had any doubts, Sebastian knew every detail about me.

The study was surprisingly easy to find, and as promised, Sebastian waited there. He was lounging in a reading chair with his feet up, flipping through the pages of some thick tome with weird symbols on the front. As I entered the room, he looked up at me with one of his dazzling smiles and set the book down.

"Trinity, don't you look enchanting…"

I blushed and sat on the chair adjacent to him. "Thanks… for everything, I mean."

"You're quite welcome. What's mine is yours and all that…" He waved it off and raised a charismatic eyebrow in my direction. "I'm glad to see you haven't run away screaming yet. I was positive you wouldn't like me anymore."

"I can't imagine too many things that would make me dislike you at the moment." I glanced down to hide my embarrassment. I didn't say anything he didn't already know, it just sounded silly to admit it aloud.

"That's good to know." He laughed, it sounded more sinister then I'm sure he intended it to.

"Well, don't let it go to your head."

He dismissed my comment with another smile. "I'm amazed by how well you are handling all this. I didn't expect you to be in such high spirits with the atrocities you saw last night."

My mind flashed to the broken images of torment, visions that didn't really answer any of my questions. "You caught that, did you?"

Sebastian reached out and laid his hand on mine, sending a small wave of electricity my way. "I stayed by your side every moment I could. Unfortunately, what you saw only explains why your abilities laid dormant for so long, and not where they originated. I'm truly sorry you had to endure such a thing."

"So it was a real memory then, they really did that to me?" I was suddenly furious. Sara and Hank had really strapped me to a bed and tortured me. They had brutally attacked a defenseless little girl.

Sebastian's calm voice broke through my thoughts. "Those humans saved your life."

"They were assaulting me."

"I'm afraid you are mistaken. They had good reason for what they did...You were possessed, my love."

My jaw dropped. "Possessed?"

"Yes. You see, some of the...weaker of us have to resort to despicable things to stay in this world. Acquiring a human body can be quite the challenge for a being of little power." He shook his head. "Children are the easiest victims. Your sensitivities apparently made you a target for a creature searching for a host body.

"The exorcism may have been brutal, but I assure you, whatever the demon had in store was worse. I'm ashamed to admit it was a being of my kind. I hope you realize the difference in caliber between me and one such as that. I have never needed a host to remain in this world. It would be far beneath me to ever pull something so vile."

Sebastian sounded more sincere than he ever had before. "As long as you are with me, I can guarantee that no one will ever harm you. There will never be anything else for you to fear."

He lifted my hand and kissed the top of it, lingering there with his eyes closed. When he finally lowered it back down, he looked utterly radiant. "Why don't we get lunch? You must be starving."

I accompanied him, arm in arm, to the elevator. I was actually hungry for once, and I felt drained, more than I ever did after a night of partying. He kept a firm grip on me when we stepped inside, counteracting the normal frigidity of being in a small room with him. Even though I knew he received snapshots of what I was thinking, I found myself wondering what it would be like to wake up here everyday. How wonderful his smiling face and affectionate greeting would be every morning.

Deep down I knew that's not what it would be like, but the fantasy was irresistible.

The dining room was in the far corner of the first floor, another enormous and professionally decorated room to match the others. More windows lined two full walls and were open to the balcony outside. The large table in the center already had two plates of food waiting for us, lobster on a bed of rice and vegetables.

We took our seats next to each other at the end of the table. Sebastian held my chair out for me. The gesture seemed old fashioned, but fitting for someone like him. He began asking me random questions about art school, what kind of music I liked, and what my favorite foods were. I was happy to answer all of them, though I'm sure he knew the answers before they crossed my lips.

I managed to finish my plate; something considered a large feat for me. He smiled and reached out to take my hand as soon as he was sure I didn't need it. "Have I explained to you how much I enjoy your company?"

I blushed again. "You might have mentioned it."

Sebastian laughed. "Yes, I'm sure I did. And luckily it appears you don't find me too disagreeable these days."

"You're very easy to like," I muttered, as I ran through images of the previous evening again. I felt my blood rush at the thought of him kissing me, and with him holding my hand, it was obvious he caught all of it.

One side of his mouth curled up in a sly smirk. It was ravishing, not at all helping my enraged hormones. "It's such a shame that our first kiss had to be under such unfavorable circumstances. I promise next time won't be quite so intense."

Next time, that was music to my ears. My undeniable joy only made his grin bigger. I wanted to pull my hand away so he couldn't gage my reaction, but found myself unable. As wonderful as he was being today, Sebastian still felt the need to dispose of my freewill.

He peered into the depths of my eyes for a second and released my hand, then leaned back in his chair with a sigh. "Well, all that will have to wait. I have a prior engagement I need to attend to. Unfortunately, I'm going to have to take my leave."

"Really?" I pleaded. I wanted nothing more than to stay with him for the rest of the day. I needed to hear more of his beautiful lies, to feel more of his touch, and Heaven forbid, to kiss him again.

Sebastian stood from his chair, and bent over to kiss the top of my head. "I'm sure you'll do just fine in my absence. I have arranged an escort..."

Always on cue, Vino strolled into the room with a frown on his face. I groaned, just the person I wanted to see. "Do I have to go with him?"

Vino gave me a mocking wave.

Sebastian laughed. "If I could spend every moment with you, I would. I'll see you tomorrow, my love."

Vino didn't say a word until we were out in his car. And even then he waited until I took off the necklace that I had been wearing for more than twenty-four hours.

"Thanks for the night off," he expressed with a big grin.

"It was all for your benefit," I added sarcastically.

"What are your plans for this evening?"

"Don't have any."

"So we're all dressed up with nowhere to go?"

"And that would be your fault, now wouldn't it?"

That only brought on a round of laughter. "It's not healthy to hold grudges, you know."

He turned the car around a sharp corner, sending me reeling into the doorframe. I heard a car honk behind us. He waited for me to compose myself before he spoke again. "Tell you what, why don't I take you out? You do look rather tempting tonight; that dress hides how malnourished you are. I could actually stand to be seen in public with you."

"I'd rather sit at home, thank you."

"You know I'm just going to be sitting right there next to you. Why ruin both our nights?"

"You're not happy unless I'm pissed off, are you?"

"I'm insulted. All I'm trying to do is have a little fun. How bad could being my date for a night be?"

"Is that a rhetorical question? 'Cuz you really don't want me to answer that."

Vino laughed again. "Was that a yes?"

"Whatever." I mumbled. This was not going to be a good night, but if he was picking up the tab…

We valeted the car and approached a ritzy Manhattan nightclub. There was a line, but Vino walked right up to the door, then gave the bouncer a dirty look when he took too long to open it for him. He didn't pay cover or show ID either. I was not impressed. That was just plain rude.

The club was appropriately named Burn. Since it was nine o'clock, Burn wasn't very busy yet, but I could tell immediately why Vino liked it. The walls were frosted plexiglass with black stencils of trees on them, and were lit red from behind. Dark purple couches, black coffee tables, and gold ottomans were arranged in rectangular patterns and sectioned off by more plexiglass. And several faux fireplaces stretched to the ceiling around a centralized dance floor.

Vino led me upstairs into a private area that overlooked the dance floor. There was a real fireplace here, and the smell of smoke completed the illusion of a burning forest. He sat as close as he could without touching me, ordered the most expensive drinks available, and flirted with the wait staff. I was beginning to notice a pattern.

The bar started to fill to capacity as the night dragged on, giving me more distractions from my loathsome date. He was back to playing the nice card, which only assured me that he had to be up to something.

"You are dead set on having a horrible time, aren't you? I thought we were past all this."

I finished my third martini and sneered at him. "If I wasn't forced to be here I might like it better."

"I've never forced you to do anything... I may have persuaded you to see things my way a few times, but I have never taken away your will," he said. "Now can you say the same about your beloved Sebastian?"

I thought about that for a second. I may hate Vino, but I was always in control of myself around him. Even when Sebastian was at his most irresistible, I was sometimes forced to submit. That realization actually made me feel better about my current company, but not much.

"I don't love him," I spat.

That brought the smile back. "So you admit it's true. I'm looking better every day, aren't I?"

"You're still an ass."

He leaned in and spoke directly into my ear. "Come on, you know you want me."

I laughed at him. He had the biggest ego of anyone I had ever met. "Yes Vino, I do want you... to go fuck yourself. I couldn't possibly like you any less."

"Is that a challenge?"

I slammed my fist on the table. "What is wrong with you?! Are you completely incapable of behaving like a civilized human being?"

"Calm down—"

"I will not calm down! You keep sucking up to me and then acting like a Neanderthal! What happened to the guy I met at my art show, huh? Why doesn't he ever show up? I've seen you be charming, did you just forget how?"

My yelling was starting to attract attention. Vino just shook his head. "Okay, I get it. You're right. Is that what you want to hear? I am incapable of acting like a human, because I'm *not one*. The person you met at the show was an act. You know what my intentions were. Now that I'm not trying to get in your pants, there's no reason to keep up false pretenses."

"But you *are* human! You already let it slip that your mother was. Didn't she teach you how to behave?"

Vino's eyebrows drew down in the center. Apparently, I had struck a nerve. "My mother is none of your business. She has been dead for a very, very long time. And no, she did not teach me how to behave, because there was no need. Do you forget, humans are *food*. My interaction with them is generally seduce, then kill. *That's it.*" He pointed an angry finger at me. "You are the only human I have been forced to spend this much time with. So forgive me if I don't live up to your expectations."

I was stunned to silence by the shock of his response. He glared at my slack-jawed expression. "What?"

"I—um… didn't mean to hurt your feelings."

Vino snorted, or made a sound close to it.

"And now we're back to the attitude."

"Maybe if you'd quit being a bitch for five minutes, I wouldn't have one."

It took all my restraint not to punch him. "If you hate me so much, why won't you just leave me alone?"

"You're not the one I hate." Vino sighed, then grabbed his drink and swallowed the last half in two gulps. He slid his glass across the table and looked out to the crowd. "As much as you think you hate me, I hate Sebastian ten-fold. Imagine being forced to spend centuries submitting to someone you have such contempt for."

"How many centuries are we talking about?"

He smiled, it was not his normal shrewd one, this one looked a somewhat tortured, almost sad. "Just shy of three."

I couldn't help but feel for him. That glamorous life of sin he was supposedly living came at a high price. "How old does that make him?"

He chuckled a little. "Worried about dating an older man?"

I rolled my eyes; of course he couldn't keep the snide remarks to himself. "I didn't realize that's what I was doing…"

"Maybe not, he is leaving you alone with me a lot. I've never seen him drag things out this long before." Vino winked at the girl who brought our next round and turned back to me. "Will you answer something for me?"

"I guess so."

"What do you feel around him?" He looked genuinely curious, another unexpected emotion.

I took a deep breath. I didn't really want to tell him, but this was the most real conversation we ever had. "I don't know how to explain how I feel around him, it's kinda dreamlike, maybe? I used to feel sick when he touched me, now it's more like an electrical current. It's comforting, most of the time, but every once in a while he'll shock me, and it just takes everything out of me."

"So it's not at all like when I touch you, is it?"

I shook my head. "Completely different feeling."

"That's great," he said. "Which do you prefer? If you don't mind me asking."

The blood rushed to my cheeks. He could tell by my reaction it was his touch I liked. Too bad it had to be associated with him.

"I thought so..."

"He's a lot more enjoyable to be around."

Vino leaned down and stared into my eyes. "Are you sure about that? The act he's putting on for you will eventually wear off. He has the power to control every aspect of your being... Do you not have a longing around him that you can't place? Don't you find yourself with strange emotions that aren't yours?"

I turned away from him and watched the people on the dance floor. Was Sebastian really controlling my emotions? Was it his will that made me feel complete when I was with him? I had never been drawn to someone like that before. I had never ached for someone so badly that it rendered everything else inconsequential.

Vino rested his arms on the back of the couch and left me to my thoughts. He seemed pleased to have been the source of such a revelation. I was miserable. The fairytale Sebastian painted was not something I would give up easily. It was the only thing keeping me together at the moment.

"Why do you keep telling me these things? Can't you just let me live in the lie for a while?"

"You prefer ignorance then?"

"I can't do anything to change it, can I? Why not let me be happy for as long as I can?"

He shrugged. "I'd rather know. But if that's what you want, then far be it for me to stop you."

"Thank you." I leaned back in my seat, slouching a little more than normal, and accidentally rested my back against his arm. That soothing wave of energy hit me instantly, intensified by the fact that I was not expecting it.

Vino paused for a moment, then gently pulled his arm out from behind me. He had a strange look on his face. "Maybe we should get you home, it's getting late."

He didn't have much to say to me after that. We rode in relative silence most of the way home. All he said when he dropped me off out front was, "See you tomorrow."

The next day started out smoothly. When Vino mysteriously popped up to rain on my parade, he sent very few insults my way. He must have been running out of ideas.

I melted at the first sight of Sebastian again. I wondered if I felt that way because he wanted me to, or if I really was that enamored with him. If he noticed my thoughts waiver, he showed no reaction. I was hoping he'd make some excuse for us not to work so I could spend my evening with him, but he was all business again.

The painting did go well, when I could concentrate on it. Sebastian's face was such a distraction sometimes. Normally when I worked I could tune out just about anything, but that wasn't the case tonight. I tried to keep from looking at him by studying the women closely and working solely on them.

Their eyes all had the same dull, lifeless stare. Why did these women look like zombies? The first group had been giggling and pawing at Sebastian, these women did nothing. I had not even heard one of them make a peep, and Sebastian barely acknowledged their presence. Had he made some sort of preemptive strike so Vino wouldn't murder the second batch?

I must have been dwelling on that too much, because Sebastian sighed and got up from his seat. "I think we're done for the evening, yes?"

I sat my brush down and smiled at him. "Yeah, that sounds good."

He studied me for a moment and came down to take my hand. "Would you care to tell me what's bothering you?"

"It's nothing, really. I'm just easily distracted tonight."

"You do have a lot to think about, don't you? Anyone in your position would have trouble concentrating." He wrapped his arms around me. His eyes were all ablaze again. "You needn't worry about the fate of these women. They are nothing. We will be done with them soon and you will never have to see them again."

That caught me off guard. He sounded as if he was talking about something trivial, like they were garbage to be thrown away. And they were still sitting five feet behind him. Not one of them so much as flinched. It sent a small wave of panic through me. Would I be that disposable to him also?

My mind immediately flashed back to Sebastian's face, or rather, his face commanded my attention. I was paralyzed again, unable to look away or speak. He smiled the most dazzling smile in the world at me. "I assure you, I would never allow anything like that to befall you. You are something truly special. And you have so much more to offer. I plan on keeping you around for a very long time."

In the state I was in, every word of that statement sounded sensational. It didn't matter who he hurt, as long as he promised to care for me.

Sebastian held me there, searching for something behind my eyes. After several long moments, he cupped my cheek in his hand, then leaned down like he was going to kiss me. My heart pounded frantically in anticipation.

Then someone cleared their throat behind us.

Sebastian turned towards our distraction with a scowl. The second he broke our eye contact, I was able to move again. I followed his gaze towards the elevator to find Vino leaning against the wall with his arms crossed.

"You're early." Sebastian growled.

Vino shrugged. "Didn't think I'd be interrupting anything."

"Well, we were just finishing up." He winked at me, any trace of annoyance gone. "Until tomorrow, my love."

"Yeah, I'll see you tomorrow."

He left me to the impatient Vino then. As usual he didn't speak to me until we drove away and I removed my necklace. I wasn't paying attention to him anyways. All I could think about were those women and their dead eyes. And how disappointed I was to miss another opportunity to kiss Sebastian.

"Hey, snap out of it…" Vino sounded annoyed. "What is your problem? Didn't you hear what I said?"

"Uh, no. What did you say?"

"I'm not going to repeat myself. Just tell me what you're thinking about."

I watched the passing lights out my window before I answered. "Those women, what's wrong with them?"

"I was wondering when you were going to ask me that." He laughed to himself. "How many weeks has it been and you're just now noticing?"

"I noticed it the first day, you ass. I was thinking about it tonight, then Sebastian caught me, and what he said was kinda disturbing."

"How did he try to excuse himself?"

"He didn't. He only said that they were nothing and I shouldn't worry about them."

Vino had the kind of 'I know something you don't know' look that sent chills down my spine. "It's the truth. They are nothing. Now that he's gotten to them."

"What did he do?"

"Have you given any thought as to what we need to sustain ourselves? I was sure you'd ask one of us by now."

To be truthful, with everything else that was going on, I hadn't really thought about it. Apparently they had to kill people; who cares why they did it. "Guess I wasn't worried about the whole how and why part."

That made him laugh. "You are one cold individual. Aren't you even the slightest bit curious?"

"Now that you mention it..."

"Well, we all have our preferences, but the end result is the same...Drain the body of energy, and consume its soul. I'm sure I don't need to elaborate on our favorite method of draining energy." He raised an eyebrow at me. I got the hint.

"Now, the consuming of the soul is where things get tricky. Simply depleting someone of their life energy isn't enough. You must actually devour some part of their being in order for them to become a part of you. This is one area where my father and I actually have similar tastes. We much prefer the taste of blood...I happen to enjoy mine still inside the heart. Amelie and Andras are partial to the flesh. I even had a brother who fed exclusively on entrails."

I tried to play it off like I wasn't bothered by this information. "You still haven't told me what happened to the women."

"I was getting to that part," he paused to drag out the suspense. "You see, Sebastian can actually remove a person's soul without killing them. Granted, it's not actual consumption, but it does give him complete control until he decides to absorb them... Those women are puppets; soulless husks for him to move around like living, breathing dolls."

Okay, that one got me. That was easily the most atrocious thing I had ever heard. "He's not going to do that to me, is he?"

"No, I'm fairly certain not ... What did he have to say about it?"

"He said I had more to offer, and that he was going to keep me around for a long time."

Vino frowned. "If that's really what he said, you might have been better off sharing the fate of those women."

I may be fooling myself, but I could have sworn he sounded upset about that.

Chapter 13

The Complexities of Dating

By Thursday, my worries about Sebastian's women had faded into the background. I was becoming numb to all this craziness. This was not the healthy kind of tolerance found through acceptance. I was merely blocking things out and lying to myself.

Vino never told me why my fate was going to be so much worse than theirs. In fact, he had been downright weird about the whole thing. I even tried to ask him about it again, but he changed the subject to avoid answering me. Imagine that, something so bad even he couldn't bear to say it.

Or what if it was the other way around completely? What if he wouldn't tell me because there was no horrific end coming? I kept telling myself Sebastian might be telling the truth. Vino could be making things sound worse than they really are. Maybe there really was a life with him waiting for me, one of endless bliss and desire. The kind of fairytale reserved for the truly wicked.

When I was staring into those enchanting blue eyes, that's all I wanted to believe. Life was great, as long as I was with him. But when I left every day, I entered a different world.

This was a world where I was alone, with Vino, all the time. It was lunch every day and drinks every night. He may have been slowly growing more tolerable as time went on, but I was fairly positive that I still hated him.

When I woke up this morning with a massive hangover, I found Vino lounging in his usual spot waiting for me. I had grown so used to this, I didn't even give him a second glance. I just stretched and went to the kitchen to make some coffee, not bothering to cover up the fact that I was in my underwear again. After all, it *was* nothing he hadn't seen before. It didn't even bother me when I caught him looking.

I turned the machine on with a big yawn, then pulled out the ibuprofen. "It's really not nice for you to keep me out all night and then show up to harass me this damn early. I feel like crap. Come back in a couple hours when I'm coherent."

He ignored me and flipped through the channels on my TV. "You blacked out last night, didn't you?"

"So, I black out all the time."

"I could have done anything to you, and you'd never know."

I chuckled. "You're running out of effective threats, Vino. You'd never get away with laying a finger on me and you know it… Hey, when did I get cable?"

"Two days ago."

"Um, thanks?" I scratched my head. So far, Vino had helped pick out half my new furniture, my new TV, and had cable installed. I didn't feel comfortable with that. "I better not get a bill," I added, so I didn't sound grateful.

He smiled but didn't answer me.

I filled my mug with caffeinated goodness and headed towards my couch. On my way, Vino's shoes distracted me again. They were more of the usual, flashy and feminine looking, with a pointy toe and a low heel. This pair reminded me of something a pirate would wear.

I laughed so hard I spilled a few drops of coffee. "I think I have a pair just like that."

"Doubt it. You couldn't afford them."

"You're such a girl. Why don't you just give in and buy a dress to match all these stupid shoes you wear?"

"Are you suggesting I show you exactly how much of a man I am?" He replied, as he reached for his belt.

I think this was a bluff, but I wasn't about to call him out. "I could use a good laugh, but I think I'll pass."

He shrugged and resumed his channel surfing. "You've kept me waiting for quite a while. It would be nice if you could get ready for the day."

"I'll get around to it." I took a few sips of coffee and sprawled across my couch. "I'm assuming we have plans if you're in such a rush."

"You would assume correctly," Vino stated blandly, without looking away from the TV. "If I said please, would you hurry up?"

"Couldn't hurt your chances." I yawned and gave myself another good stretch. I intended to drag my act out longer, but the glare he gave me changed my mind. I may feel confident talking smack to Vino, but I was still leery about pissing him off.

"Yeah, yeah, I'm on it." I took a few more gulps of my brew and went about getting ready, making sure not to be in too much of a hurry. He could stand to wait.

We drove into Manhattan again today, near Central Park. I expected him to pull up to some valet service at another fancy restaurant. Instead, he parked the car right on the street and turned to me with an expression somewhere between curiosity and agitation on his face.

He pointed a finger out my passenger window. "Tell me what you see."

In between all the skyscrapers, on the opposite side of the street, was a cathedral that stretched almost as high as the buildings around it. I recognized it immediately.

"It's St. Patrick's, why did you bring me here?" Or better yet, could he even come here?

His tense demeanor told me he probably couldn't. "Will you seek absolution, Trinity? Or do you choose damnation?" He paused and leaned closer to me, then gazed up at the pinnacles through my window. "I wouldn't stop you, you know...If you wanted to run inside and never come out. Save yourself before it's too late."

Vino sat rigidly in his seat and constantly scanned around him as he spoke. "You would be out of Sebastian's reach as long as you stayed within those doors. This is your only chance. Save your soul now, or spend eternity under his control."

I should have jumped out of the car and ran full speed into that church. But I just sat there and stared at him like an idiot. Was he offering me a chance to run away? That made no sense. Vino wasn't the type to help anyone. "I don't understand."

"What is there not to understand?" He snapped. "Make your decision now. You have thirty seconds."

I looked to the cathedral for an answer, and received nothing. Could I really do it? Could I walk through those doors and devote the rest of my life to God?

My hand trembled as I reached for the door handle. I waited for Vino to stop me, but he didn't move. Then I pulled the latch, and every muscle in my body locked up. My choices boiled down to this; spend the rest of my life hiding inside a church, or face whatever Sebastian had in store for me.

I let go of the handle.

"I can't." I whispered, staring down at the hand that just defied me.

"That's what I thought." Vino sounded confident, but he was poised to spring into action. Though I'm unsure whether it was to flee or fight. "We have to make this quick. It's not good for me to be here... So if you're staying, look up to the left spire and tell me what you see."

I peered out the window and saw nothing out of the ordinary. "What are you getting at? I don't see anything."

He sighed. "You don't see anyone?"

"I'm looking for a person?"

"Not exactly..." He turned the key, and the engine roared to life. "I can't wait. You either see it or you don't."

No matter how hard I stared, all I saw was a church. I opened my mouth to tell Vino he was nuts, then something twinkled. It looked like the sun reflecting off a window. But there was *no window*. And the more I watched it, the brighter it became. A strange feeling swept over me suddenly, almost as if I were in a trance. But it felt peaceful, like lying in the sun on a beach.

Vino chose that moment to floor it and whip the car into traffic. The tires squealed, and I got thrown around in my seat. By the time I was able to spin around and look out the back, the church was fading into the distance.

"What was that?"

He was calm again, and sending me his usual cocky smile. "What did you see?"

"I'm not sure."

"So you didn't really see him." He studied me for a moment. "You do seem hardwired to our side of things. I'm surprised you noticed anything at all."

"Um, you mind explaining what you're talking about?"

"If we exist, then logically, what else would have to be real?"

The light bulb finally clicked on, much later than it should have. All good Christians were supposed to believe in these things. I just never did until today. "Are we talking about angels?"

He nodded. "There's a whole hierarchy system like ours you don't need to concern yourself with. The only thing you need to take away from this, is that there is something more powerful than Sebastian out there. Not the one you saw, but one of a higher order could take him out. Though they wouldn't. They don't concern themselves with us, so long as we don't upset the balance of things."

"Do you think it saw us?"

"No shit, it saw us. It's not every day a demon drives up to the front door of a church."

"I—I think I *felt* it."

He laughed. "Are you saying you want to go back? Perhaps I'll walk you to the doors myself so we can see if I burn to the ground where I stand…You had your chance to run. You made your decision."

That reminded me of my torturous dream, and the pain I felt when the priest splashed holy water on my face. It felt like burning coals touching my skin. I could only imagine what would happen to Vino. "Can the church really hurt you?"

He turned back to the road, appearing uncharacteristically uneasy again. "I doubt I would literally catch on fire, but it was painful enough being across the street. I'm not about to go find out the specifics."

The day progressed normally after that. We went out to lunch, again, then he gave me a couple hours to myself. Or at least he gave me the illusion of such. I spent most of that time thinking about our field trip that morning. I turned down my only chance to get away. I wasn't convinced that was Vino's true intention, but I didn't even try. I had been given the choice between Heaven and Hell, and I chose Hell. Or maybe, I just chose Sebastian.

When I went down to the car for my daily trip to the apartment, Vino acted like nothing had happened. He even seemed to be in a good mood. I bet he only insulted me twice.

He wore the most self-satisfied grin as he escorted me all the way upstairs, something he hadn't done in a while. "He's really mad at me today."

"And that's a good thing?"

"Keeps life interesting."

I shivered as I stepped out of the elevator, and not just because the room was freezing. Sebastian sat alone on the white couch, with his feet up and a drink in his hand. His eyes were so low they were almost closed. He didn't rise to greet me like he did every other time we met. The only movement that registered at all was a slow swirling of the liquid in his glass. I had never seen Sebastian truly angry before. It definitely ranked in my top five scariest things I'd ever seen.

We stopped at the table in front of him. Vino was still glowing, and I felt completely unhinged. Sebastian glared at Vino like he was about to jump up and tear his head from his shoulders.

"Why don't you two have a seat," he stated unkindly.

I quietly obeyed and slid in next to him, giving myself enough space so that if he did launch an attack, I wouldn't be in the way. He didn't touch me, but the energy rolling off him was intense enough to make me queasy from a couple feet away. Vino sat on the other side of me, towards the edge of the couch, the furthest possible spot from Sebastian.

Sebastian never took his eyes off him. "Explain."

Vino shrugged. "It was an experiment. I wanted to see how predisposed she is to our side. That's all there is to it. You're overreacting."

Sebastian snarled at him, exposing a glimpse of teeth too sharp to pass for human. "You lie."

The confidence in Vino's face faltered for a second. Then he composed himself enough to give a snide grin. "You don't have much faith in her do you? I knew she wasn't going anywhere. She made the decision to stay on her own. You should be grateful."

I felt like a piece of meat in a crocodile den, the one they keep at the end of a stick and pull away at the last minute so the beast lunges out of the water for the audience. I could hear the applause as its powerful jaws snapped shut inches away from my flesh. I hoped I wasn't projecting that imagery.

Sebastian didn't move for what seemed like forever. Then he turned to me, and smiled like we were having the most pleasant conversation. "Is this true?"

I hesitantly met his eyes. "There was nothing for me there."

His tone changed as he addressed Vino again. "Leave. We'll discuss this at a later moment."

Vino stood silently and exited. Sebastian waited until he was completely out of sight before he spoke again. He looked positively elated. "It's me you choose then...? I must say, you couldn't have made me happier."

"It was an easy decision," I mumbled.

"I apologize if I frightened you, my love. I'm usually successful in controlling my temper. The thought of losing you was just too much for me to bear." He reached over and took my hand. "A woman like you is a rarity. Perhaps if I intend to keep you by my side, I need to make a formal declaration of courtship."

My jaw dropped. "Courtship? I don't think I'm the type that requires courting."

"You give yourself far too little credit." Sebastian paused to laugh. "Why don't we start with a proper date tomorrow night? It's only fair you allow me to take you out since my son gets you to himself all the time."

That idea sounded phenomenal. He may be terrifying, but I wanted him so much more than I feared him. "I'd love to."

"Wonderful." He snapped his fingers, summoning the women into the room. "We'll get a couple hours of work in tonight. Then I'll leave you be. I'll send Amelie for you in the morning."

True to his word, by nine-thirty, Sebastian had disappeared. Vino came to pick me up shortly after. He didn't wait for me to remove the necklace before the teasing started.

"Big date tomorrow?"

I shrugged it off. "Guess so."

"We need to celebrate my getting a day off." He looked me up and down with a disapproving shake of his head. "You're going to have to change clothes. I'm not going be seen with you dressed like that."

"Too bad, I look fine." I sneered at him. Of course I looked fine. I was in brand new clothes; more of the same jean skirt and tank top look I'd been sporting all summer.

He acted like he didn't hear me. "I went to the trouble of grabbing you something more fitting for a night out. It's in the back."

"I'm not changing my clothes. If I'm being forced to go out with you for the tenth time this week, I'm going as I am."

Vino gave me another fake pout. "Please? I really like this one on you…"

"Whatever." I pulled the garment bag out of the back and unzipped it. The black dress I purchased for my art show was inside; the one I wore when I met him. "Trying to relive old memories?"

"Just getting lost in the nostalgia of it all. I thought for sure you were going to be mine that night."

I groaned. "That might have been the only night I still liked you."

He laughed. "I thought you'd appreciate the irony… Just put the dress on. We're almost there."

"You're not going to stop for me to change? Now you're just being ridiculous." I threw the dress in the back seat.

Vino winked at me. "I promise not to watch."

"No."

"Don't be shy. I'll even close my eyes if you want me to."

"You're driving. You can't close your eyes."

He jerked the car into the nearest spot along the road, giving me a slight case of whiplash in the process. "There. Not driving. Now hop back there and change your clothes."

I took a calming breath to fight the urge to slap him. I was not going to win this argument. "Fine, can you at least pretend not to watch me?"

He gave me his version of an innocent smile, made a show of settling in his seat, and closed his eyes. I waited a few seconds to make sure they stayed closed, and hesitantly climbed in back. There wasn't much room to maneuver, so changing became a wrestling match with the tiny dress. While I struggled to pull it over my chest, I glanced up at the rear-view mirror and locked eyes with Vino, who had probably been watching the whole time.

Normally catching Vino getting an eye-full wouldn't have bothered me. But he was watching my struggles with the dress the same way a lion would watch a wounded antelope. There was something ravenous in his stare that made me feel dirty, and more like prey than I ever had.

"Fucking lecher." I snapped at him.

He laughed at me, again. I grabbed the shoes he brought for me and climbed back into the front seat. They weren't the ones I wore to the show. They were the pair of black stilettos I wore on my last date with Lucas. The thought of him brought on a whole mess of emotions I didn't want to address right now.

I must have dwelling on Lucas as I bent over to put them on, because I nearly jumped out of my seat when I felt my bra unhook itself. I knew what really happened of course. The dress was too revealing to necessitate one, so Vino took it upon himself to undo the clasp.

"I can do that myself, thank you very much."

He lifted his palms in surrender. "Couldn't help myself."

I removed my bra from the front, to avoid giving him a show, and threw it at him. "If you like it so much you can have it."

That just provoked more laughter. He lifted the lacey brassiere to his nose, and pretended to sniff it. Or at least I hope he was pretending. I punched his door, the next best thing to punching him. I had never met anyone so infuriating.

We ended up at another ritzy nightclub. This one might have been in Soho. I didn't pay any attention to where he took me anymore. He did seem to be in a better mood than normal. So instead of throwing insults at me, he was almost being complimentary. I didn't trust it one bit.

By one-thirty, I had consumed more drinks than I could remember. I'd been watching Vino closely all night, trying to figure out if he was up to something. At some point, his hair started to bug me. It hung in his face even more than mine did.

I bet he dyed it. It was so black; it looked almost blue. Like someone dumped a bottle of ink on his head and the drips solidified into strands.

When I felt the urge to rub some of it between my fingers to see if the black would come off, I decided that meant I'd had too much to drink. I needed a breather. So I pushed my drink away, and slid out of the booth.

"Where are you off to?" Vino asked accusingly.

"Bathroom, I am allowed aren't I?"

He smiled. "Of course."

I made a hasty retreat to the nearest restroom. Once inside I stopped at the mirror and leaned over the sink to check my makeup. My life was so confusing. If I ever sobered up long enough, all this insanity was going to kill me. But the pills weren't working anymore, and even the booze was getting old. Especially when my only drinking partner was someone I wanted to punch in the face half the time.

I took the long way back. I wanted to make him wait for me. I wandered around the bar area, and got a closer look at the dance floor. Then I returned to our table from the opposite direction I left from. At first, I thought I was going the wrong way, because there were two people at my table. Then my drunken brain clicked on, and I realized what I was seeing.

Vino had his arm around some slut in a blue dress. She was throwing herself at him, talking all close and rubbing her hand on his chest. Apparently, I was the only one he had qualms about making physical contact with.

I was livid. I almost turned face and walked out of the bar. But he noticed me and shooed the girl away, giving her one last wink when she spun around to tell him goodbye. I took a deep breath to calm myself, since whatever floozy he let paw all over him was really none of my business. And if I left, he'd just come after me. But as I stormed over to the table, my anger didn't subside. I sat as far away from him as possible.

"Do you mind not doing that crap when I'm around? It makes me look bad."

The sickest smile spread across his face. "Jealousy looks good on you."

"You are so full of yourself."

"Can you blame me?" He finished the last of his drink and watched in the direction the girl disappeared to. "Why don't you order us another round. I'll be right back."

He started to get up from his seat and I snapped. I would have thrown my drink at him, if I had one in hand. "You're kidding right?! I am not sitting here alone while you go bang some whore!"

Something wild went off in Vino's eyes. The smile that I thought couldn't get any sicker, did. In one swift motion, he slid across the booth and grabbed my arm, yanking me against him. One hand slipped behind my neck to grab a fistful of hair just hard enough that it didn't hurt.

I took in a ragged gasp as the rush of endorphins flooded my body. The waves of energy coming from him relaxed my muscles to the point that they all went limp. I tried to fight against the pleasure caused by the feeling so I could hit him. But just like last time, I didn't do a damn thing. I think I gave in even quicker.

The red and yellow took over his irises, and pulsed like live wires. They were so captivating a part of me cried when he looked away to lean down so his lips faintly brushed my earlobe.

"Would it make you feel any better if I said I'd much rather have you…?" he whispered. "Besides, sex is not what I had in mind for her."

A shudder run through me; I was beyond being able to control it. Vino slowly moved his lips towards my neck, and touched my skin in a way that wasn't exactly a kiss.

I had a moment where my wits came back to me, and I remembered whose arms I was in. I took the opportunity to shove him. He allowed this, and released me, moving just far enough away that we weren't touching.

I blinked a few times to clear my head. "I hate you."

"Is that so? That wasn't hate I saw in your eyes a moment ago."

I was too mad for words. I wanted to kill him. I settled for trying to leave, and turned as quickly as I could to escape our booth. But he grabbed me again, gently wrapping his fingers around the bare skin of my bicep. I'm ashamed to admit, the second that opiate coming from him washed over me, I relaxed and settled back in my seat.

He waited for me to calm down and face him before he let go of my arm. "Look, don't get your panties in a bunch. If you stay here I promise to keep my hands to myself. And as a personal favor to you, I won't leave your side. That girl can wait out there all night for all I care."

I eyed him for a moment, trying to figure out if he was lying to me. He looked sincere, but that didn't mean shit coming from him.

Vino waited for my reaction. I gave him a dirty look, so he felt the need to elaborate. "I know what will put you in a better mood. Do you see that door she walked out of? Why don't you stick around to watch for her to come back. I want you to see the look on that chick's face when she realizes she's been duped. Her jealousy of you is going to be hilarious."

He smiled at me and continued before I could answer. "That tramp came over to make her move the second you left. She felt herself above you and tried to convince me that my evening would be better spent if I left you here. So I decided to kill her... unpleasantly."

Did he just say he was going to kill her, because she thought she was better than me? In a really messed up way, that was the most flattering thing anyone had ever said to me. "I guess I could stick around for a little while."

Vino ordered another round of drinks as we waited for her to return. It took about ten more minutes, but she eventually showed. She looked around the club for Vino, and finally to our table, where she seemed surprised to find him. She scowled at me and Vino started laughing. He was right. Seeing how upset she was made me feel great.

"Humans are so shallow," he said out of nowhere. "I feel like I'm doing the world a favor ridding it of people like that. I've never taken an innocent that I wasn't forced to. The wicked taste so much better."

I caught the tangent in that statement. If Vino was telling the truth, then the threat he made against Lucas had been an empty one the whole time. Maybe he really did chase him off so he wouldn't have to kill him.

We didn't stay much longer after that. He dropped me off at the usual spot in front of my building. I stopped to say goodbye before going inside. "Have fun on your day off."

"Good luck on your date," he answered. I could tell there was a double meaning to that, but he was gone before I could ask what it was.

At nine the next morning, I was up and completely ready for the day. My anxiety about Amelie picking me up kept me from sleeping in. I hate to say I'd rather spend the day with Vino. In my defense, it was only because I was over being afraid of him.

I was also worried about seeing Sebastian. While I felt excited about spending an entire night, alone, on a real date with him, my mind kept flashing to my encounter with Vino last night. That was not something I wanted Sebastian seeing. I didn't know what to think about the whole thing, but I doubted this time had been for Sebastian's benefit.

I couldn't find a logical explanation for any of Vino's actions up to this point. He insults me one moment, wants to kill in my honor the next, gives me a chance to escape, then makes me feel like bait. I get that he wanted to kill me, or screw me, or probably both simultaneously. But did he like me, or hate me? Or maybe this had nothing to do with me at all. Maybe this was all just a game to get even with Sebastian.

Amelie didn't show up alone, but I expected her brother to be with her. They materialized out of nowhere while I watched TV. I was so used to Vino doing this, that I was barely startled.

"Hello, Trinity." Amelie said. "Apparently it's my job to make sure you're presentable enough to be seen with my father. So we have a day at the spa ahead of us."

A day at the spa sounded wonderful, being with them did not. She turned to Andras as if she was listening to him, then sneered in my direction. "I don't see why those two are in such a tizzy over someone so unspectacular. Father's toys are usually exquisite specimens of unparalleled beauty. And, well look at her... she is not up to his caliber."

I got up from the chaise, trying to hide the fact that my feelings were hurt. Andras took a step towards me and turned to look at Amelie. They held each other's gaze for a moment and closed in on me, backing me into the corner.

"Yes, I suppose you're right," Amelie said. "We'll just have to see for ourselves, won't we?"

I pressed my back into the corner, to try and make myself as small as possible. My heart felt like it was about to burst from fear. "Whatever you're thinking—"

But it was too late. They reached out in unison and each grabbed a shoulder. The pain that shot through me made my legs buckle out from underneath me. It felt like someone punched me in the stomach. I wanted to get sick. My body was on pins and needles, like every muscle had fallen asleep from head to toe.

By the time they let me go, I was on my hands and knees, gasping for air. Amelie giggled. "That was fun."

"Glad you think so," I mumbled, as I attempted to catch my breath.

"Still not worth all the trouble they're going through fighting over you," she said. "Get to your feet. We have appointments to keep. The limo's waiting out front."

I had no choice but to follow them outside. The limo was brand new and all white, some kind of Rolls Royce. I would have been more impressed, but I was too much on edge. Who knew the next time the Wonder Twins would decide to assault me.

We pulled up to an enormous and excessively lavish spa. The well-dressed woman at the front desk treated Amelie and Andras as if they were royalty.

Amelie waved a hand in my direction, and curled her lip. "Do something with this mess."

I tried to act like I wasn't offended, but I'm sure I didn't fool anybody. Luckily, they took me away separately from the twins, so I could relax while I got some well-deserved pampering.

They gave me every treatment I'd ever heard of, and more. I got a hydrotherapy soak and a massage. Every inch of my skin was buffed and polished. Then I received a manicure, pedicure, and facial. They even gave me a full Brazilian. I hoped that was a hint as to where the night's events would lead me. Lastly, my hair was trimmed and styled, pinned partially back into tiny spirals. I was practically a new person by the time they were done .

When I was all finished, one of the employees escorted me to a private room where Amelie awaited me. I was shocked to find her alone. Without her twin, she wasn't quite as threatening. She informed me that she was in charge of dressing me, in not so nice of words, and started going through garment bags and throwing dresses at me.

I was squeezing into my third dress when her mood shifted from disgust to curiosity. "Why did my brother take you to that church?"

"I don't know why that guy does anything."

"He didn't give you any reasoning?"

"Not really, just something about seeing the angel." I didn't think she needed the whole story.

She glared at me. "You shouldn't believe a word that comes out of his mouth. He's always working some angle."

"Yeah, he is pretty intolerable," *and egotistical, and rude, and lecherous...*

Amelie squeezed her temples. "I'll never understand why my father made that asshole his successor. It makes me sick."

I chuckled to myself at our mutual choice of insults, then I realized what else she said. "Wait a minute, I thought those two hated each other. Vino said—"

She started laughing hysterically. "You've been eating up every line he feeds you... stupid human. Are you too dumb to tell when someone's manipulating you?" She threw me another dress. "You look hideous. Try this one."

I held the dress in my hand without changing for a moment. I didn't ask any of the questions that were swimming around in my head. There were also a few choice words I really wanted to give her, but I kept those to myself as well. I knew one of them was manipulating me. But which one? Or was it both? And why wasn't I trying to do anything about it?

Amelie cleared her throat to pull me back to the task at hand. Once I had the dress on, she gave me a scrutinizing look. "It's about time," she grumbled, as she tossed a pair of shoes at my feet.

I strapped them on and gave myself a twist in the mirrors. The dress that finally got the okay was long and gleaming silver, with the back cut to the base of my spine, and a short train. The front dipped well below my cleavage line, and had a slit to the top of my right thigh. For a gown with a plethora of flimsy fabric, it covered very little. I felt dressed to walk down the red carpet, not go out on a date.

Amelie walked over and handed me a large jewelry box. "From my father."

I stared at the box in my hand without opening it. The last one of these I received didn't exactly come without strings attached.

"It's just jewelry," she snapped. "Don't be ungrateful. You don't deserve any of this."

Andras entered the room then, pulling her attention away from me. I opened the box while they greeted each other with inappropriate kisses on the lips. Inside was a three-banded bracelet and a pair of dangly earrings, both covered with more diamonds than I could count. It looked so expensive, I was almost afraid to touch it.

Amelie nodded to something as Andras put his arm around her waist. "It's a small improvement. I hope Father's not disappointed."

I gave her a dirty look. I don't care what she said; I looked great. Probably even better than she did right then.

They both took a step towards me. "I hope Vino does kill you," Amelie said. "I'm interested to see how he would be disposed of for it. It's time for you to go. Don't keep my father waiting."

I put the jewelry on as fast as I could and hurried out of the room. The further away the twins were, the better I felt. I didn't slow down until I reached the front doors of the spa and spotted the Rolls limo where another one of Sebastian's servants waited to let me inside. Just knowing he might be in there made my heart skip a beat. I might have floated to the door.

For this one moment, I was Cinderella stepping into her magical carriage. It came equipped with my very own dark prince, one charming and glorious, with burning sapphires for eyes. A man straight out of my nightmares that would someday be the end of me. But as I stepped out of the street and into my fairytale, I felt truly grateful just to be in his presence.

My prince welcomed me with open arms. "Hello, Trinity."

"Hello, Sebastian."

He looked even better than I had ever seen him today. That in itself was a remarkable feat. He wore an all-black, modern tuxedo with a matching fedora. The white shirt underneath was open at the collar, with no tie, and he had a white scarf draped over his shoulders.

He smiled as I slid into the seat next to him. "Ravishing... You look simply ravishing, my love."

The compliment went straight to my head. It took me a second to collect my wits enough to answer. "That's not what I've been hearing all day."

Sebastian frowned. "My daughter didn't mean any of it, I'm sure." He put his arm around my shoulders and gave me a quick hug. "I'll have to have a word with her about manners."

In his embrace, I forgot all my troubles and felt no pain. The current spreading through me was a comforting, low pulse that I had grown to enjoy. It was so intimate inside the huge limo, with all the champagne and twinkling lights. I hoped we'd drive around for hours.

"I debated bringing the Bugatti today since you enjoyed it so."

I blushed, of course he knew about that. "It's a very nice car."

"Driving is overrated. I'd much rather spend our time together a little closer." Sebastian reached out and stroked my cheek with the back of his hand. He seemed so content with such a small action. "We're nearing the completion of the painting. My estimate is you'll finish by the end of this week. Things will be much easier after that."

He hit my guess exactly. The goal I set for myself was Friday. "What happens after I finish?"

"That's when I'll be all yours. If you'll have me, that is."

I'm sure I nodded; maybe I even said yes, I couldn't say for sure. My world was sublime when it only consisted of him. I could have told him I loved him at that point. I'm not certain those were my true emotions, but I felt like that's what he wanted to hear.

Once the intensity dialed down a notch, I rested my head on his chest and drew my knees and ankles onto the seat beside me.

"Do you enjoy French cuisine?" He asked.

"Don't know if I've ever had it."

"And the ballet?"

"Do children's recitals count? My foster parents tried to force me to take lessons once, things didn't go well."

He laughed. It sounded heavenly from my position against him. "It appears we have an evening of firsts ahead of us. How exciting."

I could think of a few other firsts I'd rather experience with him, but I didn't voice those aloud. I'm sure he picked up on them anyways.

I couldn't pronounce the name of the restaurant we went to. It had white-washed brick walls, long patterned curtains, an overload of hanging plants, and paintings with gilded frames. They closed down the whole place for us. Only one table stood solitary in the center of the dining room with fresh flowers, several candles, and a white tablecloth.

The dark-haired woman who led us to our table stared in awe at Sebastian the entire way there. She stumbled into a chair, twice. I don't think he even glanced at her. Our waiter had a similar reaction, but he just stumbled over his words. I felt a lot better knowing I wasn't the only one affected by Sebastian's presence.

Sebastian helped me pick what to order and paid me an excessive amount of compliments. We were less than an hour in, and it was already the best date I'd ever been on.

"Can I ask you a few things? About you, I mean."

I'd say Sebastian smiled, but there was barely a moment where he hadn't been. "Ask away. I'll tell you anything you desire."

"When were you born?"

He didn't seem to expect that question. One eyebrow raised and the corners of his smile dropped. "Is my age of concern to you?"

I shook my head. "It's the opposite, actually. I'm… kinda fascinated. You've seen things I can only read about in books."

Even with the words of worship, he hesitated to answer. "My origins are something I prefer to keep secret," he said. "As a token of my love, I will admit I walked this earth before Christ. That is more than any human deserves to know of me."

"Wow," I said. I had difficulty wrapping my head around how much time that was. "That's amazing."

He laughed. "I suppose from your perspective that would be. Human lifetimes pass by in the blink of an eye for me."

"So why are you up here and not in Hell? I though you were pretty important down there."

"Importance does not alleviate boredom." Sebastian took a sip of his wine. "Things are in a constant state of change here. Hell always remains the same. I've enjoyed watching the world progress. Transportation gets better, and clothes are more comfortable. Technology's been enjoyable. And the women grow exponentially more attractive each century." He winked at me.

"I've spent time in every corner of this world, and seen everything it has to offer. I still keep estates in twenty-two different countries... But it all grows tiresome. These last few decades have been especially tedious. Until recently of course."

The last few decades were all I had ever known. I would never understand the magnitude of boredom he was speaking of. For me to be the cure for such an ailment was hard to swallow.

"So I guess it was just luck that you ended up in New York when I was here."

"Luck, fate, whatever you wish to call it. Either way, you've come to me now. And things are much more interesting."

I blushed, again. His endless flattery was making my head spin. "I thought demons were supposed to go after virgins and saints."

He laughed. "The virtuous can be very annoying. And as for any preference towards virgins... I don't believe they're necessary for a man such as myself."

I squirmed a little in my seat. That comment put my libido in a frenzy. Judging from the satisfied expression on Sebastian's face, he helped the feeling along somehow. I didn't mind one bit.

The food was delicious, though I paid more attention to Sebastian than what I was eating. After we finished our plates, we hopped back into the limo without ever receiving a bill. Whatever fear I used to have of him had officially dissipated. It felt right to be with him, like I was meant to be at his side. I desperately hoped he wasn't the one creating that feeling.

The limo dropped us off at a private entrance to the theater. Several employees were there to escort us inside. Every one of them stared with strange looks of fear and admiration at Sebastian as they scrambled to make sure his every wish was granted. He ignored every one of them, and kept all his attention focused on me. He sure knew how to make a girl feel special.

We were taken to a private box in the balcony that could have easily fit twenty people. Large, golden pillars stretched twenty feet up to the intricately carved ceiling, framing out our view of the curtain-clad stage. We snuggled on an antique settee as an adorable blonde struggled to pour us each a glass of champagne. She did everything she could not to stare at Sebastian as her hands shook on our glasses.

"I require privacy this evening. No one is to disturb us." He took his hat off and handed it to her. "I will send one of my servants if we require assistance."

"Yes, sir." She made eye contact with him and locked up. Then a second later she shivered and ran out of the room.

We sat in an easy silence as we watched the first dancers take the stage. He ran his fingertips up and down the skin of my arm, over my only tattoo. I nuzzled my head into his chest, and laid my hand with the heavy bracelet on his thigh. I wanted to be closer, to become a part of him. I could have fused with his flesh so that we became one being.

His heartbeat sounded so soothing to me. It didn't sound like a regular heart. It was loud, and slow, as if it was too big to fit in his chest. I imagined it supplying blood to something enormous, like an elephant, or a blue whale.

Sebastian started laughing. "Dare I ask why I transformed into a whale?"

Of course he'd been peeking in my brain again. "Your heart, it sounds huge."

He swept a loose curl out of the way and kissed my forehead. "I could spend a lifetime watching the pictures in your head float by."

I noticed he skipped the explanation. "What do you see now?"

"Right now, all I see is me… Me through your eyes, at least."

So my mind was a house of mirrors for him. No wonder he liked me so much.

We didn't speak much during the ballet. Every now and then he would ask me something, or comment about a certain aspect of the choreography. I just curled up in his arms, enjoying the comfort it gave me.

Including intermission, the show was more than two and a half hours long, and I was glad when it was over. Not because I disliked it, but because I was anxious to leave with Sebastian.

I wanted the isolation of the limo, where there was nothing to distract from him.

We rode around for an hour talking about nothing in particular, holding each other a little too closely. As much as I enjoyed myself, it was agony. That dull ache that longed for him wouldn't leave me alone. I knew he could feel it. Yet he made no move for me.

"I think it's time I took you home."

My chest seized at the sound of those words. "Already?"

"I apologize I'm always excusing myself before you're done with me. My behavior must be confusing you."

"A little." I lied.

"I may as well explain myself, since it seems my Vinicio likes to tell you all my secrets. It would probably be beneficial if you heard this from me." He sighed as he twisted a strand of my hair between his fingers. "I happen to be under serious time restraints, my love. When I leave you I am only doing so to fulfill a great need. I know you've been told what we require to sustain ourselves. Unfortunately, as my appetite increases with age, I need to consume more and more. Every six hours or so I must seek out nourishment.

"So you see, when I promised your safety, I also meant from myself. It would be wonderful to spend every moment with you, but that's not possible. If I don't separate myself to fulfill these needs I may become a danger to you." He put two fingers under my chin to tilt my face towards his. "I realize that son of mine may be out to make me look like a monster, but this is the natural order of things. This is the necessary balance of predator and prey that has been going on for all time."

The limo came to a stop before I had time to let that sink in, parking itself right outside my building. It didn't matter how terrifying what he just said should have been, the sweet way he spoke those words was hypnotizing.

"Goodnight, Trinity."

I wanted to scream no. He can't just tell me goodbye and send me on my way. That was torture. "Goodnight?"

Sebastian chuckled. "Were you expecting another night in my chambers?"

I couldn't answer him. I craved his touch so desperately it burned.

"It's terribly old fashioned of me, isn't it?" He said. "If all I wanted from you was purely physical, I would be done with you already. You would have been tossed aside like all the others. I have much bigger plans for you. So tonight you must go home."

I didn't care what he said. If he wanted me to leave this limo, he would have to do it by force. I turned around and, thanks to the high slit in my dress, placed one knee on his lap. I brought my hand up to his cheek, and ran my thumb along his lower lip.

"Sebastian, I need you... so badly it hurts."

He put his hand over mine and kissed my thumb. "After all I've told you, you still ache for me so?"

He kissed my wrist, then a few inches further, pulling me towards him as he progressed down my arm. Once he secured my hand behind his neck, he glanced up at me with his eyes burning brightly. "I suppose if it's of such importance to you... Stealing one kiss won't ruin my plans."

A devious smirk spread across his lips, and it all became clear to me.

He wanted me to beg. This had all been a ploy to see how long it would take for me to crack. But as he pulled my face closer to his, I couldn't have cared less.

Then Sebastian finally kissed me.

That soft, gentle touching of the lips sent such a charge of electricity through me, that I lost control. I straddled his lap and kissed him shamelessly, letting him feel every ounce of blind need that I felt. The waves of energy crashed into me like I was trapped in a storm at sea. I had to fight for air to keep from going under, but breathing seemed like such a trivial thing compared to finally getting what I yearned for.

Sebastian pried me off him and held me at arms length to look me over. He ran his hand down my neck and stopped over my heart. He held it there to judge my frenzied heartbeat, or possibly my frantic attempts to breathe again.

Then he smiled as if he made some sort of diabolical discovery, and said one word, "Interesting."

In a motion so quick and graceful I barely felt it, he laid me underneath him on the plush leather seat. Sebastian kissed me again, and moved the thin fabric of my dress over so he could cup my left breast in his hand. He stroked the nipple with his thumb then pinched it between his long fingers. The effect was not unlike striking a flint. Every cell in my body erupted into flames. I moaned and rocked against him, wrapping my free leg around his hip.

Sebastian's first response was a very predictable, human reaction. Then his eyes flashed to black, reminding me exactly how inhuman he was. But all this foreplay wasn't enough, and the nudge I felt between my legs drove me mad. I reached down without consciously telling myself to. Once my hand found its intended target, I latched on, and he groaned. It was a low, animal sound closer to a growl. But in the shock of what I was holding, I let go and gasped.

He chuckled and pulled away from me. I got the impression I was not the first to have this reaction. "We don't need to get too carried away, now do we?"

"I don't see any reason why not..."

The only answer he gave was more quiet laughter. He slowly adjusted my dress to cover my bare breast, and lifted me so I straddled his lap again. Then he took a deep breath and closed his eyes. When he reopened them, they were blue.

Sebastian allowed me to pull him into another kiss. I got all worked up again, and he grabbed my chin to tilt it back and give him access to my throat. He kissed a trail to my earlobe and whispered in my ear...

"Would you die for me, Trinity?"

Those words slammed into me like a freight train.

He leaned back and smiled. "You hesitated."

"I—"

"You're not ready yet."

"But—"

He shook his head. "As much as I would obviously enjoy obliging you, I have other places to be. It's time for you to take your leave."

Tears welled up in my eyes from his rejection. Sebastian chuckled, and I couldn't hold back the waterworks. He pulled me to him and kissed the spot where my first tear fell. Then he gave me one last real kiss, with the salty taste of my own suffering on his lips.

"I've indulged you enough for one night. Go inside, Trinity. I'll see you Sunday."

Two days was so long. I started to protest again, but he lifted me off his lap to get me moving. A pit formed in my stomach at the thought of leaving him. I knew he could feel my pain. He was fully aware of how much he was hurting me. I reached out to him, openly crying now, and he started laughing at me. Not just a small chuckle, this was outright laughter.

Our driver opened the door then, so I hid my face from Sebastian and climbed out of the limo. I didn't say goodbye.

That cruel laughter rang in my ears as I stood in the street, with the train of my dress lying in the filthy gutter, and watched the limo drive away. I was bawling my eyes out by the time it went out of sight.

My chest felt like it was caving in. Sebastian had completely crushed me, on purpose.

And he loved every minute of it.

Chapter 14

Vicious Natures

Much to my amazement, I was alone most of the next day. I should have been relieved to have so much time to myself. Unfortunately, all those hours in isolation gave me too much time to think. I popped a couple Xanax to take the edge off, but I didn't have the energy to drink. I even pulled out a bottle and stared at it for a while. I ended up putting it back and lying down.

I felt as if I was walking around in a dream, questioning my thoughts and completely losing touch with reality. I didn't care about searching for fame anymore. I didn't even care if I ever touched a paintbrush to canvas again. When I was with Sebastian, *he* was all I cared about. He was everything I ever wanted, wrapped up in a perfect package of blond hair and blue eyes. But now that I was away from him, the veil was lifted, and the mist clouding my eyes had cleared. I had stepped out of the fog and back into my own dismal world where nothing made sense. And I had no one to turn to.

Last night's date was already a broken memory. Only bits and pieces came through clearly. The actual conversations were blurred by Sebastian's uncanny ability to make even the most atrocious things sound benign. Deep down, I remembered he asked if I would die for him, and I knew he said he needed to feed every few hours. But the synapses firing in my brain couldn't attach those two items to anything menacing. All it wanted to register was how good it felt to be in his arms, and the rapture experienced from his kiss. For those few, brief moments, the roller coaster of endorphins was better than anything I had ever experienced. If I could feel that every day, it might not matter what he really had in store for me.

I realized something as I replayed our intimacies over and over in my head. The way he kissed, and the way he touched me were so familiar. I had kissed him before, and not the night he helped me remember. Sebastian had been the cause of my hallucination in Lucas' apartment. Even that early on he had control over me. Who knew how far under his power I had fallen. It's not like I was trying to escape. I'm not even sure I wanted to. I couldn't really be that dumb, could I?

Then there was his reaction to how much he hurt me. I wanted to be mad at him. Or to at least not want to be with him, but something wouldn't let me. I still longed for him. And if he sent for me right now, I would run into his arms without hesitation.

I sat down at my kitchen table, or the bar I was using as one, and buried my face in my arms, letting my hair flop all over the glass top. I felt weak, and worn down. My head was so overwhelmed it hurt, and I felt drugged. My arms and legs seemed to have tripled in weight overnight. What was Sebastian doing to me? The wonderful way our lips felt together was such a small part of the whole awful picture. One week, and there would be nothing to keep him from doing whatever he wanted to me. The painting was almost done. His plans would soon come to fruition.

"What's your problem?" Vino's voice broke through my thoughts from a couple feet away.

I didn't lift my head to answer. "Nothing."

"You've been sulking all day. It's starting to make me depressed." He picked up a section of my hair and peeked under it.

"Somehow I have trouble picturing you depressed."

He laughed. "I guess you're right... I was expecting you to act differently today, that's all."

I didn't answer him.

"Didn't your date go well?"

I straightened up enough to prop an elbow on the table and rest my forehead in the palm of my hand. "Why the hell do you want to know? You're just manipulating me like everyone else anyways."

He raised an eyebrow. "What makes you think that?"

"I had an interesting talk with your sister." I closed my eyes and shook my head. "Doesn't even matter. I don't care anymore."

"So she told you I'm his Second... That doesn't mean as much as you'd think. Sebastian has no intentions of stepping down. He only named me because I'd be the hardest to kill. Overthrowing him is the only real way to take his throne. I wasn't lying to you."

I sighed. "Whatever, I told you I don't care. My life is confusing enough without worrying about your stupid motives."

Vino sat in silence and watched me for a while. "So the date was that bad? I thought you were enjoying the fantasy."

"I don't fucking know, alright!" I yelled. My lovely fairytale was crumbling into pieces. "None of it felt real, I could have dreamed the whole event...I keep trying to remember the specifics and they're all blurry, like I'm watching someone else's memories. I don't understand what's going on, and you're not helping the situation!"

Vino wasn't fazed by my outburst. "I suppose that is the desired effect. The more power he gains over you, the less of yourself you're going to have left. Usually his women are so lovestruck by now that they can't function unless he's around."

"He's waiting for me to finish the painting." I mumbled into my hands. I wasn't about to tell Vino about what else he was waiting for.

"I'm sure that has a lot to do with it. Too bad that doesn't leave you with much time."

"You're not going to tell me what happens next, are you?"

"Sorry."

"Figured you'd say something like that." At least that was better than an outright no. "Will you at least tell me what the deal is with the twins? I may like them even less then you."

"And I thought I was growing on you," Vino said. "What did they do that was so bad?"

"Amelie insulted me all day, and they shocked me. It hurt, a lot, I almost blacked out."

He chuckled. "They must really not like you."

I shot him a dirty look. "You don't seem to be in their good graces either."

"That's no news to me, sweetheart. We've never gotten along. And they're not twins, by the way. Although I see where you would make that assumption."

"They're not twins? Those two are practically identical."

"Their mothers were twins. It was another one of Sebastian's experiments. They were conceived on the same night and born on the same day."

Visions of Sebastian making love to a set of twins crept up in the back of my mind. As shook-up as I was right now, the idea of him with someone else still made my stomach churn. I changed the subject. "Is Andras a mute? I've never heard him speak."

"He can talk. But trust me, you're not missing anything. Andras only likes to communicate telepathically. He thinks it's beneath him to say much of anything aloud... And he has a serious distaste for humans. I doubt he'd ever address you directly."

How many secrets did this family have? "Would I even be able to hear him if he did?"

"Easily. Any one of us could get in your head if we wanted to. That's one of the first tricks we're taught."

"Guess I should have known that," I said. "Those two aren't lovers are they? Every time I see them they're always all creepy and touching each other. It really grosses me out."

I expected Vino to laugh at me for asking such a ridiculous question. Instead, he shrugged. "That's a gray area. Those two share a bond that's uncommon for demons. They're connected much like you are to Sebastian when you wear the necklace, but the feed works both ways and it's stronger. It makes them perfect for reconnaissance. Watching you was their job before the incident with my father's women... And I don't know if they directly have sex with each other. But they do share the same prey, and the same bed. I'm fairly sure every intimate encounter they've ever had has been together."

"That's gross."

He laughed at my reaction. "We don't share human opinions of right and wrong, Trinity. There are no taboos for demons. Everything goes... Especially when it comes to sex. That's the whole point of our existence. Sin as much as possible and get everyone to join that you can."

"That's just disgusting. You could have left all that out."

"I thought you appreciated my honesty."

"You're not honest."

"Are you sure about that? I think you'd be surprised to find out how little I've lied to you."

Once I was safely out of my funk, Vino took me to a couple galleries I had never been to before. He didn't know as much about artwork as Sebastian did, but he was at least knowledgeable enough to hold an adult conversation about it. All in all, I actually had a good time. When he was on his best behavior like this, his company was bearable. In fact, he was being so tolerable today, he was almost friendly. I hated to admit it, but hanging out with Vino was a world better than sitting at my apartment alone, dwelling on the dreadful reality of my life.

I was surprised when Vino drove us back to the Bronx later that evening. He rarely ever went into the poorer neighborhoods. I was even more shocked when I realized that we were in Kingsbridge, the area Conchetta lived in before she shacked up with Teddy. It felt surreal to think about them now. It seemed like they were light years away. A distant memory from a past life.

Memories of them brought back thoughts of Lucas. I still missed him. And I'd never get a chance to make things right between us. The best I could hope for was that someday he'd forget I ever existed.

Vino pulled into the parking lot of a rather average looking Mexican restaurant, and parked the car in row among all the other vehicles. This was a far cry from the valet and full service experience I was used to him taking me to. I glanced around at the other cars in the lot; there was not one that was worth more the ten grand. The flashy Bentley stuck out like a sore thumb.

"Are you sure your car's gonna be safe here?"

He smiled at me. "I'm flattered you're so concerned, but it will be perfectly fine. Everyone around will probably go out of their way to avoid it and not even know why."

"Not gonna ask. What're we doing here anyways? This doesn't seem like your type of place."

"Maybe not. Authentic Mexican is never any good unless you're slumming it. I usually send the servants to pick up food from here."

He seemed to know what he was talking about, so I didn't question him further.

You could tell walking through the arched doorways that this used to be a really nice place, and at one time had been expertly decorated in traditional Mexican decor. However, that had to have been a long time ago, because now it just looked run down. The faux-stucco was falling off the walls and the tile mosaics on the tables were incomplete. The tile on the floor was cracked and worn, and the decorations hanging overhead were tattered.

Everyone stared when we walked inside. I'm sure they all started watching us the second he drove that shiny car into the lot. Normally, I liked all the looks people gave us when we went out, but tonight bothered me. This particular group was downright gawking.

The hostess led us to a table in the back, with torn vinyl seats, and explained the menu in severely broken English. Vino responded by asking her something in an effortless Spanish. I didn't understand a word except for margarita, which was good enough for me. She immediately loosened up and smiled, then walked away to fetch him whatever it was he asked for.

"I didn't know you spoke Spanish."

He had a conceited smile for me. "My native language actually. English was my third."

"Native language, huh?" I eyed him across the table. "What, was your mom Mexican or something?"

Vino laughed at me. "Mexico isn't the only country where they speak Spanish, you know. You're forgetting about Spain, obviously, nearly all of Central America, and half of South America. I thought you were a college graduate. Didn't they teach you anything in school?"

"I went to art school, remember? That barely counts as college," I said. "So tell me then, if your mother wasn't from Mexico, then where was she from?"

He stalled by eating some chips before he answered me. "Sebastian found my mother in the Viceroyalty of New Granada. Venezuela is what it's called now. It was Spanish territory back then and he was posing as a Spaniard."

"That would explain the hair, you're not very tan though."

Vino rolled his eyes at my attempt at a joke as our waitress made her appearance. They talked back and forth in Spanish for a minute. He didn't bother asking me what I wanted to eat, but she took our menus, so I assumed he ordered for me. I waited until she left us before I started hounding him with questions again.

"How was Sebastian passing for a Spaniard? He's one of the whitest people I've ever seen."

"I think the Spanish are still considered white."

"Whatever, you know what I meant."

He smiled at me for a moment, drawing out my anticipation for an answer. "This was almost three hundred years ago, Trinity... He was going by Cristoval. And he's traded in bodies since then. You wouldn't have even recognized him."

It amazed me how easily he gave up information these days. Even if he did beat around the bush first, Vino still answered just about everything I asked. "Oh. How often does he change bodies?"

"Every few hundred years. I've only seen him as Cristoval and Sebastian. Who knows how many personas he's had over the millennia."

"So what's his real name, if he keeps changing it all the time?"

"I can't tell you that."

"Why?"

He didn't move for a moment. His face betrayed no emotion. "I'll have more than just Sebastian to deal with if I reveal something like that to a human."

"Can you at least tell me where he gets his bodies? He said he didn't need a host, but how else would he get a human body?"

"That, I can tell you. He's actually proud of it. Have you ever questioned why he's so fond of art?"

I shrugged. "Just figured he was sophisticated."

"I never understand any of your logic..." Vino stopped to laugh. "No, he considers himself a master sculptor. He creates those bodies himself. He molds them into what he believes to be perfection. And what will arouse the most desire from the humans."

Well no flippin wonder. If I was a man who could mold my own body, I would be just as gorgeous and well endowed too.

Vino and I had a normal dinner together. If you didn't know better, we would have passed for a regular couple. Yeah, we bickered from time to time, but who didn't? At least I was completely out of my trance, and every emotion I felt around him was real. Even when I wanted to hit Vino, I was at least able to be myself. That was more than I could hope for, all things considered.

We were almost done eating when I caught Vino looking at something behind me. He was preoccupied enough, that I started to suspect him of lewd behavior again.

"What are you looking at?" I snapped.

His attention reverted to my direction a little too quickly. He had a big fake smile for me, obviously hiding something. "Nothing. Don't worry about it."

Of course that was the first thing I did. I spun around in my chair to catch what he was looking at.

A group of women had just come through the front doors. I would have chalked this up to typical Vino lechery, if it wasn't for the fact that I recognized one of them; Conchetta. She was dressed up for the evening, looking rather fetching in a low cut dress with a flowing skirt. Her hair was smoothed and curled to perfection. On a normal day, I might have been jealous.

She hadn't noticed me yet, so I spun back around. "Shit! Are you trying to set me up again? Why the hell would you do that?"

Vino showed his palms in surrender. "Look, I promise this time is a total accident. I had no idea she was coming until a second ago."

I squinted at him suspiciously, unsure if he was lying or not. "You better be telling me the truth, or I will stab you right here in this restaurant."

That made him laugh. "I swear, this is not my doing. But if you really feel the need, go ahead and stab me. You can deal with all the freaked out people afterwards."

I grabbed for my margarita, making sure to face in the exact opposite direction I had seen her in. "Maybe I'll get lucky and she won't notice me."

"Doubtful. Everyone in here has been staring at us all night. It's only a matter of time before she gets curious," he said. "I think it may already be too late. They're whispering about us as we speak."

I sank in my chair, slouching enough to drop a few inches. My heart was pounding. If she saw us, that meant Lucas would find out about this on Monday at the latest. Just the thought of

his name hurt me. I had done him enough damage; there was
no reason to rub it in.

"Just kill me now," I whined.

"Why would I want to do that?"

I glared at him. That joke wasn't funny at all.

Vino made a slight motion with his head to indicate someone was coming to greet us. I panicked; this was not going to be
good. One more swallow of my drink, and I turned to face my
nightmare.

Conchetta waltzed up to our table with an unkind smile on
her face. "Trinity, I thought that was you."

My smile was much weaker. "Yeah, how's it goin?"

Her friends were all staring at us from across the room, and
gossiping amongst themselves. Apparently, she must have told
them the whole scandalous story. Great, just fucking great.

Conchetta looked as happy as if she had caught me in bed
with Vino herself. "Aren't you going to introduce me to your
new beau?"

I turned bright red. This was so not fair. "I wouldn't exactly
call him that."

Vino laughed. "Yes, what we are is much more serious, isn't
it?" He winked at me, and reached a hand out to Conchetta. "It's
Vinicio."

The evil edge in her smile dropped as she daintily shook his
hand. My heart stopped, terrified by whatever he was about to
do to further destroy my life. It took everything I could muster
to keep from visibly cringing at sight of him touching her. Who
knew what he could do with something as simple as a hand-
shake.

"I'm Conchetta. It's nice to meet you."

"Pleasure's all mine." He released her hand and looked back
to me. He was eating this up. It made me sick. "Dear, you didn't
tell me you had such attractive friends."

Conchetta blushed, and toyed with her necklace. She was
looking at Vino with some serious goo-goo eyes.

I gave him the most murderous glare in my arsenal. "Didn't
think you'd ever get a chance to meet her."

He held my eye contact for a moment, then turned to Conchetta, speaking something in a quick, fluid Spanish that I couldn't make out. She blushed again and nodded a couple times. "Uh, yes." She then looked at me and smiled sweetly. "Great seeing you again, Trinity."

"Yeah, great seeing you too." I responded, completely confused.

She issued one last smile in Vino's direction. "It was nice meeting you, Vinicio."

With that, she walked away. I stared at Vino for at least a minute before I was ready to wage my war. "What did you just do to her?"

He grinned. "I didn't do anything. She likes me, that's all. There's no scandal for her to report if she thinks you traded up."

"I don't believe you. What did you say to her?"

"All I said was that this was a special night, and I would appreciate some privacy with you. I swear, no funny business."

I didn't say a word to Vino the rest of the time we were there. I didn't take my eyes off him either. The more I looked at him, the madder I got. All that hatred came back again, burning and building until I was ready to explode.

We had gotten in the car and driven half way to my place, when the pressure was too much and I cracked. "This is all your fault, all of it!"

Vino wasn't the least bit upset by my accusation. "Why do you think that?"

I pointed a finger at him. "If you had never showed up at my stupid show, none of this shit would be happening! I would have moved in with Lucas, and be living a perfectly normal life right now!"

He watched me expressionlessly for a moment before he answered. "You can blame me if you want to... But Sebastian would have ended up there anyways. You were calling pretty loudly, Trinity. One of us would have found you eventually. Even if you never had a show at all."

My rage was so intense; I burst into tears. "I hate you, so much."

Vino pulled the car into the nearest space along the road, and put it in park. He turned in his seat to face me, then touched my cheek with the back of his hand.

I refused to look him in the eye. But the second he touched me, and that soothing sedative washed over, my anger subsided. This wasn't the dreamlike blur that Sebastian used to keep me relaxed; Vino wasn't forcing the feeling on me. But it was just as effective.

As soon as he was sure I was out of attack mode, he dropped his hand and smiled. "See, all better."

I looked down at my lap. "I still hate you."

"If that's what you have to do, go right on ahead. But I swear, I had nothing to do with tonight, and I did nothing to your friend. You need to forget about your old life. You're never going to be able to go back to it. Holding on to this stuff is going to make things a lot harder on you. And if what happened with that girl is so important, then I can take care of it for you. There's no reason to be so upset."

I didn't want to trust him, but he sounded so sincere, like he was really trying to comfort me. And the logic in what he said was hard to ignore. I didn't have enough time left to keep dwelling on what used to be my life.

I gave him a weak nod. "Don't worry about it."

The next few days were a blur. It had been more than six weeks since this strange family entered my life and turned it upside down. Daytime was easy enough; oddly, my guard was dropping around Vino. He had barely done anything to piss me off this whole week, and I believed him about our run in on Saturday. So there wasn't much I could do about being mad at him.

My nights were a different story. Concentrating on the painting was hard. The part that required the most attention was Sebastian himself, and staring at him for hours at a time was difficult. The longing I felt peering into those fiery blue eyes was impossible to control. He was toying with me, even I could tell that much. He kept constantly breaking my train of thought, so all I could think of was him, and then disappearing into the night.

Don tried to contact me. First he called a few times, I didn't answer. Then I got a letter in the mail. I was too much of a chicken to open it. I'm assuming it contained threats of dropping me for being in breach of contract, or something along those lines. But like Vino said, it was time to forget about my old life.

Vino seemed to grow more content with hanging out at my place. He didn't force me to run about all hours of the day anymore. For the second time this week, we were sitting in my living room, sharing the couch and watching a movie together. I was on another one of my fact-finding missions, since no matter how many questions I asked, there would always be a hundred more I'd never know the answer to.

"How do you guys fit in so well if you're so old? You sound like you're my age."

He gave my question some thought, then grinned at me. "You might not be bright enough to grasp this concept."

I gave him a dirty look. "Don't be an ass, just tell me."

He laughed. "Alright... It's easiest to think of it as collective consciousness. When we devour souls, we absorb all of their being. Their entire consciousness, their strength and everything they've ever known becomes a part of us. So in essence, each one of us is a compilation of every soul we've ever devoured."

"What!? So do they just cease to be? Or do you have hundreds of voices chattering on in there?"

"Tens of thousands," Vino corrected. "I won't even take a guess at how many it would be for my father... But the voices get silenced almost immediately. Sometimes the stronger minded are harder to suppress. It doesn't happen much with humans, but I'm often ordered to take out demons. Sometimes their thoughts and memories plague me for days. In fact, about a hundred years ago, one demon was vying for Sebastian's seat, and instead of getting his hands dirty, he sent me. It was the closest

I've ever come to death. And once it was over I had to listen to him in my head for a month."

That was wrong on several different levels. "Do they do that a lot, fight for spots?"

"No one's ever successfully taken down someone of Sebastian's stature. He's fairly untouchable... unfortunately."

I asked him about ten more questions, then I stumbled onto one he didn't want to answer.

"What was your mom like?"

"Why do you keep bringing up my mother?"

"Just indulge me, I never knew my own mom. It makes me curious as to what kind of woman was strong enough to raise a little half-breed demon."

He glared at me. I smiled. "I mean a terrifying creature like yourself."

"You don't consider the one who raised you your mother?"

"You're avoiding my question."

Vino stared at me for a while longer. "Fine. What do you want to know?"

I lit up with my small victory. "Was she pretty?"

"One of the most breathtaking women I've ever seen." He looked away from me. "I look a lot like her... We all look like our mothers, since Sebastian doesn't have any human features to pass on."

"You do look like a chick."

"Do you really want to go down that road again?"

I laughed, and took my cue to move on. "Was she special too? Did she have any abilities?"

"Somewhat," He said. "She could see and feel a little of what you can, but she wasn't nearly as sensitive. She was immune to Sebastian's control though. That's why I hear those silent commands he gives, but he can't make me do anything against my will."

"Why'd she stay with him if he couldn't control her?"

"She told me that when he first showed himself she thought he was an angel, sent down from Heaven to reward her for her devotion... Then he seduced her and she saw what he really was." He furrowed his eyebrows. "After that, I became his bargaining chip."

"How long was she with Sebastian, or whatever his name was back then?"

"She died when I was ten. I was her only child so they couldn't have been together long before I was born."

"Sorry, that must have been hard losing her so young."

He kicked his feet up on my coffee table. "We're not exactly capable of feeling love, or whatever it is you're assuming I had for her. So when death comes, there's not much mourning involved. And besides, after ten years, I had aged something closer to eighteen by human standards. I didn't need a mother anymore."

I hesitated to ask the next question. "How did she die?"

Vino didn't answer me at first. He readjusted himself in his seat. "After her body gave out, she wasn't of any use to Sebastian anymore. So he killed her."

My jaw went slack. "Her body gave out? What does that mean?"

Another long pause. Vino was quiet for so long, I thought he wasn't going to answer me. "Do you remember what I said about draining energy…? Imagine what it would be like to have someone do that to you day after day for an entire decade." He gave me a second to let that sink in and continued. "She wasn't able to give him any more children, so he was especially cruel to her. She suffered a great deal before she wasted away to nothing."

I stared at him in wide-eyed horror. That was so sad. Whether or not Vino had been capable of loving her, he was still forced to watch the whole ordeal as it happened. His mother was tortured for years because she refused to leave his side. She had at least loved him. That was more than I ever had.

"Any other questions?" Vino asked, in a way that implied I was not allowed to ask any more.

"No." I felt awful for bringing up such a touchy subject. "I'm sorry."

He shrugged and leaned back again, forcing a look of relaxation. "You don't need to be. As I said before, I feel no grief for her. The types of emotions required for such a thing are simply not possible for us. She made the choice to stay. It was her own fault."

I don't know which shocked me more; the fact that he was lying about his feelings for his mother, or the fact that I knew him well enough to be able to tell.

I understood why he hated Sebastian so much now. The evil it took to slowly torture the mother of your own child to death was unreal. I marveled at how many times he had probably repeated this cycle. Vino told me the number of children Sebastian fathered would be incomprehensible, and that he made repopulation of his species a top priority. That probably meant that he did this over and over again, constantly trying to find new women to create offspring for him, and then disposing of them as they reached the end of their usefulness.

Then it hit me.

The morbid realization that made me instantly sick to my stomach. *That* was what was in store for me. *That* was the horrible fate that Vino refused to talk about. I was going to be used the same way his mother was. Sebastian wanted to see what abilities I would pass on. He was going to breed me and drain me until I was no more.

I suddenly felt dizzy, and what little was in my stomach, was about to come back up. I stood quickly and headed towards the bathroom. Vino stared after me with a confused look in his eyes. "What?"

I shook my head and tried to play it off. "Just gonna take a shower."

I'm not sure if he bought the act or not. I made a point to disappear behind the door before he could question me.

I did not want to go to Sebastian's that night. Keeping my mind clear so he didn't know what I figured out would be impossible. But staring at him and wanting him so badly when I knew what he would do to me, that was unbearable. And my time was up. I was one day, maybe two, from completion of the painting. Then there was the matter of the blood. We hadn't discussed using any, but I knew he would want it. To tell the truth, I didn't even know where it would go. No one was being tortured in this picture. No one was bleeding. Not yet anyways.

The ride to Tribeca was uncomfortable. Vino kept staring at me, but I refused to tell him what was up. I waited until the absolute last second to put on that god-awful necklace, and didn't say a word to him as we walked inside.

Sebastian was talking to the twins, or whatever I was supposed to refer to them as now. He was as happy as ever to see me, and seemed unaware of my uneasiness as he issued his normal greetings and compliments. We went to work right away. He seemed eager to get our project finished, so I obliged.

I felt just as smitten as ever. Apparently, no amount of truth could shake his hold on me. I suppose that was for the best. If all I could think of was his flawless face, then my thoughts could never wrap around anything damaging.

After three solid hours of painting, Sebastian yawned and rose from his seat. "Perhaps we should call it a night. Why don't you leave your items there and come with me."

I sat my brush down and smiled; I couldn't say no to him. "Where are we going?"

"Nowhere." He gave me one of his brilliant grins. "I was thinking we should have a few drinks together."

"Yeah, of course."

He strolled over and wrapped his arm around my waist to lead me into his bar. Amelie and Andras were there, and so were three other women. They were dancers, or strippers by the way they were dressed. Classic rock played overhead, and the lights were dimmed low. A voluptuous blonde danced on the table directly in front of the twins. The other two dancers were making use of the poles with practiced skill. They were both Asian, with long, highlighted hair, and appeared to be related.

Normally, I would have been happy to walk into a private strip club, but being accompanied by Sebastian gave a more ominous feel to it. It was hard to watch someone dance that you knew would be dead in a couple hours.

We sat on one of the couches away from the women, and Sebastian threw his arm around me as he always did. "You appeared as if you needed to relax, my love. I thought you might enjoy a peaceful night with me."

I couldn't keep myself from snuggling against him. I was in that dream again, the one where only he mattered. I didn't care about what he planned for me anymore. "I feel better already."

He smiled and swept the hair out of my face. "I'd hoped you'd say that."

We had several drinks as we sat there, talking about the usual nothing, and barely paying attention to the semi-naked women prancing about the room. I was ready to give myself to him again. His invisible leash tethered around my neck kept me lost in the fantasy world he created for me. At least the fantasy was better than the reality. If I never left, things wouldn't be so bad.

"You needn't be shy about asking one of them for a dance…" Sebastian offered suggestively into my ear.

I shook my head. That would require me to let go of him, so it was out of the question. "That's okay, I'm fine here with you."

He let out a small laugh. "As you wish. Would you care to tell me what's bothering you this evening?"

I tried to block any signs of what it really was out of my head. But when he asked that question, it was more like he commanded my brain to show him. He pulled out the pictures he needed by forcing me to think about it. I was completely powerless against his mind games as visions floated by of me slowing dying at his hands.

Sebastian aimlessly twirled a strand of my hair as we sat there together. He didn't act like he was doing anything. There was no physical evidence that he was rummaging through my head, only the sickening feeling that came over me as I lost control completely. He pulled off the ruse so well, that when he tilted my chin to smile at me, even I was questioning whether or not it had really happened.

"That's alright if you don't want to talk about it," he said. "You don't have to tell me anything you don't want to."

His words were so endearing that I melted. I was back to feeling like he was the only thing of importance on earth, just that easily. It was an out of body experience where I could watch myself as it happened, but never get close enough to reach out and stop my actions.

After a few moments Sebastian sighed dramatically and hugged me tighter. "It is getting to that hour now, isn't it? I must say, I am positively starving."

He peered deep into my eyes with the most ravenous expression on his face. Then he leaned down and kissed me, a long, deep kiss that shattered the last of my defenses and rendered me immobile.

"If you'll excuse me, my love..."

Sebastian left me there on that couch, still in a daze from his kiss. He strolled over to where the two Asian women were waiting for him, not more then ten feet away. He put his arms around their shoulders and whispered something that made them giggle. Then he glanced back at me one last time.

"Perhaps you would care to join us?"

I couldn't speak. I couldn't move. I wanted to say anything to keep him from leaving with them. Maybe I would have even joined him, if I'd have had the mental capacity to control myself. I was envious of the death that would embrace them tonight, because it meant a night in his arms. The man, the creature, who denied me his touch, still bedded whomever he wanted. And now it wasn't even in my absence.

Sebastian laughed at my pained expression. The black extinguished the blue of his eyes again. It crept out in all directions and stained his skin. Then his smile warped into that sickening mouth of fangs.

It was the most real thing I had seen all night.

I gasped, and he laughed again. Then he turned around to escort the two dancers out of the room. I didn't have the strength to move for quite some time. I couldn't tell if I was still under his power, or if I was just that terrified. When I finally was able to look around, everyone else had left. I was completely alone with not even one servant in sight.

I carefully stood up on shaky legs, and went towards the pool-room, the opposite direction I watched Sebastian take. I pulled the door open a crack and peeked inside.

It surprised me how relieved I was to see Vino waiting for me. He eyed me suspiciously from the couch. "What now?"

"Nothing."

"Doesn't look like nothing," he stated blandly, sounding completely uninterested. "Come on. Let's get out of here."

I followed him without saying a word. I didn't even make a peep the entire way home. By the time we parked in front of my place, he was staring at me like he wanted to say something. He even stepped out of the car when I did and started to walk me to the door, something he had never done before.

We were almost to the front doors when he yanked me by the arm into the walkway between my building and the next. "Tell me what's wrong with you."

He let go of me before I could get distracted by the current rolling off him. I looked down at the ground and shook my head. I did not want to say any of this out loud. That just made it too real.

Vino wasn't taking no for an answer. "You'd better start talking."

"I should have gone into that church," I said.

He leaned against the brick wall of the building behind him, and crossed his arms. "Yes, you should have. But you didn't."

"You wanted me to escape, didn't you…"

His face went blank and he didn't answer. I'd learned that response almost always meant yes.

"I figured it out… I know what he's going to do to me. He practically admitted it tonight."

Vino almost looked sympathetic. "There's nothing you can do about that now."

He was almost right. There was one thing I could do. I could die. If I was dead, I wouldn't be of any use to Sebastian. No life meant no torture.

"There's something you can do," I whispered.

He squinted at me. The sympathy from a moment ago was gone. "I'm not giving you another chance to run."

I took a deep breath and prepared myself to say these next few words. "I want you to kill me."

"No."

I started crying. "If you don't do it, I'll do it myself."

"You'll never be fast enough to pull that off. I'll stop you before you even make an attempt."

My heart sank. I had a feeling he was going to say that. "I'm begging you, kill me, please."

I could see the rage building in his eyes as he took a step towards me. "I said no."

"I thought you wanted to? It was supposed to be beautiful remember...?"

Before I realized what I was doing, I threw my arms around him and sobbed into his chest. I felt his entire body tense up as the energy flowing from him transferred to me. He froze for a moment, without even breathing, then grabbed me by both arms and slammed me into the wall behind me.

I heard a loud crack as the mortar broke free of the bricks behind my back. Pain shot up my spine as my head snapped back into the wall with blinding force. My eyes closed on impact, with showers of sparks going off behind my eyelids. I choked on my last breath as the wind was knocked out of me. When I could finally gasp for air again, I slowly opened my eyes to look at my assailant.

The second our glaze met, Vino's eyes flashed black, sinking into endless pits that wanted to swallow me alive. The corners of his mouth began to stretch to make room for the row of perfectly straight daggers that had replaced his teeth. The normally calming current from him was now piercing and intense.

His voice dropped a full octave as he spoke. "Get this straight... I am not your friend. I am not here to help you... And your fate is none of my concern!"

Vino released my arms and let me drop to the cold cement below. I let out a small grunt as I collapsed under my own weight. Tears streamed down my cheeks while I searched for him, to find some meaning as to why he would hurt me.

But he was gone, and I was sitting on the filthy ground of that dark walkway all alone. I didn't get up to head inside. Instead, I brought my knees into my chest and buried my face in my arms. I stayed there, sobbing quietly to myself, for a long time.

Chapter 15

Day of Blood

Fuck my life.

I must be the stupidest person in the history of creation. Every decision I have made up until this point was wrong. If I had only listened to Sara and Hank, paid attention in church, and maybe, just maybe, not have been such a selfish, immoral drunk, I wouldn't be praying for death right now.

Not literally, of course. I spat directly in God's face. There was no way I could bring myself to ask for His help now. No, I did something even more sacrilegious. I begged for death from the other side. I was foolish enough to ask this of Vino, and I paid dearly for it. What was I thinking? He was the last person that would show me compassion. I *hugged* him for Christ's sake. I would have attacked me too.

My whole back and head hurt. Most of my muscles were stiff. There was a sizeable lump on the back of my head and scratches on my shoulder blades. The worst part were the bruises on my arms. They were perfect prints of Vino's hands in the deepest shade of purple, and extremely sore. Luckily, my tattoo hid most of it on my left bicep. But it was so prominent on the right that I was going to have to wear sleeves for a month.

He was nowhere to be seen today. Though I'm sure he was close. I'd been waiting for the onslaught of creatures to come for me, but none showed. So that meant he was out there somewhere, watching me as I curled up on my bed in a catatonic state. The TV was on, but I wasn't watching. I just laid there, unmoving and wrapped in a blanket. I didn't eat. I didn't even want to drink. No amount of alcohol or pills could have made me feel better today.

I barely managed to get ready. I'm sure I looked like a wreck. I contemplated staying in my bed, since there wasn't much else anyone could do to me at this point. Not now that I knew what was waiting for me. But I felt compelled to do what Sebastian expected of me, no matter how much I didn't want to. So I threw on a light sweater to cover my arms, and obediently made my way to where I knew the Bentley would be waiting.

I shook as I opened the door and slipped inside. Vino didn't even look at me. He just floored it the second my door was shut. We were back to the way things were when we first started sharing this drive. Neither one of us spoke a single word the entire way there.

Facing Sebastian was none too high up on my list either, but at least he seemed happy to see me. He mentioned nothing of the previous night, and showed no signs of anger for my transgressions. It was the same charismatic man it always was who greeted me warmly tonight.

He threw his arm around me as we walked over to the enormous canvas, which now was nearly completely covered in top-dollar acrylics. He had a satisfied smile as we stood together admiring it. "We're very nearing completion, aren't we? I'm guessing done with paint tomorrow...What do you think?"

I studied my work with a critical eye. "I think you're right. By the end of tomorrow night I should be able to finish it."

"Marvelous." His whole face lit up. "So that will put us at Saturday for all the finishing touches. I have been so looking forward to that part."

There was something wretchedly foreboding about that sentence. The exuberant way he spoke it made it seem so much worse. He stood there with me, staring at the painting for a few more moments, then slid his hand from my shoulder to my bicep, and rested his fingers on top of my bruise. Then he squeezed hard enough to bring tears to my eyes.

"You hurt my feelings, Trinity."

"I'm sorry," I whimpered.

Sebastian spun me around so I was facing him and stared into my eyes. "It pains me that you would ask my son to end your life. I would hope that if you wanted to give someone that pleasure it would be me. Although I would not have done so either. You're much too important for me to allow you to die."

He paused to caress my cheek lovingly. "Not that death would save you anyways. Hell is my home, Trinity. Where do you think you're going to end up? Did you believe I wouldn't be able to reach you there? I travel freely between our two realms; finding you would be child's play... You are mine now, in this life and the next."

My spellbound mind only wanted to register his declaration of me as a wondrous occasion. But the pit in my stomach heard the words he said and tried to pull me back to reality. It was a losing battle.

Sebastian grinned at me in the most enchanting way. "And don't expect my son to help you. He may have acquired some attachments to you, but his loyalties will always lie with me. I am disappointed he wounded you. I assure you he'll be reprimanded for his brashness."

Attachments? My bruises sure didn't scream attachment.

Sebastian pulled me closer and kissed me, erasing every coherent thought from my head. I could feel myself putting my arms around him without consciously commanding them to.

He held our embrace for a long moment, and slowly released me. "We have eternity to deal with such things. Why don't we get to the task at hand?"

I nodded. "Yeah, of course."

I worked until almost two that night. Sebastian stayed the whole time, watching me with blazing eyes. I wondered how uncomfortable it was for him to stay so late without feeding. This was the longest he had ever posed for me. It disgusted me that it was his comfort I worried about in this situation.

I had another uneasy ride home with Vino. He said nothing to me the whole way, so I ignored him the best I could and daydreamed out the window. When he pulled the car in front of my building, he shifted it to park without looking at me.

"I didn't mean to hurt you," he said in a low whisper.

I had to do a double take on that one. "What?"

"I'm sorry." He inclined his head enough to look at me from the corner of his eye. "You caught me off guard. I shouldn't have reacted so badly."

"I thought you enjoyed hurting people."

Vino still had one hand on the steering wheel and one on the shifter, gripping both with white knuckles. "I didn't this time."

I don't care how sincere he sounded. I wasn't buying it. "Did Sebastian put you up to this?"

He snarled at me. "How dumb are you? He's only upset that your bruises make you less attractive. Do you really think he gives a shit about whatever pain you feel?"

"And I'm supposed to believe that you do?"

Vino didn't answer me. He looked back towards the street. "Look, you aren't the first woman Sebastian has done this to. And you won't be the last. This endless cycle has been going on for longer than even I can imagine. It's just the way things are. Things will be better if you either accept it or forget about it."

"That's easier said than done," I groaned, fully in depressed mode again.

There was a long pause before he turned to me. His eyes possessed a tormented quality that the blank mask he tried to wear couldn't hide. "I can't do what you ask of me. If you die, I die too… That much was made abundantly clear."

I hated that he was showing real emotion again. Things were so much simpler when I thought he was lying. He felt bad about attacking me. But I didn't know how to interpret that. This was a horrible, vicious person I was talking to. He wasn't supposed to have feelings. Hell, he wasn't even a person. He was a monster. I saw it myself last night. He had shown me exactly what he really was; no different from Sebastian.

But when he was acting this way, he seemed so human, so normal and emotional. Vino may have wanted to kill me, but he didn't want to hurt me. Lately he almost seemed to enjoy my company. It was so confusing.

I sighed and smiled at him. "I shouldn't have done something so stupid anyways. Consider this apology accepted."

He smiled. It was the nicest smile I had ever seen on his face. "Why don't you go inside. I'll see you tomorrow."

Translation: I'm happy you forgive me. I can't begin to explain how good that made me feel. At least my days were going to be better now. What few of them I had left.

Vino, the man I had once referred to as my own personal buzz-kill, had quite the opposite effect on me when I found him waiting the next morning. I tried to tell myself it was because I hated being alone. But in truth, we had a lot in common these days. We both had an eternity of suffering at Sebastian's hands to look forward to.

He laughed at me when he saw the expression on my face. "I think I like it better when you're mad at me."

"Fuck off." I did my best to wipe away the smile and shot him a dirty look.

He winked at me. "That's better."

Yep, still aggravating. And just when he was starting to earn some points. I rolled my eyes and plopped down on the couch with the remote. He followed and took his seat next to me.

"What do you want to do today?"

He'd never asked me that before. I was surprised enough it took a moment to answer. "How about the sea port? I haven't been there in ages."

"That's a good idea. Why don't you get dressed and we'll get going."

I glanced down at myself. I was wearing the same casual type of outfit I always did. "I am dressed..."

He shook his head. "I meant go put something nicer on."

"Such an ass," I muttered as I got up to change. It wasn't worth it to argue with him. He always won anyways.

We spent most of the day either wandering around or sitting at one of the more pricey restaurants overlooking the ocean. Aside from the occasional quip, Vino was back on his best behavior again, even holding open doors and such. I kept thinking he was up to something, but his usual deviousness never showed.

Towards the end of our stroll, we stopped along the pier and leaned on the railing to watch the boats float by. Vino looked almost happy. It felt strange to see him with such a pleasant expression on his face. "I think I'm going to take you somewhere tomorrow."

"What theory are we gonna to test this time?"

He laughed. "No, nothing like that. You're going to love it, I promise."

"Okay, where are we going?"

"It's a secret till morning... Don't want you accidentally tipping off Sebastian, you know." The sly smirk finally came back.

I knew it was too good to be true. "What are you up to?"

Vino didn't answer.

For being our last day painting, it sure was business as usual at Sebastian's. The eerie sense of foreboding was overpowered by his charisma. I got straight to work, concentrating on nothing but my brush strokes and my subjects, which was remarkably easy today.

I finished the painting around eleven-thirty, and stood back to get a look at it. Sebastian seemed to know the exact moment I was done. He came to stand at my side and wrapped his arm around my waist.

"It's perfection," he said. "Your talent amazes me."

I couldn't help but smile at his compliment. "Thank you, I'm glad you like it."

"Like doesn't even begin to describe my feelings... But yes, I am very pleased." He spun me around to face him. "You're going to love what I have in store for tomorrow. I can barely contain my excitement."

Sebastian's eyes lit up, then he reached out suddenly to grab the back of my head and pull me into a kiss. He was forceful, and passionate, and I was overwhelmed. I started to lose control again. I wanted this. And I wanted him. There wasn't a rational thought left in my brain to tell me otherwise.

But as unexpectedly as Sebastian started, he stopped, and looked somewhere behind me with a sinister grin on his face. He wasn't paying attention to me at all. I glanced over my shoulder to see what could be so important, and spotted Vino across the room.

That kiss hadn't been for my benefit. He was proving his ownership. I was nothing more than an object to him. Knowing I meant so little was almost worse than everything else he was doing.

Sebastian kept me in his arms and kissed me again, briefly this time. "I'll be counting the seconds until I see you."

It hurt me both physically and mentally when he released me and walked away. It wasn't fair to be forced to ache for someone so badly when you knew they intended to destroy you.

Vino wore that familiar emotionless mask as we left. Neither one of us mentioned the incident.

My eyes opened to a much brighter morning then I was used to lately. We stayed out until close after we left the apartment, but I didn't have a hangover. I wasn't building up a superhuman immunity to booze. I just didn't drink much. For some reason, I didn't really want to.

I gave myself a long stretch, and rolled out of bed to stumble towards my caffeine fix. My untamed tresses were a snarled mess sticking out in all directions, and hanging in my barely conscious face. I rubbed the last of the sleep out of my heavy eyelids and gave a half-assed grin to my awaiting companion.

I was delighted to see Vino this morning. He lounged on my chaise as always, but dressed differently than I had ever seen him. Vino looked like a Colombian drug lord. He wore a white, short sleeved, button down shirt, with only half the buttons actually fastened. His bold tattoo peeked out on his chest and down his arms. His khaki colored lounge pants and brown leather sandals were top dollar, but what caught my eye was the fact that his toenails were manicured. I suspected they had clear polish on them. A joke about how feminine that was popped into my head, but considering how well those comments usually went over, I kept it to myself.

"Are we going to the beach?" I yawned as I flipped the switch to my coffee machine.

"I told you, it's a surprise."

I stretched again and stared at the drops of hot brown goodness as they slowly finished filling the glass urn. "You know, if you're going to be here waiting all morning, you could at least start this thing for me."

"We'll see about that," he said. "Don't bother spending too much time getting ready today. No one is going to see you."

"That's not ominous or anything."

Vino laughed. I ignored him and went about starting my normal morning routine.

He called to me as I entered the bathroom for my shower. "In case you're wondering, we are going for beach attire today."

This was the first time I wasn't pissed about having to coordinate to his look. He said beach. That was all I needed for motivation, even if it was a little late in the season. I got ready in record time and skipped over to him.

He took one look at me and squeezed his temples. "Maybe this was a bad idea."

"Too late now," I teased. "I'm ready, let's go."

"Ridiculous."

He drove towards the seaport, and parked in a gated lot by one of the piers. We crossed the street to reach a long dock that was lined with massive yachts. Each grew in stature and size as we walked to the last one in the row.

The boat had to be a hundred feet long, and three levels high. Everything was so crisp and clean it didn't look like it had ever been used. I stood there gawking at it for a minute with my jaw hanging open. Vino laughed at me.

A man in a white shirt and captain's hat hopped down to greet us. He wore a smile, but was visibly shaken at the sight of Vino. "Good morning, Mr. Amante."

Vino actually smiled back at him. "Yes, it is, isn't it?"

The captain helped me aboard and I took in a quick survey of my surroundings. There was a full sized living room directly in front of me. All the furniture was large and masculine. Most of it was white, accented with navy. It looked more like an apartment then a boat. I could very literally live there. It was both bigger and nicer then my own place.

Vino was at my side in seconds. "I thought we were going to get a full day out here. But now that Sebastian changed the schedule, we don't have time to go far." He motioned to the room in front of me. "Let's head up to the top level."

I followed him up two sets of stairs and through a bedroom with a skip in my step. The patio on the top level had four wicker chaises, a large semi-circle vinyl couch, a bar and a hot tub. To-day was going to rock.

I plopped down on the couch and gave Vino an approving smile. "You've been holding out on me. We would have gotten along from the beginning if you just would have taken me here."

He grinned, but otherwise didn't answer.

"How mad's Sebastian gonna be when he finds out we're bor-rowing this?"

Vino took a seat next to me and threw his arms over the back of the couch. "This one's all mine… Sebastian is not a big fan of boats. Neither are Amelie or Andras for that matter. Demons are more dense than humans. They have no natural buoyancy. That's one human trait I'm actually glad I kept. They can swim, and they like water, but voyaging into the ocean can be risky. As long as we're on here they probably won't follow us."

"Then why haven't you brought me here sooner? This is way cooler then the Bugatti."

Vino hesitated before he answered. "This is my own private escape from that wretched family of mine." He leaned in and gave me a smirk as the colossal boat pulled away from the dock. "Besides, no one ever comes back alive from a voyage with me. Except for the captain of course. Poor guy's seen some night-marish things."

"Is that supposed to scare me?" I said. "I'm not afraid of you."

Vino shrugged. "Thought I'd give it a shot."

A woman in a navy skirt and white top showed up out of nowhere with two drinks and a tray of fruit. I wondered briefly in which ways Vino would rip her apart later, but she disap-peared as quickly as she came. I made Vino tell me everything about the yacht, and he generously answered every question I had. In fact, he didn't say one thing to piss me off for the whole next two hours. It was bizarre.

"Why are you being so nice to me?" I finally asked.

He thought about it for a moment, then glanced towards my violet stained arm. "Guilty conscience, maybe."

I hid the bruises with my hand. "I thought you weren't sup-posed to have a conscience."

"I didn't think so either," he said. "Why did you forgive me so easily?"

I shrugged. "I guess I'm starting to almost enjoy your company... considering all my other options."

Vino laughed. "What happened to all that hate you had for me?"

"Got tired of it." I quoted him.

"That's not very smart. It's better if you hate me." He kicked his sandals off and put his hands behind his head.

"You sure worked hard at making me hate you." I lounged back next to him, making sure to stay far enough away that I wasn't touching him. "You lied to me, you know."

He raised an eyebrow. "What could I have possibly lied to you about?"

"I'm the closest thing to a friend you've got."

I peeked at him from the corner of my eye, waiting for his possibly violent reaction to my accusation. But none came. Vino thought it over for a minute. Then he sighed.

"You're probably right... doesn't change anything though," he said. "My lifestyle doesn't exactly warrant companionship."

"Yeah, I noticed." I threw my sunglasses on and decided to tempt fate, sliding over the next few inches so that I could rest my shoulder against the side of his chest. I held my breath as I felt him tense up at my sudden show of affection.

Vino froze for a second, then relaxed, and draped his arm over my shoulder. I leaned my head back against him and let myself enjoy the flurry of tranquility that washed over me. I could have spent the rest of the day like that, but he didn't let me. It took one minute, maybe two, before I could tell he felt uncomfortable with the intimacy of the situation.

He pulled his arm back and stood up. "I don't know about you, but I'm getting in the hot tub."

He started walking toward the platform and slipped his shirt over his head. That tattoo I had seen earlier on his chest, stretched over his shoulders, down both arms and covered his whole back. It was the blackest, sexiest tribal I had ever seen, with arching forms and sharp points strategically placed to highlight the curves of his muscles.

While I was busy staring, he turned around and started un-hooking his belt. "Aren't you coming with me?"

"Yeah," was all I said.

It's hard to keep a straight face when someone who looks like that takes his clothes off. To make matters worse, he kept strip-ping. His shirt, and pants, were placed neatly on a rack adjacent to the hot tub, leaving Vino in only his swim trunks; skintight, square-cut shorts that cut off above the thigh. And, dear God, that tattoo crept out of the tiny piece of fabric he was using as swimwear, not just on his abs, but it continued down his thighs.

I take back everything I ever said about him looking like a girl, because there was *nothing* feminine about the man standing in front of me now. Every muscle in his toned body was in perfect proportion. I doubted there was a human alive that looked that good. And yes, maybe his ego might be a little justified. But I'd never tell him that.

I'm sure I was drooling. Luckily, I caught myself before I think he noticed. It felt dirty and shallow to ogle him right after we just declared our friendship. So I shook it off, and stood to follow him to the hot tub.

Vino hopped into the water in one fluid motion. I slipped off my suit cover, and slowly eased into the spot across from him. I tried not to stare at him, really. He laughed at me.

"You need to quit looking at me like that."

"Like what?" I asked, trying to play dumb.

"Like you want to eat me."

I cracked up. It took a moment to calm myself down. "You did that on purpose. You knew damn well what my reaction would be. I haven't seen a naked man in weeks."

"I'm not naked."

"Pretty fucking close."

Apparently, what I just said was hilarious. "Normally, I do go nude. But I didn't think that was appropriate in my present company."

"Of course, because you're all about being appropriate," I said.

Vino didn't react to my comment. He closed his eyes and rested his head on the rim of the hot tub. "I see you naked all the time. You don't see me tripping all over myself."

Now, I was mad. Maybe friendship just wasn't going to work out between us. "Screw you. I'm going downstairs."

I stood up to leave, but he grabbed my wrist. "Calm down. That's not what I meant."

"Then what do you mean?" I yanked my arm away and sat back down.

Vino sighed and looked at me from the corner of his eye. "What I mean is that I would never have sex with you."

"I never said I wanted you to," I snapped. "And that contradicts every lewd comment you've ever made to me."

"Again, you're not listening to me…I just said I wouldn't, not whether or not I wanted to." He covered his face with his hand. "Besides the obvious fact that my father would slaughter me in the most painful way he could dream of, you seem to have missed the point that I have killed every human I've ever been with. And even half the demons. There is no line between hunger and lust. The two are connected." He lowered his hand and looked at me. "You're thinking of things like a human, Trinity. For us, sex is just a prerequisite to death."

I didn't have any smart comebacks for that. I guess he already told me this. I just didn't take it to heart. So by saying he wouldn't sleep with me, it meant either he didn't want me to die, or he was afraid of dying himself. It also meant he'd put some thought into the subject.

"You could have avoided all this by keeping your clothes on," I said.

He laughed. "You should have seen your face."

I rolled my eyes. That was as close as I was going to get to an admission that he'd done that on purpose. "So what's with the tattoos? There's no way those were done with a needle."

"Most of the Seconds have marks like these. They're a symbol of title. But no, they're not done with a needle. I got them in Hell. And they're burnt into my skin. Supposedly, they enhance strength. I haven't noticed a difference."

"They at least make you look stronger."

"I was going for sexier, but stronger works too," he winked at me. "A hundred and seventy-five years ago, when I first got them, I had to hide them from the humans because they scared them. Now I have to hide them because they go mad with lust."

We made it back to my apartment with just enough time for me to rinse off and get ready. I threw on a casual dress I remembered Sebastian liking, in hopes it would help curb his temper about our outing today. Now that Vino and I were officially sort-of friends, my outlook on life was slightly less bleak. But my time was up. Tonight was going to be the day of blood, so to speak. The very last day I would work on the painting, leaving no more excuses to keep me unharmed.

Vino's normally erratic driving was slower paced on the way to the apartment. It seemed he was stalling. When we stopped the car out front, he turned to me with an uneasy look in his eye.

"Things might be different after tonight. I don't know what he's planning."

I stared blankly at the building out my window. "Yeah, I know."

Vino escorted me all the way upstairs, where an impatient Sebastian was waiting for us. He immediately ripped me away from Vino's side.

"We'll discuss your punishment later." He stared at Vino for a moment. I'm sure they were having a conversation I couldn't hear. When he looked back to me there was no trace of any anger.

Vino mumbled something and left the room. Sebastian paid him no attention. He was far too preoccupied with my face. His eyes were all ablaze with unveiled excitement. "You have no idea how delighted I am to see you right now."

I blushed, his doting may have been under false pretenses, but it was still flattering. "It's nice to see you too."

Sebastian reached out and caressed my cheek with his hand. "Most men in my shoes would be jealous right now... But alas, I'm too overjoyed at the sight of you to care about such trivial things." He winked at me. "Besides, I know you like me better."

His eyes were calling to me, pulling me in with that shimmering blue. He looked positively glorious basked in all his impassioned glee. I did like him more. And it made me sick. There was no distinguishing between the real me and the one he created anymore. I wanted him with my entire being, and there was no way around it.

Sebastian snapped his fingers and his harem of dolls walked in the room from the bar. They looked different today, much less like zombies and more like real people. Their eyes were alive again and bright in their admiration of him. It looked as if he had given them back their souls for one last day.

He gave me a quick kiss as they took their spots. "We have a very important reason for being here today, don't we?"

All I could manage was a weak nod. That one, small kiss left me feeling like I'd been drugged. Sebastian turned and started walking towards the group. He slowly climbed stair-by-stair and stopped near the throne. He leaned over to put a finger under one of the girl's chins and smiled down at her. "I suppose you were wondering where I was going to get all the blood you require. It is the most important part, is it not?"

A timid yes was my reply. I already knew where the blood was coming from. It was only a matter of what he was going to do to get it.

Sebastian dropped his hand and took his seat in the throne, grinning at me with the kind of ravenous enthusiasm that sent chills down my spine. "Are you ready, my love?"

I swallowed hard. "Ready as I'll ever be..."

He stared deep into my eyes for a moment, then glanced in the direction of the redhead to his immediate left. She smiled at him lovingly and leaned over the arm of the throne like she was going to kiss him. He locked eyes with me again and reached a hand up to the back of her hair, grabbing a delicate fistful and tilting her head so her neck was exposed to him.

The black engulfed his eyes again, devouring any trace of that wondrous blue I so loved. The darkness crept through the whites and spread like a shadow onto the skin around his eyelids. Then very slowly, he lowered his lips towards the bare flesh of her neck, and bit directly into her jugular.

I heard a gasp, though I don't know whether it came from the girl or me. A wave of adrenaline rushed from head to toe. I brought my hand to my chest to cover my pounding heart. This wasn't panic I was feeling, and it definitely was not fear. It was something else completely, much more driven by desire then horror.

When her body started to fall limp, he tenderly laid her at the foot of the throne and turned his attention to the other redhead, who was now climbing up his leg to him. To my surprise there was not one drop of blood on his lips, and his mouth had not changed to those terrifying jaws. Aside from the black holes that were now his eyes, he was just as gorgeous as ever.

Sebastian put a hand on the next girl's check and guided her to rise with him. He wrapped his arms around her and held her in a lovers embrace. She seemed so happy to give herself to him, even after watching him kill her friend. She smiled devotedly and tried to kiss him. But he grabbed her chin and tilted her face away so he could bite into the flesh of her neck.

He stared straight into my eyes as he drank her blood, studying my reaction. Watching him drain the life from her was easily one of the most captivating things I had ever seen. More glorious then any sunset, and more dazzling then a hundred rainbows. This woman was enjoying her death. All three of us were.

After her knees began to buckle, he draped her body across the throne. Sebastian stepped down two stairs, where the first blonde was already rising to meet him. She reached up and wrapped a hand around the back of his neck to pull him to her. As he leaned down to give her the same mortal kiss he gave the other two, my mind flashed to every vampire movie I had ever seen. Drinking their blood may not have been necessary for him, but it allowed him to absorb their souls. And with the glory of the show he was putting on for me, I agreed with his preference.

The third woman didn't last as long as the previous two. Once she lost consciousness, he let her slide out of his arms and drop to his feet. Blood pooled around the fallen women. It saturated the burgundy velvet, turned the white petals a bright crimson, and dripped down the throne. Sebastian stayed clean of any trace of the mess; completely composed and ready to move to his next victim.

She was already standing at the foot of the stairs waiting for him, wanting him probably as badly as I did. Sebastian pulled the chalice out of nowhere as they wrapped their arms around each other. Then he dipped her gracefully as if they were dancing. She smiled as she looked up at him. All the while, he looked at me with the same affection she gave him.

Sebastian grabbed the hair and pulled to force her head back. His smile changed then, but only slightly, growing just enough to allow his teeth to become closer to fangs.

One last look in my direction, and he bit through flesh and tendon, taking a chunk out of her neck and swallowing it in one gulp. He kept a firm hold on her hair as he stood and let the blood pour out of the wound, dripping down her neck and filling the chalice he placed below. Once the cup was filled, he held her out to the side of his body with one hand and released his grip on her locks, letting her fall to the ground with a dull thud.

Sebastian closed his eyes and took a deep breath. When he re-opened them, they were blue again, and burning violently. He had one drop of crimson coming from the corner of his lip. He wiped it away with his thumb, a simple act that seemed extra sexy from my point of view. His smile was radiant, and meant only for me as he strolled to my side. He peered at me adoringly and held the golden cup out for me to take.

"For you, my love," he purred as I reached for it.

Once the heavy chalice sat in my hands, I found myself compelled to lift it to my nose and take a whiff. The warmth wafting off the liquid inside had a fragrant, rusty scent that reminded me of iron. I closed my eyes and inhaled deeply.

When I reopened my eyes and looked up at Sebastian, there was something maniacal in his expression, like his act was slipping and the psychotic villain underneath was showing through. His eyes flashed black and he ripped the chalice from my hands.

The next thing I knew, I was in his arms, and sitting on the table that used to hold my painting supplies. Sebastian grabbed the back of my head and pulled me into a kiss. The surge I felt when our lips met almost made me collapse. I could taste their blood in his mouth, like a metallic sangria. His teeth were still sharp; they hadn't completely changed back. It was a miracle the kiss wasn't painful.

His hands followed the contours of my body before latching on to my hips with slightly painful force. Then he slammed our pelvises together, forcing the skirt of my dress up as I slid towards him. The savagery of it made me feel like he wanted to rip me apart rather than make love to me. For some sick reason, that made it so much hotter.

Sebastian pressed into me as we kissed, and I cursed the fabric that separated us. I was going crazy with my longing for him. I would have let him do anything to me. I hated the ache I felt. I hated him. And hated myself. I wished he'd kill me so I wouldn't have to feel like this anymore.

He took one hand away from my hip and leaned back enough to look down at me as I caught my breath. He squeezed my breast and attacked my throat with kisses.

"Would you die for me?" He asked.

"Yes." I didn't hesitate to answer this time. I felt a tear roll down my cheek.

He wrapped his hand around my throat and tilted my head away from him. And when his lips found the right spot, he sank his teeth into my neck. It was just a little nip, not enough to cause any damage. But I yelped, and he laughed. Then he kissed the slow trickle of blood escaping my flesh.

Sebastian slid a hand up my thigh and under my skirt, then wrapped his fingers around the side of my thong. He started slipping it down my leg and froze. I heard him growl and his body tensed up against mine. Then his hand balled into a fist.

He stopped kissing me and took in a deep breath. "If this wasn't the most important part, I would take you right here… And we could bathe in their blood."

"I don't think they're going anywhere," I said.

He took his hand out from under my skirt and kissed me again. "I think you may be my favorite yet." The most satisfied smile spread across his face. "I'll leave you to your work."

Sebastian kissed me again before he walked away. He left me sitting on the table, staring after him with my longing tearing at my soul. As he reached the door to the bar, he turned back to me one last time. "We celebrate tomorrow," he said, "I've left a gift for you."

Once he disappeared it took a few minutes to clear my head enough to check out the carnage he left behind. Upon closer inspection, I noticed that all the women were alive, barely. I watched them with morbid fascination as the last of their blood dripped from their bodies. One by one, their breathing gradually slowed to a halt. The scarlet liquid remained everywhere, oozing out from the soaked velvet drape and spreading across the marble floor in front of me. It was breath taking.

When I was sure they had all expired, and the blood was in its final resting place, I went back to my long forgotten canvas. What awaited me there stopped me in my tracks. This was not the same painting I had been working on for the past six weeks. All the same aspects were there, and it was obviously my brush strokes. But it was drastically different.

Sebastian was perched as I remembered in his throne, with that sexy, sadistic grin he always wore. But the women were different. They were all exactly as they were now, bloody and drained of life. They were even in the same positions. The only discrepancy was that the one draped over the throne was now placed over Sebastian's lap.

Had I really painted this? Was I in that much of a trance that I thought I was painting something else the whole time? That would mean that either he killed them to match my artwork, or that I had known all along exactly how he would end each one of their lives.

My shock and confusion were overwhelmed by a strong need, an urgency to finish what I had started, to make the picture I was working on mirror the magnificent scene in front of me. I grabbed the chalice and my nearest paintbrush, then went to the large painting with determination. A smile spread across my lips as I dipped the brush into the syrupy liquid and touched it to the canvas.

Chapter 16

Falling and Obsession

"You're a mess."

Vino's voice snapped me back into the present. I'd been so lost in my painting, I didn't notice him enter the room. Well, I guess I never notice him entering a room, ever. A quick survey of myself verified what he was talking about. I was covered in blood. The largest blotches were on my hands and forearms, but my dress was stained with crimson dots and smudges. I'd never be able to wear it again.

"Yeah, I guess I am. How long have you been here?"

"Half hour or so. I didn't want to bother you."

I put a bloody hand up to my forehead. "What time is it?"

"Midnight."

I set my brush down. Every last drop of blood in the over-sized chalice had been used. I must have been painting in a frenzy. "Seems like it should be later..."

Vino turned around and started heading for the door, a not so polite way of saying it's time to go. When we got to his car, he threw me a blanket from the back seat. "Do not get blood on the leather."

"I think it's all dried by now," I snapped. "Why is it such a big deal? You like blood."

"Just because I like the way it tastes, doesn't mean I'd enjoy it smeared on my upholstery. And I don't eat in my car."

I felt pretty stupid after he said it that way. At least he wasn't making me take my clothes off before I got in. I took special care to make sure the seat was completely covered. I wouldn't want to mess up one of my favorite vehicles.

Vino didn't say anything else until we drove away, and my necklace had been safely removed. "It doesn't bother you to have that much blood on you?"

I glanced down at my crusty, burgundy colored self. "Not really, this sometimes happens when I paint. I just forgot to wear a smock this time."

He lifted his hand off the shifter like he was going to touch me, then changed his mind and put it back. "You're bleeding."

I reached up and felt my neck. Sebastian must have bit me harder than I thought, because I had a couple good gashes in my skin, and a nice-sized blood trail that dried all the way down to my cleavage.

"Oh," I said. I felt ashamed he noticed that. My personal battles with giving myself to Sebastian weren't something I wanted to share. I tried to wipe some of the blood away, but it was too sore. So I stopped and stared out the window.

"You don't seem disturbed by all the death you saw tonight," Vino said.

I kept my eyes fixed on the passing lights. "I—I think I liked it. They enjoyed dying, they gave themselves so willingly. Then he left them there to die in front of me. I listened to them choking on their last breath, I watched the blood pool around them, it—it was beautiful."

Vino was quiet for a moment. "What he showed you, that's not how things really are... It was an act to give you a glimpse of what your subconscious wanted to see."

I nodded. I had a feeling that's not how he normally killed people. "I take it you watched too?"

"I was ordered to stick around, yes."

That meant he saw the other moments too. The ones of me and Sebastian. That hurt. I sighed. "So was the painting always like that? Have I been that much under his control from the beginning?"

"Since the first day."

I felt my tears welling up again. I remembered falling into his eyes and his face changing that evening. It was already too late for me, on the very first day.

"I would have told you," he said. "But it wouldn't have made a difference. You couldn't have seen what it really looked like until he let you… And you never would have believed me without seeing for yourself."

I looked at Vino and gave him a weak smile. "What's one more fucked up thing to add to the list? He's just going to keep doing whatever he wants to me, nothing I can do to stop it. You've already helped me more than you should have."

He didn't answer.

We pulled up in front of my crappy apartment building shortly after that. Normally when we got back from Sebastian's this early, we ended up at some pricey club, but my present condition would have raised alarms. So that was out of the question tonight. I opened my door to get out, but the way Vino was staring at me was too distracting.

"What?" I asked.

He didn't move. Not one muscle flinched. I hated when he did this. I took a deep breath and reached for the door handle again. "Good night?"

"Good night," he said.

I waited to see if he would say anything else. He didn't, so I stepped out of the car, and pushed his odd behavior to the back of my mind. There was not one single item that wasn't strange about the last few weeks. I didn't have the strength to worry. It was time to get some rest and turn my brain off for a while.

I took a long shower and crawled in bed. But sleep wouldn't come. On one hand, I was pretty sure I was going to sleep with Sebastian tomorrow. I shouldn't be excited about that. But I was. So I was also now experiencing a new level of self-loathing.

On the other hand, I knew my life was about to drastically change, in a really bad way. I didn't know what Sebastian had in mind for celebrations. Something told me it would involve blood, and death, and it was probably going to be very painful for me.

Four o'clock rolled around before I knew it, and I still wasn't tired. I climbed out of bed and stumbled to my kitchen to find something to drink. The dim light inside my fridge blinded my weary eyes as I bent down to grab a bottle of water. I stood up and chugged it, since restless nights always made me extra thirsty.

When the entire bottle had been depleted, I shut the fridge, extinguishing the light and leaving me in darkness. I turned to the side to toss the bottle in the sink, and caught something moving from the corner of my eye. I spun around as fast as I could manage.

The temperature dropped drastically as the shadows on the floor swirled around like smoke. A black mass slowly swelled up from the center like it was floating through the floor from the apartment beneath me.

I pressed myself into the counter and held my breath.

The shadows spun faster and faster and energy charged the air around me. The mass grew taller than me and started to take shape, growing bulkier and filling to a solid being. Then a pair of glowing red eyes appeared in the middle of a face too dark to see.

I shrieked.

A low laugh answered me from the darkness. I recognized it immediately and almost collapsed with relief.

"Jesus!" I gasped.

"Not quite," Vino answered.

I put a hand to my chest and bent over to catch my breath. My racing heart apparently didn't get the notice that I wasn't really in any danger. "You're an asshole."

"I said I'd show you how I get in here someday... Now you know."

"That was actually kinda cool." I straightened up and laughed, a little. "But don't you ever do that to me again." I pointed at him to add emphasis. "And what're you doing here at this ungodly hour?"

"I was in the neighborhood." Vino took a step forward so we could see each other better in the darkness. I would have never guessed he was just a collection of shadows a moment ago if I hadn't actually seen it.

"You're always in the neighborhood. I meant why are you here right now? Don't you ever sleep?"

"Of course I sleep. Just not as often as you do... It doesn't look like you're getting much rest tonight anyways."

As my eyes adjusted to the lack of light, I could see he was smiling at me. But I couldn't tell if he was up to something. "You didn't have to sneak up on me like that."

"But it's so much fun. You scare easily."

"Anyone would be frightened by a monster rising out of their floor. There's nothing special about that."

"You're right," he said. "Then I guess I'm just making excuses to drop in on you."

"No really, why are you here?"

Vino shrugged. "Why not?"

I couldn't think of one reason for him not to be there right now. "Valid point."

We threw in a generic action flick to pass the time, and took our spots next to each other on the couch. I bet I was asleep within the first ten minutes.

I woke up the next morning on that same couch. The TV was on in front of me, and someone else was flipping through the channels. There was a blanket draped over me that I didn't remember grabbing. It fell off when I sat up to stretch. "Good morning."

Vino smiled at me. "Morning."

I went to the kitchen to slap myself in the face with some caffeine, and found a Starbucks bag on the counter. "Couldn't quite bring yourself to start my machine for me?"

He chuckled but didn't answer. I took that as a yes, and went back to the couch with my cup. I wrapped myself with the blanket and pulled my knees into my chest. The coolness of the room still got me sometimes when he was around.

"Are we doing something today? You're here awful early."

He shrugged. "If you want to we can... I never left, except to get coffee. So it doesn't count as waiting for you."

I giggled quietly to myself. "So we had a sleep over? That's so cute."

"I'm cute now?" He sighed. "Ouch."

"Sorry, but you kinda are. Don't think I didn't notice you tucked me in last night."

"I did no such thing."

"Then where did the blanket come from?" I laughed so hard I almost spilled my coffee. I guess I should have been more grateful for how nice he was being, but it *was* pretty funny. He owed me some kicks at his expense.

Vino didn't answer me, again. He just shot me a dirty look and went to the kitchen to spice up his coffee with the last of my three hundred dollar bottle of scotch. I glared at him. But in truth, I didn't mind in the slightest.

We hung out at my place for a few hours. It felt so natural having him around now, that the time flew by. We were both sitting on the couch watching some trashy daytime talk show, when I started to get hungry. I glanced at the clock. It was almost noon. "Are we going out for lunch today?"

"If you want to."

It still felt strange to have him so agreeable. "What about the yacht? Can we take it out for a few hours?"

Vino's expression turned sour. "There is no yacht anymore."

"What?! What do you mean there's no yacht?"

"It's at the bottom of the harbor now. That was my punishment for whisking you away for the day. Sebastian set the damn thing on fire." He gave me a crooked smirk. "You owe me a new boat."

"Well, I would have felt sorry for you," I said with an eye roll.

He laughed. "So where are we eating?"

"Let's go to Central Park, get a hotdog or something."

"You're kidding… We have all the money in the world to eat wherever we want, and you're choosing a hotdog cart? That's disgusting."

"I'm not choosing the hotdogs, you jerk. I'm choosing the park. So, just get over yourself for one minute and spend a day living like a normal person. It's really not that bad."

Vino squeezed his temples. "We can go to the park. But we're eating at a restaurant first."

I tried covering the gashes on my neck with some band-aids before we left. I came to the conclusion that I would make a terrible nurse, and ended up leaving the wounds uncovered. They were really tender today. And I looked like I'd been attacked by a wild animal.

We had lunch at a restaurant with a view of the park. It was high-priced and stuffy. And it's a good thing I didn't like large portions, because there weren't any here. Our waitress, a classy looking blonde with blue eyes and tits big enough to stretch the buttonholes on her shirt, dropped off Vino's third scotch of the meal. I was still on my first Merlot. He winked at her as she left, and she almost dropped her tray.

My first reaction was to get mad. Though I'm not sure why, because that's just what Vino did. I think I was starting to fig-

ure him out. I mean, why does anyone flirt? It's for the attention. And the more I thought about it, I really believed that
deep down, under all the violence and all the ego, Vino was just
lonely.

I started to feel sad when I realized that this was probably going to be our last day hanging out. He was my only friend right
now. That fact was even more depressing. Something horrible
was going to happen tonight, and it was hanging over both our
heads. We avoided talking about it.

"Will you be honest with me about something?" I asked.

"Always am."

I could have called him a liar, but I needed this answer.
"There's something I don't understand. If Sebastian can make
me do and feel whatever he wants, why bother with all the flattery? Why would he waste time tricking me into falling for
him?"

Vino frowned and took a long drink. "Are you sure you want
me to answer that? You'll feel worse after you know, trust me."

"I don't care. I want to know."

He avoided eye contact with me by looking at the trees out
the window. "It's all about feeling worshiped. He wants you to
not only accept the pain he causes you, but thank him for it in
the name of devotion. He says there's more satisfaction in hurting someone who loves you."

My tears started to betray me again, but I caught them in
time to keep them hidden. "Thanks for telling me."

"You shouldn't thank me. I didn't do you any favors by telling
you."

He kept me at the restaurant longer than I wanted, but gave
in quickly when I complained about his promise to go to the
park. I tried to put my thoughts of impending doom aside, and
enjoy my day out with him. We walked around the trails and
talked smack to each other for a while. As twisted as it sounds,
I actually liked arguing with him. Exchanging the occasional
quip felt more like flirting then insults.

A couple approached us from the opposite direction with a
large German Sheppard. The second it saw Vino, it growled.

Then he looked at it, and the dog put its tail between its legs and yelped. It tried to run away and ended up yanking the man holding his leash off the path and making him trip.

I covered my mouth with my hand to hide the fact that I was laughing at them.

Vino grabbed my arm to direct me in the opposite direction. I could tell he was about to laugh too. "Maybe we should go sit somewhere away from the path. We don't need to make spectacles of ourselves."

I nodded and complied, mostly because I was distracted by the fact that he actually felt comfortable touching me in a casual way.

He led me over to a crooked tree about two hundred feet off the trail. It overlooked a small metal bridge with a curved archway. He took a seat beneath it and leaned his back against the trunk. I followed suit and sat down.

"Does that happen with animals a lot?"

"Sometimes," he said. "Supposedly animals can sense evil. These days it's never a problem. But when horses were the main source of transportation, it made things more complicated."

"Yeah, you seem real evil right now, Vino."

He sighed, and I laughed. Apparently, when you tell a demon he's not scary or evil, it's about as emasculating as telling them they have a small dick.

I relaxed under that tree next to him, drinking in the moment. I was sure I wouldn't get too many more like this. I doubted Sebastian would want to come sit at a park with me once he'd begun his rounds of torture. At least I had a decent date today, though I was surprised that he agreed to come here with me. I knew this wasn't his type of outing, but he seemed to enjoy himself as much as I did.

Vino stared off in to space, looking completely at ease. I watched him, wondering what he was thinking about as the light breeze tousled his shiny, ebony hair. I smiled as I noticed how handsome he looked with the little flecks of sunlight dancing over his skin. I couldn't think of anyone else I wanted to be with right now.

Wait a minute… what was that last part?

Was I… falling for Vino?

I suddenly felt dizzy. This was bad. I took a couple deep breaths to calm myself down. It didn't work.

No, no, no. I pleaded to myself. But it was too late. The realization already hit me. I wasn't falling. I already fell, and I was now a broken mess at the bottom of an endless pit.

What the fuck was wrong with me?! How did I not notice this happening? How on earth did the person I had once hated the most in this life, now become the object of my affection? I'd been so fixated on my annoyances with Vino that I wasn't paying attention to how much I actually liked about him. This was no fleeting crush that swept over me. This was powerful and intense. This was a lot closer to…

No, I couldn't even think the word. But it was there, waiting for me to give in and pluck it out. All his arrogance, all his viciousness, the cruelty paired with the uneasy kindness; I wanted it all. I was obsessed with his tormented soul and all the death that surrounded it. I loved him.

I put both hands over my face and tried to pull myself together.

Vino noticed. "What wrong with you all of a sudden?"

"Nothing, I'm fine."

"You don't look fine." He leaned closer to get a better look at my stunned expression, stopping with less than six inches between our faces.

That made things so much worse. I tried to avoid his eyes, because mine might give me away. But I couldn't bring myself to do it. I stared right into them with a dumb grin on my face. A strange new urge was starting to tug at the back of my mind. I wanted to kiss him.

I did my best to hide it. "Guess I'm having a blonde moment."

"Must be rough." He raised an eyebrow at me. I'm not sure he bought it, but he leaned back against the tree.

I laid on the grass to put some distance between us, and threw my arm over my eyes. I didn't move for at least ten minutes. It was agony. Nothing good was going to come of this.

Why hadn't I loved Lucas? It would have been so easy, so normal. Lucas could have made me happy. He would have loved me back.

Vino was never going to love me. He was simply incapable of reciprocating the feelings that were now ripping me apart. Falling for him was one of the worst things that could happen right now. Not just for my sake, but for his. Sebastian would find out. There was no avoiding it, and the repercussions were going to be terrible. This kind of love could only end one way; my death, and very possibly his too.

"Are you planning on ignoring me all day?" Vino asked. His voice came from closer then it should have.

I removed my arm and peeked in the direction I heard him. He was lying down next to me, propped up on one elbow. I was delighted to see his face, and did a horrible job of hiding it. "I wasn't ignoring you."

"Right, you were just trying to take a nap and leave me here to sit alone. That's almost as bad."

"Unintentional, I promise." *Play it off Trinity.* He can't figure this out. I can't let him know. This was so, so wrong. But the way he was lying next to me, being so casual in such an intimate setting, felt like pillow talk. I was about to break in two.

"I can probably forgive you," he said. "We're being watched, you know."

"By who?"

He laughed a little. "The a... twins as you call them, have been ratting me out for every move I make the last couple weeks. They're a tad closer than normal, trying to hear what we're talking about. They seem to think I haven't noticed what they're doing."

My heart broke. No wonder Sebastian knew everything before we showed up. "Then why are you here with me? This can't be safe for you."

"I doubt they can hear much. Besides, all Sebastian can do is kill me, and I haven't crossed that line." He laid back and threw his arms behind his head. "I'm surprised you're so worried about me."

Don't look at him... I closed my eyes and took a deep breath. "Didn't say I was."

"I'm sure that's the case."

I snuck a peek at him to make sure he wasn't looking at me. His eyes were fixed on the branches above, and there was a smile on his face. I had to close my eyes again to keep from staring at him, but he was there too, waiting behind my eyelids. It was almost like the forced ache I felt for Sebastian, a blind need where all I could think of was him. But this time it was caused by me. And this hurt more.

I was almost in tears when his voice broke through my thoughts again. "Maybe we should take off."

That was a good idea. This was way too intense for me right now. "Sure, why not."

Vino stood and grabbed my hand to help me up. My chest seized when the current hit me. I couldn't even look up at his face. I think I was ashamed. I felt like I had committed some horrible crime against him. He must have felt my hesitation, because he dropped my hand the second I was on my feet.

He didn't turn to leave. He just stood there watching me, trying to figure out what was going on without asking anything. His face went blank again, and I wondered what conclusions he had drawn. It felt so awkward, wrestling internally over my craving to reach for him, but needing to keep my infatuation a secret. Being around Vino lately had been as easy as breathing. And I had to go mess that all up.

He glanced towards the path and slipped his hands into his pockets. "Lets go. We don't want to be late."

I nodded and followed him quietly across the grass. I was so compelled to touch him, that I caved in. I wrapped my hand around the inside of his thick bicep, so that we were walking almost arm in arm. His pace slowed, then his eyebrows dropped in the center and he looked down at my hand. But he otherwise allowed this action. I couldn't tell if it was the energy coming off him, or my own butterflies, but I was floating. Such a ridiculous amount of joy from such a trivial thing. It was pathetic.

We walked that way the entire distance to the car. By the time we got there, it was second nature. Even Vino seemed completely comfortable with it. I'm sure Amelie and Andras were getting a kick out of this, and Sebastian was going to be livid. But I didn't care. I wondered why Vino would oblige me in such a way. His punishment was probably going to be worse then mine. I hoped it meant that he did care for me, even if it was only a little.

The ride back to my place was quiet; more of the uneasy silence I'd orchestrated. When we parked out front he popped the trunk and pulled out a garment bag. "I'm supposed to give you this."

"Another dress? What's that for?"

His face was blank again, and his voice was quiet and detached. "We're celebrating tonight, remember? I was informed that you needed to look presentable."

I watched his expressionless eyes waiting for something, anything to change. He looked away from me. "Guess I forgot about that," I said.

Vino carried the bag upstairs for me, and sat patiently on my couch while I changed into its contents and fixed myself up. The dress was exceptional, as they always were. It was black and shorter than was comfortable, hanging off both shoulders with sleeves that were just long enough to cover my bruises. I would have enjoyed wearing it if the circumstances were different.

He smiled at me when I emerged from the bathroom. "Looks good."

I blushed, that was the first normal compliment he'd ever given me.

I sat on the couch next to him and pulled my ankles up on the cushion. We only had fifteen minutes before we had to leave. It took all my strength to not burst into tears. "Do we really have to go?"

"You already know the answer to that."

Yes, I did, but I was still pleading into his eyes. "That sucks."

"I'm not happy about it either." One side of his mouth turned up in a sad little smile. Then he put his arm around me. "I'd kill him if I could… But I don't stand a chance against him."

I took that as his way of apologizing for not being able to save me. That act of friendship carried so much more meaning coming from him. "I've already given up on getting out of this. I know you're in almost as bad of a situation as I am."

Vino was quiet for a moment. "I want you to prepare yourself for what we're about to walk into."

I nodded. While I was in his arms, I felt at ease. But I knew what kind of trouble today caused. I closed my eyes and snuggled into him. He rested his cheek against my head.

I felt like I was having a heart attack when we pulled in front of Sebastian's apartment. I realized I hadn't taken a single pill, and I only had one drink. Going into this sober seemed like a really bad idea. My guilt was eating away at me so bad, I debated coming clean with Vino, and admitting how I felt so he would be prepared when he was attacked for it. Naturally, I was too chicken to do such a thing. I was still having trouble admitting this to myself.

We didn't speak to each other as we went upstairs. There was a lot I still wanted to say to him, but I couldn't find the words. I didn't put on the necklace until we were in the elevator.

Amelie and Andras were standing together with the most twisted smiles on their faces, looking like much more evil versions of tattle-tailing children. They were dressed for a special occasion. Amelie wore a long, teal dress that made her look like a movie star. Andras was in all black, except for a tie that appeared to have been specially made to match Amelie. She leaned into his chest and toyed with his collar while he had his arm around her.

Sebastian sat in front of the twins, directly adjacent to where my painting had been set up for viewing. He stayed completely composed as we walked in, and gave me the same dazzling smile he did every other day. He looked just as handsome, just as debonair. He was the same majestic, god-like creature he always was.

But my thoughts were on someone else entirely. There was no switch that went off, focusing my entirety on him like I was used to. Vino was all I could think about. His face was the one in the front of my mind.

As Sebastian strolled over to meet me, I forced myself to picture the scene from last night to get Vino out of my head. I dwelled on the sound of the last breath of one of the women, and visualized Sebastian's smile as he handed me the chalice. I even focused on my memories of kissing him. Anything to distract from what was really on my mind.

"Hello, Trinity," Sebastian purred, sounding completely devilish. He cupped my cheek in his hand and leaned towards my face. "I heard a vicious rumor today. For your sake, I hope it's not true."

I would have made an excuse, or come up with some lie to tell him. But my whole body went numb and I couldn't open my mouth to speak. Sebastian forced pictures of my day to float past my eyes. Every image was of Vino, and they grew steadily more vivid as we reached the part in the park. My heart seized as I saw him sitting under the tree with the breeze in his hair, and started reliving the feeling I had at that moment.

Sebastian's smile vanished. He lowered his hand away from my face so quickly I thought he was going to slap me. Only his eyes went to Vino, though I could tell something passed between them. I started to panic at the thought of Sebastian killing him. I wanted to scream to tell him to run, but I was unable to move.

My anxiety only irked Sebastian more. His lip curled and he glared at me. When he spoke his words came out as more of a growl. "That's unexpected, isn't it?"

Amelie laughed in the background. "Told you they looked friendly."

Sebastian lifted a hand to silence her. "I must say, I never saw this one coming." He smiled, and I knew he was about to do something really nasty to me. "Thankfully, there are ways to remedy such a complication."

He grabbed me and pulled me against him. Every fiber of my being screamed *submit.* I went limp and my breathing slowed. My heart only beat because he told it to.

I saw Vino take a step forward out of the corner of my eye. Sebastian snarled at him and he stopped in his tracks. "And you... You are going to suffer so many lifetimes for this." His eyes started to shift to black. "If I ever catch you in the same room with her again, you die. Leave now or I will rip you in two."

Vino didn't move. Sebastian's energy surged and threatened to rob me of my consciousness. "Perhaps you're not the one I need to threaten," he said.

He grabbed my hair and tilted my head back, then bared his fangs and smiled at Vino. Though I couldn't see him well from my rag doll position in Sebastian's arms, I could tell he bowed his head and started to move away.

Sebastian released his grip on my curls, but otherwise kept his hold on me. "Isn't that sweet," he taunted.

Heavy, silent tears rolled from my eyes. I couldn't see Vino anymore. This was all my fault. Who knew how many centuries Vino was going to pay for my indiscretions. I wanted to at least watch him leave, to see him one more time. But my body was not under my control anymore.

"There's no reason to celebrate now, is there? And I had been so looking forward to tonight." Sebastian's eyes stopped mid-change. There was only a sliver of blue left in the outer ring of his irises. His words were dripping with venom as he inched closer to my face. "*No one defies me,* Trinity. I will have my way. And you will submit to my every desire."

His hand latched onto my side and his fingers dug into my flesh. It felt like he was stabbing me with hundreds of needles. I screamed and recoiled from the pain. But he just held me tighter and drove the feeling deeper.

"I had pictured our union as being much more beautiful... But you had to go and ruin my plans, didn't you?" Sebastian released my side, and dropped me to the cold floor at his feet.

The room spun around me as I fought to keep my eyes open. The pain radiated through my insides and burned me to the core. I could feel the abyss coming for me, slowly covering me like a warm blanket.

I heard Sebastian growl from somewhere above me. "Get this trash of my sight. She'll be worthless for days."

Then everything went black.

I awoke on the middle of my floor. I was unable to get up, and I had no idea how long I'd been there. I laid there for hours, fighting against the pain and nausea. I screamed, and cried, and prayed for death. When I was finally able to will myself to move, I crawled to my bed and pulled myself on top by climbing my blankets.

I reached up to remove the heavy chain that hung around my neck. I fumbled for the clasp, but couldn't find it. Panic sank in as I frantically pulled at it, trying to find its weak point. There was none. The necklace was now a solid band fused all the way around. My own personal, platinum noose.

With great effort, and unsteady hands, I lifted my dress to inspect the damage where all the pain originated from. I wasn't bleeding. There had been no real needles. Instead, there was a large dark spot, too black and deep to be a bruise. It was layers under my flesh, and had shadowy veins spiraling out from all sides and pulsing under my skin.

Another wave of pain hit me, and I curled into a ball, shrieking as tears poured down my cheeks. All hope was gone now. This was only the beginning of my torture. Sebastian was done playing nice. I had been successfully reduced to property.

The pain tunneled deeper into my body, sending spasms down my spine. I buried my face in my pillow to stifle my screams. Tremors began to overtake me, and I clawed at my mattress, trying to hold still.

Then a hand gently touched the back of my head. A calming current flowed through me. It wasn't nearly enough to make the pain go away, but the tremors slowed. I knew it was Vino, and I tried to look at him, but another influx of pain shot through me. My vision went out, and I curled into a tighter ball.

Vino grabbed the front of my necklace and I heard a loud snap, then felt him slide it out from around my throat. The second it was off the pain subsided, fading into a dull numbness and clearing my sight.

"You shouldn't be here," I whispered, as I started to become more coherent.

"Bought myself some time. Thought I'd help ease your suffering."

I pushed myself up on one arm so I could look at him. His eyes were shining in the dim light, giving off a deep red glow. It was the happiest sight I could have seen at that moment.

"I can't do anything about that mark... But it shouldn't hurt as much now."

A new set of tears flowed from my eyes. These were filled with joy. I threw my arms around his neck and pinned myself to him. "I didn't think I'd ever see you again."

Vino wrapped his arms around me, and hugged me back. He held me there for a long moment. "I can't stay," he said. "Sebastian would have felt the necklace being severed. If I want to live through the night I need to go beg forgiveness... Now that he knows he can use you against me, it might help your chances."

He had to pry my arms from his neck to step away from me. But I didn't stop him from walking away, even though every step he took was another blow to the chest. The only person I ever loved was about to walk out of my life forever. I wouldn't allow myself to call out to him. He was going to go suffer enough because of me. I didn't need to make things worse.

Vino made it almost all the way to the door, then stopped and peered at me from the corner of his eye. He took a deep breath, then looked down at the floor. "I have this... obsession with you," he said. "It's eating away at me, driving me mad. I can't let him have you... But I don't know how to save you."

He laughed uneasily and shook his head. "It's terribly aggravating, you know. Not being able to get you out of my head. Having to spend nearly every second of every day with you, and not being able to do anything about it." He took his last two steps to the door and started twisting the doorknob. "You're probably going to haunt me for the rest of my life."

All reasoning left me, and with a great amount of effort, I jumped out of bed on wobbly legs and ran to him. "No, wait!"

He didn't look at me, but he also didn't open the door. I stopped a couple feet behind him, and begged with tears in my eyes. "Please don't go—don't leave me."

Vino didn't move for a second, then he slowly took his hand off the knob. "So you'll condemn us both to die then?"

My heart sank. That's really what I was doing, killing us both by begging him to stay. After everything I had been through, I was still so selfish that I was willing to let him die for a few more minutes together. I was putting another man in danger because I couldn't put his needs above my own.

He spun around to face me, then reached out and pulled me to him. And he smiled. "I suppose I can live with that."

Vino put one hand behind my neck, and leaned closer to my face. He hesitated a few inches from my lips. It seemed like he was bracing himself for impact, debating the sin he was about to commit.

Then he closed the distance, and crashed our lips together. A surge of raw emotion passed between us. The desperation I felt coming from him almost matched my own need. But the energy transferring to me left me feeling like I'd been dropped underwater. I clung to him, and gasped for breath.

I knew he'd probably kill me. I didn't care. I wanted death. One night together made everything I'd been through worth it. I'd die happy.

I was so lost in the feeling of his lips as they moved against mine, that I didn't notice we made it back to my bed until I was already lying on it. My head started swimming, and darkness crept in from the corners of my vision. I reached up and grabbed a handful of hair at the back of his head, and kissed him harder. No, I was not going to pass out now. I would not allow myself to lose consciousness.

Vino eased back to let me catch my breath, and used the opportunity to grab my dress and tear it open in one clean rip. He paused to look down at me, and his eyes went black. Then, being rougher than I'm sure he intended, he ripped my dress the rest of the way off. I eagerly pulled at the buttons of his shirt, but he beat me to it and lifted it over his head. He didn't wait for me to help him with his pants either. And somewhere in the throes of things, my underwear disappeared too.

He laid himself over me, bringing every inch of our naked bodies together. We kissed, and we touched, and I surrendered to the euphoria. I wanted to scream that I loved him, and let him know that I was his, and always would be.

I could feel myself slipping again, slowly fading into the black. I wasn't ready to let go yet.

Vino backed off, like he could tell I was fading. I took a few short, ragged breaths and opened my eyes. He kissed my neck, wrapped his hand around my throat, and tilted my face away to give him better access. It was the perfect balance of forceful and tender. I knew he was trying not to hurt me, but I kind of wanted him to. I'd forgive him if he killed me. I hoped he knew that.

He hoisted his body weight onto his arms, and looked down at me with the sexiest grin I had ever seen. I bit my lip as I stared up at him, admiring how beautiful he was. I grabbed his neck and pulled him back down to me. His hair tickled my temples when it hung in my face as kissed. He slowly slid his hand to my hip, where he grabbed hold and tilted it towards him. He broke our kiss just long enough to allow me to scream from the first thrust.

Chapter 17

The Man She Hated

Well, I didn't die. Though that's probably what my neighbors thought occurred. They pounded on the wall a couple times, which Vino seemed to think was hilarious. Every time they did it, he would intentionally do something else to make me scream.

I gave myself a good stretch in the emptiness of my bed. I didn't expect Vino to be the type to cuddle after coupling, but I was still disappointed I didn't wake up in his arms. I frowned and rolled to my side. Almost every muscle in my body ached, and I was weak and sluggish. Moving my legs was the hardest part; my hips felt like they had been pulled out of the sockets.

So worth it. I grinned to myself, remembering the bliss of our union. We had both been a little emotional, which made things intense at first. But it did become a lot easier. And I was able master the art of breathing again. What happened last night was not sex. The mechanics of it were the same, mostly, but what went on beneath the surface was something else entirely.

I must have been doing it wrong all these years.

What can I say about Vino as a lover? Most of it's not repeatable. But I was convinced he was a mind reader now. That man could write a book on pleasing women. I could draw the illustrations for him. He's commanding, and personal, and only liked positions where he could look me in the eye. Which was weird, since his were empty, black pits. He's also a biter. I'm sure I didn't have a mark on me, but I didn't want to think about what that meant for the people he normally bedded.

And yet, the emotional experience was even better than the physical. I had never experienced *love* before, not in any form, or for anything. Now that I knew what it was like, I would never be able to have plain old sex again. I never wanted to be intimate with another person, ever. Vino may not love me the same way I loved him, but he was willing to sacrifice his life for me, and that was close enough.

So was the sex that great because he was just that good? Or because he wasn't human? Or because I was completely, insanely in love with him? I guess I'll never know, but I bet it had to do with all three.

Once I pulled myself out of my musings, I sat up and searched the room for Vino. At first glance, I didn't see him and panicked. Then I noticed a pair of flashy shoes propped up on one of the bar stools in my kitchen, and knew he was just out of my sight.

I braced myself and slid out of bed, threw on my robe, and headed over to him. Once I was up and moving, my ailments became quite tolerable, though the bowlegged feeling was hard to shake off. I felt like skipping, or maybe running full speed and pouncing him.

Vino was reading a paper with a coffee and a doughnut. He was fully dressed, I'm assuming because he had to step out to retrieve his breakfast items. It was a completely normal, human scene for him to appear in.

He lowered his paper as I neared, then winked at me and pulled his feet off the chair. "Didn't expect you to be getting around so easily this morning..."

I weaseled my way close to him and threw my arms around his neck. "Pain is how your body tells you it had fun."

He gave me a truly happy smile. "I did a stand-up job of not killing you last night, didn't I?"

"I wouldn't have been mad if you did."

"I'll keep that in mind." Vino teased, then kissed me. I shuddered when our lips made contact. He laughed and pulled away. "You should probably eat. There's coffee and doughnuts on the counter. I couldn't go far, so our options are limited."

"Thanks, I am pretty hungry." Starving was more like it. I felt utterly depleted.

I took his advice and went to the counter to rummage through the doughnuts. I stuffed three in my face and chugged half my coffee. Then I went to the bathroom to freshen up. As I washed my hands I realized there was blood under my nails, and two were broken. I hoped they weren't still embedded in his back.

When I emerged from the bathroom, I grabbed Vino's hand as I walked by, and tugged him towards the couch. He offered no resistance, and draped his arm around me as we took our seats together. I nestled in against him with a very satisfied smile endowing my face. This is exactly where I wanted to be right now, and who I wanted to be with. Who needed drugs or booze anymore? All I had to do to get my fix was touch him, and voila; instant tranquility.

"You floored me in the park yesterday," he said.

I reached out to take his hand, then threaded my fingers through his. "How'd I do that?"

"Your emotions... That need. I've never felt anything like it before."

"Neither have I," I mumbled. That sucked all the happiness out of my moment. He knew I loved him. I guess I wanted him to, but sharing such an intimate emotion was terrifying. "So you can tell what I'm feeling too?"

"Only when I'm touching you." He winked at me. "Definitely made for an interesting night."

I elbowed him in the ribs. It hurt my elbow. "That's cheating."

Vino laughed. "I didn't hear you complain."

"Why didn't you tell me? It would have been nice to have a heads up about something that potentially damaging."

"You never asked. And I'm glad you didn't know. Everyone I come in contact with always feels the same shallow, sinful emotions towards me. But you were so different. And then whatever happened yesterday... that was so intense and pure, and you were ashamed to feel it." He pulled me tighter against him. "I never expected, or wanted, you to feel that way. Because I knew what it would mean for you. But Trinity, it's the most wonderful thing I've ever felt."

I sighed. "That's still a serious invasion of privacy. I would have preferred to admit that when I was ready."

"When would that have been? I wasn't supposed to ever see you again. And you haven't had a moment of privacy since the night I met you."

"Please at least say you can't see in my head. I don't think I could take it," I pleaded. I swear, if he said yes, I was going to cry.

He chuckled. "I only wish I could."

"Thank God."

Vino rested his head against mine. "There's something I should probably tell you," he said.

In my experience, nothing good ever followed those words. A pit of doubt formed in my chest. The fact that I knew he could feel it turned it into a swirling vortex.

He let go of me and turned to give a reassuring smile. "It's nothing like that. I just thought you might want to know who we really are. Who Sebastian really is. When I told you he was third in line, that was a half-truth. His real name is Asmodeus."

I gave him a blank look. "Is that supposed to mean something?"

Vino laughed. "I guess not... There's mention of him in the Catholic and Hebrew versions of the bible."

"Still not ringing any bells."

"This isn't getting me anywhere," he said to himself. "Many of the stories are contradicting anyways. But there is a grain of truth to them… Have you heard of the seven kings of Hell?"

"No."

"Do you at least know who Lucifer is?"

"I'm not that dumb."

"Okay, that's a start. Ultimately, Lucifer is in charge of everything, but there are six others who rule alongside him; two more fallen angels and four demons. Each one represents a different cardinal sin. Lucifer is Pride, Beelzebub is Gluttony, Leviathan is Envy…"

I could see where this was going, and I was having a hard time keeping a straight face. I covered my mouth with my hand.

"Asmodeus is Lust. He's the highest ranked demon and the only one able to infect others with desire. It's an ability passed down to everyone in his bloodline."

I broke out in laughter. I laughed so long and hard my eyes watered. I even snorted. "Oh my God," I choked out. "That makes so much sense."

Vino wasn't amused. "This isn't funny."

"You're right, it's not funny. It's completely fucking hilarious. I mean, no wonder…" I tried to quiet my laughter, since I could tell it was bothering him. I just wasn't very successful. And the more I looked at the serious expression on his face, the funnier I thought all this was. "Damn, Vino, how do you expect me to react? Just look at you two. Of course he's the demon of lust. You might as well be wearing a sign."

He shook his head. "And I normally have such good taste in women."

"Screw you."

"You already did."

That comment sent my mind in a completely different direction. My memories of last night flooded me, and a familiar stirring tugged at my more delicate areas. A big grin spread across Vino's face.

"You're an asshole."

He laughed. "You wouldn't like me if I was nice to you all the time."

I climbed on his lap and straddled him, then grabbed a handful of his hair and yanked it so he had to look up at me. "Oh please Vino, tell me what an idiot I am. You're so sexy when you insult me."

His body shook from laughter underneath me. I was still naked under my robe, and having him between my legs put me right back into the danger zone. He grabbed my face with both his hands and pulled me down to him.

"You're such a moron," he said. Then he kissed me.

The energy hit me with the force of a tsunami. I almost collapsed on top of him. The black started closing in a lot faster this time. I pulled back and smiled at him to disguise the fact that I needed a moment to breathe. Then I realized he would have already noticed. Not fair.

Vino grabbed the tie to my robe and tugged it loose, exposing my bare skin to him. He paused for a minute and just looked at me. Then he shook his head and started laughing.

"What?" I snapped.

"Different context..."

"Huh?"

"Seeing you naked, when you actually want me to," he said. "You glow, you know. It's intoxicating. Like you're in color and everything else is in black and white. If there was ever such a thing as demon bait, you're it."

I didn't know whether to be flattered, or completely freaked out. "More things you just didn't feel the need to tell me?"

He laughed. "Didn't want to admit it."

"Your sister sure didn't think I was special."

"She was lying."

He wrapped his hands around my back, and lifted me enough so that my breasts were at eye level. He nuzzled his face between them, and kissed and nipped at them. "I still think you're too skinny. I'm not supposed to see all your ribs."

I pulled his hair to show my annoyance, but I knew he only said that because he was uncomfortable admitting everything else. He paused at the left nipple and rolled it between his teeth.

I squeezed him with my thighs and tightened my grip on his soft hair.

As his lips, and teeth, moved skillfully along my flesh, I started to become lightheaded again. It was enough that my vision started to go out, and I felt like I was swaying from side to side. Vino felt it, and immediately backed off.

I pulled his face back to mine and forced him to kiss me. I had to have him now, even if it made me blackout. I skipped over his shirt and reached for his belt.

He grabbed my hand. "I don't think you can handle that right now."

The dizziness made it hard to speak, but I managed to snap at him anyways. "Who the Hell are you to tell me what I can or can't handle?"

"Do you not remember anything from last night?"

"I have very fond memories of it actually, which is precisely why you need to take your pants off."

Vino kissed me, but he was laughing so hard it didn't count. "I'm not good with self-control, Trinity. I really don't want to kill you, and with as sensitive as you are, that takes a lot of effort. You kept talking me out of stopping, and like a fool, I gave in every time. Eventually you blacked out completely. You're already so weak I doubt you'd last five minutes before you reached that point again. I could suck the life right out of you without even meaning to."

I did remember all the fighting I had to do with my consciousness. I was just hoping he hadn't. I shut my robe started to climb off him. "Then you shouldn't have touched me at all!"

"It's extremely difficult not to." He grabbed me and kept me on his lap, then wrapped his arms around my back and hid his face in my chest. "You know there's no happy ending coming for us," he said. "Even if by some miracle we live through today, I can't stay with you...We can't be together."

His words came at me like a steamroller, crushing my heart into dust. I knew what he was saying was true, but I didn't want to believe it. I would lie to myself until the day I died if I had to. Which probably wouldn't be a very long time.

Vino looked up at me. It looked like what he said hurt him just as much as it hurt me. "Whether I mean to do it or not, I'll destroy you the very same way he would. Night after night, depleting you of your life force until you waste away to nothing. Every time I touch you, I'm sucking a little more away."

"I don't care."

"I suppose you wouldn't… but it's not fair of you to ask me to watch as I do the very thing I'm trying to save you from. Besides, you don't really want me anyways. Just because there's one human I don't want dead, doesn't transform me into a good guy. I've killed a lot of people, and I will continue to do so for the rest of my existence."

"I said I don't care. Kill everyone in the city. Kill everyone in the entire country. I don't give a fuck." I said. "I know I'm being selfish, but I won't allow you to make excuses. The only thing that's going to kill me is if you leave."

His eyebrows squeezed together in the middle. "Trinity, we're not going to live long enough to worry about such things. Take comfort in the fact that we had one night together. We've got a few hours, if we're lucky, before Sebastian comes for us. He already knows what happened. They're biding their time now, waiting to see what our next move is. My siblings are staying just far enough away that if I go after one of them the other can get to you."

I sniffed back a couple tears. "I'm sorry. I should have never asked you to stay."

He chuckled. "I was dead the second I showed up here. I wasn't really going anywhere. I just wanted to hear you beg."

"You're lying."

Vino shrugged. "You think so? Why would I need to use your door to leave?"

I punched him in the arm as hard as I could, which was feeble, at best. He cracked up, and kissed the tight line that was my lips. "Told you I'm not that nice."

"I still think you're lying to me."

He ignored me. "If we go somewhere public it might buy us a few more hours. Sebastian needs to keep a low profile, so I doubt anyone will come after us out in the open." He kissed my neck and took in a deep breath. "You should go take a shower. You smell like sex."

I sighed and started getting off the couch. "Will you at least come with me?"

"I've seen the size of your shower."

"That's what makes it fun, a quickie won't hurt anything."

He shook his head. "You haven't listened to anything I've said at all, have you?"

I pointed an accusing finger at him, intentionally using the arm that had been holding my robe shut. "Quit making excuses. If we are going to die today, you are going to have sex with me again, and there's not a damn thing you can do about it!"

Vino erupted with laughter. I glared at him, but he wasn't looking anywhere near my face. His eyes were glued on the section of skin revealed through the open part of my robe.

So I dropped the robe.

His eyes widened and looked up and down my body. Then they started to turn black, and I knew I'd won the argument. I turned around slowly and started walking towards the bathroom.

"I guess you know where to find me," I said.

I made it about three steps before I found myself spun around and pinned to the wall with my wrists above my head. Vino's eyes were completely gone now, and he leaned close to my face.

"You fight dirty."

I giggled. "Does this mean I win?"

He released my wrists and ran his hands down the length of my body. Then he grabbed my ass and lifted me off the ground. "It means you might have a point about how we spend our last moments... and that I have control issues."

I wrapped my legs around his waist and kissed him, then he carried me into the bathroom.

Vino can be surprisingly gentle when he wants to be. He was obviously putting forth a lot of effort not to kill me. It was probably a good forty-five minutes before he decided I was too weak to go on. The water was ice cold by that point, so it did an excellent job of snapping me back into consciousness every time I started to black out.

I did feel like I hadn't slept in a week. I was dizzy, my head felt foggy, and my body felt heavy. But I didn't care. I still had an excellent after-sex glow that made all the other crap inconsequential.

I stood in front of the mirror in my bathroom and tried to pick out the snarls from my curls. Vino was leaning in the doorway watching me like a hawk because he was positive I was about to keel over at any second. Neither one of us had bothered to redress yet.

"I just want to stress the importance of us getting out of here as soon as possible," he said.

"Yeah."

"Which means you should be getting ready..."

"Uh huh."

"Trinity..."

"What?"

"I'm up here."

Only when I looked up and saw the smirk on his face did I realize that I hadn't actually been combing my hair. I was just standing there holding the pick up to it, and staring at his junk. What can I say? The man's real impressive without his clothes on.

I laughed. "Maybe you should put some pants on. Otherwise we're never gonna get out of here."

He slid around me to grab his pants off the floor, making sure to bump into me in as many places as possible. I watched in fascination as he pulled them on without underwear. I always had a sneaking suspicion he went commando.

Vino put his shirt on too, which was disappointing, but I understood the reasoning behind it. He reached out to touch the sore spot on my side where that hideous black mark was.

"Have you looked at this today?"

I did a quick twist so I could see it in the mirror. The black was gone, it looked like a faded scar, and it was half of its original size. The skin was wrinkled and gray, but it was nothing compared to the gruesome, rotted-flesh look it had the night before. That brought new hope to our dismal situation.

"Did you do that?" I asked as I ran my fingers over it.

"I don't know how I would have. I didn't think that was possible."

I poked at it some more. It barely hurt at all. "What was it?"

"A mark. It cements his hold on you and claims you as his property. I suppose you could compare it to branding cattle... if the brand gave you complete control over every thought and action." He struggled to add the next sentence. "It also prepares your body so it won't reject impregnation."

Isn't it called the vapors when you suddenly feel like you're going to faint? Well, I think I got the vapors. "Right to the point that one is..." I started to calm down, then another terrifying question came to mind. "I'm not pregnant now, am I?!"

Vino laughed so hard it bordered on rude. "I'm not the one who marked you," he said. "And I have no plans to further my bloodline."

"That's a relief."

"We do need to hurry though. I can't believe I'm going to say this, but it's a good thing your apartment is the size of a closet. It's not big enough to fight in. There would be no way to hide it, so confronting us here is risky... You don't live as long as Sebastian has without learning some patience. No matter how mad he gets he'll wait to make his move. But it's still not safe for us to stay here long. He'll eventually figure out a way in that he can get away with."

I did the best I could to rush through the rest of my morning ritual. I threw my hair up in a ponytail, and grabbed my makeup to apply it in the car.

We headed the opposite direction of Sebastian's apartment, trying to distance ourselves even if it was pointless. We went to a restaurant we had actually been to before, and snuggled in next to each other in another private booth. I appreciated the accommodations much more now that I had a different view on his company.

I curled up in Vino's arms and closed my eyes. I felt downright groggy and feeble. So yeah, Vino was right about sex being a bad idea. Well, big deal. I was going to die today no matter what happened. If I was a tad drained for my last few hours, so what.

"Do you want me to let you sleep?"

I must have dozed off, because I jumped when he spoke. "Don't you dare. Slap me or something next time I do that."

He laughed at me again.

So much of Vino's strange behavior made sense now. One particular moment stuck out. I spun around and gave him a wide-eyed smile.

He raised an eyebrow. "What?"

"You were totally jealous of Lucas."

"I was not."

"Oh please, why else would you make it look like we were sleeping together? There were a hundred other ways you could have scared him off. You had to prove you were more desirable."

"I wouldn't need to do anything to prove that."

"Come on, just admit it..."

He sighed and looked away from me. "I didn't like the way you looked at him. And... it's uncomfortable when you're upset. With you mad enough to want to kill me I didn't have to deal with that."

Put another victory in the Trinity column. I giggled and kissed him.

When we disengaged, he took a moment to look me over. "You look like shit by the way."

Typical Vino fashion, take all the bite out of admitting something by distracting me with insults. "Don't care, totally worth it."

"I told you what was going to happen."

"Still alive, aren't I? Besides, you aren't listening to me much either. How many times do I have to tell you that I don't fucking care."

Vino glared at me. "You don't understand the severity of the situation, Trinity. We are in a load of shit right now and everything is about to blow up in our faces. The fact that you are now so pathetically debilitated only makes our situation worse."

"I'll be fine. I'll order every piece of meat in this restaurant if it makes you feel better. But like I said, if we're dying anyways, what does it really matter? Unless you have some bright idea as to how we are going to escape all of this."

He sighed again. "No brilliant schemes, sorry."

I was hoping for a more reassuring answer then that. "We can't run? I thought you said he didn't like the ocean. Maybe we could go steal a boat or something and disappear into the sunset."

"That might last a couple days, but I've tried it before. Sebastian has hundreds of other children roaming around. I'm not the only one who kept that particular human trait. And he could bring forth an entire legion from Hell if he was compelled enough."

"So there's really nothing we can do? I thought you said one of the angels could kill him? Can we ask for help?"

Vino laughed. "Think about what you just said. No angel is going to get involved in a demon squabble over a lover. Maybe you should give some serious consideration to becoming a nun."

"That's just as stupid. I'd have to go outside the church at some point in my life, and he'd just get me then."

He squeezed his temples. "Lost cause..." He muttered under his breath.

"What was that?" I snapped.

"You are a completely lost cause. And by far the most aggravating person I have ever met... And for some sick reason that's completely irresistible."

"Feeling's mutual." I grabbed him and pulled him in for a long kiss.

We were interrupted by the sound of our waitress setting drinks on the table. Vino barely looked away from me as he ordered us each a T-bone, mine well done and his bloody. He also ordered two different appetizers.

"That's a lot of food, I'm assuming you think you're gonna make me eat all of it."

He grinned. "Possibly."

And of course, he did. But I was actually hungrier than I ever remembered being in my life, so it turned out to be a good thing. We spent a good hour just enjoying being with each other before the issue at hand came up again. I could tell Vino was troubled but he was smiling anyways. "My brother and sister are going to show up any minute. They're really close... and they're pissed."

My jaw dropped. "They're coming after us now?"

He laughed. "Those two hardly pose a threat, so long as we're not separated. But I'm afraid our time is up. We need to face our demons, so to speak."

"That was a horrible joke."

Vino shook his head. "Hardly a joke. But we might as well face this head on. As far as I see it, our only chance is an outright challenge. It's a long shot. And it most likely has a zero percent chance of working. But I won't go down easy and they all know it."

My heart sank. The thought of him fighting for me was painful. "I'm still in favor of running."

"There is not one corner of this universe that is far enough to escape the wrath we've inflicted upon ourselves." He stopped for a minute and looked towards the door of the restaurant. "They're here already anyways."

I immediately went into panic mode. I didn't have the nerves for this kind of stuff. Vino put a hand under my chin and tilted my face towards his to give me another smile. "Those two are nothing to worry about."

Vino kissed me again, pretending not to care about our soon to be guests as they entered the front door. He didn't pull away until he was sure they noticed. That didn't make me feel any better. He leaned back and casually rested one arm around my shoulders and the other on the back of the booth. He didn't appear the least bit worried to see his siblings walk over to our table.

I pressed myself as close to him as I could. He may not have been scared, but I was petrified. Amelie and Andras sauntered over to us, gliding in unison as they always did. They looked so much more evil today, tensed and ready to spring into action with shifty, murderous eyes.

"Something on your mind?" Vino asked with a smile on his face.

"Aren't you going to ask us to have a seat?" Amelie snapped.

"No."

Both of their faces turned sour. Andras' lip curled as he glanced in my direction. Amelie looked to her brother and then followed his gaze to meet my frightened eyes, holding me there for a long moment before speaking to Vino. "You have one hour to deliver her to our father. After that he's going to summon the others and every single one of us will come after you."

Vino sounded just as cocky as ever. "The estate is more than an hour away."

"Then I guess you better hurry."

"Message received. You can go now."

Amelie started laughing. "He's going to kill you for this. You might as well come with us now and get it over with."

Vino winked at her. "Why don't you go ahead and try to make me?"

Andras took a step forward and his sister grabbed his arm. They both looked like they wanted to rip us to shreds. "I'm going to take great joy in watching him destroy you, both of you." She pointed at Vino and leaned over our table. "I have been waiting to watch you die since the day I was born. You are a disgrace to our family."

Vino laughed at her. "And you were the one who was treated like garbage. That's got to be eating you up inside."

Amelie lunged forward this time, and Andras caught her. She snapped her head in his direction as if he were yelling, then calmed herself down by smoothing out her shirt and taking a deep breath. She nodded in agreement to some silent comment from her brother. "I suppose I'll watch you get your justice soon enough."

Andras was staring at me again. I tightened my hold on my protector. Amelie seemed to speak whatever he was thinking. "Your slutty little human is the one who's going to pay the most for this. I hope it was worth it."

She smiled at me with a true intent to kill, then they turned and marched out. I buried my face in Vino's chest, trying to stifle the tears that were ready to break loose. He wrapped his arms around me and kissed the top of my head. I waited for words of encouragement, but there were none. Our situation was beyond pep talks.

"Still think you don't want to become a nun?" He finally kidded.

"I'm not going anywhere that you're not." I growled into his shirt.

"Thought you'd say something like that."

Vino paid our tab and we left for Sebastian's apartment. The decision to make this particular venture had been an easy one. It was either face Sebastian alone, or wait for him to assemble an army. And splitting up was also out of the question. I refused to leave his side for one, but more importantly, if there was even a split second where I was left vulnerable, someone would come for me.

Vino was driving slower than I had ever seen. He still exceeded the speed limit, but otherwise obeyed the basic traffic laws he normally found beneath him. Neither one of us said much.

We valeted the car just like we had every day previous to this. The only significant difference in our arrival today was that Vino put his arm around me to escort me inside. I clung to him like a frightened child, trying to channel his natural sedative to numb my anxiety. It didn't work as well as it usually did. My legs didn't want to move and my heart was about to explode.

Vino was patient with me. He let me just stand there with him and try to calm myself down.

He didn't seem nearly as nervous as I was, though he did maintain a protective grip on me as we walked slowly through the lobby. I'm sure he was mentally preparing himself for the inevitable fight that was just ahead. His eyes didn't look troubled anymore. They were determined and glowing a deep crimson.

I was trembling by the time we stepped into the elevator. As soon as the doors closed, I started crying. Vino grabbed my face in both his hands and smiled at me. "I told you I hate it when you do that."

He leaned down to kiss me one last time; a passionate, sad kiss that felt more like a goodbye. My senses were overwhelmed by the sheer force of it. It may have been my already weakened condition altering my perception, or his emotions causing him to lose control over the current he emitted, but that one powerful kiss nearly knocked me out.

Then the elevator doors opened.

Chapter 18

War

We stood in that elevator, gazing in each other's eyes, trying to drink in every last detail of each others face before we would be torn apart. Vino smiled at me. I could tell it was forced. Then he led me into the empty apartment ahead of us. The room was silent, and deathly still. There was no sign of any servants anywhere, and it was much colder than usual.

"He's in the gallery," Vino stated.

All I could do was nod, my voice deemed frozen or non-existent by fear. The second elevator was harder to get into than the first. There was no kiss waiting for me in here, just a whole thirty seconds of anticipatory anguish. I held my breath when those doors parted, revealing our awaiting executioner.

In preparation for what was to come, the sliding panels that housed a majority of the artwork had been pushed back, opening the room to immense proportions. The massive room was even colder than downstairs had been, forty degrees, tops. Cold enough that I couldn't control my shivering and the steam of my breath hung in the air around me.

I could feel Sebastian before I saw him, as if his energy had leaked out to consume the whole room. It hung like a miasma in the air, charging the particles around us and making it hard to breathe. He sat directly ahead, on the couch against the far wall of windows. He had both arms on the low back of that leather sofa, with the ankle of one leg rested on the knee of the other. His eyes were burning so bright that I could see the murderous intent in them from across the room. He looked positively villainous; a vicious monster straight out of a comic book. Only this kind of evil was unfathomable by any human standards.

As we approached him, Vino's grip on me tightened, and Sebastian's lip curled in a sneer. His voice was low and menacing. "Would you look at that. It seems my treacherous son has come to return what's mine."

"You'll have to kill me to get her," Vino replied.

Sebastian laughed. "What a coincidence. That happens to be exactly what I had in mind."

Amelie and Andras were standing off to the side, huddled in a corner. I only noticed them because she started to giggle at that comment. Only Sebastian's eyes darted in her direction and she shut up.

"I'm very disappointed in you, Vinicio. After you die, who will I have to take your position? Those two over there are worthless, and the others aren't strong enough to serve my purposes." Sebastian paused for one of his dramatic sighs. "I knew the day would come when you would challenge me. But I never imagined you would do so over something as disposable as a mortal. You disgust me."

I was nothing more than a frail, fleshy statue at Vino's side. Vino was willing to die for me, and here I was cowering behind him and letting him take all the blame. Yet he stayed cool under the pressure, and grinned back at Sebastian. "Are you afraid I'm going to beat you? I've already taken your most prized possession."

Before I could blink, I was shoved to the side and Sebastian had his hand around Vino's throat. I stumbled as he lifted Vino off the floor with one hand. I hadn't even seen him twitch in his seat on the couch, let alone make his way over to us. Vino grabbed his hand with both of his, and tried to pry the fingers from his neck.

"Possession is the right word. I own that pathetic creature. She is mine to do with as I please. And now you have completely defiled her." Sebastian's grip on Vino's throat tightened. Then his eyes flashed to black. "You are delirious if you think you would be a challenge to me."

Vino grinned at him as his own eyes changed into the black holes that mirrored his fathers. He let go of Sebastian's arm and brought both fists crashing down on top of Sebastian's head with a thunderous crack. It was enough force that it broke Sebastian's neck. His head snapped backward at an awkward angle and hung limp.

But Sebastian didn't even teeter in his spot. He let go of Vino's throat and let him drop so that he could grab his head with both hands and set it straight. With a snap of bones he righted himself, then flexed his neck to both sides and rolled his shoulders.

"That's how it's going to be, is it..." He raised a hand towards Vino, and Vino went flying into the wall. "You know how much I dislike fighting."

I felt vulnerable standing in the middle of the room by myself. I wanted to leap to his assistance, but there wasn't anything I could do. Sebastian turned his attention towards me and smiled. Then he cocked his head to one side and wave of energy smacked into me. My knees buckled and I landed on all fours.

Sebastian took a step forward, but Vino jumped in the way and took a swing at him. Even though the punch was so quick I barely saw it, Sebastian managed to catch his fist before it made contact. Vino swung at Sebastian with his other hand. This time he connected, because Sebastian didn't try to avoid it. The sound of impact echoed around the room. But he took the blow to the chin without flinching. Then Sebastian returned a punch to Vino's face that sent him crashing to the ground. His cheek split open from the force of the hit, but the wound healed before the trickle of blood made it to his chin.

I could see the direction this fight was going. Things did not look good for Vino. I couldn't bear to watch Sebastian hurt him. And I had no plans to abandon him, but I didn't want to end up in the middle of those two. So I decided to run for cover.

I scrambled to my feet to try to get out of the way, but I didn't make it far. Both twins were in front of me instantly, and poised as if they had always been there.

"Where do you think you're going?" Amelie hissed.

They reached out in unison and each grabbed an arm. It shocked my heart into stalling and sent me reeling to the floor. They kept hold on my arms and lifted me to present me back to our attacker.

Sebastian took a second to straighten out his tie. He didn't bother to look in our direction as he scolded them. "An intelligent child would stay out of this. Unless of course, you two wish to die also. Leave her be. She can't escape."

They both released me and took a step back, pain on their matched faces. Amelie's voice was a meek whisper. "Yes, master. I'm sorry, we were out of line."

Sebastian turned to Vino, who looked ready to launch another attack. His face transformed, stretching the corners of his mouth into an inhuman smirk and decaying the lips, exposing his jagged fangs. "Try not to die too quickly for me. If I'm being forced to fight, I want to at least receive some enjoyment from your pain."

Another flash and he crashed into Vino again. A series of blows rang out that I couldn't follow. Then Sebastian slammed Vino into one of the display cases. The glass shattered, and Vino went through the metal supports, crushing some of the priceless artifacts inside and coating their remnants with blood.

Vino shoved Sebastian off, sending him a good five feet into the air above him. He stood fast enough to kick Sebastian before his feet hit the ground. There was a loud thud as Vino's foot made full contact with Sebastian's stomach. Since Sebastian hadn't touched the ground yet, this knocked him off balance, but only slightly. He leaned forward on impact and grabbed

Vino's ankle with both hands. In one swift movement, he hurled Vino into the wall of medieval weapons, knocking almost every item off its supports and toppling them on top of his broken body.

Sebastian raised his hand again, and several swords lifted up and aimed at Vino. Vino was healing fast and trying to stagger to his feet, but it was useless. Sebastian gave his wrist a small flick and the swords ran Vino through. Every one of them skewered his chest and emerged from his back. Vino stopped moving, and a pool of blood formed underneath him.

I shrieked the loudest "*No*," my lungs had the power of producing, and tried to run to him. Two steps in, I wasn't on my feet anymore. Sebastian slammed me into the nearest wall and pinned me several feet off the ground with his hand around my throat. I frantically clawed at his fingers for relief.

"Do you think I hit his heart?" He glanced over his shoulder at Vino's limp body and snickered. "He's still conscious, I believe," he said. "Tell me, Trinity, does he know how you begged me? Or how you cried when I rejected you?"

I started to grow lightheaded from lack of air and Sebastian's grip on my throat loosened. He pressed the full length of his body against mine and put his lips right next to my ear. "He watched us the other night. Without me ordering him to. Wouldn't it be sublime for his last moments to be spent watching me take you here in front of him...? I promise to make sure you don't enjoy any of it."

I started to sob quietly. "No, please, no. I'm sorry. I—"

"The time is late for apologies, my love." He removed his hand from my neck and used it to yank my hair and tilt my head back. Then he bit me again, hard. I screamed.

Sebastian didn't drink my blood. He wasn't even controlling me. He just held me there with his teeth, the way one dog would show dominance over another. I tried to squirm away from the pain but I could feel my skin tearing where his fangs sank in. It burned and I shrieked and cried. He didn't let go until I gave up and was completely still.

"I can taste your fear," he said. "I wonder how scared you'll be when I finish off your lover."

"Please, I'll do whatever you want—I won't fight you. Just please, don't kill him."

"You offer complete submission in trade for his life?"

I nodded.

Sebastian lowered his lips to where they brushed mine. "I'd prefer to have you struggle. No deal."

I pushed against him as hard as I could and twisted violently to try to get away. I knew my efforts were pointless. But I cried and hit him repeatedly in the chest anyways.

He laughed at my futile attempts. "That's it. Fight me..."

My will broke then. I stopped hitting, and let myself sag into him and cry.

"Father," Amelie interrupted.

Sebastian growled and turned his head to look at her. "Stay. Out. Of. This."

"But he's moving."

"I am well aware he is alive! How dare you presume I need assistance against the likes of him! I forbid you from speaking again!"

She didn't answer, and I couldn't see her reaction from where I was.

I tried to look around Sebastian to get a glimpse of Vino. He was still on floor, but one of the swords had been pulled out. And he was grabbing the handle of another.

Sebastian's face commanded my attention. My eyes reverted to the emptiness of his. "I believe we were in the middle of something," he said.

He ran his hand down the skin of my right arm, caressing it the way he used to. When he reached my forearm, he put his middle finger on one side and his thumb on the other. With a quick snap of his finger, both bones shattered. I screamed and my hand went limp.

"I'm going to teach you a thing or two about pain, Trinity. I think you can scream louder than that."

Sebastian put his hand on my right shoulder and pushed. I heard a loud pop, immediately followed by a flood of immense pain. My entire arm went slack. It tingled and throbbed in tune to my heartbeat. He was right, I could scream louder.

"What a beautiful sound," he said. He caressed my cheek with the back of his hand and smiled at me. "You are going to suffer like no human has ever suffered. I will never allow you another pain-free moment *for the rest of existence.*"

The pain was so intense, I started to black out. My vision faded and I closed my eyes. Sebastian slapped me. "You don't get to sleep. Your punishment is just beginning."

He laughed and dropped me to the floor, then kicked me to the side. I skidded to a stop about five feet away and just let myself lay there. I clutched my ruined arm against me and rolled from side to side. Sebastian walked over and nudged me with his toe.

"To think of all the trouble I went through," he said. He kicked me lightly again and brought his hand to his chin. "I suppose I shouldn't break too many of your bones. I want to leave enough fight left in you to keep this entertaining... And you need to at least remain pleasing to look at." He studied me for another moment then grinned, showing his fangs. "I know a fun game we can play."

I felt a wave of energy pass over me, followed by a surge of desire and that familiar ache. "No—"

"No? Why that doesn't sound like you at all." Sebastian knelt and grabbed me by the face. He lifted me up with him and pinned my back against the wall again.

My body reacted in ways I didn't want it to. My breath quickened, and my skin was on fire. I pressed against him and started to surrender to my longing. I cried, but I couldn't stop myself. Sebastian laughed. Then he kissed me. And I didn't just let him; I kissed him back. The energy that hit me stalled my heart and lungs. I almost passed out, but I enjoyed it. And I wanted more.

A voice inside screamed for me to come back to reality. It clawed at my mind and showed me what I was doing, trying to separate the real me from the one he controlled.

Sebastian pulled back from our kiss. "Tell me you'd die for me, Trinity."

Tears flooded my eyes, and my internal voice finally caught hold. "No."

Rage overtook Sebastian's face. He let out a snarl and punched me in the stomach. I choked and spit up blood on his shirt. My vision started fading again and my head slumped down. I wouldn't last much longer at this rate. That punch had to have damaged something internal.

Sebastian threw me to the floor. "You got blood on me, you disgusting human."

"Father!" Amelie shrieked.

He clenched his fists and growled. The entire room shook. "I forbade you from speaking!" He lifted a hand and she went flying across the room and slammed into a wall. He looked back down at me. "Now where were we?"

Then a blade hit Sebastian on the top of the head. It connected with such force that it sliced right through the center of his skull and continued all the way to his stomach before it stopped. Sebastian's eyes flew open with the shock of the attack, and very slowly, each half of his body started to separate. Blood sprayed out in all directions. Strings of tissue pulled apart as his right and left sides fell opposite each other, knocking his body off balance. He collapsed to the floor.

Vino stood behind him, holding the handle of the ancient battle-axe that had just chopped his father in half. He was covered in blood, and his shirt was filled with holes, but he appeared unharmed. He gave the axe a yank, and it came free of Sebastian's body.

Vino lifted the axe and took another swing at Sebastian. My vision started to fade again, and I lost a moment. The next thing I knew I was in Vino's arms, away from the carnage.

Amelie was screaming and kneeling with Andras next to their father. They each had one side and were frantically trying to push the two halves of his torso back together. Almost instantaneously, the areas where the flesh met seemed to reach out and grab each other. Blobs of red goo fused to close in the gaps.

"I'm sorry," Vino said, as he sat me down and inspected my injuries. "That's not going to stop him for long."

I nodded, but I was in too much pain to speak. I couldn't imagine someone coming back from being split in two. Vino wrapped his arms around me and held me close for a moment. I broke into tears instantly.

He glanced over his shoulder at his family's attempts to put Sebastian back together. The twins locked eyes for a moment, and Amelie nodded to some silent question.

Andras rose and glared at Vino. I assume he said something I didn't hear. Vino winked at me, then stood for the next round of battle.

He motioned Andras forward with one hand. "Do you think it's wise to try to take me on?"

Andras closed the distance between them in a fraction of a second, and took a swing at Vino. He didn't connect, and as his body twisted with the near miss, Vino grabbed his face with one hand and brought his head crashing towards the ground. He hit the floor with a deafening crunch as his skull broke open and shattered against the marble. The sound echoed about the massive room, drowning out the splash of all the soft tissue that exploded from impact.

Vino stood and wiped the scarlet liquid and chunks of white brain matter onto his torn shirt. He grinned at Amelie before removing his shirt and tossing it aside. "There's no coming back from that one, now is there?"

Andras' body shook with a few postmortem spasms. Amelie screamed like she was the one dying. "Andras!"

Vino laughed. "I guess he's not going to get to watch me die after all."

Amelie let out a war cry and leaped to attack Vino. But a hand reached out and grabbed her arm, a hand from a body that was still not quite put together. She looked down at it and stopped in her tracks, weeping uncontrollably for the loss of her brother.

Sebastian's body had all but sewn itself together at this point. Only his head was still slowly pulling closed by invisible zippers. He sat up before the last of the wound shut, and released his hold on her arm. The bloody line down the front his face climbed upwards and disappeared into his burgundy stained hairline. His shirt hung down each arm and he was covered in blood, but he was whole. And he was pissed.

The look on Sebastian's face was monstrous. He stood and glared at Vino, and the pressure in the room changed. The air weighed me down and pushed me to the floor. He removed the shreds of his shirt and ran his fingers through his hair.

"How dare you," he said.

Vino just smiled.

Amelie sobbed into her hands at Sebastian's feet. He grabbed her by the back of her hair and lifted her off the ground. "Stop your whimpering! You're of no use to me without your brother!" He twisted her around and stared into her leaking eyes. "Well, there is one more purpose you can serve..."

His face flashed back to the black eyes and jagged teeth. Then he bit down on her neck, removing a piece of flesh and swallowing it. He chomped down on her one more time and drank from her open veins. Blood dripped to the floor as Amelie struggled helplessly in his arms. He drank only a few swallows before he tore off another chunk of flesh and ate it. She shrieked, and he smiled down at her. Then he grabbed her head, and in one strong yank, tore it free of her shoulders, removing a portion of her spinal column with it. He dropped her limp body to the floor and tossed her head over his shoulder.

Sebastian closed his eyes and took a deep breath, letting the energy from this quick feeding fuel his newly repaired body. Blood dripped from his mouth and chin. He wiped some of it away with his arm before opening his eyes.

"You won't get another lucky shot," Sebastian said. He flexed and the room dropped another ten degrees. A breeze swirled around from nowhere, changing the air pressure again. "I'm really quite fond of this body...It's a shame I'll have to replace it."

Vino's attention reverted to me. I saw a flash of panic cross his face, and I wondered what I missed. Then Vino darted over and picked me up again, clearing the distance to the elevators in less then a second.

But Sebastian was faster. Vino came to a screeching halt directly in front of the elevator doors, where Sebastian had already slapped his hand to block our path. The steel doors buckled under the force of his palm as he leaned into it and laughed wildly at us. Vino slid me out of his arms and positioned me behind him.

Sebastian waved his finger in a scolding motion. "You weren't trying to leave, were you?"

He winked at us with what used to be his eyes. A wave of energy smacked into me and the smell of sulfur emanated from him. The skin on his hands began to crack and peel, burning from underneath the way that bark would peel off of a log in a fireplace.

Vino started backing up, towing me with him but always staying between me and Sebastian. I clutched at him with my good arm and managed little more than a whisper. "What's happening?"

He didn't take his eyes off Sebastian when he answered me under his breath. "He's shedding his shell, showing his true form. First chance you get, I want you out of here. I should be able to keep him busy long enough. He won't be able to follow you if he can't pass for human… You know where I want you to go."

"I'm not leaving you," I cried.

"Don't argue with me! Just do what I say!"

I nodded, but I didn't mean it.

Sebastian's skin continued to burn off and fall into clumps below. His pants caught fire in a few spots, and tore as they stretched to allow something much larger to break free of his flesh. Claws burst from his hands, long bony talons attached to gangly arms so dark red they were almost black.

His back hunched over, and in and explosion from within, a separate spine emerged in unreal proportions. In a shower of blood and searing skin, a set of bat like wings unfolded out of his back. They opened and shook now that they were free of their confines. He pulled his new head out of the old one, although this one could not logically fit inside. Large, backwards-facing horns came out from either side of his temples, paired with a set of smaller spikes where eyebrows would normally go. The eyes were the same black holes as before, but otherwise there was no trace of Sebastian's previously flawless features. His new face was hideous. The nose was rotted away, resembling that of a corpse and his now enormous jaws were filled to the brim with uneven, crooked fangs.

Dragonesque legs with clawed feet emerged as he stepped over the smoldering piles of flesh that five minutes ago made up one of the best looking people ever created. This new look came complete with a long reptilian tail that he started tapping against the floor in a slow rhythm. This Sebastian was easily three times larger than the original, and it smelled of all the scents of Hell: sulfur, brimstone, and death.

When the transformation was complete, he spoke again in a new voice, one raspier and several octaves lower than the earlier version. "It's much more comfortable being free of that cramped disguise." He stretched and looked himself over. "It's not as good looking as the other body was, but I'm sure you'll find the trade in power to be nothing less than spectacular."

Sebastian started taking slow steps in our direction. He tucked his wings back and wagged his tail. Vino tensed, and gave me a gentle shove behind him, then launched himself at Sebastian.

Sebastian didn't try to avoid the punch Vino landed to the side of his ribs. He just looked down at him and laughed, then flicked him away the way you would a fly. That simple little slap sent Vino sailing across the room, where he landed on his feet and slid to a stop. He immediately charged again, but this time Sebastian grabbed him by the shoulders before he could try to attack.

He lifted him off the ground and held him at eye level. "There's not a thing you can do to me now. You may be strong compared to the others, but you are nothing next to me."

He tightened his grip on Vino and dug his claws into his back. Large amounts of blood oozed out of the holes that Sebastian's fingertips disappeared into. A loud crack echoed around the room as one of his bones gave way to the pressure. Vino's back arched and he growled, but he otherwise showed few signs that he was in pain.

Sebastian slammed him into the ground with an insane amount of force, cracking all the marble in a six-foot radius and splattering blood around them like raindrops.

Every muscle in my body was telling me to run, to leave now and save myself. But I couldn't bring myself to do it. I couldn't leave Vino to suffer his horrible fate alone. I knew there was no way he would survive. And this was all happening to him because of me. The very least I could do is stay with him, and offer myself as penance for my sins once he was gone.

Vino rolled to his side and sat up. The wounds on his back had already healed. Sebastian waited for him to stand, laughing and whipping his tail back and forth. Vino grinned back at him, baring the daggers that replaced his teeth.

Vino dashed to the side and picked up one of the swords that had impaled him earlier. He spun the sword around in one smooth rotation and walked towards the abomination that was his father. Sebastian swung at him as he neared, missing by a hair. Vino ducked to the side and thrust the sword into his chest. Sebastian's other hand came around as it happened, catching Vino's side and knocking him to the ground.

Sebastian shook his head and pulled the sword out, tossing it aside. He laughed as it clanked to the floor in the background. Then Sebastian slammed Vino into the wall across the room. He leaned down and snarled in his face, one long drip of saliva hanging from his mouth. Vino reached one hand behind his back and pulled out a small dagger, then stabbed Sebastian in the side of the neck.

Sebastian dropped him to the ground and pulled it out, the tiny wound disappeared immediately. There wasn't even any blood. Vino attempted to kick his legs out from underneath him but Sebastian stomped on his calf, visibly shattering everything that was inside. The crunch of bone on bone echoed in my ears and I winced as if he did it to me.

Sebastian stomped down on his midsection next; the ripple of cracks coming from his ribs brought tears to my eyes. Vino grunted as the air was forced out of his chest. Sebastian continued to stomp and kick at him, growing steadily more ferocious as he went on. Blood splattered everywhere as Vino's skin repeatedly broke open from the barrage of blows. Sebastian must have broken every bone in his body before he got tired of it and booted him across the room.

Vino was still breathing, barely. His body twisted and contorted in disgusting ways while it tried to set itself straight again. Once his arms were back the way they should be, he rolled to his side and started pushing himself up, trying to get on all fours.

Sebastian looked like he was enjoying himself. He stretched his wings and smiled in my direction, drinking in the anguish on my face. "I'm going to take my time for you. Give you a chance to enjoy the show."

All I could do was shake my head and weep. Sebastian was going to drag this out as long as he could. And since Vino would continue to heal after every beating, who knew how long death would take.

Vino was almost kneeling now. He leaned forward on one fist as his regeneration finished. His ebony hair hung in his face in a tangled, bloody mess.

Sebastian sauntered over to him and brought a fist towards the back of his head with lightning speed. Vino spun around and caught his hand mid swing, stopping the assault in its tracks. All his muscles flexed and he shoved Sebastian back. Sebastian teetered, and rocked on his heels, balancing himself with his thick tail.

The room grew colder again. Another wave of something that felt like a gale force wind hit me. Vino's skin looked like it was cooking; scorching itself and turning darker like a piece of grilled meat. His shoulders spasmed and cracked, suddenly growing wider and ripping the skin at the blades. Wings tore free of his flesh. They snapped open and sprayed a thin mist of blood into the air.

Vino rose to his feet, and horns sprouted out from either side of his forehead. They twisted and framed his head like a dark halo. Vino's back arched as another violent tremor rocked his body. His muscles enlarged and he grew another six inches taller. His pants stretched and ripped in several places to allow for his new size. Even his hands transformed into claws, though they retained most of their human shape. The black abyss in his eyes was gone now. The actual eyeball had come back, only the whites were still dark and the pupils were nothing but a red glow.

He still looked like Vino, sort of. All the basic features were there, but this was no man that stood before me. The only person I loved was not a person anymore. He glanced in my direction and we locked eyes for a moment. He quickly looked away. As terrifying as he appeared right now, he seemed ashamed for me to see him like that.

"Well, well, well," Sebastian said, as he brought his hands together for a slow clap. "I must say; I am impressed. A transformation from a halfling... that's unheard of."

Vino reverted his attention to his father. They never looked more related then they did now, dark creatures of horns and wings, with blistering skin and sharp claws. The power rolling off them was so thick I could almost *see it.*

Sebastian threw his head back and laughed wickedly. "You look shocked, son. Have you been struck mute?"

Vino's lip curled. "No."

"What, no smart remarks? You should see yourself, remarkably frightening." He looked in my direction and smiled. "Look at the poor girl. She's completely terrified of you."

As awful as it sounds, I was. I was more afraid of him now than ever. My Vino was gone, and I was alone with two monsters. Vino didn't look at me with Sebastian's accusation. He actually shifted a little so that I couldn't see his face at all.

Sebastian's laughter erupted. "You're never going to pass for human like that. And you won't be able to control yourself. I'll have a new body in days. I'd wager it would take you a century to figure out how to change back. And the thought of all the power that I'll gain by devouring you..."

A low growl rumbled in the back of Vino's throat. "Shut your mouth, old man."

Sebastian charged Vino. They clashed together so quickly I barely caught it. A shockwave spread through the room from the force they exerted. I heard the exchange of blows, but couldn't follow who was throwing them or where they landed.

They locked claws and came to a standstill, pushing against each other in a classic power struggle. They both grinned sadistically, wings straight out behind them like a violent, choreographed dance.

They shoved away from each other and charged again and again with movements too fast for my slow human eyes to comprehend. Sebastian threw Vino across the room, only to end up on his back a moment later. The fight seemed to be evenly matched, despite the size difference.

Another strong clash, and they both stopped. Sebastian had bit down on Vino's shoulder, fitting the entire portion of his body in his mouth. Blood poured from Vino's back and his arm looked unusable, his feet were barely touching the ground. I heard a suction and ripping sound come from somewhere, and Sebastian's eyes flew wide open.

Neither one of them moved for a moment. Then Sebastian's mouth slowly opened and released Vino's flesh. Vino pulled his free arm out from underneath him. It was covered in blood past the elbow and he had something in his hand, a huge, crimson lump of flesh and muscle that was throbbing to a slow cadence.

It was Sebastian's heart; and it was still beating.

Vino took a step back and kicked Sebastian square in his chest, knocking him to the floor. His humongous body hit the ground with a thud that shook the building. Vino stood there, staring down at him for a long minute as Sebastian closed his eyes and chuckled softly.

"You haven't won… this isn't over," he said.

"Looks like it to me." Vino kicked him again, crashing him into the nearest wall.

Sebastian took a deep breath and rolled to his side, clutching at the gaping hole in his chest that wasn't closing itself. His laughter grew louder. "Go ahead, devour me. I'll be in there with you forever. I may even be able to take your body."

He coughed towards the floor. Blood dripped from his teeth and pooled around him. "Once you've gained all my power you won't be able to handle it. You're going to lose all control of yourself. You'll kill every human in sight…" He raised one hand and pointed in my direction. "Starting with her."

Vino walked towards him with the giant heart in his hand. It still beat as if it was in his chest. Sebastian was fading fast, bleeding out onto the floor and choking through his low laughter.

"Your only choice will be to retreat to Hell and take over my throne for me," he said. "My will is done regardless… I win, even in death."

Vino brought his foot down hard on Sebastian's face, crushing his jaw and pinning it shut. He lifted the beating heart to his mouth and ripped a chuck out of it with his fangs. He chewed slowly and swallowed, then took another bite. The last growl emerged from Sebastian, followed by the sound of him choking on his own blood. His breathing halted, and the dripping heart in Vino's hand no longer beat.

Sebastian decayed in fast forward. His flesh rotted and fell apart, becoming a smelly mess on the floor. Vino stood in silence and stared down at his father.

And then it hit.

Another shockwave, a flash emanating from him and pressurizing the room around us. It had enough force to push me back and stun me, nearly knocking the wind out of me.

He took in a deep breath and flexed as his newfound strength coursed through him. He was easily thirty feet from me and I could still feel it. An almost visible aura surrounded him and wafted in my direction. I held my breath and waited to see if he would turn on me. I was terrified that the love of my life had become a soulless monster.

Vino glanced over his shoulder at me without moving, and my heart stopped. He watched me from the corner of his eye for several seconds and uttered one word.

"Leave."

That word sounded so tormented, so sad. It was still Vino in there, no matter how frightening he looked. I stared at him, tears streaming down my cheeks.

"Vino…" I sobbed.

He looked down at the now almost non-existent pile that had been Sebastian. "I told you to get out of here."

I stayed put. That was his voice coming from that creature, pleading with me to go so that I would be safe from him. That was all the more reason to stay. He didn't want to hurt me. He was still trying to protect me.

I shook my head.

"I said go!" He roared, spinning around and opening his wings to their full extent. His eyes erupted in flames as he released that swirling shockwave again, knocking me backwards and scaring me into submission. He pointed to the elevator doors and they flew open on command. "NOW!"

I scrambled to my feet and stumbled into the awaiting lift. I hyperventilated as I pushed myself to the back corner. The doors shut before I pushed any buttons, and thirty seconds later I was at the living room downstairs. I tried to bolt towards the second set of doors but got lightheaded and tripped over myself.

A servant reached out and caught me. He looked completely calm, unaffected by the chaos that had gone on upstairs. "I'm to escort you out, Miss Morgan."

I pushed him aside with my one good arm. "I'll be just fine on my own."

The man just smiled at me and held up a jacket. "Master Vino's orders, ma'am. I must obey. I'll take you to the hospital, everything will be taken care of."

Why was he so calm? And what was all this 'Master Vino' crap? I opened my mouth to yell at him but the room started spinning. Now that my adrenaline was wearing out the pain was too much to handle. My right arm was completely useless. It throbbed and burned, and I couldn't even move my fingers. I doubted I'd ever paint again. My stomach ached and breathing was difficult. I felt like I was having the worst cramps of my life. My cheek stung from being slapped, I had a deep bite mark on my neck, and I was so weak I was about to fall over.

I was also completely covered in blood from head to toe. I had been splattered so many times during the fight, that my clothes were completely ruined, and my hair was a sticky, red mess.

The servant draped the jacket over my shoulders. I pulled it shut across my wounded limb and leaned into him to let him support my weight. "Maybe the hospital is a good idea."

Chapter 19

Trinity Alone

I passed out on the way to the hospital. The servant woke me up at the emergency entrance. He smiled at me and said something about Master Vino making arrangements again, then two aides put me in a wheelchair. That was the last I saw of him.

Once inside, I was taken directly to a private room, bypassing all the other waiting patients. A handsome doctor saw me immediately. He asked no questions about how I managed to get into the state I was in. He gave me a full examination, including X-rays, stitches for the two worst puncture marks in my neck, and an ultrasound to see what was damaged in my stomach.

I didn't say a word the whole time. I cried, a lot. I'd never been in so much pain. Physical or emotional. No human was ever supposed to see what I just saw and live to tell about it. But I did. And Sebastian was dead. So now I was free.

But I was alone.

Vino might as well have eaten my heart too. Because that's

what it felt like. I don't care what his reasons were, or how scary he looked right now. He wasn't allowed to leave me. I had no one without him. There was a good reason why I rejected love my whole life. It was the worst agony a person could put themselves through.

The doctor gave me a long list of injuries, most of them small. But my shoulder was dislocated and the tendons were torn. Plus my arm was broken in three places. I needed surgery and months of rehab before I would regain full use, and that was if I was lucky. He also told me the bite marks on my neck would scar significantly, and I had a contusion of the spleen.

So what did all these injuries have in common, besides the fact that Sebastian inflicted them upon me? They were all non-lethal, would barely affect my overall appearance, and were all things that would have left me well enough for Sebastian to continue his torture indefinitely.

Had to give him credit for that. Sebastian had enough restraint to keep the big picture in mind while getting his revenge. And he managed to take away everything I cared about; my artwork, and the only man I ever loved.

Surgery wasn't bad. I welcomed the sweet numbness the medicated sleep brought me. And the morphine afterwards helped tame the mental anguish almost as much as the physical pain. They were keeping me overnight for observation but I was otherwise ready for discharge.

I awoke in the middle of the night, despite the fact that the drugs were still heavy in my system. My dreams were haunted by Vino, and the epic ache I felt for him. In my intoxicated stupor, I expected him to be waiting for me, the way he always was when I woke up. But he was nowhere to be found.

It took an awkward minute to push myself into a sitting position with my left arm. I blinked a few times and swayed back and forth as I tried to collect my wits. It was almost pitch black in the stale hospital room. The only lights were the dim glow coming from a computer screen to my right and a small green dot from the nurse's call button.

I stared at the monitor, watching the screensaver change

scenes. Then it vanished. I rubbed my eyes and looked at it again. It was still there, doing the exact same thing it was before. I shook it off, must be the drugs.

Then something else moved, not five feet from my uncomfortable bed. I snapped my head in its direction to find a pair of creepy black eyes staring up at me. I screamed.

This creature was similar to the ones I had seen before, its face was decayed like it had risen from the dead, and it was not quite solid. It looked gangly and deformed, and had four scrawny arms and a short tail that looked cut off at the end

I screamed again and chucked my pillow at it. My aim was surprisingly spot-on for using my left arm, but my projectile went right through it. The little demon dissipated into the shadows.

The door flew open, and a nurse turned the light on and ran to my side. "Are you ok?"

"I'm fine," I snapped, as I laid down and fumbled with my blankets.

She helped tuck me in and did something to my IV before leaving the room. A fresh wave of grogginess washed over me. She obviously sedated me again. I had enough time to start crying before I fell back asleep. There was no one to keep those little creatures away anymore. They were going to be a constant part of my life now.

The doctor didn't let me leave the next morning. I threw such a fit about it that he decided to sedate me even further. Apparently my mental state was now just as much a concern as my injuries were to these people. During the next two days, I was down right rude to anyone who dared to enter my room. I even tried to escape once, unsuccessfully.

When I wasn't crying, or screaming, I was sleeping. But it brought no relief. Conscious or unconscious, I was filled with the same pain. And when night came, and the shadows filled the room, I had more visitors.

They were easier to ignore this time. I remembered what Vino told me about them. They weren't even strong enough to hold their shape, and therefore couldn't harm me. These demons were nothing compared to what Sebastian had been, and what Vino now was.

My depression was in full swing when I woke up the next morning. Someone brought in breakfast while I slept, but I had no interest in it. However, I did pull the cart over so I could reach the tiny cup of coffee that was probably cold already. When I picked up the plastic cup, I heard something jingle, so I set it back down and felt behind it. My fingers found a smooth, rectangular object.

The black rectangle had a diamond encrusted B with wings on it, and two buttons on the back. I pushed on the side and a key popped out of the bottom. Tears welled up instantly in my eyes. It was the key fob to the Bentley.

Vino was saying goodbye, giving me something to remember him by before he disappeared forever. He wasn't coming back for me, and where he was going he wouldn't need a car. Not that he could drive one anyways. I doubt he could have even fit inside the drivers seat with the massive wings he sprouted.

I held the key to my chest and bawled my eyes out. The doctor came back in and I ignored him. I barely registered the fact that he told me I was being released. All my new prescriptions had been filled and were waiting in a bag for me, along with fresh clothes, since the ones I wore when I came in went straight into the trash.

Everything had been orchestrated for me, but there was no sign of whoever did it. I didn't even have to sign any paperwork. I'm sure Vino didn't have any direct contact with any of this. But it appeared the servants remained loyal to the family, no matter who was now in charge.

The shiny, silver Bentley was parked out front for me, in an area meant for unloading fresh patients. My heart sank when I saw it and I burst into a fresh set of tears. I walked to the passenger side out of habit and rested my hand on the doorframe. I stared at the empty interior, trembling as I fought back hysteria.

I walked around the car and slipped into the driver's seat. I held my breath for a moment, then leaned forward and rested my arm and head on the steering wheel. I closed my eyes and pictured the face of the man who was supposed to be sitting here. My mind ran through images of how sexy I thought he was the night we met, the angry expression on his face the first day he picked me up, the smirk he wore when he was up to something devious, the sensual smile he gave me on our only night together... and the terrifying burning of his eyes as he commanded me to leave.

It was a full half-hour before I could pull myself together enough to even start the car. The hospital staff kept giving me dirty looks, but I didn't pay them any attention. I hoped I remembered how to drive. I hadn't owned a car the entire time I lived in New York. I only kept a license so I could prove I was old enough to drink.

I took a moment to reacquaint myself with the workings of the vehicle, adjusting mirrors and tilting the wheel. A brief flash of panic crossed my mind as I specifically remembered this car being a stick shift. I knew how to drive one, but with an unusable right arm, I wouldn't be going anywhere.

But now the Bentley was an automatic. A brand new shifter had been installed. The car had been altered so I would be able to drive it.

That fact only brought on more tears. I punched the steering wheel the best I could with my left hand, hurting myself in the process. I shook my hand out, waiting for the stinging to subside, then threw the car into drive. I went straight to my apartment; though that was the last place I wanted to go.

My apartment was horribly lonely. The bed and shower were particularly revolting to me. I saw him everywhere I looked. I wanted to destroy every piece of furniture he helped pick out, and set fire to the areas where we had been intimate. To make matters worse, my torn clothes from our night together were still on the floor.

I'd start looking for a new place tomorrow, and sell all my

furniture in the process. The chaise and my new bed would be the first to go. It might take all the money I had left, but I didn't care. His memory was going to kill me.

I spotted movement out of the corner of my eye. Two pairs of eyes stared back at me from the opposite end of the room. I was beyond being afraid anymore. I was so pissed I was about to explode. I picked up the nearest item I could find and threw it as hard as I could at them, missing, but chasing the eyes away. This was getting old fast.

I was up early the next morning. Even with sleeping pills, I was restless, just waiting to open my eyes and find a creature on top of me. I had to sleep on the couch, because Vino's scent was all over my bed. Every time I got a whiff, the porno would start playing behind my eyelids, and my chest would cave in.

I got ready as fast as I could, cutting my shower down to just a rinse-off so I wouldn't have to relive that episode either. I stopped to check the balance in my account from my computer. I would find a new place today, even if it took every cent.

Something glimmered on the floor next to my feet. It was the necklace, broken, and without a clasp. I'd have to pawn it. Even in its condition, it was still a lot of platinum, and probably worth tons. I'd sell the other jewelry Sebastian gave me too. That'd be enough to support me for a while, since my career was now down the toilet.

The Internet pulled up effortlessly, and I navigated to my banks homepage. I hardly used this new computer since I bought it, and the miniscule amount of joy its speed brought almost made me smile.

Then the balance in my account showed. And I threw the laptop across the room. The screen cracked and the back popped open. It was destined for the trash.

There had been a wire transfer from Sebastian's estate, and the number was ridiculous by my standards. A one followed by seven zeros: ten million dollars.

I slammed my fist down on my desk, then collapsed on top of it and sobbed. Vino was never going to come back to me. He was still out there, and still enough of himself to make sure I'd have everything I needed. But he was unwilling to let me be at his side. I didn't care if he was a monster now. If he had to kill me, so be it.

I grabbed my cell phone and dialed the number Sebastian gave me for the estate. It was disconnected. No surprise there.

My next move was to grab the key to the Bentley and storm out of my place. I drove straight to the Tribeca apartment, and skidded to a stop in front of the valets. I walked right past them, not letting them touch the car, or me, and marched inside the building to confront the doorman.

"I need to go upstairs," I ordered.

It was the same guy that always worked the front desk, the one Vino constantly ignored as we walked in. He smiled at me politely. "Who are you looking for? Maybe I can page them for you."

"I don't want you to page anyone! I want you to open the damn doors so I can go talk to him myself!" I yelled, pointing towards the elevators.

"Ma'am, if you don't tell me who you're looking for, I can't help you."

I took a deep breath to try to calm myself down. It didn't work. "Vino Amante, the same fucking person you see me walk in here with everyday!"

He frowned and rustled through some papers. "The Amantes have left strict instructions that they are not to be disturbed. I'm sorry, but I have to ask you to leave."

Why didn't he recognize me? "I'm not going anywhere until you let me upstairs!"

"Don't make me call security, ma'am... Why don't you just calm down and go home."

"Go ahead and call them! I'm not leaving!"

He picked up the phone and murmured something into the receiver. Two large men entered the room and stood on either side of me, trying to appear intimidating by staring at me through their sunglasses. I wasn't fazed. These guys were wimps after everything I'd witnessed.

"It's time to leave, ma'am," One of them said.

"Make me," I hissed.

They did exactly that. The other man grabbed my left arm and dragged me out the door. I was too weak to put up a fight. Once they had me safely outside, I was released and allowed to straighten myself out. Apparently they didn't see me as a threat.

They asked where my car was and I pointed to the Bentley, which shocked them. I'm sure they knew who normally drove it, but they escorted me to the door anyways. I hopped inside without much resistance. This was already a failed mission. It was time to give up.

I went straight to the nearest bar and drank until I blacked out. I'm guessing I drove home, because that's where I woke up the next day. I was on the floor with a blanket. In my inebriated condition, this must have sounded like a good solution to the issues I had with my bed. Most people probably would have just washed their sheets.

I made coffee, and dumped whiskey in it. Pills came next, my pain meds from the doctor, and the usual unprescribed ones. My stash was getting low. So I phoned my "pharmacist." He was surprised he hadn't heard from me in so long, and promised to come over within a few hours.

My next phone call was to a real estate agent. At first she said she'd pencil me in by the end of the week, but when I made it clear I was ready to buy something today, at first glance, she made an appointment for six tonight.

I walked down to Kearney's to kill time until my pharmacist called and took my usual seat at the bar. Jackson greeted me with a smile, asked where I'd been, and commented on the arm sling and cast being a good fashion accessory. I wondered if it dawned on him that I was right handed.

As I sat there staring at the dust-covered bottles behind the bar, I relaxed a little. I was already three sheets to the wind. I reminded myself that I was free now, and that things would get better. I had ten million bucks, a flashy car, and Sebastian was gone. I could move on with my life, find some normal guy, settle down, buy a puppy, have some kids. Maybe Lucas would forgive me...

Who was I kidding? That was never going to happen.

As if I needed extra verification, I saw something moving in the shadows about ten feet away. Demon bait. That's what I was. They would come for me everyday until I died. And probably even after.

I slammed my drink then ordered another, and a shot.

After meeting up with my pharmacist, and purchasing everything he had on him, I drove past the Tribeca apartment. I even parked across the street and stared up at the windows for a while. They were too many floors up to see anything, but a girl can dream, right?

I stayed there so long I was late to my appointment with Melissa Perkins, the real estate guru. Her office was in a high-rise in Manhattan, on one of the top floors. She was an attractive woman of about forty, with curly brown hair and a big, fake smile.

Her smile faded when I stumbled into her office. "Can I help you?"

"I'm Trinity," I said.

She looked me over, with disapproval written all over her face. "Maybe we should reschedule. You don't seem to be in any condition to view properties."

I dropped my purse to the floor. "Look lady, I need to move, now. You want me to write you a check this very second? I am going to buy an apartment *today*. If you don't want to sell me one, somebody else will."

She nodded. "Why don't you have a seat? I'll get all your information."

We filled out a bunch of pointless paperwork. She asked me a series of personal questions to see what I was looking for. I told her I was an artist and gave her a bogus story about getting dumped, which ended up being remarkably close to the truth. Minus the stuff about demons. She took pity on me after that, and apologized for being rude earlier.

An hour later, we were on our way to a three-bedroom in Soho, with a good-sized balcony. She drove, since I was wasted, and she felt uncomfortable with me behind the wheel. The apartment was listed for just over three million, and deemed ready for immediate possession.

"I'll take it," I said.

Melissa gave me a shocked smile. "Okay, what kind of offer would you like to put in?"

"No offer, I'll pay full price. I want to move in right away."

"You're sure you don't want to see any of the other properties?"

"Positive," I said, reminding myself I wasn't just purchasing this one because it was only a few miles away from Tribeca.

Within two weeks, I was moved in to the new apartment, fresh furniture and all. I had to pay extra to speed up the process, but since I was paying cash and had no loan to deal with, things were fairly painless.

I drove past Vino's everyday. I parked across the street and wondered if maybe he was up there looking down at me. The pain in my shoulder and arm was quickly fading, but the ache in my heart was not. No matter how much I drank, or how many pills I consumed, the pain never subsided. Even being out of my apartment wasn't helping much. The fact that it was his money that bought my new place, and his car that I was driving, weren't making it easy to forget.

The demons came more often now. Even during the day, if there was somewhere dark, there would almost always be eyes watching me. It was wreaking havoc on my nerves. Every night not spent being rude to people in a bar, was spent throwing half my possessions around, trying to scare away disgusting little creatures.

As far as I could tell, if there were no shadows around, no demons could get in. So I eventually resorted to buying every light I could get my hands on, and keeping them on twenty-four hours a day. I had to wear a blindfold to sleep, and even then I could only sleep for an hour or two at a time.

Today, I was torturing myself as usual, and I was so messed up that I was barely conscious. I'm not sure how many weeks it had been at this point. The cast had just been taken off my arm, but I hadn't been attending my physical therapy so it was still confined to a sling. I laid under the tree in Central Park where I decided I loved Vino. I knew this was self-destructive behavior, but I couldn't help it. At least I wasn't sitting outside his place again… I did that earlier in the day.

Every time my eyes started to close, I could see him there, leaning against the tree with the breeze in his hair, the light peeking through the canopy and dancing against the skin of his face. I forced my eyes to stay open to get rid of him, and burned every detail of the tree into my brain.

The sun went behind the clouds, casting shadows all around me and darkening the branches above. Most of the day had been cloudy, so I knew it would be a bad day for demon spotting. I braced myself for what would be waiting to come out of those shadows. And sure enough, something had been preparing for this moment.

A demon slowly materialized in the center of the tree, where the highest concentration of darkness was. It was more of the same; holes for eyes, rotting flesh, silent screams. It crawled down the trunk towards me, stopping only when there was too much light for it to continue. I pulled my arm out from behind my head and reached upwards, holding my middle finger up to give it a big 'fuck you.'

Apparently, it didn't like that. It started jumping around, frantically trying to find a dark enough route to get to me. I grabbed the nearest stick and launched it in the creature's direction, missing by several feet. Normally this action scared them off, but this particular creature seemed angered by my taunting.

It started to suck in all the darkness around it, giving its body more definition and making it appear solid. It then lunged off the branches towards my face. I yelped and tried to scoot out of the way before it landed on me. But I was so intoxicated my movements were sluggish. And having only one good arm made getting up from a prone position difficult.

Then the clouds shifted and the sun shown through the branches again. The creature vanished in thin air, less then a foot from my face.

I started hyperventilating. None of those pestering little monsters had ever done something like that before. They mostly seemed curious and cautious around me. This one was ready to attack and completely unafraid. It also had a lot more depth than the others. It looked like I would have been able to reach out and touch this one.

I shivered at the thought of more powerful demons coming after me. This one might not have been much, but I knew there were so many more out there. How long would it take before one of the stronger ones came?

Would news get out that Sebastian died because of me? He supposedly had hundreds of children left roaming around the world. Would any of them show up for revenge? What about the other six kings, or whatever they were… would they want me too?

I got up as fast as I could and took off down the path.

I saw something else under one of the bridges I walked past. Then I snapped. Something deep inside me had reached its limit and shattered. I starting running full speed towards the car, where I locked myself inside and wept into the steering wheel.

This was all too much. I couldn't take it any more. I needed some form of relief or I was going to have to kill myself. It seemed the only way out right now, the only way to end all the pain.

Don't think like that… it's only been a few weeks. Things will get better. Those creatures can't be everywhere…

That's right. They aren't everywhere. I had never once seen one near this car. It must still reek with Vino's essence. They wouldn't dare go near it. It was an easy jump to where else they wouldn't be. I had never seen any while I was stalking the Tribeca apartment.

There was somewhere else they wouldn't dare go near. The one place Vino tried to convince me to seek refuge.

Church.

I go could back to St. Patrick's.

I had completely forgotten there was a whole other side to this. I was one of the few people on earth who knew, beyond a doubt, that God was real. If I had asked for His help when Vino first put the idea out there, I would have saved myself a lot of heartache.

I wiped the tears and running mascara from under my eyes, and started the car. It was time to finally seek out my own salvation.

The second the massive cathedral came into view, I started to feel funny, like someone was pushing against my chest. I ended up parking the car about half a block down, hands shaking on the steering wheel. Very slowly, I opened my door and got out, searching the spires for that glimmer of light I found here before.

The light was easy to spot this time around. Even though it was in a completely different location. In my head, I felt like it noticed me too, although there was no way to tell. I took this as a good omen, and started walking towards the church.

Today was brisk, and I had a coat on. But the closer I got to the church, the warmer I became. By the time I was at the far end of the building, I felt overheated, and had to lose the coat.

That feeling in my chest was beginning to intensify, and I started getting antsy. My adrenaline was pumping and telling my body to flee. But I pushed on. I didn't stop until I was at the steps in front of the brass doors.

I looked up to find the light again. It had moved closer and was brighter. That peaceful feeling I sensed last time came over me. I smiled. It was the first good feeling I'd had since the war in the apartment. It gave me a new bout of courage.

My whole body tingled as I placed my foot on the first step. I reached out to take the thin metal railing, but let go immediately. With as chilly as it was today, the railing should have been cold. But it was warm, almost hot.

I gave another glance upward. My twinkling light was still watching me. I had trouble calling it an angel, since I couldn't see it. But I felt like it was urging me forward. I took a deep breath and turned back towards my goal, the intricately carved doorway in front of me.

I forced myself to climb the few stairs separating me from it. My body temperature rose, and I started to panic. I reached out to open the door and halted, terrified of what was about to happen. Then I shook my head and shoved the door so I could slip inside.

It felt like I caught on fire. I couldn't breathe. The cathedral was almost empty, shy of a few tourists. But one of the reverends happened to be only fifteen feet from me. He noticed me come in right away, and stared at me in shock. I'm sure I looked like a wreck; eyes red from crying, hair disheveled, arm in a sling, and completely freaking out.

When my breath finally came, I gulped at the air in gasps. The reverend walked towards me to try to help. I could tell he noticed something out of the ordinary about me.

"Do you need assistance?" he asked.

I opened my mouth to speak, but nothing came out.

"Please, come inside. We can help you," he said.

I grabbed for the door to make my escape. But in my panic my coordination was compromised. He took the last couple steps towards me and touched my hand.

It burned. I screamed.

I yanked the door open and sprinted down the stairs. I didn't stop until I was at the car. I jumped in and sped away without looking back.

So much for that idea.

I should have been expecting something like this. I'd been through an exorcism before. I knew it would be painful. No matter how I saw him, Vino was still a demon. He was still a creature of Hell, and I had willingly given myself to him in every way. There was not one fiber of my being that didn't belong to him. Whether he wanted me or not.

Then there was the object of what Sebastian did to me. That mark may just be a spider-like scar now, but it was still there. Its effects had to still be lingering somewhere deep inside me.

Maybe if I endured the pain I could free myself of the hold Sebastian still had on me and keep the demons away. But that might mean losing my ties to Vino too. And that was something I just wouldn't do.

No, I would not be allowed asylum. I was too weak to seek the salvation waiting for me inside those doors. I had rejected God one too many times. Hell was the only place that would accept me now.

To say I became a mess would be a gross understatement. Days flew by as my sanity dwindled. Weeks turned into months, and winter came and went, leaving my mental state much the same. In fact, things were slowly getting worse. My arm regained almost full usage, but I couldn't bring myself to paint. I couldn't bring myself to do much of anything these days. Aside from my obsessive trips through Tribeca, I never left the apartment. I had officially become a shut in.

Food lost all appeal, so there was no reason to go to the store. The only thing I ever consumed was alcohol, or drugs of various sorts, so my body started to revolt against me. I lost another twenty pounds, which for most people wouldn't be detrimental to their health. But I was already too thin before. Now I was completely emaciated. My cheeks looked hollow, and I had permanent bags under my eyes. Most of my bones were protruding from my jaundiced skin, and my clothes hung off me like they were hand-me-downs. Bottom line... I was not attractive.

Death was starting to look really good. I just hadn't gotten up the guts to pull the trigger, so to speak. Hell had to be better than this. Who knows, maybe Vino would be waiting for me there. Sebastian talked of keeping me to himself for eternity. Why couldn't Vino do the same? And I remembered Sebastian saying something about Vino retreating to Hell to take over his throne, maybe that's what he did. If all I had to do to see Vino again was die, then my choice was simple. But there was no way to know if he was down there or up here. So I waited.

I was lying on the floor of my apartment, trying to will myself into death's sweet embrace, when I blacked out in the middle of the day again. This happened often, a mix of all the poisons in my blood and exhaustion from starving myself.

One of the spring's first storms was rolling through, and a loud crack of thunder roused me from my slumber. I awoke in a panic. Night came while I slept, which meant I'd been out for at least six hours. And all my lights were off. I always kept the lights on. The storm must have knocked the power out.

That meant that I would not be alone.

I was too weak to run, so I stayed as still as possible and waited for my eyes to adjust to the lack of light.

On the ceiling in front of me was another demon, much larger then the usual, and much more creepy. It hung upside down on all fours. Its legs were hinged backwards and its arms and hands were elongated.

Otherwise it looked almost like a man, a hairless, contorted man. This creature had the same empty eyes and rotted skin as all the others, but it stretched its mouth open into a huge, round hole and screeched. It could vocalize.

In my terror I screamed too, abandoning my plan to stay unnoticed, and it started to crawl towards me. On instinct, I threw the pillow I was using at it… and it made contact.

This demon was whole.

That meant it could hurt me.

And that was my final push, the one thing that made up my mind and sent me over the edge. It was time to end this. It was time to kill myself.

I scrambled to my feet and stumbled towards my balcony, then slammed the door behind me. I ran through the downpour to the railing. The wind whipped damp tendrils of hair around my face, and the pouring rain stung my eyes. I shivered from how cold it was, but it didn't really matter. I wouldn't be conscious long enough for it to bother me.

I leaned over and looked down at the street. The lights below illuminated the passing cars as they sprayed water trails behind them. Only a few pedestrians braved the weather, so the sidewalks were nearly empty.

There was no sound coming from behind me. That thing must not have wanted to follow me outside. I was grateful for that. I would rather jump on my own accord than be forced into hurrying because it was at my tail. I didn't see any other demons out here either. Usually there was at least one. Maybe it was powerful enough to scare them off. It definitely scared me.

I put one foot on the bottom of the railing, never taking my eyes off the cement below. I pushed myself up and steadied myself on both arms. It sent a jolt of pain up the right one. I wavered slightly and shifted my weight to the left. I leaned forward and closed my eyes to summon the strength to go through with this.

My mind showed me the man causing my pain. Five months, and he was still clear as day in my head. Every last detail, of both versions, the one I loved and the one that sent me away. I chose to concentrate on the earlier copy, one last happy thought of him smiling at down at me before we kissed.

I smiled. I was ready for death.

I had to use the pillar to be strong enough to swing one leg over the banister. I stopped for a moment, straddling the railing as the adrenaline coursed through my veins. I was surprised I had any left at all. I had been in such a weakened state lately, nothing seemed to get my heart pumping anymore. It was racing right now.

My grip on the railing tightened and I steadied myself enough to pull my other leg over. I was trembling violently, and the railing was slick from the rain, so it took a great deal of effort not to fall on accident. I perched on top of the metal banister and took a deep breath. I loved the smell of rain. It washes everything clean. Maybe it could do the same for my soul once my body was splattered across the sidewalk.

There was not one aspect of my life that was worth living for anymore. I had money, but that was worthless. My career was a distant dream, and there would be no family left to mourn me. My closed casket funeral would be empty. My foster parents wouldn't care enough to make such a long trip for a lost cause. I bet they'd say they always saw this coming.

I'm sure Lucas would show up, and I felt bad about that. He may hate me, but I know he didn't want me dead. He'd have to hear a eulogy performed by some priest I never met. And the priest would say something about me being loved, and being a good person, and that I would be going to Heaven to experience paradise. All of which would be a lie.

Yeah, my funeral was going to be a joke. I had to laugh at myself for that one. There was no one to blame but me. If I hadn't been such a horrible person my whole life, maybe things would have turned out differently.

I shook my head at the irony of it all, and carefully slid my feet to the thin ledge below. Another wave of adrenaline hit, and my knees started shaking. I leaned forward and gripped the railing with white knuckles.

Vino came to mind again. He wouldn't be attending my funeral either. My only hope of seeing him again was waiting for me on the cold cement below. And my chances were fifty-fifty, at best.

I locked my hands as tightly as I could around the cold metal and leaned myself outward. I felt weightless as the wind and rain swirled around me, throwing my hair violently in all directions.

This wasn't going to hurt at all. Nine floors up, that was plenty high enough to kill me on contact. A quick plummet, and then I'd get to see for myself what Hell was like. It'd be so easy just to let my fingers go limp…

"This is a horrible way to thank me for all the trouble I went through saving your ass."

My eyes flew open, and I pulled myself back against the railing. That voice was like a punch to the face, immediately snapping me out of bleak hopelessness and waking me from the nightmare. I couldn't have really heard that, could I? I had to be hallucinating.

I tightened my grip and braced myself. Then I slowly turned around to look behind me. What I saw had to be a dream.

He was really there. If I wasn't clinging so tightly to the one thing keeping me from falling nine stories, I could have reached out to touch him.

Vino was hardly wet, like he had just poofed onto the scene. And his clothes were all black, with no flashy shoes, as if he were trying to blend into the night. Vino looked older, like he had aged ten years in the last few months. Crows feet just like his father's lined his eyes, which were now deep crimson, the exact shade of fresh blood. His hair was down past his shoulders now, and there was even a streak of gray in it. He was several inches taller, and seemed to have filed out more.

I stared at him in disbelief with tears streaming down my cheeks. This couldn't be real. I must have already fallen to my death.

He smiled at me and lifted me over the railing. I threw my arms around him and sobbed into his chest. The calming energy that I was accustomed to feeling from him had intensified to the point that it froze my lungs made the muscles in my chest burn.

"Is it really you?" I managed to choke out.

"It's me... or close enough anyways." He held me tight against him and turned so he was shielding me from the rain.

I hid my face so he wouldn't see what a mess I'd become. "I thought you couldn't change back."

"I was motivated. Some crazy woman kept driving past my home everyday and tormenting me." He chuckled. "Had to cut the wings off the first few tries."

"You saw me?"

"Every time you came."

Vino tried to gently pull me away from him, but I wouldn't release my grip. I clung to him with every ounce of strength I had left in me. There was no way I was going to let go now, even if it was getting more painful by the minute.

"That hurts you."

I shook my head. "No, it doesn't."

"You're lying," he said. "I'm sorry, I can't control it as much as I'd like to. And I can't hold this form long. I shouldn't have come for you, but you left me with no other choice."

He wiped the wet hair out of my face and tilted my chin so he could look in my eyes. "How could you do this to yourself? I bet you wouldn't have made it another week the way you were going. But… being with me won't delay death much."

"You're really going to stay with me?"

Vino smiled at me the way I'd been imagining in my head for so many months. "I guess I have to, don't I? I want you to live, and you're not cooperating. I kept thinking you'd snap out of it. I should have known better."

I was too happy for words. My tears shook my entire body as I pinned myself to him.

"You look… disgusting. You need a doctor. And a sandwich," he said.

I laughed. I don't remember the last time I did that. It felt good. "Well, your hair looks stupid."

Vino joined my laughter, then pulled my face to his to kiss me. My heart and lungs both went on strike the second our lips made contact. He eased back and rested his forehead against mine. I forced him into a repeat performance.

He kept the kiss brief, since it was so overwhelming for me. "It was painful staying away," he admitted.

"I'm moving in tomorrow," I said.

"I've already made arrangements." Vino scooped me up into his arms to carry me inside. "Besides, how else am I going to keep you in line?"

We were really going to be together now. Who cares if it hurt to touch him, or if he couldn't pass for human long? I was going to get my happy ending. No matter how brief it may be.